# A.M. JAXON

# MADLY
## TOO MUCH, TOO SOON

HEMBURY
BOOKS

# ABOUT THE AUTHOR

A.M. Jaxon is a dramatic romantic suspense writer who grew from wild child in small-town tropical Queensland to become a pharmacist in Brisbane. She travelled and worked around the world, then went slightly insane – if that's possible! – to undertake study to gain a PhD in Business.

Passionate about coaching women's hockey, it has taken her to Barcelona, Rotterdam and the UK, as well as the Gold Coast and Perth in Australia. These different paths of her life have seen her experience many adventures and misadventures, which give a unique edge to her writing.

In 2014, A.M. decided to leave her pharmacy career to focus on her writing, and has since written seven novels. She enjoys writing about resilient women of all backgrounds and temperaments who endure what life throws at them.

A newcomer to the romantic suspense genre, A.M. loves highlighting human nature's complex, uplifting and dangerous aspects – and all its glorious frailties. She lives with her husband and wily Westie terrier in Perth, Western Australia.

Check out my website at: www.amjaxon.com
Or use the QR code

Or connect with me at: facebook.com/amjaxon

If you enjoyed reading this book, please consider leaving a review on
Goodreads or your preferred platform.


ALSO BY A.M. JAXON
Saoirse's Story
Joshua's Story

**HEMBURY**
—BOOKS—



First published by Hembury Books in 2026
hemburybooks.com.au
info@hemburybooks.com

Paperback ISBN 9781923517295
Ebook ISBN 9781923517271

A catalogue record for this book is available from the National Library of Australia

# DEDICATION

For all the Natashas out there:

They snarled, shouted and screamed at her.
But it was the soft whispers of her mind that
damned her.
Only the feminine steel and beauty of her
soul saved her.

# PLAYLIST

**The MADLY playlist:**

'Desire' – U2

'Let it Roll' – Flo Rida

'Locked Out of Heaven' – Bruno Mars

'Cherry Bomb' – The Runaways

'I'm Outta Love' – Anastacia

'Nasty Naughty Boy' – Christina Aguilera

'All Nite (Don't Stop)' – Janet Jackson

'Sexual Healing' – Marvin Gaye

'Big Girls Cry' – Sia

'You're So Vain' – Carly Simon

'Son of a Gun (I Betcha Think This Song Is About You)' – Janet Jackson (feat. Missy Elliot)

'Human Nature' – Madonna

'You Better Run' – Pat Benatar

'What Goes Around Comes Around' – Justin Timberlake

'Life for Rent' – Dido

'Thunderstruck' – AC/DC

'All I do is Win' – DJ Khaled feat. Ludacris, T-Pain, Snoop Dog, Rick Ross

'Waiting on a Friend' – Rolling Stones

'Cream' – Prince

'Bring Me to Life' – Evanescence

'Come Undone' – Robbie Williams

'Born this Way' – Lady Gaga

'Secret' – Madonna

'A Moment with You' – George Michael

'Love and Affection' – Joan Armatrading

'Should I Stay or Should I Go' – The Clash

'Slow' – Kylie Minogue

'Come On Over (Turn Me On)' – Isobel Campbell and Mark Lanegan

'Start Me Up' – Rolling Stones

'Permission to Shine' – Bachelor Girl

'Hymn to Her' – The Pretenders

**QR Code to MADLY Spotify Playlist**

# CAST OF CHARACTERS

CAST OF CHARACTERS

| | |
|---|---|
| Natasha Perry | Pharmacist/ex-stripper/ex-addict//friend/lover |
| Dr Sebastian Mancini | Oncology/haematology doctor/son/businessman/lover |
| Joanna (Jo) Sanderson | Chief pharmacist at Sir John Cartwright Hospital/Nat's friend |
| Chelsea Taylor | Oncology/haematology nurse/Nat's friend |
| Sage Thompson | Street clinic head doctor/Nat's friend |
| Donald Ford (Dodge) | Sage's partner, Natasha's friend |
| Charles Ford (Chevy) | Sage's friend, Natasha's friend, Donald's brother |
| Rick Bates | Clinical ward pharmacist/Nat's ex-boyfriend |
| Dr Rachel Cartwright | Doctor at Sir John Cartwright Hospital |
| Mr Charles Cartwright | CEO at Sir John Cartwright Hospital |
| Mr Byron Cartwright (Lord B) | Consultant surgeon at Sir John Cartwright Hospital |
| Cole Hexum | Mancini and Aida Foundation lawyer |
| Holly Draper | Dietician at Sir John Cartwright Hospital |
| "The Boss" | Street thug |
| Pauly | Street thug |
| Archie | Nat's ex-boyfriend in Sydney |
| Sharon Townsend | Director of nursing at Sir John Cartwright Hospital |
| Averill Green (Avarice and Greed) | Oncology/haematology head nurse |
| Ruby Brown | Elderly chemotherapy patient |
| Jonothan Brown | Ruby's husband |
| George Long | Head of hospital security |
| Renzo Mancini | Seb's father |
| Aida Mancini | Seb's mother (deceased) |
| Pia Gallo-Mancini | Seb's sister |
| Antony Gallo | Pia's son |
| Michael Gallo | Pia's son |
| Renzo Gallo/Mancini | Pia's ward |
| Guiseppi Mancini | Seb's brother |
| Dominic Mancini | Seb's brother |
| Nina Panetta | Pia's personal assistant |
| Tony Gallo | Pia's husband |
| Elva Mancini | Dominic's wife |
| Wolf | Strip club owner |
| Paul | Seb's bodyguard |
| Sofia Mancini | Mancini family (deceased) |

# CONTENTS

We all sin.
It's the choices made after that define us.

# PROLOGUE

*A tragic day. Sydney, Australia, 2007.*

Wolf topped up with a line of blow. He had to be at his best for this one. Who did the bitch think she was? He owned the joint now, and things were changing. By morning he'd top her. She'd be on her knees and, like all the others, his. Then he'd do whatever he wanted. But first, she'd make him money. Men would pay good for her. He'd rebuild the empire taken from him.

'Yeah, mojo's kickin' in now.' Things were so much better when he had some coke on board. The knife became an extension of him. Picasso had a brush; Wolf had the blade. It was art, his art. This time he'd leave her looks, her smooth golden skin. He'd still stick her good, but not with his knife – yet. She'd make more money for him if she was pristine. On the outside, anyway. The animal that was Wolf would take that sweet candy, which, according to Archie, no man had tapped.

# ONE

## STRETCHING THE KINDNESS OF STRANGERS

*An ordinary day, Fremantle, Western Australia, 2015.*

'Incoming!' The emergency room charge nurse barked over the chaotic buzz of human misery and the sounds trying to remedy it. 'Dr Thompson's bringing one in. Female, OD, critical.' She gave a resigned mutter. 'Like there's any other kind.' Her bleak tone corralled the staff strewn around the ordered department, their battered minds and duty-bound hearts prepared for another fight with death.

Sin and life had led Natasha Perry here. Thankfully, she was only an observer today, but not that long ago, the shadow of a powerful synthetic master had enshrouded and threatened her too. Today, she had a stronger hold on a better life. She'd prevailed, to now work as a pharmacist at the Sir John Cartwright Hospital. Still, others weren't so resilient – the combination of bitumen-melting heat, a shortage of meth and MDMA, plus the purity of the latest batch of heroin to hit the streets, had sent some of the less fortunate over the edge. Fremantle had gone crazy in its lust for release. Cool detachment never felt so good as escaping a Hades-hot reality by slipping the needle in.

Chelsea was frustrated. 'What the eff is it with Harry's high? I just don't get it.'

'Russian roulette, with a hot shot,' Nat nodded, handing Chelsea a pack of ampoules.

'Yeah, why?'

Natasha shrugged. She could say, but now wasn't the time to try to frame the irrational and elusive with logic. Chelsea wouldn't have understood. Being an ER nurse was the closest she had come to any irrationality. Her life, like her beauty, had been free and easy. This was one of several differences between the two women.

All morning the Sir John Cartwright Hospital emergency room had been treating a procession of patients who'd overdosed on heroin. Natasha shuddered as thoughts of others still duelling with an addictive death slithered through her mind. The telltale blare of the siren found the ER staff ready.

'Hot seller this morning, this week for that matter.' Chelsea waved the naloxone ampoules at Nat.

'Yeah, thought you'd need a top-up.' They'd need the naloxone, a drug given intravenously to counteract the effects of heroin. 'Hope they work.'

'We'll know sooner or later. God, I hope this one's only a heroin OD. But given Sage's coming in from her clinic, there must be some other crap going down.'

'Catch you later.' Nat made to skate towards the exit door.

Chelsea called over her shoulder as she hurried to the arrival area, 'No, Nat, stay. We might need some added drug advice if treating this one gets tricky.'

'Okay.'

To watch the ER staff work was to witness practised chaotic precision collide with desperate inspiration. Kids rarely said they wanted to grow up and specialise in emergency medicine. People seemed to just fall into it. It wasn't money-making medicine, but the staff were priceless. The emergency department was usually the last vestige of the injured, non-responsive, desperate and vomiting. Unfortunately, also the crude, rude and vile. At times like today, it approached being a childcare centre for recovering druggies. Outwardly, the staff coped and tried not to judge the sins of their patients. The patients, for their part, mostly never acknowledged how far they stretched the kindness of these ER strangers, their guardian angels by proxy.

The room surged into action as Dr Sage Thompson, an addiction psychiatrist, jogged beside a gurney. Her silver-streaked black ponytail bobbed from side to side in time with her calm and calculated pumping of the patient's bag mask. Her knee-high leather boots tapped out the urgent beat of the situation as she crossed the concrete walkway into ER proper. As the doors swung open, Sage took a noticeable deep breath as the familiar, reassuring smell of hospital-disinfected cleanliness greeted her. She then she shouted hand-over instructions to the ER doctors and nurses that joined her.

Chelsea started removing blood-soaked bandages from the face of the emaciated girl on the bed. On each side of her mouth, where her lips met, deep slashes jagged and split her cheeks. Example A of the other crap Chelsea had mentioned. This poor wretch's malnutrition and track marks showed she was a regular street user.

Chelsea and Sage's real work began. Natasha walked behind a glass partition as her mind whirled and scattered at the sight, and she was there again, there on the other side, transported back to a time when cold sweats and her demons reigned supreme and she was scared to her core. It was why she understood the flawed logic of an addict. Back then, she'd thought about escaping her hell with just one more hit – a hot one – and sleep for good. Luckily, the last time Natasha had ended up on the other side of the glass, Dr Sage Thompson had found her. The doctor saw the goodness in Nat and wrapped her in a warm, protective blanket of compassion.

A groaned cough caused Natasha to refocus on reality and Sage to pause. The doctor calmly encouraged. 'Good girl, come on. Come back to us.' The naloxone had started to work. The young junkie's breathing began to return to some semblance of what was needed for life.

'Your soul's not leaving us today,' Sage said with a wrinkled brow.

The high-pitched staccato of the heart-rate monitor told the doctor that this poor soul wasn't out of the woods yet. Sage sighed, 'What else have you got on board, my love?'

Some other unknown synthetic invader travelled the poor girl's veins. Most likely it was a speedball – a heroin and cocaine mix. It was hard to know. Maybe she had meth or MDMA on board. But as the doctor waited for the results of a more detailed tox screen, the girl began to flail around as a seizure took hold. Sage had to play a calculated medicinal guessing game. What drug to give next to counteract the unknown substance or substances still affecting the life of a waif who once was a father's little girl and a mother's pride and joy.

The controlled frenzy continued until a range of legal drugs worked their magic to contain the effects of the illicit ones. There was no one magic pill. Fortunately, this time, the homeless soul was brought back to her life. A life she may not have wanted back. Calm ensued and the ward soon settled. The ER staff tidied and stabilised the patient while others prepared for the next emergency or attended to the more benign medical problems that flowed through the ER each day.

*The same morning: Holly Draper and Dr Mancini*

Holly was a man's woman, and she knew it. Dumber than she looked but smarter than she acted, Holly was still trying hard to prove her worth, and for that she needed a man. She'd realised at an early age that there were many ways a woman who affected men as she did could get ahead. But Holly was yet to properly catch the eye of the connected, brooding and impressively toned Dr Mancini. Seeing he'd entered the doctor's office alone, she decided to make her move.

Holly began setting her honey trap, aiming for professional but with more than a whiff of over-familiar, friendly overtones. She'd heard that outside of work he was known by another name. 'Hey, how's The Boss this busy morning?'

Mancini turned quickly, glaring. 'Uh, good. Look, don't call me that. Dr Mancini to you.' His father had been The Boss in his Italian home town a whole other life away, and Sebastian didn't want to take that part of the family business on. It also gave rise to his utter hatred of people trying to kiss arse. They were only ever trying to weasel their way into the new life he was carving out. Holly had been trying to isolate him for a while. He'd not socialised much since coming home, apart from a few unsatisfying one-night stands. Knowing what Holly and her curvy body were after, he decided to make light of it. 'Hey, I'm just a simple guy trying to make a bit of a difference.'

'Oh, I think we both know you're far from a simple guy or that you're only striving to make a bit of a difference.' She glided towards him. She wasn't his type, but was easy enough on the eye. 'Are you doing anything tonight?'

Just as Mancini was wondering if it should be this easy, Rick, the ward pharmacist, bounced into the room. Mancini had observed this guy from afar. More of a harmless try-hard than a conniving sycophant, but there wasn't much of a margin for error. It's why Mancini had kept a wide berth.

Rick smiled and thought, *finally!* 'Howdy, Holly. Ahh, Dr Mancini, I don't think I've had the pleasure.'

# TWO

## THE LUNCHTIME UNDERWEAR ENLIGHTENMENT

Constrained and contained, Natasha Perry made her way back to the pharmacy. She met up with Jo, a lady who had never let anything constrain her. Jo hadn't only broken into the male-dominated, upper-management, lycra-clad cycling posse, she'd corralled them to fall in behind her. This woman had become the chief pharmacist of the Sir John Cartwright Hospital – or JCH as it was known – in record time. The only time lycra, Jo and a male would find themselves together was for a totally different riding scenario.

Jo and Natasha headed out to have lunch with Sage and Chelsea. Ever since Natasha had left Sage's clinic to work at JCH, and when all their rosters aligned, the four looked forward to sharing a Friday lunch catch-up. Sometimes they called themselves the Amigos. The silly name stuck after one particularly drunken night of fun – Mexican and margaritas. The four idly chatted as they made their way to a table at today's chosen cafe.

The port city of Fremantle was an eclectic mix of old-world charm blended with modern, sleek seaside architecture and graffiti-anointed dilapidated warehouses. The jewel in Fremantle's crown was the many amazing restaurants and cafes lining its winding streets. There were the enchanting smells of different foods and strong coffee, which lured countless curious passers-by into the cafes. The Friday afternoon buzz around the markets and the Cappuccino Strip was contagious, even in the bone-baking heat.

The waitress took their orders. The morning's trauma began to wash away as they relaxed, enjoying the air-conditioned energy of the lunchtime crowd and the sumptuous smells of tapas wafting out from the kitchen. Then the party sound of LMFAO's 'Sexy and I know it' rang out from Nat's handbag.

Chelsea rolled her eyes, 'You're kidding. Rick chose that, didn't he?'

Nat shrugged. 'It's not that bad.'

'Really? Come on. You know better. Oh, I get it. He's being ironic. That makes sense.'

Nat ignored Chelsea to attend to her boyfriend's call. Although lately he'd become less of a BF and more of a FB. Nonetheless, at least he was her fuck buddy.

'Hey, what's up?' Things were generally up and down with them.

'Good news! Instead of it just being us tonight, I've organised a foursome with Holly, the dietician, and one of the doctors up here on my ward.'

Her heart filled with lead. This would be one of the down times. 'But I wanted to be with you. Just us.' She hadn't seen him for the last couple of days. The last time they were together it was short, as fulfilling and frustrating as trying to pot an eight ball with a floppy piece of liquorice. As unsatisfying as sex with Rick could be, she craved the semblance of intimacy and belonging. Real love.

'Come on, for me, please. I've been trying to get closer to Dr Man—'

'No, you prom—'

'Yeah, but anyway. You come to mine around six-thirty and then we'll head out. Oh ... and Tashy, don't be late this time.'

The sudden silence made her swear as she punched her phone into her bag. Natasha had the perfect venting environment.

Jo obliged. 'What's he done now?'

'I thought we were going out, just us. Instead, he's agreed to meet up with some doctor and the dietician from his ward.' She groaned. 'So tonight ... um, well, you guys know I'm not great at the small talk thing, especially with new people.' Her dissatisfaction grew. 'Do you know much about Holly the dietician? Or this Dr Man—whoever?'

'It's Mancini. Uh ... um, he keeps to himself. Something fishy there, you know,' the usually direct Sage rambled. It was odd for her. 'Hey, we need some water here. Where's that waitress? She hasn't taken our order yet, right?'

Natasha pressed Sage. 'Hey, you can't just hang something like that out there. Mancini, come on. What's the goss?'

'Let's just leave it at ... he might have been in some kind of trouble. I can't remember the specifics. It was a while ago. His family got him out of it by sending him overseas, Italy I think. Ever since coming back, he's kept pretty much under the radar, squeaky clean.' She paused, 'I mean, that's the word on the street.'

When she talked streets, Sage knew her stuff. Mean streets were her speciality. She rubbed her wrinkled forehead. 'Not sure I want to talk too much today. I have a massive headache. Busy day and all that. But I will say, Holly ... mmm, that one. Her reputation precedes h—'

'Trollop is an apt term that comes to mind,' Jo added.

'Serial doctor-effer is another.' Oddly, given Chelsea's penchant for using an array of boundary-pushing adjectives, she drew the line at dropping the f-bomb. 'Slutty slut slut alert there.' Chelsea and subtlety had never entirely been introduced. Now would be no different. 'Bonks anything with balls.'

'That's more than fair.' Jo chuckled, causing her ample bosom to jiggle just a bit. Her industrial-grade bra was restraining her, but nothing could hold back the broad smile that crinkled her English-rose complexion. 'You can't help but wonder what egotistical prat she'll be sniffing around.'

Nat's words were as dry as the desert to the east. 'Thanks, that really puts my mind at ease.' Nat turned back to Chelsea. 'Do you know about this doctor?'

'Let me think. Speaking as the table's appointed connoisseur of the male form—'

'Self-appointed,' Jo mumbled.

'I'll get back to that.' Chelsea waved a finger at Jo while turning to Nat. 'Dr Mancini, hmmm. Heard a few rumblings about dark and stormy, but that's all I've got. I don't believe I've laid eyes on him – yet.' She shot Jo a wry look. 'Could be because he works up in the clouds with you, and poor simple me just works down on the ground with the little people in ER.'

'Don't give me grief. I hear you'll be moving up into the clouds soon enough.' Jo brushed her reddish-brown hair aside. 'I haven't laid eyes on him, either. I understand he works for the Aida Breast Care

Foundation, up on eleven.' Before Chelsea could say a word, Jo nodded. 'Yes, in the clouds.'

'Let's Google him.' Chelsea chuckled, 'Maybe a bit of friendly Instagram and Facebook stalking.' Chelsea's voraciousness for social media rendered her immediately useless. Her attention was instantly drawn to her phone.

Jo persisted. 'I know he's been appointed to the Sir John Cartwright Hospital Board, and if he's working on JCH's oncology/haematology ward as well as for Aida, then he's someone Rick feels he needs to brown-nose.'

Sage seized her chance. 'Nat, you deserve better than Rick. You know that, don't you?'

Nat started sweating, which had nothing to do with the weather. She hated being in this type of spotlight. 'Hey, think where I've come from.'

'That's the past. Now you deserve better. This guy, well, he doesn't … you're just so much more than him.' Sage's piercing green eyes burned into Nat's, making her soul squirm.

'So, I take it your headache isn't stopping you from talking now? Can we just leave it?' Natasha was made of glass when it came to Sage.

Sage was comfortable in her skin. Who else could pull off being a leather-clad, Harley-riding doctor with heeled boots and a stethoscope? Such a snugly fitting outfit worn by a female in her late forties, even a trim one, would typically shriek mutton aiming for lamb, a woman tragically trying for an all-too-late stab at attitude. But Sage, she who was never sheepish, only ever commanded respect. Being a specialist addiction psychiatrist she cared for some of the most troubled and broken people society had discarded. All the same, her compassion was not to be toyed with. She shook her head, worried that all Natasha's hard work tackling her dark, heavy baggage would be wasted on Rick.

It was true. Nat had fought fiercely to find her way back. No one ordered her around anymore. 'Enough. From where I've come from, who'd have thought I'd ever have a life close to this? Who knows what Rick and my future holds?'

'No crystal ball needed. A train wreck and you hurt,' Jo mumbled dryly.

'Don't be a cow.'

'Sorry, but I'm worried.'

Nat hung her head. 'It's … I mean, he's all I deserve at the moment. I know it's not perfect. God knows I'm not perfect.'

'Nat, forget perfect. It's an intangible construct. He's seriously selfish, which is clearly tangible.' Sage squeezed Nat's shoulder, her eyes softening. 'I haven't seen it for the past year. You're settling for second-best. You deserve better.'

Chelsea came back to the conversation. 'Can't find much on this Mancini guy. It's odd. Who can't be found on Instagram, Google or Facebook? I just keep getting bumped to some company site. There are a few business function photos of him with various stunning babes hanging off his arm. Doesn't seem to have a main babe, could be a bit of a player. Not much else. Seems strange. But ...' Her tone was more frustrated than mean. '... as for Rick, well, Nat, I know it's hard to hear, and since Sage has brought it up. I agree.' She widened her gorgeous hazel eyes while giving her patented, sanguine, let-me-educate-you stare. 'You're a babe. You could have so much more. God, I'd turn for you if I didn't like cock so much.'

Ahh, vintage Chelsea. She'd never had to settle. She shone, even in her nurse's uniform. Chelsea may have been someone Natasha envied. Instead, they'd instantly clicked as Chelsea smoothed the way for Nat when she was an ER pharmacist newbie.

On this far too hot day, silence settled over the table like a thick, prickly blanket. Natasha looked towards the Fremantle port as a distraction from the Spanish Inquisition at the table. Cranes dominated the docks in the busy port like giant robotic dinosaurs baring their large skeletal frames to the world as they loaded and unloaded both legal and, given today's events, undiscovered illegal cargo. These monoliths, their carcasses shimmering in the waves of heat, constantly changed the landscape of the port as they built up and then broke down the mountains of containers.

Nat smiled despondently. She could relate to the cranes. Her innermost defences were laid bare to her friends as she strained under the heavy load of always building her and Rick up. She glanced at Jo. 'Anything else to add?'

Jo tried to lighten the mood. 'Well ...' Her shoulders rose on a dramatic pause, as was often her wont. 'Does he take your breath away? You know, when you see him first thing in the morning or when you're about to do the horizontal tango?'

Nat aimed for indignant. 'Ahh, none of your business.' Her shoulders dropped along with her head. The only thing that took Nat's breath away lately was the sprinkling of icy water at the start of her solo morning showers.

'Nat, given your less than convincing response, let me say honestly, Rick's a smart-arse, and that's not only my professional opinion – I don't trust him.' Jo's lips curled in a smirk. 'If you're using him for s.e.x., that's fine. As long as you know that's all it is. You must know we care for you dearly when we say he's not good enough for you.'

'Please, don't hold anything back on my account.' The death stare Nat flashed Jo was anaemic.

'If you want to get some, have a hot affair, but not with someone like Rick.'

Exasperated, Nat said, 'Stop it. It's for me to work out.' The prickly silence settled once more.

Finally, Sage broke it, reaching out for Nat's hands. 'You're right. I'm sorry, we forget ourselves sometimes. We don't want Rick to come between us. I don't want to see you hurting again, that's all.' Her smile creased lines around her eyes, and her face softened. 'I'll always be here for you.'

Jo and Chelsea nodded in unison. It was what they did. They thrashed things out, but only the Amigos got to criticise each other. To anyone else, they presented a united front.

Natasha shared her real worry. 'But what if he's the one, and I miss my one big chance?'

Jo spoke, reflecting the expression on all their faces. 'If you've got to ask that, then he's not.'

Not for the first time, Natasha pushed down an unsettling feeling about Rick. He did have his good moments too. 'Okay then. I'll think about what you're saying.' She was mostly happy, better than she'd been for a while – no attacks, a point in Rick's favour, surely.

Their lunch arrived and thankfully, the topic moved on. Chelsea led the way. 'I've discovered a new underwear etiquette.'

Jo couldn't help herself. 'Really, pray tell. Was this a personal discovery on one of your nights out with the latest Mr TDD?'

Chelsea and Jo's man codes always intrigued Nat. 'You've lost me. Mr T-what?'

'Mr Tall, Dark and Delicious.'

'Oh.'

'No, not a Mr TDD. Purely an observation from work.' Chelsea smirked and continued to hold court, 'With all those designer names and labels branded all over men's underwear, I've noticed they're getting bigger and bigger.' Chelsea took a long sip of water, 'So way, way more is covered than just the rod and the reel. Yet young women's underwear is getting smaller. It's barely there, or not at all, the whole commando thing.'

'Whatever happened to always wear your best underwear in case you get hit by a bus?' Jo giggled. The lightness and happiness were returning.

Chelsea cleared her throat. 'Forgetting the bigger problems of the women's no-undie issue, I sometimes find that with these young men, I have to fight through all the extra material to save them. So, my dear friends, revenge is not only best served cold, but with a bloody big pair of scissors.' She gave a smoky laugh. 'Straight through all those expensive Tommys and Calvins because, seriously, it's a matter of life and death, no less.' And there it was. The fun was back.

Sage was still a little quieter than usual as she watched Natasha. Her worries filled her already thumping head. Was Rick sending Natasha back into an abusive cycle? Sage remembered the discarded, desperate waif she'd taken in. Delving through the outward grime and abject desolation of Nat's spirit, Sage discovered Natasha's mind had splintered from the vicious abuse she'd been subjected to by her father, and then more so when she ran away from home.

The young woman had fought back against all odds. Sage remembered how her chest warmed with pride when Natasha had finished her time at Sage's clinic as a fully graduated and registered pharmacist.

Then her gaze drifted to Jo, who laughed so easily with her friends. A bold and loyal woman, she took Sage's word that Natasha would never let her down if she took a chance on her. Jo met Nat with an open mind. With ever-present grace, balanced with shrewdness, Jo employed Nat as a pharmacist. That long-ago conversation returned to Sage as if it was yesterday.

*Sage's Fremantle clinic, three years ago.*

'She's had an abhorrent time of it. Yet, given a chance to change, she's made such stunning progress.'

Jo rested her chin on a fisted hand. 'Tell me about the underlying need for *such stunning progress.*'

'I'll let her detail the worst of her past if you need it. It began with domestic violence and a father who tortured her. She was forced to flee her home. That's when her circumstances went from bad to worse.'

Jo didn't flinch. 'Okay, tell me.'

Sage began to walk her long-time friend through the rubble of Natasha's circumstances. 'Back then, to survive, she disconnected from her surroundings and let an alter-ego take charge as she was forced into addiction.'

'Okay, but I can't employ someone whose mind might wig out and who's been an addict.'

'*Forced* into using, is different to *becoming* addicted,' Sage added.

Jo countered, 'You're splitting hairs.'

'She threw off addiction as soon as she could, meaning a *wig out* is unlikely,' Sage continued. 'We've worked hard to give her coping mechanisms. She's aware of the triggers that bring forth the personality that causes severe panic attacks, which sometimes leads to violence and blackouts. If necessary, she knows how to manage it with meds. She's so strong these days, it's unlikely she'll completely submit to an attack.'

Sage sipped some water. 'We've figured out that guilt over the enforced drugging caused her mind to split. However, at that point in time, she already had overwhelming feelings of guilt about how she was making a living. Given she's out of that environment now, being totally controlled by her alter egos is unlikely. She calls them her alters, for want of a better term. One alter ego, Trixie the Slut, did what was necessary to survive. Now Nat just calls this alter ego The Slut. The other, Goldilocks, punished Nat for what The Slut did. The terror Goldilocks brings is the most worrying – at its worst, Goldilocks can lead Nat to violence or suicidal thoughts and actions.'

'Just to be clear. This type of behaviour is very rare now, if it happens at all?' Jo asked.

'Yes.'

'Will she ever regain a complete and together mind?'

Sage's brow furrowed. 'That's the million-dollar question. There's one main block we're yet to unearth and have her remember. I'm certain that if she does, we'll be able to rid her of her alter egos forever. We've all but banished them, for the most part, from her everyday life. Mostly now her alters are voices, if they appear at all, like negative self-talk.'

'Can she manage these alters without meds if they do start to appear?' Jo said.

'Yes, music is the main key. Playing, singing, or if her guitar isn't handy, remembering the fingering to play songs and their lyrics. It calms her. Nat plays the guitar so well and has an amazing voice. Clinging to a song, whether out loud or in her head, settles her down.'

'Okay. Could work stress bring on an attack?'

'Unlikely, because three very rare triggers must occur all at once. All of which aren't ever likely to occur at work.'

Jo's eyebrows winged up, 'And her names for her alters are The Slut and Goldilocks, really?'

'Yes, I know it seems dramatic, but that's the core of what we're dealing with. They're opposite sides of the same coin – pleasure and punishment.' Taking a breath, Sage said, 'Nat hasn't had an uncontrollable attack in years.'

'Reassuring, but still ...'

'She's a work in progress, but she very intelligent and giving her a fulfilling job will help even more so. She been working as a pharmacist for me, and there's been no issues. In fact, because of her life experiences, she's very good with patients.'

'I'll need more. It's a lot to take in and trust a person over.'

Sage could see Jo was coming around.

'Why pharmacy, of all things?' asked Jo.

'Yes, it's an interesting career choice, given her background. I think because of her trauma she wanted to understand more about drugs and help those addicted. She's top of her graduating year and has experience beyond her years. She's been invaluable at my clinic, but needs to broaden her horizons now.'

On that day, Jo's generosity was tested, but Sage convinced her.

Jo nodded. 'Okay, I desperately need another pharmacist. I'll give her a three-month trial period to begin with and we'll go from there.'

Now, years later, neither woman had been let down by Natasha. Looking at her now, Sage was so proud, and was reminded that even rubble could be used to build new towers of strength. Nonetheless, she didn't want Rick to be the wrecking ball that brought down Natasha's progress.

After lunch, the Amigos dispersed. Jo and Natasha walked back to the pharmacy department, struggling against the heat that caused acrid vapours to waft up off the semi-liquefied bitumen road. When they neared the hospital's entrance, Jo could see relief in sight and asked, 'How's Rick feeling about you applying for his oncology/haematology job?'

The doors slid open. 'He's fine with it.' The cool, clean hospital air refreshed them as it washed over them. 'He sees his move to ICU from oncology/haematology as a step up the ladder. It'll give him more chances to show off how much he knows about all things medical. He's been trying to prep me for my job interview, but he's pretty busy with his own career, and just makes me feel inadequate.'

'Oh, please. You should have had a senior role ages ago.'

'It's okay, things are coming together now.'

'I'm so happy you have an interview.' Jo's voice dropped a little. 'You know I'll be on the interview panel, right?'

'Yep. I guessed that, given you're chief. Who else?'

'Pia Gallo, the CEO of the Aida Breast Care Foundation. Her family set up the foundation. And there'll be a rep from JCH's HR department.'

'Sounds fine to me. I'm just glad to get an interview.'

'Nonsense. You're intelligent, experienced, and more than qualified.'

They had to catch the lift to reach the pharmacy on the fifth floor. The mission-brown cube smelt of hospital-grade cleaner and sick people's regret. Dr Rachel Cartwright joined them, entering the lift just as the doors closed. She ignored Jo and Nat, punching the button of the floor she wanted.

Natasha had been working with Dr Cartwright for weeks now. 'Hi, has ER settled down?'

The doctor gave a gruff, 'Yes,' then gazed upwards as the floor numbers lit up, enforcing perfect lift etiquette.

Jo broke the silence. 'So apart from Rick, what prep are you doing for the interview?'

'I thought I'd go over some journal papers and read through some oncology texts this weekend.'

'How about we go over some onc and haem stuff this Sunday night, accompanied by a bottle of wine?'

'Isn't that a conflict of interest?'

Rachel's ears pricked up. *What was this about?*

Jo chuckled. 'Oh dear, no, the wine won't care.' She nudged Nat. 'No, I'm not going to know anything specific about the interview. I don't meet with the panel to sort that out until next Tuesday. I'll only be able to prepare you for what to expect generally, as any friend would do.'

'Don't you have anything better to do?' said Nat. Jo might have been divorced and married to work now, but she still entertained a rich social life, although not as much as Chelsea. 'No hot dates this weekend?'

Jo winked. 'No, not this weekend. I thought I'd have a quiet one. Besides, I'm working Sunday, which puts a dent in one's social life. I don't mind coming to your place after work. We can order food in and make a night of it?'

'Sounds like a plan.'

Jo's nose crinkled as she laughed. 'Sounds like a grand plan. By the way, did you know that Chelsea is moving up to onc/haem from ER as well?'

'Yes, but I don't know if you should say *as well*.' The lift doors opened and they stepped out, leaving Rachel to enjoy her own company.

'You'll be fine. You're one of the smartest women I know.'

'Flattery will get you everywhere. But I'd better get back to work. Don't want to get fired by the boss. I hear she's a real cow.'

'Really. How interesting ... I've heard that too.' Jo pulled a face. 'Moo.'

# THREE

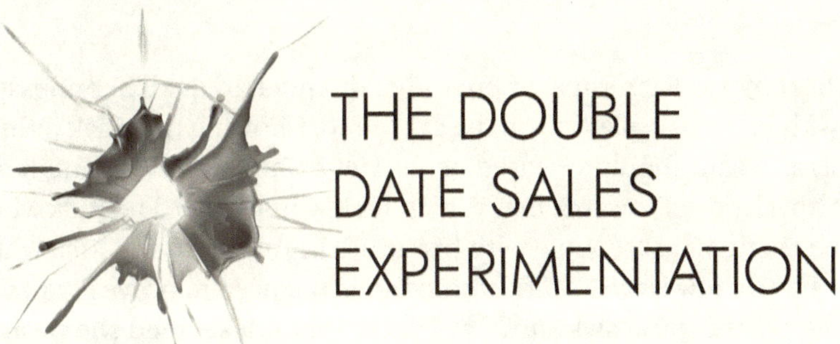

## THE DOUBLE DATE SALES EXPERIMENTATION

Natasha worked through until 5.30 pm then headed home, relieved the steady flow of overdoses had eased. She still had to drag her reluctant feet, which morphed to autopilot as she prepared for the night ahead.

Nat dressed, dreaming of caring and intimacy, wanting more from Rick tonight. *Stupid*, she thought. Safe was enough. Although the afternoon had been armpit-dripping hot, Natasha chose jeans for the evening. She'd been bitten so many times that it had left her far beyond twice shy. Life for Natasha was easiest when draped in the camouflage of ordinary.

To achieve this mundanity, she'd selected nameless skinny jeans snagged from a bargain bin at a budget store. To keep her a little cooler, she wore a white polyester shell top. Same store, different bin. While the fabric hugged her torso, it was not too tight. Her hardly bare shoulders were all the skin she was prepared to display. The only small eccentricity she entertained was knock-it-out-of-the-park shoes. Shoes were the one item she frequently stretched her budget for. Tonight, to set off her outfit, she'd chosen her intricately strapped white stilettos with silver heels.

Her straw-like hair sat up in a simple ponytail. She really should've tried to do more with it and let her beauty shine through. That was for another night when the date was more than a social experiment to improve Rick's job prospects. As it was, she wore only light make-up and did nothing extra to her hair.

---

The short trip to Rick's apartment didn't do much to quell her unease, even with her music playing on the car stereo. Knowing that Rick didn't see this as a date should've eased her anxiety. She was never confident about how he'd act towards her. Which Rick would it be? The Rick who showed them off as a couple with his future in mind? Or the Rick who only want to show Natasha off? Both satisfied the need to prove Rick was a solid guy, not some awkward, intelligent loner. It seemed she wasn't the only one with different personalities. Nevertheless, when it came to Rick's personalities, none were enough for Natasha. Maybe tonight Rick would show her more.

At this frustrating thought, the negative voices began. The Slut struck out, first, *Oh, don't be so sucky sentimental. It's only sex, and pretty bad at that.* The Slut was uninhibited, with questionable morals, but she'd had her uses for far more than trying to vamp it up on a date.

Such was Nat's life that for any Slut action, there was always a very unequal and opposite Goldilocks overreaction. *You're trash, that's why he only shows you the affection you deserve.* This reaction was mild. In the past, these two alters fought over Nat like two rabid dogs competing for a scrap of food. Goldilocks, the puritanical bitch liked to punish Nat severely for any of The Slut's transgressions.

Thankfully, now, Nat had better control but sometimes her mind entertained these two negative voices for a little longer than Nat liked. Goldilocks accepted Rick. He fitted her lore. He was not too hot, not too cold, not too soft and not too hard. He was just right. Hence Natasha's name for this alter. *You can't be trusted. Follow MY rules, bitch.*

*But he's a soft-cock.* The Slut barely tolerated Rick. Back in Sydney when Natasha was defenceless and had things done to her against her will, she would retreat and let The Slut take control. *And you survived.*

*As scum,* ranted Goldilocks. If The Slut strayed and sinned, Goldilocks released a beastly creature of fear, panic and loathing that sent The Slut, and ultimately Natasha, spiralling into a chasm of horror and violence, a full-blown psychotic storm. Natasha, even with Sage's undying patience, hadn't been able to unlock what this creature represented and why Goldilocks used it to torture Natasha.

The Slut was bored. *Come on, let's have some fun. Ditch Rick the stiff, or in his case, not so—*

'Stay on MY righteous path tonight, skank, or you'll pay.' Goldy spat.

'Arghh!' Nat fought back. She had enough energy left this day to shout all of them down, especially when she turned up the music. She mumbled to herself, *Yes, I'm settling,* Nat pushed The Slut and Goldy back to the dark side of her mind, silencing them.

As she parked her car, her overpopulated mind quietened. For the past year, beige banality was the only path she'd found that came close to ridding her of her alters. One day she'd be confident enough to play with all the colours. Until then, all she had was the black and white of her alters and the beige they coloured her in.

Natasha's knight in beige armour looped his wiry frame through the barely open door. His body was not too wimpy, not too great; perfect for Goldilocks. Natasha was comfortable with the safe techno-geek thing he had going on. Leaning up with minimal effort, he gave her a peck on the cheek. She moved her head and tried to linger on his lips. He moved away, and she sagged.

Jo's words sprang forth, invading Nat's thoughts like a struggling weed that had finally found the sun. Okay, he hadn't taken her breath away just now. Then again, he was in business mode and she was nervous. Rick didn't do much to improve his chances when he impatiently ran his hand through his greasy brown locks and shut the door. The tetchy jangling of the keys in his hand signalled there wouldn't be any pre-dinner couple time.

Rick's greyish-blue eyes swept upwards, appraising her. There was no spontaneous delight, a reaction she thirsted for. Instead, he dealt her a backhanded compliment. 'Hey, Tashy, you look hot, but not in *that* way. It's been so hot today. I thought I'd get to see your gorgeous legs tonight.'

'If this was a real date you would've.' There was a hint of satisfaction in her eyes as she looked down at him from her heels.

His eyes did a quick droll roll. 'Jeez.' He stood back slowly, shaking his head from side to side, practising his Steve Jobs circa 1970s look. 'Tashy, don't be like this. Tonight will be good for both of us. You know you need to raise your profile around the hospital. Sell yourself more, especially if you want my job on the onc/haem ward.'

'I'd rather let my work speak for itself.'

He adjusted his glasses. 'But there's no harm in giving yourself a bit of an edge. Once the doctors know you, your work doesn't just speak for itself. It announces you.'

'Yes, but I don't want it to announce, *here comes a complete tosser*.'

His eyes dulled, and silence became the only thing they shared as they walked along the stuffy corridor to the apartment block's garage. Natasha reached over and tried to hold his hand, pleading for a skerrick of attention. Her reward was another mood-deflating, economical peck on the cheek.

Rick coiled himself into the driver's seat, yelling from the open door, 'Come on. I know you, you're stalling.'

Natasha hated that he thought he knew her MO. She was so much more, if only he'd take the time to find out. He used to once.

Nat slid into the passenger seat as Rick reached over and squeezed her hand. Another brief touch, her chest ached for more.

'Can you relax? I know you're shy, but you can be mesmerising. I've seen you with your patients, your friends. You're brilliant. It's one of the reasons I'm with you.'

'I'll take that as a compliment, shall I?' Natasha's lips struggled with a skittish smile.

'Yes, you should. You're rarely like that with me, but I know you can be, so for tonight, if you could, please. It's important for my career ... and yours, of course.'

Rick was nothing if not consistent. A predictable, narrow path. It had to count for something. Natasha was tired and briefly disheartened, allowing Goldy to return to sit on one of her shoulders. *He's all you deserve. He's safe.*

The alters began to bicker as The Slut climbed onto Nat's other shoulder. *Safe's for young kids and churchgoers. You're made of hotter stuff. Set it free.*

Natasha wouldn't let the voices stay, fighting back, she let the lyrics and music of a song playing on the radio lighten her mind. Then she shifted the focus of the evening from an alleged sales opportunity to the safety of banality. 'Where's dinner tonight?'

'The Red Herring.'

She scoffed as her lips now found an easy smile. 'How apt.' *It summed up the date*, she thought.

Rick frowned, starting the car and crunching the late-model appliance into reverse gear. He liked this type of car. It was reliable. A practical vehicle that delivered serious people from A to B. Rick's dull white car looked and handled like a washing machine: a cycle of monotonous predictability that gave limp results. It wasn't Natasha's type of car. She liked power and performance, a car that gave the driver thrills and excitement. How she dreamed her partner might be. Her car – like her shoes and her friends – was one of the few not-too-ordinary things in her life.

Their dinner companions were late, so Rick and Natasha sat at the bar. He ordered a berry cider. *Not an adult drink*, thought Natasha. She settled her nerves by ordering champagne. She gulped more than the first half. She was rostered to work the next day so she'd go hard early, quell her nerves, and ease up later.

Holly arrived, apologising for her late date. She was more than a little pissed at him. 'I was all set to come in his car.'

*I bet she was*, thought Nat.

'Then he called, going on about some meeting, so I had to get an Uber. A meeting, you'd think he'd come up with a better excuse than that.' Not missing a beat, she shifted to flirty as she got the bartender's attention. 'A dirty martini.' Her lips hovered over the words, 'heavy on the *dirty*'. Once she'd joined them for a drink, her troubles slipped away. She thrust her curvaceous body Rick's way. 'Trust you to be on time.'

Rick jutted his chin carelessly towards Nat. 'Yes, still had to give Tashy here the hurry up.' Then he swept back to focus on Holly. 'H, have you two met?'

'Oh, sorry, I didn't see you there. Tashy, is it?'

Unlocking her grinding jaw, Nat managed, 'No. Natasha.'

'Of course it is.' Holly swiped her hand dramatically over her ample chest. 'I'm Holly, but you know that.' Nat's nostrils were assaulted by Holly's sickly-sweet perfume. Overpowering and cheap, it was a fitting calling card.

Rick rested his hand on Natasha's shoulder. 'You two should get to know each other. Tashy might be up on onc/haem soon—'

'So, where ya going, Richard?' Holly stroked back her long, copper-chestnut hair. Natasha suspected that's what the dye colour printed on the bottle read. Holly flicked her locks back, revealing more of her porcelain face. It was a perfectly practised move. Her scantily clad breasts swayed hypnotically in the direction of her locks. All pure sexual precision.

Rick's hand fell from Nat's shoulder, and an icy awkwardness engulfed Nat. So much for the scorching day. She drained her glass, wondering how Holly flirting with Rick was helping his, or for that matter, her, career. His cloaking of Natasha made time seem to skulk by. Rick ordered a second round of drinks for Holly and him, ignoring Nat.

Natasha wanted the floor to swallow her up so she could be as invisible to the rest of the world as she seemed to be to her boyfriend. Her eyes drifted. They swept around the restaurant, wondering if anyone had noticed that she was uncomfortable – self-conscious and being ignored by her boyfriend. Natasha's gaze became fixed on the entrance as a gorgeous man appeared. The doorway framed his tall, dark and definitely delicious features – a perfect Mr TDD. Chelsea and Jo would've been impressed.

Smouldering dark chocolate eyes burned Nat, and her breath hitched. 'Desire', U2's sexy anthem, started to power through Nat's brittle psyche. They stared at each other for a moment longer.

'Oh, finally. There he is the man himself.' Holly fussed, as Nat's Mr TDD smiled politely.

*Damn.* He'd have to be the doctor sniffing around Holly for more than her keen intellect and bubbly personality. Despite her disappointment, Nat couldn't take her eyes off him, nor stop the music. The last of the dusk sun seemed to light the way for him as he walked towards them. She was captivated by his face and smooth, tanned skin. He swept his long, sexy fringe across his face, causing his hair to catch the sunlight in a particular way, glistening blue-black. He was worth a second glance.

A brutal desire flooded Nat as her heart started to pound. The beats ran faster together like the heavy drumming of the music in Nat's head. She had to stop the drumming. She wasn't sure if it was driven by her, or if sometimes just the mere thought of The Slut appearing caused Nat to be wary about the feelings pumping through her. When The Slut became DJ to the soundtrack in Nat's head, Natasha was simply screwed. Still, she couldn't take her eyes off Mr Tall, Dark and Delicious, and desires born from a whole different kind of screwed flowed through her. For his part, he seemed indifferent.

Natasha couldn't help but appraise Mancini's sublime lines. He looked carefree but there was a kind of fiery restlessness in his manner, tinged with an edge of underlying darkness, maybe sadness. Soon it was hidden as a flash of annoyance flickered across his face. Natasha recognised a man it was best not to anger. Yet she had this irresistible urge to challenge him. There would be a certain excitement in testing how far his buttons could be pushed.

Before Nat could think any further, Goldilocks said, *This one is too hot for you. Too dangerous. Stay with Mr Just Right.*

Nat tried to hang onto Goldy's beige beads of wisdom and the control she needed even as The Slut added, *Just right is for breakfast cereals. Let's spice up life with Mr Deliciously Devine.*

As the doctor came close he extended his hand, and Natasha understood the flash of annoyance. Rick had hopped off his bar stool to shake the doctor's hand and fawn. 'Sebastian, I mean Dr Mancini, great. Good to see you. Glad you made it.' It was like the doctor was Rick's date.

'Apologies, all. I got caught up at a board meeting.' The doctor's voice was so smooth and deep that it vibrated to Natasha's core. Oh, it was hot again. He reached over and with a quick nod and a slight smile, shook Holly's hand. Not what Nat had expected at all.

Rick prattled on. 'Oh, those hospital meetings. Sometimes I wonder why we have them. They just stop us from getting to the real work.'

Another flash of annoyance hit Mr TDD's face, until he moved away from Rick. Then his eyes brightened as he extended his hand, turning his full attention to Nat. 'Hello, I don't believe we've been properly introduced.' His smouldering sizzle was paired with old-world charm. 'Sebastian Mancini. My friends call me Seb.'

Nat took his hand. 'Hi Seb, pleased to meet you. Natasha Perry. My friends call me Tash.' As she echoed his words, a glorious smile spread across his face. A charge shot through her as his eyes widened. Nat shifted her focus as he seemed to see into her soul. Her eyes darted to the light dusting of dark curly hair on his broad chest. It poked above the top button of the crisp navy shirt that hugged his svelte torso.

Suddenly, she had to fight outrageous notions as 'Desire' ramped up again. Its powerful bluesy swagger drove an erotic longing, daring her to find out what it would feel like to drag her fingernails through his chest hair and follow the rich path down, down. Southwards could be fun, below where his black trousers highlighted his lithe hips and toned butt.

Nat fought to heed Goldy's rules and banish Trixie the Slut. The feelings he inspired surprised her. She'd suspected this depth of passionate need had shrivelled up and died at the hands of partner tedium forced upon her by Goldilocks's control. It was Natasha who defiantly wanted to run wild and hot with Mr TDD. Wow, Natasha's desire, not The Slut's.

Holly pushed between them, grabbing the good doctor's arm. 'Shall we eat?'

Rick crashed through Natasha's trance. 'Yes. C'mon, Tashy.'

Natasha hadn't realised that while her thoughts were cascading over themselves, she was still holding the doctor's hand. With the contact broken, U2's power was pulled. Bono's gravelly sexiness yielded to that noise heard when a vinyl record became stuck, tracking around and around in a well-used rut. Natasha's familiar safety zone.

Mancini cleared his throat. 'Um, yes.' Cocking his head, he gave Natasha a quizzical look. Rick grabbed her hand and not so subtly pulled her away. The waitress, who recognised Sebastian, rushed to seat them near the windows, a prime position overlooking the Swan River and the Norfolk pines lining the opposite bank. Natasha sat next to the window, with Rick on her right. She was amazed to be at a table with such a view. Dr Mancini waited and pulled Holly's chair out so she could sit across from Rick. Mancini chose to sit across from Natasha.

Given the view, Natasha was relieved she could make safe small talk. If Rick monopolised their companions, all would not be lost. She could enjoy some delectable food and magnificent views. Not to mention the occasional sneak peek at Mr TDD. As if on cue, Rick highjacked the conversation and it followed his path.

Finally, there was a pause in Rick's domination of the conversation as the waitress delivered their mains. Natasha noticed that Sebastian had also ordered seafood. She loved seafood. Rick, on the other hand, had come to one of the finest seafood restaurants in Fremantle and Perth only to order steak. That was Rick, one of his many quirks. Holly had ordered oysters and proceeded to eat them luridly. Predictable, yet still stomach-turning. Natasha couldn't help but notice that Dr Mancini was also repulsed.

This doctor wasn't at all what she'd expected. Unlike Chelsea's description, he was considerate and respectful. He didn't seem to be a player. Then again, she hadn't spoken to him that much. There was still plenty of time for cheesy pick-up lines and pretence. He was here with Holly, after all.

With Holly and Rick's mouths full, Sebastian finally had a chance to speak. This woman he'd organised to sit across from held his attention. He'd had his fill of skin-deep. Something about her whirl of blue eyes and simple beauty made him want to see what made her tick. He wondered how far he'd have to dig to see if he affected her like he wanted to. 'Nat, do you like sailing? I see you looking out at the boats on the river.' She seemed much more like a Nat to him than a Tash and certainly not a Tashy.

Natasha became knot-in-her-stomach surprised. She almost choked on her fish. *No, no, no.* Only her closest friends and family were allowed to call her Nat. Stumbling past his first curveball, she swung at the second. 'Um, only from afar. I've never had the chance to sail, but I like the water.'

'Me too.' Sebastian thought he saw a hint of a blush. He became intrigued by her challenging level of self-discipline. Women rarely surprised him these days. Could he break through her control? He added, 'I love the water.' Then, he surprised himself by blurting out, 'I have a sports cruiser. Maybe one day you could come for a cruise with me.' He frowned inwardly. He was trying to break her down, yet he was the one cracking.

His words made the knot in her stomach tighten. Nat's brain crashed as she contemplated his invite, which included her all on her lonesome. She kept her face impassive, mask in place. Goldilocks had trained her well.

With Nat's thoughts stalled, The Slut surfaced. *Oh yesss! You know you want to.*

Goldilocks hissed, *Get a grip. With this Italian prince, you'll be dirt and then mine to hurt.* Fear of Goldy rebooted Nat's brain. Yes, pompous Italian prince. He needed a peg or two knocked out. She was with Rick. Didn't it look like it? From the glares Rick and Holly shot her way, Nat knew she had to shut this down, not only because of her alters' ire.

The good doctor's bottomless brown eyes pinned her as they danced with mischievous delight. To be safe, Nat moved the conversation. 'I've always thought I'd like my first sail to be special, maybe a motor yacht around the Greek Islands.' She gave Seb a back-off stare.

He found that intriguing. Most women fawned over him. Although maybe there was a chink in her armour. This woman could be the challenge he thirsted for. Tonight may be more entertaining than Seb had anticipated. He wondered how much she was attached to this guy Rick. 'It sounds like a fantastic adventure to share with someone special.'

Nat decided this arrogant bastard needed a lesson. Risky to rely on Rick to help teach Sebastian Mancini, but Nat tried. 'Yes, I think so. Hey, Rick, how about it, you, me and a small yacht with the beauty of the Aegean surrounding us? Sounds good, don't you think?'

Rick shook his head and grunted. 'No, not really,' and continued to chew his steak.

His dismissal forced Natasha to save face with cheery ambivalence. 'Then there's the architecture and history. Some of my friends have done it. They make it sound so good.'

'So you're living precariously through them?' Holly chipped in with an airy giggle.

Seb raised his eyebrows as his eyes met Nat's.

Rick sniggered. 'I think you mean *vicariously*, H.'

Knowing how terrible it felt to be on the end of a Rick put-down, Natasha spoke. 'You're both kind of right. At the moment, I am living through the stories my friends have told me, but given I haven't sailed before, when I finally do, the trip might be fairly precarious.'

Everyone laughed. Holly quickly recovered from her faux pas.

'Totally rules me out, then.' Rick put his very own hurtful cherry on top. Rick and Holly downed their wine and struck up a conversation about the food.

A pang of sympathy hit Seb. It was his fault she'd been left high and dry by Mr Flaky. He lowered his voice, focusing on Natasha. 'I've been around the Greek Isles, but not on a yacht. It would be fun.'

Surprisingly for Natasha, she slipped into a relaxed conversation with Dr Mancini. His musical tastes were almost as eclectic as hers, her love of books nearly as diverse as his. He liked Hemingway and was reading one of his books. She liked to run along the same beach track as he did.

'Maybe I'll see you out there. I usually do a Sunday run.'

Natasha pushed down strange feelings. 'Um, I'm working this weekend, so probably no run.' The discussion moved on to work where she found that Dr Mancini the oncologist empathised as much with his patients as Natasha did with hers.

His brow creased. 'Sorry, the last thing you probably want to talk about is work.'

Natasha was impressed; something she hadn't been in some time with a man.

He refocused on her. 'Where have you travelled?'

'Not far. Sydney to Melbourne once by car for a family holiday. And a cheap flight to Perth, obviously. That's about it. I want to travel more.'

'Me too.'

'You sound like you've already been to so many places.'

'Only Europe, the usual cities, Paris, Rome, Barcelona. I lived in Italy for a time.' Again, he found himself giving away more than usual. 'Once I hit thirty, it was time to come home. I've only been back about six months.'

'Ahh, I'd love to see Europe, but then there's Machu Picchu, or Ethiopia and the sunken—'

'Churches of Lalibela.'

'Yes!' They laughed at their easy familiarity and the meal passed almost too quickly.

As they organised to pay the bill, Holly, who was quite tipsy, declared, 'The night's young. Who's up for more?'

Natasha pulled Rick's hand, trying not to look desperate, yet desperately trying to hint that she needed this sales experiment to end. Without looking at her, he spoke to Holly. Not really to her face. His boob fetish was coming to the fore. With Holly's girls swinging around unhindered, Rick slipped into a boob-inspired hypnosis and smiled his let's-have-fun smile.

'What a great idea, bring it on.' He was a little inebriated, but it didn't excuse his leering.

'I really can't. I've got work tomorrow, and Rick, you shouldn't drive.' Natasha nudged Rick's shoulder, her anger rising. She restrained her urge to slap him silly. She was losing patience with dismissive, public Rick, especially given the day's lunch conversation. And now there was Mancini's Greek Odyssey challenge so fresh in her mind.

'Oh, Tashy, since you've been such a goody-two-shoes, you can drive. Come on out and play.' Rick's miniaturisation of Natasha knew no bounds. 'You're only in the dispensary tomorrow. It's not like you'll need a lot of brain power there.' Nasty Drunk Rick had appeared, and Natasha had thought she was the only one with a few nasty alter egos.

Not totally sure why, Sebastian felt someone needed to rescue her. 'I have to work tomorrow too. What if we go for a little while? Then we can see how we all feel after that?' He saved the shred of pride Natasha had left.

'It's settled then.' Holly grabbed Seb's arm and gleefully proclaimed, 'To Metropolis, and don't spare the horses.'

# FOUR

## SHIFTING GEARS TO SEXY

Rick threw his car keys at Natasha as he fell into the passenger seat. Her rage bounced from her grinding jaw to her words. 'How dare you ignore me like that?'

'No choice, you were flerrrting soooo much with the doctor.' Rick's snarly slur pushed a button, but not the type Mancini had been pushing.

'I wasn't flirting.' She clenched her jaw and echoed his words, 'I was being *mesmerising*. Isn't that what you wanted me to be?'

'Yes, but to help our careers. How does talking about the Greek Isles do that?'

She yelled, 'How does talking about the bloody food help either?'

'She's a dietician.'

'Give me strength,' she groaned.

'Anyway, she's not the sharpest tool in the shed, but she looks the goods.'

His words were like gasoline on Natasha's fire. 'Yes, I saw you looking over her goods like you wanted to sample them.'

'Oh, Tashy, don't be so jealous and needy. It's not a good colour on you.'

'And you're a first-class arse.'

Rick thought he had all the answers. He was confident that he was all Tashy could handle. After all, he knew what made Tashy tick, no surprises there. 'Look, if we're going to be in this for the long haul, then you have to understand that I do everything to get a better-paying job and make things better for us.'

She grimaced. He'd pulled out his old chestnut that had her feeling guilty. She didn't need any help in that department. Tonight would be different. All Natasha saw was Rick's roaming eyes and his lecherous smile at Holly's breasts. There'd be no guilt trip tonight. 'I'm happy with what I have. And don't treat me like a handbag.'

'Handbag? What the hell are you on about now?'

'I'm not just a fashion accessory for you to hang off your arm, show off, drape over a chair and only care about when you're arriving and leaving.' His silence only deepened her fury, further exacerbated by her inability to find a park quickly or close to the club.

When they finally joined the queue outside the nightclub, Nat couldn't see Holly or Seb anywhere. She suspected they'd probably gone elsewhere, so Holly could finally come in his car, which the over-sexualised trollop was known for. As these mean-spirited thoughts began settling over Nat, she saw Seb come out of the club with a huge guy dressed in black, who promptly waved Rick and Natasha through.

Rick prattled on. 'Way to go, Sebastian. You're a prince. I knew it was an excellent idea to hook you up with Holly tonight.'

Nat was back to grinding her teeth at the realisation that Rick was the matchmaker and architect of the evening. She thought, *Shit, he could be such a dick.* She was livid when she entered the club. The DJ was pumping out Flo Rida's 'Let it roll', which usually would have helped her mood. It didn't. She was so in-her-head angry there was no room to focus on anything other than her rage. She didn't recognise the danger as a woman teetering towards her tripped on her skyscraper heels, causing her drink to fly everywhere. Sebastian grabbed Natasha around the waist and pulled her back into him, away from the flying liquid.

A sensual, electric pulse ripped through her as she turned in his arms, looking up into his deep, Old Gold chocolate eyes. His alluring cologne had her swooning. Mmm, all real man. She steadied her weakened legs by resting her forearms and hands on his ripped chest. His arms were so strong and safe. She wanted to run her fingers down his washboard and brush them against his—

No, not this again. Natasha had to stop these uninvited fantasies before Goldilocks took over. She pulled back abruptly, almost falling over the woman struggling to get back on her feet. Seb grabbed her forearms and smiled as he gently steadied Nat back on her heels.

'Thanks.' Reluctantly, she tore her eyes away from his, as she tried to put some distance between them. Yet her arms remained in his hands.

Sucking in a sharp breath, Seb thought this lady was *too ... something* for him. Nonetheless, he held her a little longer and leaned in close, his lips on her ear. 'Don't mention it, my pleasure.'

An unnamed emotion flowed over his face as she backed up. It floored her for a beat and then it was gone, shrouded in the good manners that dropped over him as he distanced himself from her. Rick and Holly hadn't noticed anything, allowing Natasha to slip back into normalcy as well. That was until Seb leaned in again. She raised her ear to his lips. Rick wasn't the only one who could play this game, and she might as well try to teach Mancini a thing or two.

'Would you like a drink?'

She frowned, 'No, I've had enough, and with work tomorrow ...'

Flo Rida pumped out around them while mischief played in Seb's voice. 'When we talked music, you said you liked Flo Rida. You look like you'd move well to him.' He flashed a cheeky grin. 'How about it? A dance instead?'

Taken by the moment and not his player pick-up line, Nat took Flo Rida's advice. Fuck Rick and his stale love. 'Why not. Let the good times roll!'

Seb treated Natasha to a Dr Mancini megawatt smile. It triggered an empowering feeling. As they pushed past Holly and Rick, Rick stopped mid-sentence and sullenly rocked his head from side to side. Holly gaped.

Once he was on the dance floor, Seb pulled Natasha to him. His presence flooded through her once again. No longer wanting to fight it, she succumbed to this good-looking man's hold. That was the last Natasha saw of Rick or any other reality for a while. Strong, gentle hands found her hips. Flo Rida morphed into Bruno Mars's 'Locked out of heaven'. Dr Sebastian Mancini had indeed unlocked something heavenly. They moved together like they were fated to know the steps each other would take.

Goldy tried to shout. *Stop! Dancing like this doesn't lead to bliss!* For once, Goldilocks failed. Seb banished her as his hands caressed Nat's hips with reverence.

In the past, she had been repulsed by the lust-filled trance her dancing provoked in some sleazeball's eyes. The emotions that claimed her when strange men placed their hands on her had nothing to do with pride or veneration. But the look in Dr Mancini's eyes made her body tingle.

With her so close, Seb found her too captivating. He had to turn her because he couldn't trust himself – her eyes seemed to peel him apart. With her back towards him, his hands caged her waist and they lost themselves in the freedom of the song. He felt her relax and he couldn't resist moving his hard body against her butt cheeks.

Seb leaned down, his lips at her ear again. 'You're a great mover.'

At his words she expected her guilt to rise, so she spun around to explain she wasn't normally like this. Then her lips accidentally brushed against his. A stronger sensual charge rippled through them both, causing them to linger a little longer, until reality bit and they sprang apart. Nat was confused at how much she liked it. The barest of tastes, yet it evoked a powerful feeling she couldn't define. Even more of a surprise was there were no voices, no guilt.

Seb's chest hummed as his teeth bit into the fleshy part of his bottom lip. He held it there while his whole body stilled and felt warm at the taste of her.

Stumbling back, her words did the same, 'I like you, um ...' It took her a beat. 'I mean, I like how you move too.'

In that finger-snap of time, her mask of ordinariness slid back into place. Before it did, Seb witnessed a glimpse of the fire and vulnerability that resided within Ms Natasha Perry. It left him wanting something he hadn't wished for in a long time: to be a better man.

Pragmatism returned, causing Natasha to muddle through a quick exit. 'I really should go now. It's late, with work and all that.'

Also scrambling, he said, 'It's okay, I didn't mind. Sorry, I didn't mean to. But yes, with work tomorrow, we should go.' The earlier restlessness she'd seen in his eyes returned.

Rick and Holly were still sharing a drink and a far too intimate conversation at the bar. Nat reached for him, trying to ignore his proximity to Holly. 'Rick, I need to go.'

He was in a spiteful, drunken place and yelled, louder than needed, 'I don't. You're such a wet blanket. I'm gonna dance with Holly.' Rick stumbled a little as he stood, grabbing at Seb's shoulder to steady himself. He slurred as he seemed to joke with Seb, but a heavy hint of sarcasm infected his words, 'You take her home since you two seem to be hitting it off.'

Seb's muscles coiled tight as he clenched his fists and stood taller. Two guys, one of whom could have been the bouncer who'd appeared outside the club with Seb, began edging closer to the bar. They'd taken an interest in the conversation's escalating heat. Seb curtly shook his head, and they stepped back.

Holly giggled, running her hand up Seb's arm. 'If it's okay with you, it's okay with me.' She seemed to be the only one with no idea what was happening. She was either extremely understanding or completely clueless. Natasha's money was on the latter.

Seb asked, 'How are you getting home, Holly?'

Rick turned to Seb, realising he needed to keep him on side, while showing Natasha who was in charge. 'Don't worry, I'll look after Holly. At least she seems to be able to handle more than one dance. Am I right?'

'Rick, stop this.' Natasha leaned in close. 'Jealous and needy don't look any good on you either.'

He jerked his head away, shouting, 'You speak in clichés. You know that. It's really boring.'

Seb couldn't believe how his insides churned. He'd just met this woman, yet he wanted to punch Rick's lights out for being such a bastard. He needn't have worried as he watched and learnt more about Ms Perry.

She gave Rick a sickly-sweet smile, treating him like a precocious child, bringing her head down to get in his sullen face. 'What can I say?' She pushed him back as her face flooded with disdain. 'I learnt from the best.'

Rick stumbled back. Seb smiled. Ms Perry could stand up for herself.

Natasha didn't like seeing them like this, but at least Rick was showing some emotion towards her in public. 'Rick, give me your car keys and promise me you'll get a cab.'

Holly slurred, 'An Uber's fine.'

Nat held his gaze. 'We can thrash this out later.'

Rick jutted his chin out at her. 'I don't think I'll wanna talk to you later.'

'And I'm pissed at you too.' She shot Rick a withering look, thinking *just give me the keys, dumbass*. Her patience was wearing thin.

Seb took note. He didn't want to be the cause of that look.

Rick baulked and fumbled with his keychain, unhooking his car's keys. He had no idea what was eating Tashy, but he knew he couldn't be picked up by the police for a driving drunk. It wouldn't suit anyone's plans. Tashy's overwhelming need to be good and avoid guilt would shine through. Ever reliable, she'd look after his car and go home alone. 'Same drill as before. Park it out front, keys in the letterbox.' He wasn't sure if Nat had heard him until she snatched his keys, making him smile. She made it so easy for him.

Once Natasha and Seb were on the street, he was talking. 'Can I drive you home? My car's just over there.'

Her body slumped as she looked at her feet. 'Thanks for offering, but I'll do as Rick asked.'

'That makes sense.' Seb didn't want to push her. He couldn't help but think he was responsible for Rick's anger towards this breath of fresh air of a woman.

'It's less complicated.' Natasha was trying to take the safe path, like always, still afraid to be who she wanted to be, although tonight an inkling of that person poked through her plain persona. *Stuff Rick. He can have some pain*, she thought. She'd already made it too easy for him. 'You know what? Drive me to Rick's place. My car's there. I'll put his keys in his letterbox. He can pick up his own damn car.'

Seb stepped out onto an unusual limb for him, 'I hope you don't mind me saying, but he doesn't deserve such a hot girlfriend.' His gaze levelled Natasha.

She had no doubt he was referring to her in *that* way. The way Rick hadn't. She almost blushed, dropping her head to bring herself under control.

He surprised them both by gently lifting her chin so he could look into her eyes, hopelessly blue, even in the streetlight. 'I'm sorry. I didn't mean to embarrass you.' He leaned forward, coming in too close.

'Oh,' whispered from her lips.

The Slut's voice was more than a whisper in her head. *Bet he tastes gooood. Yesss, please.* As The Slut was about to break free, Natasha flinched slightly, causing Seb to catch himself.

Shaking his head, he said, 'Sorry, I'm really not like this.'

She nodded and tried not to pant. Of course he'd come to his senses. Natasha wasn't his type – too bland and unsophisticated, unlike the hot women Chelsea had described him photographed with. He was a player, after all. They walked along the footpath in nervous silence until Nat saw a magnificent car and couldn't help herself. 'Now, Dr Mancini, I bet that moves well.' She cringed, sure she'd removed any doubt about her lack of sophistication.

'Yes, Ms Perry, you're so right.' Seb pushed the key fob in his hand and the doors clunked, the lights flashed and the inside of the car illuminated, revealing a plush bone-coloured interior.

'Oh, I didn't realise it was yours. It's a Maserati Grand Turismo.' She found herself slipping, hypnotised by his car. It was black, with the sleek lines synonymous with Italian automobile craftsmanship. A dangerous beauty, like its owner, and she was drawn to the danger as much as the beauty. Somehow Dr Mancini had pierced through her mask. Natasha was in trouble with this one. 'V8, right?'

His eyebrows shot up. 'Yes, it is a Maserati V8. I'm impressed, Natasha. You know your cars. Where does that come from?' There was more to Ms Perry than met the eye, and he liked what met his eyes.

'I have a couple of friends who're mechanics. They're kind of like big brothers. They've encouraged my love of cars.' Rick didn't know about her love of cars. Then again, Rick didn't drive a car that warranted such a discussion. A rare spark of real excitement ignited. In her moment of weakness, The Slut started the music stylings of The Runaways.

'I'm glad. I love cars too.' He stopped and quipped, 'And this is my Maserati Granturismo Sport, 4.7 litres, V8.' This woman seemed too innocent. Then she'd flash a side of her that surprised. She had him off balance and unable to help himself, he blurted, 'I like a car that looks like it can eat the road.' He sent her a sizzling gaze as he opened her door.

Nat was enthralled. Goldilocks was too slow. Trixie appeared, and The Slut pounced. 'Stunningly dangerous, like a chained predator pulling on its collar.' Now The Slut purred. 'Captivating. The fusion of strength and power is almost sensual.' The Slut was present. Nat was lost.

His eyes widened. 'Yes, a very keen observation, Ms Perry. I'm glad. I'd like the chance to take you in her.' He closed the door, the pause getting her engine running. He walked around to slide into the driver's seat, 'For a ride, that is. Argh, that's what I meant to say.'

'Either way, yes. Why not?' The Slut was in control, guiding Nat's tongue over her top lip while her legs parted a little and her hips suggestively moved forward, like she was seeking a more comfortable position in the seat but wanted so much more. The Runaways started to play 'Cherry bomb'. Goldilocks had been left behind.

Seb's mouth ran dry, 'Excellent. I get to spend more time with someone that understands the performance of my ride.'

'Again with the double entendre. I'll make it simple. Yes, your car is a turn-on, Dr Mancini. That's where it ends tonight.' Goldilocks was up to speed, taking control. Joan Jett was forced to pack up her guitar, and The Runaways had left the building. The Slut had been thrown back to the darker recesses of Nat's flawed mind.

Seb was confused. Had he misread the signs? Such a hot come-on and then a cold rebuff. He scrambled to dial it back. 'You've misinterpreted what I meant. It's rare to find someone who understands why a car like this is such a joy to drive.'

'Did you want to finish that sentence with, *especially a woman?*'

'No. Not in the least. I can see you know your cars. Nothing else was implied. I apologise if I offended you.' Seb's mind tilted slightly. She was fiery, challenging him, and that intrigued him. His playboy smile and name didn't affect this one.

'Oh, I see.' He'd surprised her. 'That's nice to know.' His apology and the sincerity in his eyes had brought Natasha back, and with Goldy gone, she had a notion that she needed to say, 'Thanks.'

The car roared into action as he pulled out into the traffic. It was truly a dream ride. 'I love the sound of a powerful engine being shifted superbly through its gears. It's hot.'

'Yes, exactly.'

'Oh, shit. Did I say that out loud?' Now he'd not only believe she was unsophisticated, but he'd also know she was a revhead bogan. Jeez.

Seb chuckled, beaming at her. 'You did. It's okay. You're upfront about your thoughts. I like that.'

'Since we're being upfront. You and Holly, what's that about?'

He laughed, dropping his head. 'Ah, not me. Rick thought it would be a good idea if we all went out together.' He rolled his eyes back up to the road and grimaced. 'When he asked, I was trapped in the doctor's office with Holly and him. I didn't want to appear stuck-up, so I said yes.'

'Ha, that makes sense.'

'Which leads me to ask my own frank question, Ms Perry. You and Rick, what's that about?'

'Yes, well, that's an interesting question. After tonight I'm not sure. Obviously, we have a few things to talk over. We've been seeing each other for about a year. I thought we were good together, but over the last couple of weeks, well …' Nat's frustration bubbled up. 'Fuck buddies is more like it.'

'Oh!'

'And … I can't believe I just shared that either. Jeez, I seem to suffer from a serious case of foot-in-mouth disease around you.'

Seb laughed. Natasha joined him. A pang of regret stilled the mood in the car as the ride neared its end when she gave him the final directions to Rick's .

Seb parked and swiftly opened his door and rushed out. Nat suspected reality had finally claimed his sensibilities. She was not in his league. His folly realised he wanted to rid himself of her quickly, alleviating the need for the crushing awkwardness of the end-of-ride-home conversation. A conversation usually filled with false platitudes, yet inevitably a let-down, or worse: the contrived goodnight pity peck on the cheek and maybe the oh-but-I-*will*-call-you.

To show she was thinking similarly, Nat opened her door. Part of her wished she could be different, like years ago, and dare to make him want her. She wondered, when had it become all or nothing in her life?

Wanting to show Natasha that she deserved more – chivalry, at the very least – Seb was going to open her door for her. Of course, she had other ideas, so he changed tack. Gently he took her hand, helping her leave the low-riding car. He then kissed along the top of her knuckles. He hadn't intended to go that far, but she made him forget himself and be that better man he hadn't seen in a while.

Natasha melted and almost fell back into the car. She thought guys like this would never exist anywhere on her radar. What was she thinking? She had no radar, certainly none that would pick him up.

He found her eyes and, while still holding her hand, mouthed, 'Hey, you okay?'

'Yes, well, um, thank you, Sebastian.' He was too close again.

'Will I see you tomorrow?'

'I don't think so. I'm in the dispensary.'

'Do you get lunch?'

'Yes, but only half an hour on weekends, so I tend to stay in the pharmacy.'

Tilting his head to one side, he opened his arms, raising his shoulders playfully. 'Any chance we could catch up again sometime?'

What did he want from her? 'I want to talk things over with Rick. Give him a chan—'

'Really. When he let you come home with someone you'd just met so he could be with the hospital floozy.' Playful Seb was banished. Annoyance tainted his words, creased his face and cooled his eyes.

Her anger rose at his arrogance. 'Excuse me. I still owe him a chance to explain. I'm sorry if that cramps your style, but that's just me.' Bastard entitled Italian prince.

He restrained his cynicism, but not by much. 'Forgive me, of course. Even if you're only just fuck buddies.'

'Oh, touché, Dr Mancini.' She seethed. Of course he'd be bent out of shape because she hadn't fallen for his player moves.

Seb bristled but couldn't take his eyes off her. Instead of storming apart, they stepped towards each other, drawn by the heat. Her sad, stormy eyes broke his need to prove his point. 'Sorry. You're right. I mean this sincerely, you're far better than me. I couldn't – listen, I don't want to leave you like this.' He took her hands in his, hoping his words and hold could melt their combined anger.

Natasha had never known a man not to fly totally off the handle in such a situation. 'Now that's taken the wind out of my angry sails. You're quite the surprise, Dr Mancini.'

'And you're a pleasant surprise, Ms Perry.' Then, with a mystified whisper, he said, 'Just ... mesmerising.'

Natasha smiled unashamedly. She'd been mesmerising enough for at least one person tonight. While her heart sang, she realised she needed to escape before she became trapped and gave up too much. 'Goodnight, Sebastian.' Breaking their contact extinguished the electric energy pulsing through her. Nat's hand still tingled as it fell by her side.

Captivated by her smile, especially it made her eyes sparkle, he offered, 'Thanks for a far more entertaining evening than expected.' Giving her back a sizzling, megawatt Mancini smile.

Breathless and vulnerable, she turned and walked away, not daring to look back until she reached her car.

Seb didn't want to leave her, but he had no choice. She was leaving him. It made him want her more. She seemed resistant to him, except for a fleeting second when discussing his Maserati. He slid into his car, utterly bewildered, waving as he sped past.

Natasha waved back, sagging against her car. A slow realisation crept over her as she sat behind the wheel. That was what it felt like to have her breath well and truly taken away.

# FIVE

## THE SAFE ENCOUNTER FARCE

Natasha finally fell into bed at around twelve. She was fearful. Slutty music had spontaneously broken out in her head, and she'd used The Slut's words. An attack from Goldilocks could be close. She left her curtains open the prescribed ten or so centimetres, letting a skinny, muted ray of moonlight through. Her phone was by her side, with Anastacia's 'I'm outta love' piercing the silence as she scrolled through photos of herself, her mum, brother and sister in happier times. She wasn't alone or in the silent dark.

With all her triggers covered, a new feeling of satisfaction settled over her. Fighting back against Rick and holding the line against Mancini seemed to have dulled the sharpness of Goldilocks's negative voice – for now. The music carried Natasha to welcome numbness and peace, and she didn't stir until seven-thirty.

It was going to be another scorching day. The morning was already too hot for the day to evolve into anything other than an air-conditioner salesman's wet dream. Natasha had a cool shower and dressed, settling on a plain light-blue shift dress and bone-coloured heels. With her hair in a neat work-ready ponytail, she'd succeeded in camouflaging herself in ordinary.

Work rolled by with no hiccups and no visits from Mr TDD. Everything seemed back to normal until her phone pinged as she finished lunch.

R: Where r my car keys & car?

Shit, she'd been so sidetracked by Mancini she'd forgotten about Rick's car keys. They were still in her bag.

N: Have at work. Car where parked last night

Nat hit send, knowing her news wouldn't be well received.

R: FUCK!!!!!!!!!!!!!

'Bastard,' she hissed. Rick was the one who got pissed and left her high and dry, all to try and prove a point.

N: Nice to hear from U2 arsehole. Shit happens. Pick keys up at work

or later. IDGAF

R: How do you suggest I get to work?

N: You got a brain use it

She was in no mood for his diva antics. Rick got the message.

R: CU in 10

Natasha returned to work to fill a prescription for morphine tablets. Morphine was classed as a dangerous drug because it was addictive, so she had to go to the pharmacy's safe to retrieve the tablets. The safe was the size of a small room, with a heavy iron door. A handle shaped like a small ship's wheel was used to open and shut it, and a rotary combination lock was used to secure it. If it were in a bank, it would have housed safe-deposit boxes. It was large because it stored the entire supply of dangerous drugs, or DDs, for the hospital. They had to be kept securely, with their usage recorded meticulously so that every ampoule, every millilitre of liquid and each tablet could be accounted for.

Strict regulations were in place so these drugs wouldn't fall into the wrong hands. If records weren't accurate and drugs went missing, Jo could lose her licence to run and manage the JCH pharmacy. Anyone caught trafficking or stealing the drugs would be prosecuted, and if they were a pharmacist, nurse or doctor, they would be fired and stripped of their licence to practice and most likely the police would become involved.

Natasha was in the middle of counting out the grey 100mg morphine tablets and recording the prescription in the DD register when Rick strode into the safe. He decided to work his well-rehearsed angle. Once he made her feel guilty, she'd forgive anything. 'Hi, Tashy. I just came to get my keys. How come you didn't drive my car home, put the keys in my letterbox like you said you would? Anything could have happened to my car last night. What happened to *you*?'

'Is that all you've got to say for yourself?'

'Don't be like that.' He hadn't planned on her still being in last night's belligerent mood. He'd have to work harder. He moved closer. She sat at the desk, buried in DD paperwork. 'You got to know Mancini, and if you get my old job, you will have your foot in the door there. Hey, no foul.' He reached for her hand, squeezing it before she pulled it away. He smiled because she'd let him touch her. She was coming around. Tashy was so dependable, nothing if not pragmatic. But it was her body he loved having on his arm. Everything Holly wasn't, but the busty redhead had other qualities that didn't disappoint.

'I'm sorry. I drank too much again and forgot myself.' Rick reached for her once more. 'How about I make it up to you tonight?' He leaned in and kissed her, whispering tenderly, 'You know you're the only one for me.' He knew how to act sometimes.

Even though he looked like reheated leftovers, Natasha sighed. If she was truthful, her foot in Dr Mancini's door was all a girl like her could expect. She felt a sad frustration and acquiesced to reality. 'Okay, okay. Now witness this DD transaction for me.' Another regulation that had to be followed was that all dangerous drug transactions in the hospital had to be witnessed by two people. Any combination of nurse, doctor or pharmacist must sign the record book and a patient's chart. It was a double-check to ensure a complete paper trail of drug usage.

Rick looked like reheated leftovers as he shuffled across Natasha to sign the register.

Her nostrils were immediately treated to an overpowering sugary smell, a stark contrast to the stale, musty smell of the safe. She cringed. He must have tried to freshen up this morning with a shower-in-a-can, another annoying Rick quirk.

When he finished countersigning, he stooped and embraced her. For the first time in a while, he took the time to give her a sound kiss. He relaxed and smiled as he felt Natasha kiss him back. She was going to make it easy for him yet again.

Multiple signs of affection were unexpected but more than welcome. A hint of need ignited within Natasha. Just as it was intensifying, Rick pulled away.

'Tashy, I've someone for you to meet.' He stepped out of the safe and returned a few moments later with Dr Cartwright.

Natasha's joy crashed back to what had recently become her usual level of disappointment in Rick. This was another down for their up and down relationship, except lately there didn't seem to be any upsides coming her way.

Rick scrambled a little. 'Ahh, I bumped into Rachel on my way here. I thought I'd show her around the pharmacy. She's going to start working occasionally on ICU with me and onc/haem with you. If you get the job, that is.' He cleared his throat a little nervously. 'I thought since I was coming here, I'd introduce you two.'

'Really, Rick ... you have no idea.'

Rachel couldn't care less about the girl pharmacist's coolness towards her. It was how useful Rick could be that held her attention. 'I hope you have some sort of serious security down here to make sure all these DDs stay safe.' He was like a not-so-cute mongrel puppy that followed you home. She could understand the fascination, how unconditional doting stroked the ego. Ultimately, he was the wrong fit for her plans.

Rick turned his back to Natasha. 'Yes, the latest, and we're always updating it.'

Natasha bottled her irritation. As if he knew anything about Jo's management plans to keep the pharmacy's security up-to-date. Rick's easy dismissal of Nat saw her fume.

Cartwright then tried to ingratiate herself a little more. 'It's impressive. Of course, you'd have to keep them somewhere. Good to know they're so safe. Rick, I suppose you as a senior pharmacist would know all about the security here.'

Trying not to vomit from the foul taste the sycophantic atmosphere was leaving in her mouth, Natasha shuffled them all out of the safe. She slammed the door leaving the noise to angrily echo around the desolate weekend pharmacy. Turning the wheel handle and spinning the combination lock hard, the safe was locked.

Cartwright continued. 'Do all the pharmacists have access to the safe?'

Natasha had no interest in answering her, but Rick jumped right on in. 'Only the dispensary pharmacists and some weekend rostered pharmacists.' He proceeded to ramble on about security, record books and the duress alarms in the pharmacy as he ushered the doctor along the corridor. 'I'm not on the weekend roster. That's usually reserved for pharmacists more junior than me.'

As they moved into the dispensary, Rachel found herself mildly impressed. 'Good to know that there are such good security measures in place.'

Rick chortled. 'Yes. See here. These are the duress alarms. We have them near the outpatients' and inpatients' counters. They're like a bank might have. If the pharmacist or assistant is threatened, they press this button under the counter, and hospital security and the police will come running.'

Rachel Cartwright nodded. Her eyes darted swiftly around, appraising the dispensary layout. 'My great-uncle didn't mention anything like this.' They continued their conversation as Natasha trudged off to retrieve Rick's car keys.

Seething at his uncanny ability to cloak her in nothingness, Natasha threw his keys at him while he waited at the exit door. Cartwright had already walked off towards the lifts. With no one around, Rick gave Natasha a soft kiss on the lips and a lame hug. 'Until tonight.' Adding softly, 'Have patience with me. I'm trying to do the best for both of us.'

'Oh please, you've hurt me on so many levels.' She slammed the pharmacy door in his face. She wouldn't hold her breath about him sharing the evening with her.

As the night rolled on, there was no sign of Rick, so Natasha stewed over a quick noodle-and-vegetable dish for one. When the doorbell rang, her tired eyes were halfway through her third journal paper. She snatched the door open to see Rick's freshly showered and shaved face smiling at her. He was back to being her safe, ordinary Rick. She was restless and didn't want to engage in a blow-by-blow running commentary about who did what to whom. Yet she snapped, 'Come in.'

'Are you *still* mad at me about last night?' He sounded contrite as he grabbed for her. 'I'm sorry. Nothing happened with Holly and me.'

'Why would you open with that?'

'Um ... isn't that why you're still mad?'

'God, you're relationship deaf.'

'What, why ... what did I do?'

She pulled out of his grip. 'I really don't want to get into this. But let me say that apologising to me and then, in the same breath, bringing in Cartwright, supposedly to introduce her to me, was pathetic. Don't think I didn't know what you were up to. And then, to top it off, you just ignored me to show off to her.'

'Look, I was getting in good with her for *you and me.* Since it was clear you weren't in the mood to talk to her, I had to fill the void.'

'Don't throw it back on me. All I want to do is spend some time with you. Just me and you, no one else, no ulterior motives. Simple, safe.'

'I'm sorry, I really am, but I had your best interests at heart.'

'Bullshit! I want the truth.'

'Okay, the truth. I should have come home with you, Holly means nothing. I didn't like Mancini monopolising you. I was jealous. There, I admit it. I tried to make myself feel better by staying out with Holly.' He put his arms around her, pulling her to him, and kissed her shoulder. 'I know you're the best thing for me.'

Natasha wasn't sure if he was trying to convince her or himself. 'I'm sick of hearing that, Rick. Especially when you forget it once we're in public.' He clumsily moved her hair to plant an all-too-sloppy kiss on her neck. *Yuck*, she thought, but said, 'It's not good enough.'

'I know.' His sticky, hot breath tickled her ear. 'I promise I'll try. For you, I'll try. It's hard for me. I'm just not the romantic type. It doesn't come easily.' She jerked away from his whispering.

'It should if I mean anything to you. It should be a reflex, spontaneous, because you want to. Like I feel and do for you. Not something you have to think about or be told to do.'

He turned his head away. 'You're right. Look, I'll try. How about dinner tonight?'

'I've already eaten.'

'What about tomorrow night, just you and me? We'll have a meal, split the bill, share the night.'

Her heart twisted. 'I can't. Jo's coming over. We're going over stuff for my interview.'

With a hurt whine, he said, 'What happened to me helping you?'

Natasha didn't want him to wriggle out of feeling bad because he thought he'd been snubbed. 'You seemed too busy, that's all. With starting the new job and your MBA, I didn't want to bother you.'

'Of course, you're right, plus Jo's on the interview panel. Good thinking to use her.'

'It's not like that.'

'Oh, I didn't mean anything bad. Jo's a good friend.' He wrapped Nat up once more.

He smelt like good, familiar, safe Rick. Nat weakened. 'I promised Jo.'

'How about I make it up to you tonight, then. I'll be back. Just wait here.' He kissed her and ran out.

After around twenty minutes, Rick returned with petrol station flowers and a bucket of vanilla ice cream. 'I know it's not great, but it's a start. Am I forgiven?' He dropped to one knee and presented the flowers and ice cream to Natasha.

He was right, it wasn't too brilliant, but it wasn't too dull, either. For Rick, it was a big step. 'Yes, you are.' She gave a heavy sigh. 'Up you get. I'll get some water for the flowers. You get two spoons.'

# SIX

## MR EVEREADY: MORE BANG FOR A GIRL'S BUCK, OR IS THAT F@#K?

An hour later, they were naked in Natasha's bed. Safe and predictable, Rick was back and he started his veritable pre-coital checklist. There was no ephemeral zing like Sebastian Mancini's touch. A sensation that, if it were noise, would sound like the dangerous sizzle that radiated from high-voltage power lines. Natasha tried to yield to Rick's will, desperate for their lovemaking to sizzle. She wanted to drive out any fanciful thoughts of the out-of-her-league Mancini.

Rick twiddled Nat's nipples like he was rolling his fingers over the tuning knob on a radio, searching for better reception. Natasha was finding it hard to get tuned in. She tried to concentrate more fully on Rick. Her mind still drifted as the slightly painful pressure of his furtive fingers felt like he was checking her left boob for lumps. This was swiftly followed by sucking on her nipples. It was the next step in his very ordered sexual routine. An astronaut checking an ignition sequence with mission control before blasting off would've been proud.

Tonight, Natasha found it hard not to laugh. She closed her eyes to concentrate on the act they were about to share. It should have been beautiful; a shared, sensual dance. The noise drifting from the darkness as he moved his lips over her breasts seemed contrived, like he was slurping up a long strand of spaghetti.

Natasha had to take control. Otherwise, she wouldn't get what she wanted. Reaching for his soft cock, Nat massaged it tenderly. The thin sausage-like shaft responded to her coaxing and stiffened. Natasha tried to lure herself to some level of eroticism by fantasising about the promise of the exquisite friction to come. She worked him, wishing she could coax him to want to stay with her and grow so his size might fill her, but he wasn't sharing tonight. Signalling this sojourn was all for him, Rick grabbed her hips, pushed her legs apart and rolled fully onto her, jerking his way home. This wasn't the beautiful, sensual dance Natasha hoped for. This was a polka, jolting and indifferent.

Rick then set off on his odyssey, his eyes looking upwards. At times, Natasha wondered if he knew what it meant to share. Holding his backside, one hand on each cheek, she tried to match his rhythm. Hoping to propel him deeper, to feel him more. Finally, her body began to react. A weak sensual wave began to build. It tantalised her. Much more was possible, and she wanted it. She tried to nurture this bud of eroticism by gripping his butt cheeks harder, pulling him into her, and pumping his cock deeper. She urged him on, moaning her need. It helped her too. But, all too soon, he stopped thrusting to rest and gather himself, leaving her hollow and frustrated as her fragile, slow-growing arousal shrivelled and died.

'Come on, baby, harder. Go again. Give it to me,' Natasha moaned, knowing if she commanded salaciously, it would restart him.

He grunted, pushing up, locking his arms on either side of her shoulders. Scrunching his eyes tightly shut, he started again. 'Yes, yesss, Tash.'

She tried to work her way back to where she had some semblance of arousal. She started rocking hard against him, rolling her hips up to meet him. She wrapped her legs around his thin, bony hips, trying to force his penetration to be more pleasurable, closer to hitting her there, but Rick wasn't awakening much in Natasha tonight. She needed to climax soon because now it was a race between them. Nat had an ever-shrinking window of opportunity. If she didn't get there before he expired, she wouldn't reach the summit by Rick's dick tonight. He wouldn't keep going for Nat. She sensed he was close as his grunting and jerking increased. She was nowhere.

Too late. Rick fired, unloading into her, grunting, 'Oh baby, that's it. Yeahhh! That was *all of it* and more.' Nat was left short as an exhausted

Rick pulled out of her, limp and squashy, puffing as he rolled off her. 'That was a blast.'

Restless and unsatisfied, Natasha sagged as she rolled to her side of the cold bed, saddened she said, 'I deserve better.'

'Huh?' Rick ran his hand against her thigh and patted her hip, then settled with his back to her. He might as well have been lying in a bed a whole suburb away. Make that a world away.

It was going to take her ages to settle. She had to release this pent-up, frustrated sexual energy and anger. They lay there in silence, Nat burning with unsated desire and Rick dead-to-the-world sated. After a short while, she heard Rick's breathing slow and deepen.

Grabbing her phone and two pillows from her side of the bed, she went to the bathroom and locked the door. Natasha cleaned herself up a little. From their hiding place underneath some handtowels in a vanity drawer, she took out a tube of lubricant and her vibrator. Nat needed to finish off tonight, as sexual frustration and despondency about her relationship meant sleep wouldn't come easily.

It used to be so much better with Rick. At least, she thought it had been. A pang of guilt rose momentarily but was quickly smothered by practicality. At least this way her climax and the level of pleasure she chased were controlled and acceptable. The queen of her splintered mind, Goldilocks would be placated. The Slut would be disgruntled but manageable. Everyone won, and it was unlikely Rick would miss her warm body next to him in bed.

Nat was reliably informed that no woman had ever given up the real thing for a vibrator. After Rick's efforts tonight, she wasn't so sure. Her vibrator was bigger and harder than Rick, lasted longer, and had far more options in speed and stimulation.

She lit a couple of honeysuckle-scented candles and extinguished the bathroom light. Positioning her pillows on a chair, Nat created a soft nest to recline in. With her bum on the edge of the chair, she placed her feet up on the vanity's edge. Pushing in her earbuds and setting down her phone, Nat hit up her carnal playlist. She lubed up her vibrator and fingers. Given her mood, Nat didn't expect to last until Mr Sweet Love-juices himself, Barry White, tonight.

Now she fantasised that Mr Eveready was the man she wanted. He'd help her release the sexual frustration wound tightly within her. She started slowly with Christina Aguilera's 'Nasty naughty boy', creating the ambience she craved. The seductive, warbling sound of a trumpet and the sensual sweep of brushes on snare and cymbals were perfect for the sexual dance Nat desired.

Closing her eyes, she tenderly moved the vibrator over the lips of her sex, lubing herself synthetically until the touch had her natural arousal and wetness pulling her deeper into a lone odyssey. She was taking the time to appreciate and luxuriate. The time he wouldn't. Christina, with her accompanying strong, sexy voice dripping with innuendo, was the tour leader. Yesss.

Nat lay back further, resting on the pillows. She turned on the vibrator to use the small, bunny-like ears that protruded from one side and rubbed them gently against her clit. 'Ohhhmm!' Spreading her legs further, 'Oh yeah.' The first sweet pangs began to grip. 'Yeahh!' Increasing the speed as the scent of honeysuckle filled her lungs, her core awoke. The rest of the vibrator, the shaft, the pleasure beads, were vibrating and rotating on slow. Captivating, dark eyes, sensual mouth, chiselled lips and dangerous charm now stormed her thoughts.

She began rocking her hips against the vibrator as she rubbed the shaft against the cleft of her sex. She moved her hips upwards, higher, turning the vibrator around so she could tease herself with the now vibrating head, moving it in and out of her most sensitive place. She slowly, oh so slowly, plunged it into her. It was hard and big. Just what she wanted, and this cock wasn't quitting for a rest.

Nat drove further along a road to fulfilment as her locked-away, unreleased arousal started to break free in the flickering half-light of her bathroom hideaway. She drove Mr E all the way into her. 'Yesss! Come on ...' Christina and her big band urged Nat on. She dreamed of male underwear models, toned torsos and abs glistening from sex sweat.

Moaning, she caught herself before she became too loud. Mr Eveready would give her absolution tonight. Nat slowly increased the rhythmical pace of Mr E's shaft and beads, harder and harder into her. Perfectly timing the rise of the pulse of the friction to the introduction to Janet Jackson's 'All nite (don't stop)'.

Her core clenched and rippled, awakened by the glorious friction. The beautiful wave that had ebbed earlier grew to powerfully roll through her. Building, building and spinning on and over itself, again and again. She forgot where she was and what was driving her exquisite pleasure. She simply went with the high and lifted off.

Now that she was naturally lubed, Mr E helped her chase freedom. Sans control, she wanted to be captured and beguiled by attentive, bottomless eyes. 'Oh!' No stopping. Not now. Nothing mattered. No yin–yang alters. Using Janet's breathless voice and the song's staccato beats, Nat's sensual rhythm intensified as she chased the wave to its crest to freefall and crash into a seemingly endless sea of pleasure, only for another wave to form.

She wasn't pretending to be beige any longer. Her final orgasm was different, a rosebud unfurling at the call of the sun in a long, languid blossoming that consumed her. Then came the climax, the bloom exploding like a champagne cork popping from a shaken victory bottle, shooting through her and bubbling over. She tensed her feet, curling them up towards the sky, contracting her leg muscles, squeezing the maximum erogenous sensation out of the act. Pent-up sexual frustration released.

Nat kept moving Mr E, slowing her pace, trying to prolong the last feelings of desire that radiated from the remaining sensual aftershocks. Then there was only the sound of her emptiness and that of her racing heart as it slowed to melt into the satin smoothness of Marvin's 'Sexual healing'.

The freedom of release – sweet. The heaviness of satisfaction was sufficient. Yet her soul wanted more. Marvin was whispering soft words, delivering them with silken tones of escape. Her soul, just once, wanted to experience the pleasure that ignited all her senses to the dizzying heights of that sensual dance. This wasn't it, although she moaned softly, draped over the bathroom chair in a semi-boneless, synthetic afterglow.

Her retreating climax was consumed by the lingering regret of the high's demise. Nat was always reluctant to come down, needing to stay firmly wrapped up in the extremes of the high – for completeness. Reality bit back big time as she cleaned up herself and Mr Eveready. It had been pleasing, but artificial, nonetheless. She slipped into the straitjacket of her imperfection, moving back to the protection of ordinary. Taking small solace from her climax being safe, all alter egos appeased.

# SEVEN

## IS STALKING EVER BETTER THAN BOYFRIEND NEGLECT?

Natasha woke to the harsh sounds of her kitchen being raided. The fridge door slammed, glass bottles rattled, coffee cups clinked and the cutlery drawer clanged as the kettle whistled. Nat groaned. Instant coffee again. She had no idea why Rick refused to use her much quieter machine. Then there was the pièce de résistance in Rick's cacophony of morning breakfast preparation: the high-pitched, frenetic tink-tinkling of her spoon in Rick's hand as he rapidly stirred his coffee, the finale being the vigorous tapping of said teaspoon on the edge of the mug. Then the final note of annoyance, the used spoon clattering into the sink. It was times like this she wished she had a bigger place with her bedroom far, far away from the kitchen.

Hearing the telltale scraping of chair legs across the tiled floor, she knew it wasn't coffee for her. *Christ.* It was early Sunday morning. She'd worked yesterday after little sleep. All she wanted to do today was to sleep in. Sleep would never come now. Not with the constant tinks of her spoon in his hand moving against her cereal bowl as he ate her out of cereal and milk, not to mention slurping her coffee everywhere. All of it left for her to clean up.

Natasha dragged herself out of bed, snatched her robe and staggered out to the kitchen. Rick was sitting at her small dining table, reading the news on his phone. He smiled up at her. 'Hey there, rough night? Good sex will do that to you.'

The need to hide in banality stopped further harsh thoughts as her perfectly lacquered mask slipped back in place. 'Yes, you seemed to enjoy it.'

'Ohhh.' He grinned, leering at her with the same intent she'd seen in his eyes as they had swept over Holly. Now his eyes were moving up her body, openly gawking.

She followed them and saw that her robe had slipped open. 'Enjoying the show?'

'Yes, muchly, but Tashy, I can't fool around this morning. I've got to get going. There's this big assignment for my MBA due Tuesday. I need to work on it today.'

'Oh.' It hadn't entered her mind that sex might be on the breakfast menu. Past experiences had cooled her desires. It didn't matter if she was up for it. Morning work-mode Rick usually softened him to the consistency of soggy toast. Although, as she paid more attention to him, she could see he was more than a little up for it now. Maybe she could still raise some spontaneous reaction out of him after all. In a mischievous, unguarded moment, Nat decided to play a little. Knowing her robe would slip open further, she leaned over to stroke her fingers up and over his bulging zipper, finishing with a gentle squeeze. Her girls swayed unfettered in front of his eyes. 'Mmm. Don't worry, I was only going to get a cup of coffee.' She gave him a quick peck on the cheek as she heard his breath shudder and hitch.

Rick swallowed as his voice wavered. 'Really, Tashy, I must get moving. Sorry. I'll text you later, okay.' He started packing up to leave.

'Yep, fine.' Nat was oddly relieved. There was no familiar ache within her for his attention. As she slipped a pod into the machine, the coffee aroma reminded her. 'Hey, have you changed your cologne or something?'

'Why d'you ask?'

'Nothing, I just thought I smelt something different on you yesterday when you came into the safe.'

He fumbled his car keys. 'No, I haven't.' As he grabbed them off the floor, his no-nonsense demeanour flared into a searing sulkiness. He didn't meet Nat's eyes as he ground out, 'Mixing me up with Mancini, are you?'

'Of course not. Why would you say that?'

'Why didn't my car keys end up in my mailbox? Why didn't my car end up at my place, safe and sound? What did you get up to after Metropolis? Guilty much,' he sniped, feeding the sudden spitefulness between them.

'All he did was offer me a lift because you were a little shit, and I decided you could have the trouble of picking up your car. He dropped me at your place. I forgot about your keys because I was tired and in a rush to get home; it was late and I had work the next day. If you hadn't insisted on going clubbing and drinking too much, your car would have been home safe and sound.' She groaned. 'I was just asking, so if you had changed, I could tell you it smelt like a cheap whore's, not a *real* man's.' Nat wanted her words to hurt, returning his spite. 'Why would you jump to such a conclusion? Guilty much.'

'No, not at all.' He tugged at his shirt struggling for control. He wasn't used to her pushing back. 'I guess it's just, well, where *he's* concerned, I see red.'

'You brought him up, not me. You're the one who arrived at work the next day looking shag tired. You don't hear me going on about Holly.'

'Don't you dare! I knew you'd bring her up.'

'Look, Rick, I don't want to fight, least of all about Mancini and Holly.'

'Me neither,' he grumbled, 'and I haven't changed my cologne.' He turned towards the door. 'Goodbye.' Slamming it shut, he left Natasha in the silence of her messed-up kitchen and mind.

As the sun set, Jo walked into Nat's living room, shining her love of life Natasha's way. 'How was your day?' With a mini pause, she said, 'Have you done something different with your hair?'

'To answer your first question, I enjoyed a tough workout and then a swim at Leighton Beach. It was relaxing, so I didn't feel like straightening my hair after I showered.'

'Oh, my dear girl, you need to get out more if you call that relaxing.' Jo kept it light. She'd interrogate Nat about the double date after what she had in her bag did the trick. 'This is precisely why I'm here with wine. Let's order some food, then we can prep for this interview.'

Looks were deceiving. Jo's straitlaced appearance and correct phrasing hid a stinging wit, a sharp mind and a constitution that could drink any sailor under the nearest table. As they finished up the evening's interview prep, Jo began some friendly fishing. 'You didn't mention how your double date went.'

'No, I didn't, did I.'

'Come on. Don't play the innocent with me. In the long run, it'll only make the interrogation even more painful, especially if I get young Chelsea involved. Give it up, Ms Perry. All of it.'

'As double dates go, it was fair. I didn't get up to much because, as you know, I had to work Saturday. Holly was as predicted.' Natasha switched topics to escape further questions. 'Hey, I've just remembered something from work yesterday.'

'Oh?' Jo was suitably sidetracked by the mention of her beloved business.

'It's probably nothing, except Rick brought Dr Cartwright in to show her around the pharmacy. He said it was good PR.'

Jo gave a tired sigh. 'Ahh, that one. He's always scratching someone's back, hoping they'll scratch his.'

'Yeah, I guess, but what worries me is I was finishing up a DD script and he brought her down into the safe. She carried on like she had a say in the running of the hospital, going on about the dangerous drugs and their security. I guess with a name like Cartwright, she thinks she has a say.'

Jo's brow knitted.

'Rick went off on a spiel about the pharmacy's security and showed her the duress alarms.'

'What! All of them?'

'No. Not the ones in the safe, but he did show her the ones in the dispensary.'

'Bloody hell!'

'Sorry, I didn't mean to upset you.'

'No, it's good you told me. Rick's compromised our security, and it's my arse on the line. I know where he's concerned, I have to watch my back and my arse.' Rubbing her forehead she said, 'He has aspirations for my job, which is why he's doing that MBA crap, probably why he brought Dr Cartwright, of all doctors, down to the dispensary. He must think her name gives him the connections he lusts after.'

'Is that what all his brownnosing the senior consultants is about? To go for the top job?'

'Yes, partly that, and the fact he's an obsequious little bastard. Um ... s-sorry. It's why I find it so hard that you're with him. He must be great in bed. That's all I can say.'

'Excuse me!' Nat couldn't work out whether her anger was at herself because Rick wasn't that good in bed or if the resentment was aimed at Jo for thinking she was so superficial. 'That's not fair, and hardly called for.'

Jo's arms swung up in despair. 'I'm sorry. Of course, I don't believe for one second that you're that shallow, and I've upset you about Rick – again. I care about you and ...' She paused and made a face like she'd swallowed something foul. 'It's just that I've been through the whole settling for what you think you need in a partner rather than what you want and deserve. For me, it led to divorce. You're so great, and Rick ... sorry.' Shaking her head, Jo said. 'I guess I'm just a little touchy about the pharmacy at the moment. To top it all off, I've heard from Charles Cartwright that he's under pressure to review my pharmacy contract with the hospital.'

'Is he Rachel Cartwright's great-uncle? She mentioned something about a great-uncle.'

'No, that's Byron Cartwright. He's the Chief of Surgeons. You may meet him on onc/haem. He's a real stuffy toff and a distant relation of the hospital's benefactors. Charles, he's the hospital's CEO, a nice guy and the real deal. He's the grandson of *the* Sir John Cartwright.' Jo composed herself. 'If someone's looking for a reason to force a pharmacy contract review, a problem with the DDs and a security breach would give them enough ammunition to have one called. It's not a bloody coincidence he's brought Rachel Cartwright down to the pharmacy. Rick probably thinks if he gets her on his side, he can use her to work his way into the upper echelons of JCH and maybe cause some hardship for me. Fortunately, I have a good relationship with the *real* Cartwrights, especially Charles. He's well aware of Rick's aspirations and his talents.'

Nat was stunned. 'I had no idea. Can I do anything?'

'Thanks for asking, but no, nothing at this stage. Just don't tell Rick you've let me know. I'll make a record of the breach and inform JCH security. That way, it's official. Then I'll wait and see what happens. Let it play out.'

'People know you're a clever businesswoman. The pharmacy runs like clockwork because of you. I don't know what's going on with Rick. Now, if I'm truthful, my feelings for him are a little all over the place.' Nat released a frustrated sigh.

A gracious smile warmed Jo's face, 'Ultimately, it's up to you, Nat. You'll figure it out.' Jo rose from the couch and gathered her things. 'I know you have a day off tomorrow, but I must be there bright and early. I hate to love and leave you, but I'd better get going.'

Natasha gave a wry smile. 'It's been happening to me a bit lately.'

As Nat locked the door, she heard her phone ping. Thinking it was Rick, she swiped it open, only to find an unknown number.

> Enjoyed meeting you Friday night

> You distract me. If you want to catch up sometime give me a call.

> Seb

So many questions, so much frustration with so little release. Nat hadn't even given Seb her number. She wasn't sure if she should be creeped out or flattered.

She headed to bed with an oncology/haematology text and the hospital policies and procedures in her hand. They should've easily taken her mind off her MIA boyfriend and possible stalker. It didn't work, and in a weak, lonely moment, she caved and texted Rick.

> N: RU Ok?

Nat had to wait about twenty agonising, self-recriminating minutes as her heart sank and her ire rose.

> R: Flat out with MBA. What U up 2?

> N: Not much. How about lunch tmrw?

She hoped for a shred of warmth from him.

> R: Can't. CU tmrw night?

> N: Can't.

She didn't want him around the night before the interview. He'd make her feel vulnerable, inadequate and nervous with all his confusing advice. Then came strike three.

> R: CU at work then. TAY.

Throwing her scraps of affection like *thinking about you* wasn't enough to feed their starving relationship. Nat freed her frustration.

> N: So much for trying harder. You A-hole.

Sitting restlessly on her bed knowing she wouldn't find sleep, Natasha grabbed her guitar. Initially, her mood fed her fingers. They angrily struck out at the taut strings, causing harsh, jarring sounds of disharmony. Her attack on the strings had the same effect as Rick's callous rejection had on her. Disharmony and an awful jarring filled her crowded head. She regained control, using the strings for release as her fingers skated over Sia's 'Big girls cry'. She relaxed, sitting on her bed, losing herself in the melody.

Finally, silence fell on her guitar and mind. Natasha pushed the guitar aside, scrunching up her eyes in despair, her pitiful existence highlighted by sharing her bed with a hollow, wooden instrument. She hadn't even been able to entice her hollow, wooden boyfriend away from his MBA to come over and help warm her bed.

---

*Tuesday morning: Interview time.*

Natasha entered the interview room to see Dr Sebastian Mancini sitting between Jo and the JCH Human Resources representative. It was like being hit in the head by a cushion filled with stones. Jo threw her a concerned stare, having noticed Nat's face turn the colour of sour milk, accompanied by an expression that looked like she'd swallowed the whole carton of that rotten milk. Seb smiled innocently while Natasha's heart was suddenly trying to pound its way out of her chest.

Brenda, the HR rep, introduced herself. She was bubbly and warm, trying to settle Nat into the interview. The jolt to Natasha's equilibrium made this pointless. Any focus she'd entertained was gone. It hadn't rushed out the door but thrown itself out a window.

Brenda continued. 'Ms Perry, let me introduce you to Dr Mancini, the CMO of the Aida Foundation. He's a bit of a surprise for us today.'

A bit of a surprise? Wow. Natasha wanted Brenda to review her definition of *a bit*. Chief Medical Officer. Of course he was.

Brenda gestured to Natasha to sit in the only available chair at the interview table. 'Dr Mancini has joined us at the last minute, stepping in for his sister, the foundation's Managing Director. Ms Gallo has been unavoidably delayed in Melbourne on foundation business.' Brenda finished her spiel as Natasha chastised herself for not taking more notice of the foundation literature. She'd figured the technical stuff would be more critical. Now, she tried desperately to corral her galloping mind back into the room. Too late.

Jo began the interview proper.

---

At lunch after the interview, Natasha grabbed some food, and as a treat added a cupcake to celebrate turning her interview around and salvaging her pride. As she almost skipped out of the coffee shop, her Seb-dar pinged as she sensed him, and everything tensed. He fell in beside her and they walked in silence to the lift. They were alone as the doors closed, compressing the atmosphere between them to hot and heavy. Natasha was only catching the lift to the fifth-floor pharmacy and decided to follow strict lift etiquette, keeping her eyes locked dead ahead and her mouth shut. Seb pushed the twelfth-floor button. They only had five floors to share. He knew it, so he stomped over any etiquette, deliberately slipping in front of Natasha to face her.

He could usually cause a woman to quiver if he ran his hand through his thick black hair, sweeping it off his face to trap her with a commanding gaze. She gave him nothing. It threw him. So much about her intrigued him.

'Ms Perry, you interview very well.'

The joust began.

'Yes, at least as good as your stalking. You keep showing up in the most unexpected places in my life.'

'Ah, some loquaciousness – an improvement on your texting.' He gave her a glib smirk.

'Sarcasm – not an improvement on your self-importance.' She fleetingly met his eyes and fought the pull towards him. She made herself take a step back as an unanswered question surfaced. It solidified her defences against his charm. 'How long have you had my job application?'

'Since Sunday afternoon. Pia and I reviewed the applications to prep her for the interview.'

'I'm guessing that's where you got my phone number, since I never gave it to you.'

'Yes, it was a pleasant surprise indeed to see your application, given how little you give away.' He leaned in so close that the intoxicating mix of Dr Mancini and his cologne immediately took her back to falling into his arms on Friday night. No sickly-sweet smell here.

'You're a real mystery, Ms Perry.'

Those same sensual feelings from Friday began to rise. Natasha managed to hold him at bay and string some words together. 'Are you allowed to do this?'

His husky breath brushed her ear. 'Over the last couple of days, I almost dropped by. I have your address as well.' His voice was soft yet persuasive. 'I knew it wasn't right. Then again, at that time, my sister was interviewing, not me. I was tempted.'

Natasha asked more forcefully, 'Are you allowed to do this?' It was kind of hot but more than a little threatening.

He blanched, frowning as he pulled back. 'Shit, sorry.' He shook his head, tossing his fringe to one side with an annoyed flick. 'What are you doing to me? Yes. Unprofessional, Mancini.' He answered with a mutter. 'I become an uninhibited fool around you.'

Natasha's mouth went dry. 'I don't think it's my fault. I'm just me.' Then before she could stop herself, 'Maybe you're just a fool.' She gripped the rail of the lift. Jeez, not a good thing to say to a potential future boss. Way to go, Perry.

His eyebrows rose. 'You're right, of course, and being remarkably humble.' His face dropped, 'Has that boyfriend of yours been treating you right?'

'That's none of your damn business.' Such an arrogant Italian prince. She convinced herself she wasn't interested in this player. Her anger suddenly usurped any schoolgirl infatuation. 'You need to check your ego. I'm not sure this is the place or the time for you to intimidate me regarding my personal relationships. Especially since you've just interviewed me for a position where I might be under ... um, working with you.'

He stepped back, gaining the control he always exercised over his desires, especially when at the hospital and attending to business. 'Once again, I've lost my manners around you. Of course, you're right. Forgive me.' He gave her a heart-melting half-smile that extinguished her anger.

'Of course.' Nat managed to mumble.

The fifth floor was nearly upon them. Seb sensed her eagerness to escape and rushed his words. 'Please, let me make up for my bad manners. Let me buy you a proper drink, my shout, at the Sail and Anchor, no stalking. Rick can even come. Maybe tonight or Friday, or even Saturday?'

'Dr Mancini, you really are exceedingly flattering, but I'm busy those nights – with Rick.' She chastised herself inwardly. *Exceedingly flattering, jeez, did she just step out of a Jane Austen novel?*

A determined look swept over his face as the lift pinged and the doors opened. 'I'm not going to give up on having one more drink with you. You should know that, Natasha.' His voice was quiet and resolute. She stepped out.

As the doors were closing, she turned defiantly, facing him. A smile graced her lips. She met his dark brown eyes, and his face brightened as a new adventurous feeling swept through Nat, fuelling her words. 'Don't give up.'

She stood stone-still for a full minute, asking herself where the hell the sass had come from. Of course, Rick and Natasha hadn't planned anything. Dr Mancini didn't need to know that.

# EIGHT

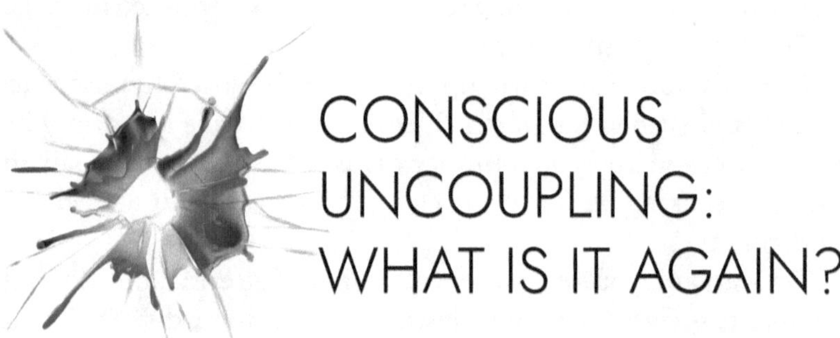

## CONSCIOUS UNCOUPLING: WHAT IS IT AGAIN?

The week went by, both fast and slow. It sped by when Nat didn't want to know her fate regarding the job. Then it slowed inexplicably when she decided she desperately needed to know if she'd been successful. Friday came around and, mercifully, final judgement was handed down. At lunchtime, Brenda from HR called. 'Hello, Natasha, I'm calling to inform you that sorry ...' There was a harrowing muffling sound as she coughed and spluttered. 'Sorry, I have the dreaded lurgy. Where was I?'

*Killing me.*

'Yes, that's right. We would like to offer you the job. You're the successful applicant.'

Her spirits, which had plummeted during Brenda's coughing fit, now soared. 'Oh, thank you so much.'

'My pleasure. You were easily the best applicant.'

'Thank you.'

'I'll email you the details and send you an official job offer letter. Sign it and send it back. We want you to start next week. Okay?'

'Yes, certainly. Thank you.'

Friday night after work, Natasha made her way to the Sail and Anchor. She sat across from Jo at a high corner table in the crowded bar. Nat had nailed the sexy professional look in her shortish, powder-blue pencil skirt and matching jacket. She'd undone her white silk blouse to show a reasonable hint of cleavage. The ensemble was topped by a light-weight, long beige overcoat to ward off the sudden cold snap – and Goldilocks. All long, sculptured, sheer-stockinged legs, high heels and power suit. Not so camouflaged, because new confidence flowed through her. She had released her hair, allowing it to flow freely around her face. Empowered by her success, she felt beautiful and sexy. Not from The Slut's sleazy sexiness. It was Natasha's own brand, and this new brand had loosened Goldilocks's straitjacket.

Natasha felt she was finally making her way, creating the person she wanted to be. That meant she wanted to see less of her alters. Things were good. She shouted above the noise. 'If you had told me eight years ago I'd be dressed like this, with a new job like this, I wouldn't have believed it. Thank you, Jo.'

Jo's lips widened to an impressed smile. 'I'm so pleased for you. After a shaky start, you were great in the interview and deserved every bit of your success. When will you believe that?' She raised a champagne-filled glass, and they clinked.

'Okay, okay, thanks. Thanks for the help.'

'My pleasure, but I had quality material to work with. Now let's have some fun.' Jo nodded in the direction of the bar. It was like an official summons had been sent to a few of the Friday night regulars. The guys made their way over to the two ladies, and the night truly began. Chelsea had christened these guys the Bootylicious Builders. Natasha could never remember all their names. Soon they were all talking, and Nat was energised. What a day. Stuff Rick. She could still enjoy herself if he couldn't be bothered to celebrate with her.

Jo and Natasha laughed, flirted and chatted with the guys. One of the more adventurous, Casey, leaned down and reverentially kissed Natasha's cheek. In total awe, he hoarsely murmured, 'My God, you're gorgeous. Congratulations, Natasha.'

Being in this extraordinary mood, she didn't shrink away from his compliment. She turned, smiling warmly up at him. He smiled back, his sparkling blue eyes shining out from under a mop of blond, sun-bleached hair, then he sauntered off to the bar.

His attention gave her a heady, warm, powerful feeling. It wasn't the alcohol causing it. Most of all, she wasn't ashamed to admit it. A stranger's warm, chaste kiss crystallised Nat's realisation. She wasn't in a fairytale. Rick was never going to suddenly awaken from some selfish slumber and realise she was the one. The reality was that any romance with him would be lukewarm, lean, and always beige. Her phone pinged and lit up, drawing her attention to a flashing neon sign reading WAKE UP. She read the text.

> S: Not stalking, just CONGRATS on your new job.

> Checking my ego at your door.

> Looking forward to working with you.

> S

His words made up her mind. Sebastian had shown pleasure at her being more verbose, so she attended to him first.

> N: Thank you kind sir.

> I look forward to working with you too.

> Don't give up on that drink.

> Nat

'I need to go and see Rick.'

Jo frowned. 'What, now?' She motioned to the attentive tradies. 'You want to put a dampener on this?'

'Yes. I have to do it tonight. I'll text you later.'

'No matter what time, right?'

Nat nodded and headed out.

On the short drive to Rick's, she started to give him the benefit of the doubt. An MBA was a serious workload. He had said he was swamped and would try to catch her on the weekend. Unsure of what she wanted to achieve, Nat knew she'd have to convince Rick to interrupt his work and spend time with her.

No surprise who agreed with her. *Spend the time. No harm. Best for you to stay on the narrow path. Only one celebratory night missed. It's not a crime.*

And no prizes for guessing who didn't. The Slut offered, *Oh, please. More than the night missed. His prowess in the bedroom alone is a crime.*

Nat dismissed this psychotic storm before it reached any significant lows. The rants in her head were becoming less troubling, making rejection easier.

Regaining control, Natasha knocked on his door. There was nothing, so she banged it harder. 'Hey, Rick, it's Natasha.' She heard scrambling and what could have been a woman's giggle. Rick could be effeminate, but not even he sounded that girly. Gradually he appeared, all legs and arms, barely opening the door. Natasha recognised his just-fucked look. And there it was, the undeniable sickly-sweet smell of deceit. Of course, it was Holly's perfume clinging to his guilty heart and body. Yep, Nat had finally fully admitted it to herself. It had been Holly's smell all along. It signalled his betrayal just as blatantly as the smudge of harlot-red lipstick on his cheek.

Her heart sank and her anger rose. Rick had already been lured away from his MBA. Nat had been so stupid, and he'd been, well, he'd been so Rick – disloyal and narcissistic. He tried to scramble. 'Tashy, I wasn't expecting you. Look, I'm still a bit under the pump. Can you come back later?'

'There's not going to be a later for you, you fucking bastard. I take getting on top of your MBA is a euphemism for getting on top of whatever slut would let you *do* her.'

Natasha's vitriol surprised even her. Rick stood awkwardly in front of her, trying to pull his clothes together while making sure he stopped Natasha from entering or seeing much past the door. 'Tashy, come on. Let's be reasonable. What are you saying?'

'That Holly needs to trade up, starting with her cheap perfume, and then you.' The real Natasha was breaking free. 'It's over, you arrogant shit.' Rick had ripped her open. She'd never given him her heart, so only her pride was torn. Nat caught a glimpse of the harlot herself, running from his bedroom, semi-naked, with the rose-pink stain of sex on her cheeks – all her cheeks. Rick was nothing if not a creature of habit. He liked it doggy more than anything. This final realisation bit only a little.

She relished her new-found strength, yelling a little louder. 'Oh, by the way, you can tell Holly good luck from me. She'll need it. Someone with her numerous and varied sexual encounters is unlikely to ever get satisfaction from a soft cock like you.' Natasha was learning about love.

No matter how deep or shallow, it could quickly turn into hate; a hate that ran deep in the blink of an eye.

Rick fired up. 'Piss off. What would you know? Maybe it was just your frigid ways that couldn't get me there.'

'If she wants to get her rocks off, fully, she'll need to buy some batteries. That's if she stays with you. Knowing Holly, you'll be on the fuck heap before you know it.'

'That's not called for, bitch.' He tugged at his shirt, angrily trying to straighten up. 'Oh sure, it's easy for you to complain about me. But I'm sick of you tagging along on my coat-tails. You can't even socialise with the right people at work because you're too scared. I won't be your whipping boy anymore. '

Nat was can't-help-herself furious, giving away more than she should have. 'Believe me, and I know from experience, you're not good enough to be my whipping boy. You're just plain whipped.'

She took a moment before staring him dead in the eyes and said, 'Read my lips.' And then flipped him the bird.

Natasha left, a storm clouding her mind, feeling lighter but embarrassed. Now the torture started, centring around humiliation and broken trust. She called Jo.

'That good-for-nothing arse.' Jo seethed. 'I'm coming over.'

'Thanks for not saying I told you so.'

'Ah, Nat, what you fail to realise is that solidarity is what's needed. The night is still young and perfectly open to any number of activities to cleanse your soul of Rick the Dick. Perhaps even burn him in effigy.'

'I'm all out of effigies.' Nat sighed.

'What about pins, a lock of hair and a voodoo doll.'

Hearing the laughter in Jo's voice gave Nat a lift. 'Darn. I'm fresh out.'

'You're in luck. I just so happen to have—'

'I'd like to see that.'

'Of course. I have them for all my troublesome employees.'

'Of course you do.' Natasha was surprised at how easily Jo's lightness imbued her, although her heart was starting to weigh heavy in her chest.

Jo wouldn't let her wallow. 'No, but seriously, I have the next best thing. I have alcohol and lots of friendly support that should help cleansify you.'

'Cleansify? Is that even a word?'

'Probably not, but it fits,' she chuckled.

'A night of female solidarity then.'

'You bet. You up for it?'

'Definitely, twist my rubber arm.' As Natasha hung up, the heaviness of disappointment and a healthy hint of sad embarrassment sunk the lightness. She'd been stupid and tolerated his prima donna routine because it was easier than facing the greater terror of Goldilocks's punishment with someone more adventurous.

Natasha should've known. Rick wasn't the way to defeat The Slut and Goldilocks. She had to keep searching and pushing for the love she thirsted for. Then maybe her alter's would give up the final block that they held from her like a hostage. Although when it came to love, how could she know what to look for? The concept of real love was foreign to her. Her dad and mum didn't have that type of relationship. Her mum had been a lone hand in the love department.

All Natasha kept uncovering was shallow, belittling love. Exactly what her dad had shown her mum. Nat was beginning to believe that she'd only ever experience sex, not the intimacy of lovemaking. That was out of her reach, a fairytale. This thought weakened her.

The Slut was back. *Why do guys, who think they know it all, fuck like fifteen-year-old boys?* Out of the two of her alters, The Slut had always been the better observer of reality. On hearing The Slut's sarcastic observation, there was no way Goldilocks was letting it pass without comment.

*But he was safe. Kept your slutty spirit under control and the gutter whore at bay.*

Nat called Sage, and the bickering voices of her alters stopped, even when Nat's call was answered by the gruff voice of Sage's long-time partner, Dodge. His real name was Donald Ford. He and his brother Charles Ford, known as Chevy, had lived with Sage for years.

Dodge explained, 'Sage's in bed, girl. She's had a headache for a couple of days. She's been flat-out at work and needed an early night. I'll pass on the message about your job. Congratulations, it's great news, and I'll tell her about Rick. I suspect she may want to congratulate you on that one herself, but I'm not touching that news even with a ten-foot pole.'

Natasha smiled.

# NINE

## A SOUNDTRACK FOR A DEFIANT HEART

Jo soon arrived at Natasha's with the best medicine for the situation: two bottles of Pol Roger champagne and a bucket of gourmet cookies-and-cream ice cream. 'I think we should celebrate, but I know you'll be hurting. It's a loss, after all. So I've brought demonic comfort food for commiserating and champagne for celebrating.'

Just seeing Jo made Natasha feel less of a fool. 'You're so right, as always.'

'Chelsea will grace us with her presence once her shift finishes.'

'Okay, the more the merrier.'

Soon Chelsea materialised. She didn't hide her intentions. In each hand she held a bottle of the most exquisite, girl-on-a-budget sparkling, Jansz Premium Cuvee. This was a celebration.

'Come on, Nat, let's get your happy on.' Flashing a wicked smile, Chelsea set down the bottles and hugged her sad friend. 'We're gonna get you through this. Come on,' she winked, before saying, 'You know what you need?'

'No, but I'm sure you'll enlighten me.'

'A sexy rebound guy.' As they laughed, Chelsea asked, 'Are you going to play for us tonight?' Nat had played the guitar on other nights when they needed to help one another through what life had thrown at them.

'No. I'd rather pick some songs to kick this break-up on its arse, and sing and drink Rick out of my life.'

'Then it's settled, my lovely ladies. This is definitely a celebration. I'll put the ice cream in the kitch—'

'Freeze, Sanderson. Stay right there. I'll get spoons. There's no rule that says we can't celebrate and cleanse with champagne *and* ice cream.' Nat felt the sadness trickling away.

Chelsea's face broke into a broad smile. 'Now you're talking.'

A little later, sucking on a spoon of ice cream, Chelsea mumbled, 'Okay, Nat, it's the soundtrack for your break-up, so choose the first song. Set the standard.' She poured Nat a very generous glass of champagne. 'No pressure, of course.'

'You're on. I'll start with a Carly Simon classic followed by a reworking of said classic by Missy Elliot and Janet Jackson. Any ideas what the songs are?'

'Of course not,' Jo huffed. 'More hints, please.'

'The classic was thought to be written about Warren Beatty, but the singer-songwriter has never revealed her secret.'

Chelsea took a big sip of champagne. 'It must be Carly Simon's 'You're so vain', followed by 'Son of a gun', Janet Jackson, Missy Elliot and Carly's remix and fattening up of the classic.'

'Know the first, absolutely no clue about the second,' Jo chuckled. 'Let me listen to them while I take a long sip here and a spoonful of this. Then I'll tell you if you're close.' Jo was always confident, even if she wasn't entirely sure of her path. She just trusted she would prevail. Nat knew she had much more to learn from Jo.

She loaded the songs. They all knew Carly Simon's song, and Jo nodded her approval at the second. The evening started to warm up as the mood lifted.

Chelsea couldn't help herself. 'Good start, especially the second. Hey, what about the queen of female sexual independence, Madonna, and her anthem railing against insipid men, 'Human nature'? I was only young when I first heard it.'

Jo smirked. 'Are you sure you were even born when it was released?'

'Yeah, and I loved it as soon as I heard it. Later, I used it to help rid myself of a nasty piece of work who tried to control me,' said Chelsea.

Nat frowned, 'I can only ever imagine you in a scenario where your partner would absolutely adore you.'

'Not so. Men always underestimate me. They only ever look at these.' Chelsea's finger circled her face, followed by her breasts. 'They think I wouldn't have a single intelligent thought in my being. Just an easy lay. I learnt my lesson early. A guy tried to make me feel less than, like I didn't deserve better. I soon got rid of him. Anyway, he made love like a bad basketballer.'

'A bad what?' Jo gave a puzzled smile.

'He always drove straight to the hole, the quickest root! You know, never understanding the concept of taking time to touch and build the moment. He was uncoordinated, came up short, and never really scored.' Chelsea laughed, 'But he was quick, I'll give him that.' She shook her head. Her words were laced with bitterness. 'One night, I vowed *never again* and said goodbye, wishing all sorts of shit on him.' Her lips formed a triumphant smile. 'I growled out "Human nature" to my rather confused dog and felt so much better.'

'Excellent.' Jo was up for a good night. 'Don't despair in the slightest you two. We'll find someone.' She sighed. 'And he *or she* will be the best. And love us for being who we are!' Her whole body wobbled with laughter.

'Thanks for opening up my dating life to a completely uncharted world of possibilities. Although Rick was the worst root I've ever had, he hasn't turned me just yet ...'

'Not that there's anything wrong with that.' Chelsea gave Nat a light-hearted nudge.

'I've considered it,' Jo murmured.

Chelsea and Nat nearly choked on their drinks, blurting out in unison, 'Really?'

Words tumbled out of Nat's mouth. 'It wouldn't be a problem.'

Chelsea finished her sentence. 'No, not at all. As long as you're happy.'

'Yeah, I know. But I like men too much.' Wistfully, Jo added, 'What's not to like about the feel of a guy's warm body next to you in bed in the morning, the gentle brushing of stubble against your cheek for a tender wake-up kiss,' sighed Jo. 'I'm doomed.'

'Aren't we all?' Chelsea took a sip and steered them back on track. 'Rick was too ordinary for you.'

There was that word again, thought Nat. She needed to set her sights on the *extra* in extraordinary.

She returned to the conversation just as Chelsea said, 'It's just so predictable that he'd cheat on you with someone like Holly.'

Jo took another sip. 'Definitely. He was holding you back.'

Their kind, supportive words were soothing Natasha's wounded pride. Then Jo chose a song. 'This was my anthem to get me through my divorce. It became like a vow I made to myself when getting rid of him. It's Pat Benatar's, 'You better run' – best yelled at the top of our voices!' Nat scrolled her playlists and hit play. Their collective voices screamed out the song until they were laughing, fully empowered by the mood the music had engendered.

Chelsea almost spilt her sparkling wine. 'Not fair, Perry. Even shouting, your voice is so bloody good. Honestly, you're wasted as a pharmacist.' Chelsea swayed into Nat, messily filling her glass while swaddling her in a warm hug.

Jo was just as enthusiastic. 'Yes, but apart from sounding like Annie Lennox—'

'No, Pink,' Chelsea cut in.

Jo persisted. 'Nat is now not just a pharmacist. As of next week, she's a clinical pharmacist. We must toast our esteemed colleague.' The Amigos had all reached that time of the night when they felt silly enough to scull, draining their glasses.

They descended into fine female banter and thoughtful reflection on the male gender. Chelsea grinned, 'I'd like a bit of "What goes around comes around" by Justin Timberlake. The song has some excellent sentiments, and he's a gorgeous man.'

'He's not a man. He's a boy.' A predatory look crossed Jo's face. 'But I wouldn't kick him out of my bed for being too young.'

'Come on, you'd need jumper leads.' Chelsea took another swig. 'Then again, it's you, and you have boundless energy, so maybe he's just the right age for you.'

'Fair point.' Jo raised her glass to Chelsea.

Chelsea took centre stage and Natasha started drinking water. Hours later, with empty champagne bottles gathered around them, the Amigos decided a sleepover was in order. Chelsea collapsed on Natasha's couch.

With Nat leaving Goldilocks's Mr Just Right, it could precipitate an attack. Understanding Natasha's history, Jo shared Nat's double bed. The newly single woman wouldn't be alone tonight. Also the curtains were open a sliver, as Jo noted. 'I can fall asleep even with the lights on.' Nat also had one of her phone's playlists at the ready. All triggers were covered.

Jo's words became infused with care. 'You make sure you're happy tonight and always.' She gave Nat a warm hug. 'You're a beautiful person, and this, what you've done, all of it, is good.' She rolled over to her side of the bed and fell asleep.

Settling down, Nat was in a far better state than she'd expected. She'd paced herself with water. Too much alcohol broke her defensive walls, and Goldy became beyond uncontrollable.

Natasha shed no tears. She hadn't cried over lost love since she was ten. It wasn't that she was heartless; it was practised survival, sentiments taught to her by an untrustworthy father. No man had ever proved himself to be different. The lesson learnt, Natasha had vowed never to shed a tear over a man, or let one see her cry. She never gave anyone the satisfaction, and would never show the world her pain or weakness. Now she only cried alone when she became beyond-crazy emotional after an attack.

Nat chose a far softer song to numb her mind. Dido's 'Life for rent' brought clever lyrics and calming music, painting Nat's time with Rick in its true colours. Rick leased, Nat rented, only Goldilocks invested fully.

In the morning, a lighter, less troubled Nat woke. Jo was still blissfully asleep as Nat slipped out to the kitchen to grab a cup of coffee. She found Chelsea had the coffee maker already fired up.

Bleary-eyed, Chelsea looked up from her coffee. 'How are you feeling?'

'As bad as I should. Far happier than expected.'

'Not liking the first comment. I share your pain there. Although I definitely like the sound of the second. But really, are you okay?'

'I don't think it's fully hit me. Between you two and having to get to work, I haven't had a chance to wallow.' Nat half-smiled, then said softly, 'Thank you for last night.'

Chelsea reached over and reassuringly gripped Natasha's forearm. 'We've joked with you about this split, but you know that if you need a shoulder, you can always give me a call or text, okay?' It was Chelsea's caring tone, but delivered as a heartfelt command.

They chatted as Nat grabbed some breakfast and sipped more water.

Chelsea, bless her, was always working the angles. 'You know he's working today.'

Alarm spiked. 'Who, Rick?'

'No, Dr Mancini.'

'Oh, should that interest me?'

'Let's see. There was the double date, which I will interrogate you about later. But, man-oh-man, Mancini, well. He asked me about you when I bumped into him on onc/haem the other day. While you might not be interested in him, he's interested in you.'

A thrill ran through Nat. She pushed it aside. 'It's too soon, Chelsea.'

'You don't want to leave it too long because you know what they say.'

'No, what do they say?'

'Let's just say, if you don't keep,' she smirked and pointed downwards, 'you know, down there in regular use, it'll seal over.' Her eyes danced with fun. 'You know, like pierced ears.' Her throaty laugh was contagious. 'Don't take too long getting back in the saddle.'

Between a gasp and a chuckle, Nat managed, 'On that note, I've got to get ready for work.'

She left Chelsea and Jo discussing the plan for the evening while they hooked themselves up to Nat's coffee machine. She knew they'd lock up when they left.

# TEN

## THUNDERSTRUCK

The pharmacy was busy and the day passed quickly. Late Saturday afternoon, Natasha stopped at the onc/haem ward to take any final drug orders. It seemed fate was on her side for once. As she arrived, Seb was at the nurses' station. The ward was buzzing with visitors and they smiled at each other through the mass of moving faces. The nurse who was talking to him soon left.

Uneasiness swirled in the pit of Nat's stomach as they drifted closer while others streamed past. Her voice was a squawk with a strange upwards intonation at its thankful demise. 'Is that offer to meet at the pub, um, tonight, um, Sail and Anchor, for a drink, still open?'

Seb was in full doctor's mode. 'No. Not now.' His frank no-nonsense composure dissolved as her scent, all fresh and jasmine, flooded his professional manner. Lured away from work, he softened his rebuff. 'Ahh, sorry.' He suddenly became desperate to tell her he wasn't blowing her off. 'When I saw you last, I'd forgotten I had to attend a casual JCH board dinner.'

Somehow this woman loosened his lips. 'It seems luck isn't on our side.' Drawn to her beautiful face, he leaned in, transfixed by her full red lips. 'Maybe we can work at changing that.'

He was no longer young and stupid, so how could she reduce him to being this ridiculous? He didn't seem to affect her, he thought, except to make her angry or clam up, or both. He had better control this, whatever *this* was. He'd made one big past mistake. Once was enough. Lesson learnt, he'd made himself impervious to women, other than to relieve the occasional carnal itch. Then along came this woman and he was weak with an overwhelming, all-over tingling itch that only she seemed to soothe.

Natasha couldn't help smiling back at him. 'Yeah, luck can change.'

People continued to flow busily around them. They were still.

Seb leaned closer, mouthing, 'I think together we can make our own luck.' While no one noticed, he gently squeezed her forearm, lingering a little. His tantalising touch drifting down her arm called to Natasha. 'Maybe there's another time we can make work?'

With her mind somersaulting down a soft grassy hill, she quickly chose a song to halt any nonsense from her alters. Natasha's eyes widened momentarily, the only hint of disquiet showing outwardly. Inwardly, she was the beginning of 'Thunderstruck', the AC/DC song, her mind spinning and cascading like the opening guitar solo. Her heart, having skipped a beat and slowed, was rapidly picking up speed like the drumming and chanting accompanying the guitar riff. Natasha's mind, heart and soul seemed to collide to produce only one thought. Yep, she'd been ... thunderstruck.

Seb didn't want to feel her temper again, so he asked, 'Ahh, will Rick ... be with you?'

Her eyes fixed on his mouth and then flitted to his bottomless brown eyes. His heart leapt. She shook her head, and he felt strange. Excited and sad, he cocked his head.

Natasha shook her head again, trying to derail her adolescent desires. Thankfully it helped as she scrambled to find words. Finally, 'No, not him,' dreamily left her lips.

They were like two rocks lodged together in a stream of people surging around them. They remained motionless, resistant. He wanted it to last. 'What about Monday night drinks and dinner?' His full megawatt Mancini shone. 'Say yes, and our luck will have changed.' He fixed her with a caring gaze. 'Especially if we can finally be alone, just you and me.'

Her mind, although thunderstruck, finally caught up with his words. Sebastian Mancini was already granting her wishes she'd waited months for another to deliver. Faking calm, she answered, 'You're on.' Gawkiness returned as Natasha tried flirting with a playful swat at his shoulder, but she missed.

Seb took heart. He'd flustered her, albeit briefly. His voice like molasses, 'So how about we say seven on Monday? I'll meet you at The Norfolk. Then what will be, will be.'

Internally, Nat was putty in his hands. Right there, that thing he did with his voice, the smooth, deep, treacle thing, made her clench in ways she never thought she could. He could talk to her all day about sorting socks in that tone, and she'd be his. Nonetheless, Goldilocks had trained her well, and externally, all these torrid thoughts appeared only as a mild smile. 'Sounds fine.' He was indeed the finest of temptations.

At six-thirty there was a knock at Natasha's door. Chelsea stood before her. As always, she was stunning, with just the right amount of sexual allure on show. She had a bottle of Jansz tucked under her arm and gripped a large bag, contents unknown. They were in for an epic night.

She was wearing her favourite bum-hugging leather mini. It sat just right around her taut butt. The deep blue sequined blouse with a plunging neckline dazzled Natasha as the late afternoon sun danced across it. On anyone else, it would have screamed cheap. Chelsea made it look sophisticated. She had completed her man-eater outfit with thigh-high black leather boots with killer heels. Her chestnut hair was loose, hanging around her face and shoulders in a stylish, wild, soft-wave look.

On seeing Natasha, a scary look swept across Chelsea's face. 'Oh, come on, Nat. Aren't you even trying to pick up Mr Sexy Rebound guy tonight?'

'What's wrong with this?' Natasha was comfortable in her jeans and black halter top.

'Look, Perry, I haven't worn my lucky skirt just for the sake of polite conversation. I want to get some serious action tonight. You should want too as well. Come on, let me help you start again.'

Chelsea was early. She knew Natasha would dress to blend in – just another wallflower. Not on her watch. She had the cure in her big bag of tricks. Various sexy pieces of clothing and an array of hair and make-up products soon materialised, the likes of which Chelsea knew Natasha seldom let grace her body. She and Nat were the same size, including shoes. Over the course of their friendship, she'd learnt a thing or two about Nat's tastes.

A while later, and a couple of glasses of Jansz in, Chelsea had finished. Natasha had enjoyed the sparkling wine while enduring the curling of her hair, brushes of blush, the smearing of eyeshadow and the primping of many combinations of clothes. Finally, Chelsea had Natasha sorted in a revealing black skirt, which Nat seemed to be borrowing. If it 'worked', Nat could keep it. Natasha didn't dare ask what Chelsea meant by 'worked'. The black halter top stayed.

'Oh, my God, your shoe collection is to die for.'

'Yeah, I love a good shoe. Imported all the better, of course. I stretch my budget when a pair catches my eye.'

'Okay. Well, Perry, these ... you should wear more often.' Chelsea held up a pair of electric-blue patent leather heels. 'These are stunning and will make your body even more irresistible to any mere mortal of the opposite sex.'

Chelsea's confidence in Natasha had her feeling brave and more comfortable in trying on a new skin. Tonight was the time to expose a little more of it. She was stepping out from the camouflage. No Slut or Goldilocks needed. Guys would know Natasha had a heartbeat and was willing to use it – no dead wallflower tonight.

Her hair ended up slightly less wild, but like Chelsea's. Her friend had assured her anything could be achieved with the right amount of blow-drying, the curling of a hot wand, different hair products and the right amount of hairspray. Natasha had a moment of doubt. She used to dress up and do her hair like this, albeit far wilder and with a lot less clothing.

When Nat saw herself in the mirror, with an appreciative Chelsea watching, her fears were dispelled. She had a new job and a second chance at life on her terms, no one else's. Her outfit wasn't Slut style. This was revelling in her beauty, her power, accentuating good things. This was Natasha style.

Soon Sage and Jo joined them, and the night came alive. Jo excitedly told them she'd booked a table at Nunzio's.

When they arrived at eight, the restaurant was buzzing, like them. They ordered their meals, drank good wine, chatted and, above all, laughed. Natasha had truly found her place.

Nunzio's was made up of several rooms. To visit the ladies, Jo and Natasha had to walk through the restaurant. On their way back, their attention was drawn to a large table.

One of the group, a dashing older man, stood. 'Joanna, is that you? Of course, it is!' Jo chuckled and greeted him warmly. They briefly kissed each other's cheeks. Natasha recognised the guy as Charles Cartwright, CEO of Sir John Cartwright Hospital. Clearly, it was a JCH board gathering and he was more of a friend of Jo's than she would have had anyone believe.

Natasha's eyes drifted expectantly, finding their target. 'Natasha. What a pleasant surprise.' Sebastian stood, coming in close, running his fingertips across her shoulder. A fleeting touch, but once again a zing of sensual pleasure rippled through them her. He smiled and spoke softly, the background noise of the restaurant masking his words to anyone but Natasha. 'Are you stalking me?' His soft laugh put Natasha at ease. 'Unfortunately, we're just finishing up.'

If Natasha hadn't been with Jo he might not have recognised her. Natasha's windswept-style blonde hair fell alluringly around her face. Her smoky-eyed make-up gave her eyes a sultry, irresistibly hot edge. Seb skated his hand around her exposed back. Ms Perry had more than one facet to her, and so far, he found all of her intriguing.

Seb enjoyed the feel of her smooth, soft skin skating under his fingertips and lost control of his thoughts. He was ensnared by a desire to taste her. Visions materialised of running his tongue around the orbit of one of her breasts, across the narrow, tanned valley to the other breast. Once there, he'd roll his teeth over the nipple perfectly outlined by the black fabric holding her beautiful, pert breasts loosely to her body. He shook his head.

*Whoa!* Nat had to work hard to stop falling into him. He was all captivating cologne and gallant knight.

He proceeded to introduce her to the rest of the table. Besides Charles Cartwright, the table was full of other JCH luminaries. Natasha could only smile sweetly, not registering much at all, although there was something about Cole Hexum, the Aida Foundation's legal representative. It was his predator-like, hooded blue eyes. She couldn't help but notice they were scanning her very efficiently. Not in a sexual way – he was calmly evaluating her.

She broke away from Hexum's gaze, peeking up at Seb. She suspected from the delight on his face that all his innocent-looking touching, seemingly necessary for gentlemanly introductions, was giving more than only Natasha pleasure.

All the other guests soon rose and made to leave. Sebastian didn't want to go without seeing if he could make her react to him. He needed to know if he affected her as much as she affected him. She never gave much away, outwardly at least. On an impulse, his hand brushed up her bare, exquisitely tanned skin, which was stretched tight over her spine. He then ran his hand all the way down her arm. Finally, a reaction, albeit reflex, registered at his touch. Goosebumps trailed after his fingertips. He smiled, leaning in, mouthing against her ear, 'You look amazing. I would love to stay, but I have other business to attend to tonight.' His heart tripped when she turned, fixing him with her piercing blue eyes – then nothing, only a coy smile as she nodded.

His breath jolted out as he was lost in the pure blue of her gaze. She was escaping him again, seemingly unaffected as she stood back. How could he concentrate on the not-so-sweet work he had to undertake tonight when all the sweetness he wanted to taste walked away from him? He needed to take control and rein in his ill-discipline.

As she and Jo sat back down, Natasha wondered just how much Jo had noticed. She figured she had enough ammunition to divert any prying questions by asking what was going on between Jo and Charles Cartwright. Then the bottle of Dom Pérignon Brut Vintage arrived at the Amigos' table.

The waiter addressed their quizzical looks. 'Courtesy of the gentleman just leaving, who says congratulations to Ms Perry.' The Amigos looked across to the restaurant entrance where Seb stood. He gave them the full megawatt Mancini, focusing his dark eyes and smile on Natasha. Seb bid the ladies good night with a small salute. Unlike Rick, he had no qualms about showing his fondness towards Natasha in public. Also unlike Rick, Seb had the whole table of Amigos swooning.

'It would seem our good friend has already found herself a rebound guy, and she hasn't skimped on the sexy.' Chelsea smirked.

'Natasha, is there something you should be telling us?' Sage interjected.

'At least bring us up to speed.' Jo completed the rapid-fire barrage of questions.

'There isn't much to tell. It all began on the double date.' Nat recounted her brief encounters with Dr Sebastian Mancini, finally divulging details about her upcoming Monday night date.

'Ahh! So that's *the* Dr Mancini.' Sage said, 'His reputation, well, at least his family's, precedes him. His father's ruthless – my mind's like fairy floss these days, nothing of substance in it – I can't quite remember, but there was something. It's old news. Still, something tells me you should be careful with that one. His family are ...' Then Sage smiled. 'But that's for another time, because tonight is about celebrating how far you've come, and there are no limits to how far you can go.'

Natasha decided it couldn't be that bad, or Sage would be on her case. Chelsea wasn't letting an old rumour stop her from enjoying the exquisite champagne. She motioned to the waiter. 'Just leave the bottle.' She happily poured generous glasses for all. Sage, who didn't often drink, had a small glass to toast Natasha's new job and the hopeful resurrection of her love life.

# ELEVEN

## HANGOVERS AND LEFTOVERS

The rest of the night was full of fun, friendship and support, with no complications or moral dilemmas. It passed far too quickly, unlike their Sunday, which passed painfully slowly. Natasha woke up late, tired from lots of dancing and happy drinking. She was relatively unscathed as, once again, she had tempered her drinking to be safe. Not because she was a present-day saint but because she'd been a past night-time sinner.

Chelsea spent another night on Natasha's couch, its convenience and her giddy mood winning out over any lumpy-couch discomfort. Also the fact her car was at Nat's and she wasn't up to driving, met she stayed.

Chelsea's lucky skirt had worked its magic yet again. Although luck and her skirt weren't her only advantage. Late in the evening, or was it early morning, several hot hunks were found twerking around Chelsea. She was working up some very *nice* moves of her own. All the action led to Chelsea having her pick of the very keen admirers' phone numbers. She was a real heartbreaker, keeping the guys buzzing around her at arm's length – the evening was for the Amigos' friendship; no men were needed to complete the picture.

They left before any of the guys – or the night, for that matter – became too shameless. A hint to timing their exit was when everyone started dancing with their hands in the air and moving in ways like they didn't care because they really, really didn't care.

With oversized dark sunglasses firmly in place, Chelsea and Natasha walked their fragile constitutions to a nearby cafe for brunch. With the morning becoming an octogenarian, their mojo coasted along to the tempo of the Rolling Stones' 'I'm just waiting on a friend'. Nowhere close to the frantic doof-doof beat of DJ Khaled's 'All I do is win', to which their energised bodies had moved sublimely when the morning was a mere babe.

Chelsea left mid-afternoon with a bottle of water and some ibuprofen tablets for company. Natasha decided to take her confidence out for a spin.

> N: Hope ur enjoying ur day. Thank you very much for gorgeous bubbles.

> Take care, Natasha

Within minutes her phone pinged.

> S: You're very welcome. Can't wait till tomorrow night.

> Seb XX

Of course, now her thoughts were filled with velvet voices, dark-chocolate eyes and gorgeous smiles. Mr TDD.

---

Chevy's head sang, but not with any harmony. The pain grew with every thought and mumble. 'Where is he?' Then he screamed, *Where the bloody hell is he?'* He picked up a can. Maybe he needed a drink to stop the screaming in his ears. He was so hot. The flames, they were licking at his body yet again, engulfing him. He had to go back into hell. 'Gotta find Dodge,' he shouted to no one. Even the winos and grifters stayed away – too big, too ugly, even for them. Half his face was damaged and scarred. He hunched over to shield the world from his disfigurement because he looked like a hulking Hunchback of Notre Dame – and not the Disney version.

He couldn't find Dodge, the brother who'd always looked after him. Charles and Donald Ford, two boys from the Western Australian wheat belt, where the land was open and flat. It wasn't right that they were fighting a war in the humid jungle, surrounded by walls of green. He hated it, the smothering green claustrophobia, stopping him from seeing the horizon. It was too hot, the flames and smoke too thick.

'Gotta see where the sky meets the earth. Man needs that. Don't know where to go otherwise. Can't find my brother. They had no right, no right. Wasn't our fight.' Now he couldn't see the horizon, too many buildings closing in. The heat of the sun searing his skin was sending him back to the heat of the burning jungle.

The throbbing of his brain felt like it threatened to split his skull. 'I gotta keep going. Find Dodge. He's hurt.' To try and settle, he muttered, 'Chevy is the name of one who walked ... who walked. Ahh fuck.' He couldn't remember. He crushed the life out of the can, which had only yielded a mouthful of rancid beer and street dregs. The aluminium crumpled and disappeared into his massive paw. The way he crushed the can, it could have been one of those tiny paper cups the tablets came in before they forced them down his throat at the military hospital.

He needed that woman, Sage. She wasn't frightened of Chevy. When he came back, she'd cared and even touched his scarred face while looking him in the eyes. She sorted him out while Dodge fell in love with her. He sobbed, forgetting his last thought, 'Sorry, mate, I can't find you. I'm so sorry. I promise, just a bit of a rest, then I'll find you. You won't burn.' Finding a quiet, slightly cooler doorway down an alley, he curled up out of the setting sun.

# TWELVE

## THE FIRST DATE CONUNDRUM

Natasha left work late, not because she'd been busy, but because she'd procrastinated. Her nerves weren't about seeing Sebastian – this time her anxiety jittered over what to wear. She'd decided to revel in the power that surged through her when Seb's eyes heated and his gorgeous mouth bowed up into *that* megawatt smile at seeing her. Sebastian was helping her to draw the real Natasha slowly but steadily out into the light. Tonight, she wouldn't worry about the wrong men noticing her. She only cared that the right one would notice.

For a moment, Natasha gave way to Goldilocks checking her enthusiasm. *Wrong men after you. Why don't you see what you can't have? Around and around we go. He'll debase you, then I'll punish you.*

The Slut was licking her lips. *Let's have fun. Finally taking our great bod out for a spin again. Make him hunger for you.*

A stronger Natasha dismissed the mind fuck before it could gain any bluster. As a safeguard, Nat added one piece of clothing, heeding some of Goldy's fashion tips. 'Shit,' Natasha moaned. While Goldy's words were small, they still found a place in her reality.

Finally, at quarter past seven, she stepped out of an Uber and into The Norfolk. Appropriate Ferrari-red skirt – short, tight, but not too tight. She'd chosen a spaghetti-strapped, clingy white top with a sufficiently low back – not too low. Showing some cleavage, but not too much. A red silk scarf to top it off, covering her a little more. The concession to Goldilocks, not fashion. No stockings. Tanned legs, which after a shave were looking smooth, shapely and brown. Her white high-enough-but-not-too-high strappy stilettos were giving an encore performance for the good doctor.

Her face fell to her silver-heeled shoes upon seeing Rick and Holly talking to Seb at the bar. Holly was draped over Rick like some cheap superhero's cape. The trollop reached out to place her hand on Seb's shoulder.

Seb stepped back and turned to avoid Holly's clutches. That's when he saw Nat gliding towards him on legs that went to the sun. Their eyes locked. And there it was, the sun itself – her beautiful smile lit her face. Refreshingly, she hadn't caked on the make-up, not like Holly. She needed only a little eyeliner and mascara to accentuate those mesmerising orbs of blue. A hint of blush and some lip gloss highlighted her natural beauty. Her hair was straightened, falling alluringly around her face.

Seb's eyes fired. She was so sexy, yet she seemed to fear it, tried to hide it. That must've been what the scarf was about. Seb gleamed as he sighed, 'Thank goodness.'

Score. That was the gaze Natasha had aimed for. Rick and Holly also took note. Smiling sweetly, Nat looked at each of them in turn and addressed the trio in level of importance. 'Hi, Seb.'

Seb reached across and snaked his arm around her before whispering in her ear, 'You look fine, so fine.'

'Thanks, apologies for being late.'

Rick chuckled. 'Oh, Tashy's always late.' He'd stuck around the bar with Seb to rub it in Natasha's face. He and Holly were an item now. Knowing Mancini's reputation, her bland ways would see the well-connected doctor tire of her soon. Rick could help there. 'Tashy can never seem to get a little thing like being on time right.'

'Maybe you weren't worth being on time for,' Nat muttered.

She'd struck a nerve. Drunk Rick's jealousy countered, 'Sebastian, if you're going to go out with this one, you should know some things. I can fill you in.'

Sebastian pulled Nat in a little closer. 'That's not necessary, Rick. I like finding things out for myself.' He flashed his cheeky grin, captivating her. They shared a moment as attraction sizzled between them.

While Rick didn't fully recognise what was happening between the couple in front of him, he knew it didn't make him feel good. He had to break their silent connection. 'I bet I can tell you loads of stuff. Have you seen her god-awful tramp stamp?'

Holly's lips curled up into a sly grin.

Natasha had forgotten the nastiness Drunk Rick harboured.

Seb's eyes narrowed, and his mouth formed a hard, downturned line. 'Nice to bump into you two. We've got a dinner reservation, so it's time we were going.'

'Careful, Sebastian, she'll just use you like she did me. Get a leg up the ladder and kick you to the kerb.'

Seb felt Natasha's body tense. She tried to step towards Rick, only for Seb to tactfully swung her around a little, shielding Rick from her.

Rick wanted to bait his ex into a scene and ingratiate himself to the influential doctor. 'You won't want the Mancini name associated with a girl like Tashy.'

'Watch yourself.' Seb's grip around Nat's waist intensified. 'You know nothing of what the Mancini name can and can't be associated with.'

The doctor's wrath dumbfounded Rick. Seb's voice was low, pure Mancini menace, with an added arrogance. 'Keep this up and you won't walk out of here.' Seb wanted Rick to understand he had the power to harm him, and he wanted Natasha to know he thought she was worth defending.

Natasha was reeling. It was like Seb had stepped out of some bad Mafia movie. He looked so threatening. It scared her. Confusingly, she was also attracted to the protective power pulsing from him, all in her name.

Still, Nat didn't need Seb fighting her battles. His commanding voice had drawn the attention of two man-mountains dressed in black, seated at the end of the bar. They'd both looked up from their soda and lime pints. Seb curtly shook his head, and they looked away. Nat had seen similar interactions before. With her emotions running high, she couldn't grasp the memory as Rick interrupted her thoughts.

'I'd watch out. She's not worth it. Her family didn't even want her.' Rick thought he was on a roll, outing the real Tashy to the prominent doctor.

Natasha's icy glare could have frozen the Sahara. 'You're pathetic.' She pushed out of Seb's hold to square off against Rick as her control shone. 'What Rick fails to understand is that his mind is as small as one other certain part of his anatomy.'

Seb suppressed a smile. Yet again, Natasha had handled herself with assurance. Maybe she could take on his family.

Rick was speechless and staggered. Holly stumbled backwards.

Natasha spoke to Rick. 'Don't ever—'

'Speak about a lady like Natasha that way again.' Although he knew she could stand up for herself, Seb had been taught it was his duty to protect the ones in his care. It was almost a reflex. 'Rick, you've had too much to drink. And I wasn't joking about what could happen to you. Leave Natasha. She's none of your business anymore. She's mine. My business to care about.'

Resentment and frustration ripped through Natasha as Seb kept talking.

'It's been, for want of a better word, tiring.' Seb glared at Rick while ushering Natasha away. They squeezed out of the entrance between the two big guys, who had also decided to leave. The lump brothers split, one heading out ahead of the couple. The other man mountain waited patiently for them to leave before exiting.

The cooling evening breeze didn't counter Nat's temper. 'You do realise I can take care of myself. And I can certainly take a lightweight like Rick, of all people!' She didn't want Seb's protection; didn't feel she deserved it.

'Yes, I know. I've got it.' Seb softly cupped her chin between his thumb and finger. He wanted to kiss her but given her temper, decided to brush his thumb across her full, red lips instead. He hoped his touch could derail her anger as much as the silken feeling of her lips was scattering his.

She shrank a little at his touch. Her voice remained firm. 'You don't have to handle me.' But he'd brought her back.

'I saw that. I thought the look you gave Rick would make his head explode.'

She took heart from the pride in his voice and smiled.

He relaxed. 'Would you like to go to the Sail and Anchor for a drink? I've suddenly gone off The Norfolk.'

'Y-yes. Bit of dry argument here.' She smiled wryly. 'Didn't we have dinner reservations?'

He flashed a sheepish smile, 'A bit of a white lie. Just making an excuse to get you on your own – and all mine.'

She was about to object to the *all mine* quip until he took her hand, raising it to his lips, kissing the back of it, rolling his fingers over her knuckles as his gaze heated. Who did things like this, especially in public?

# THIRTEEN

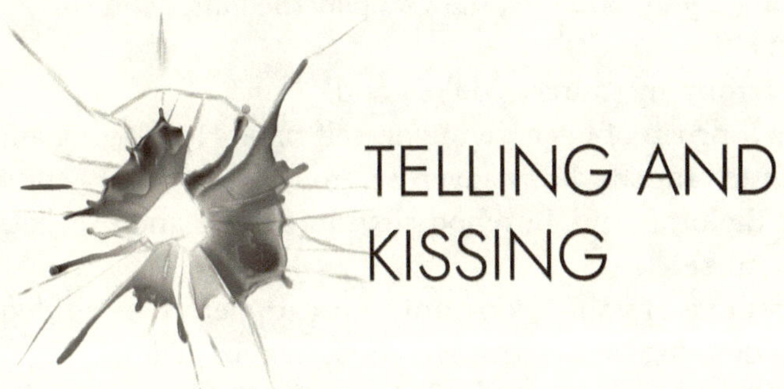

## TELLING AND KISSING

It was early, and the Sail and Anchor was quiet. 'Will I be forgiven for my rash actions if I finally buy you that promised drink?'

Playful dark brown eyes met simmering blue cooling her anger. 'You are a stirrer, Mancini, and yes, you can buy me a beer.'

'Any beer in particular?'

'I'll have a Peroni, please.'

Grinning, he said, 'An excellent choice.'

'Because?'

'It's Italian.'

When he returned with their beers, he asked, 'So, you and Rick, done and dusted.'

'Yes. Splitsville. All my friends think it's a good move.'

'I bet they were asking why such a beautiful woman was with such a jerk.'

'Is that what you were thinking?' She cringed at sounding so needy.

'Yes.' Taking a pull on his beer, he offered, 'That and why I'd never laid eyes on you around JCH.'

'Oh.' Before Natasha became too carried away, a small, nasty voice tried to make her acquiesce. *Too hot for you, too good to be true.* Natasha pushed Goldilocks easily aside. 'You probably hadn't seen me because

I was working in the ER and outpatient areas, not on the upper wards like oncology/haematology.'

There was a mischievous spark in his dreamy eyes. 'When we talked about music, you didn't tell me you play the guitar and sing.'

'No, I didn't.'

'I've heard from my sources you're good.'

She took a long sip of beer, giving herself time. Her singing and playing were something she didn't advertise. 'You have sources? Let me guess, Chelsea Taylor, friend, busybody extraordinaire and excellent new onc/haem nurse.'

'Very perceptive of you.' It took only a breath before he chided, 'Come on, stop dodging the subject.' His smile was contagious.

'Okay, I play and sing. I've had a few pub gigs. I don't get to play as much now because of work and distractions, like my friends. I'm deciding if you, Dr Mancini, will also be on that list.'

'I'd like to be your distraction. Speaking of which, would you like to go, maybe … somewhere else?'

'Um … for what?'

His mouth curved up as he thought, not *that*, yet. 'For dinner, Ms Perry. Just dinner. I love the spicy Mexican tuna steak here. Let's see if they can fit us in.'

'Maybe …' Her nerves returned.

'You don't sound too sure?'

'No, I mean, yes. I've never been good at these things.'

'What things? It's just dinner. You know, eating. Not sex.'

'Wha …' She spluttered.

'Shit, I mean. Sorry.' He scrambled. 'I, I didn't mean to put you on the spot.' How the hell did his thoughts escape his mind? This woman had him in a whirl.

Natasha found Seb's stumble refreshing. 'Seems you've caught my foot-in-mouth disease.'

'Yes, way to go, Mancini. I don't usually tend to be so forward. I usually leave that to the rest of my family. Let's start again. How about a casual dinner, Ms Perry, no strings?' He ran his hand through his hair and tried to pin her with a smoulder. A look that usually had them begging.

'Seb, let's leave it at just a drink.' Nat was taking the safe Goldilocks path as she went to slide off the chair.

Stunned, he thought, *this woman is just so immune to the usual moves*. Reaching for her hand it was Seb who begged. 'Hey, wait, I'd like to have dinner with you.' He found he landed on an old-fashioned ploy: honesty. One he hadn't used in a while. 'I'd like to get to know you. I don't bite. Get to know me. Just dinner between friends.'

She decided to stay and break away from her regular camouflage. 'Since you've made good on the promise of a drink, I guess, yes, I'd like to see if you could distract me some more.' Nat couldn't believe her candidness, sadly realising she hadn't been brave in a relationship for a long time because of her alters' security detail.

Once they were eating, he found it easy to talk to her – too easy. He began babbling about his family, sharing how his sister, Pia, amazed him with her seemingly bottomless drive and energy. She balanced looking after her children while managing the Aida Breast Cancer Foundation. The foundation was set up by his mother to give something back to the community. 'Pia and I run the foundation now.'

'I gathered that much from my interview.'

'Yes. One of the more enjoyable tasks I've stepped in to help Pia with.'

'I could see that. You made it tough for me.'

An eyebrow winged up. 'How so?'

'Only by turning the volume up on my nerves about three hundred per cent. Talk about pressure.'

'See, another reason you got the job. You handle pressure well. What else do you do well under pressure?'

*Smart-arse*, she thought. 'Do you do anything else besides Aida and JCH?' She wanted the spotlight back on him.

'There are several facets of the family business that I have no interest in, and only a few that I do.'

'Oh, there's a family business?'

Slightly confused, he decided to play along. 'Yes.'

'What's the name of this family business?'

A quizzical look furrowed his brow. 'Mancini Enterprises, of course.'

'Shit!' Escaped her lips with no chance to haul it back. '*The* Mancini Enterprises?'

The Mancinis were one of the best-known families in Fremantle. They owned and ran a multitude of businesses in and around the city, the world, for that matter. It was an impressive family. 'Oh my God,

I never put two and two together.' She was guileless when it came to powerful family trees. For that matter, big business.

Sage's warning must have been about this connection. While she may have been high-society deaf, she knew enough to understand he couldn't be involved with a girl like her. She slumped.

'Oh my God, you really didn't know.'

'No. I guess in the time between studying, working and ... sorry, I don't have much interest ... well, I don't keep track of business or the Freo gossip pages.' Her brain had disengaged from her tongue. 'I didn't make the connection. None of my friends did either, or if they did they failed to mention it.' She thought, maybe this was really what Sage had hinted at. 'I guess I just see you as Dr Mancini. Not anything to do with Fremantle royalty or world domination.'

His soul smiled, 'Don't apologise. It's refreshing.'

'I'd never have thought a Mancini son would be working so hard for a living as a doctor. But you can't—'

'Hey, don't let my family's name scare you. I'm only involved with bits and pieces of the business. The foundation and real estate.'

'Oh, well, of course, that makes all the difference!' She tried to settle the shock. 'Tell me, what's it like?'

'What?'

'Being part of such a big, successful family.'

'It's not like we're the Kennedys or anything, although it's still a lot of responsibility.' A hint of a frown formed, 'Especially from where my dad sits. The family name is everything to him.'

He started to talk about his mum, sister and two older brothers. She sensed he respected and loved his father, but it was nothing like his deep connection with his mother. She was surprised he'd opened up so readily to her about his family's tragedies.

Sadness dulled his eyes. 'Money means nothing to death.' He was in the middle of revealing the pain while simultaneously wondering why he felt compelled to tell this woman so much, so easily. 'It hit us all at once. My oldest brother, Giuseppe, was killed in an accident, and soon after, Mum died of breast cancer. That left Dominic, the next in line, to run the rest of the family business with Dad.'

The bad vibe Sage had projected seemed to be about what his family did to others, not what had happened to them. Nat's head and shoulders dropped at the shambles of her family life.

Seb saw the surrender, so he stopped abruptly. 'I'm sorry. I've been monopolising the conversation. Tell me about you?'

'Not much to tell.'

'Come on, what's your family like?'

He had chosen to ask her about one of the two most traumatic parts of her life. 'Oh, Dr Mancini, we're not going there yet. You have to do a lot more work before you get me to tell you about that part of my life.'

'Come on.'

'Can we leave it?' She shrugged, trying to shift the heavy weight of her past off her too-small shoulders.

'I'm sure you can't tell me anything I haven't heard.'

Her eyes became an ocean of tempestuous blue. Belatedly, he realised things were teetering on the edge of going very pear-shaped.

'Look, no! I've said I'd rather not. Can we just leave it at that?'

He pulled back in his chair, looking confused but wary, while she slumped further before gathering herself. 'Sebastian, I don't feel the need to go into my family story tonight. Not when I'm enjoying your stories so much more. Okay?'

He saw the unfathomable hurt in her eyes, and although she tried to dodge his gaze, it sent a raw jangle through him. She looked down at her wine and took a sip. When she peeked up, she'd set her mask back in place.

His eyes softened as he threaded his fingers with hers. 'I've put you on the spot again. I'm rushing you. Sorry. You're a mystery, and it seems I can't help myself.'

Another pleasing revelation, which was soon surpassed by her worry that the possibility of them being together was zilch. This thought left Nat shaking her head.

Seb knew he could find out about her family using other channels within the business and he would use those methods, if necessary. Yet, for a reason he couldn't grasp, he wanted to give this woman the chance to tell him her story, all on her own. 'I apologise, of course we can't get to everything on a first date.' He leaned forward once more.

With a skittish smile, she said, 'You've said I should take some time to get to know you. I guess you're going to have to do the same.'

'I can live with that. Don't ask about the family yet. Then I won't piss you off.'

'Yes, Dr Mancini, but it will take a bit more than asking about my family to do that,' she lied.

'Let me make it up to you. More wine?'

And they had moved on. No lingering retribution like she'd encountered with Rick and – long ago but never forgotten – Archie.

It was late when they finished dinner. They discussed books, music, art, more books and, ironically, the food. It was a bit spooky how much they had in common.

Goldilocks lingered. *He's pretending ... just to fuck you, bitch. Get another notch.*

It hadn't felt like it. Natasha had experienced feigned interest before. If he was a player, he was a patient one. Players didn't usually invest this much time and effort if they only wanted to jump her bones. Again, in Seb's presence, Natasha found it easy to shake off Goldy.

As they walked out of the restaurant, Natasha noticed that the two lumps of men she'd seen at The Norfolk were sitting in the front bar of the Sail and Anchor. They had a view of Seb and Natasha's table, although from where Nat was seated, she couldn't see them until she walked out.

Rational thoughts about them scattered as Seb wrapped an arm around her waist to move her into an alcove. His lean, hard body pressed against hers, as he backed her into the wall, his voice was a heavy rasp. 'I've wanted to do this all night. Truthfully, ever since Metropolis.' Seb's eyes had turned to soul-simmering Old Gold chocolate. His hands gently cradled her face as he tilted her lips to his.

Nat arched up into him, wanting, needing to taste too. It began as sweet, electric release. Nat closed her eyes, and the kiss spiralled deeper as a sensual white heat arced between them, all wrapped up in a silky smoothness of their lips. Time stood still, and she could only hear their combined heartbeats, no illicit music. His lips were tender as his tongue coaxed her lips to open wider. Sensual licks tantalised her. He tasted like desire.

Pulling away, Seb whispered, 'You never disappoint.'

They found each other's eyes when another flow of attraction pulsed through them. With no noise from Goldy or The Slut, Natasha threaded her fingers through his thick hair and pulled him to her. Their tongues danced, and it felt like a warm sun had come out from a long, dark shadow to brighten their lives. Velvet electricity wrapped around them like a ribbon binding them together. It energised the couple.

# FOURTEEN

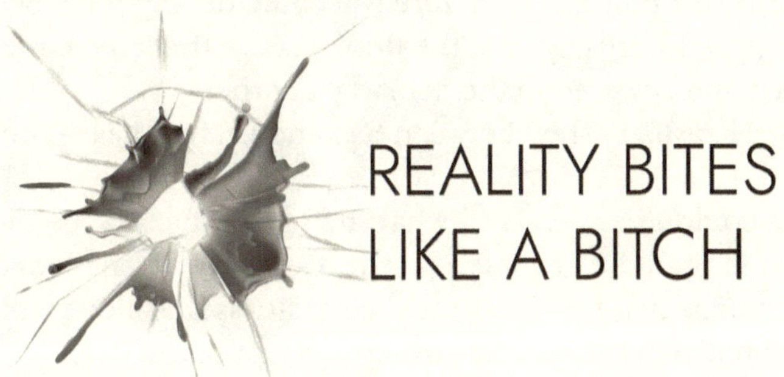

## REALITY BITES LIKE A BITCH

As they pulled back, Seb slid into a nervous ramble. 'Shall we get a taxi home, you know, to our homes, each of them, separately, or if, like me, you'd like to spend a little more time … talking. I know a fantastic bar up the street a bit, or whatever you'd like.'

Nat found his nerves eased hers. 'Lead the way to a taxi. Maybe coffee at my place?' This man made her feel bold.

'Excellent.' Seb slid his hand around hers, and she followed him onto the street.

'I make a mean cup of coffee …' Natasha's voice trailed off as she noticed a shadow of a man crumpled in the doorway of a nearby store. The guy was a living-on-the-streets dirty brown, with soiled jeans and a grimy t-shirt. He was a sobering sight. The tattoo on his arm drew her attention. The panther surrounded by jungle and flames was unique but familiar.

'Natasha, what is it?' Seb's voice fell away.

'Just a moment.' Almost overcome by the smell of putrid street dirt, Natasha made herself step closer and put her hand on the street guy's shoulder. 'Chevy, is that you?' He stood quickly. His glazed, pale blue eyes had no focus.

'Chevy is the name of one who walked with his brother in the forest of fire while Jesus watched over us. We go together into the eye of the firestorm. Forever we walked. We will persist. We will live and stay strong until redemption.'

He grabbed Natasha's hand off his shoulder and pushed her away, with more incoherent mumbling. Before Nat could do anything, Seb slammed Chevy backwards against the door, 'Leave the lady alone.' Chevy crumpled and cowered in the doorway's corner.

'Stop, Seb!' Natasha pushed between Seb and Chevy. 'Leave him alone.'

'What!' He couldn't understand what she was doing. Maybe the vulnerability he thought he saw was a facade. Could the strength and fire within be her true nature? A frustrated curiosity spiked along with his anger. 'He could've hurt you, the grubby piece of scum.'

'No, he's not. He needs help.' Nat reached over and tenderly grazed Chevy's face where it was scarred. 'Chevy, I can help. Trust me.' Her words and touch soothed the broken man's angst. They did nothing for Seb's.

'You're kidding me. Help? He's chosen this life. Leave him.'

The menace in the young man's tone caused Chevy to huddle into a ball, rocking back and forth in the doorway corner, whimpering, 'Please don't hurt me. I'll be good.'

'Nat, don't fall for his con job.' Seb hissed, eyes hostile and mouth set in a foreboding line. He grabbed Natasha by the arm, trying to pull her away.

She shook him off. 'You don't know anything. This guy is a Vietnam vet. He's been through hell.'

'How do you know he's a vet?'

'Let's say I just know and leave it at that.' Natasha bent down to Chevy and patted his shoulder. 'You're safe. I'll phone Dodge for you.'

Chevy stilled and stopped muttering.

Straightening, Nat glared at Seb, who glowered back at her. 'You can't be serious. You want to help this guy? Let's go home. We both have work tomorrow, and it's late.' He thought she was smarter than this.

'You go home.' Sarcastically, she seethed, 'Get your beauty sleep.'

Seb's eyes narrowed. 'I'm not leaving you with this low-life.'

She looked away but didn't back down. Once again, their tempers drew them closer. Seb grabbed Natasha's arm. They were toe to toe, chests heaving, each breath ragged. A few passers-by had stopped. The man-mountain twins had come out of the Sail and Anchor to check on the commotion. Another mountain man stepped purposefully towards

Nat, albeit with a noticeable limp. He wore his long salt-and-pepper hair tied neatly back in a ponytail. His face was leathery and rough, with a long beard the same colour as his hair. He had a menacing biker look, reinforced by his barrel-like chest, tatts and formidable shoulders.

'Hey, what's goin' on? Mate, let the lady go.'

Looking over Seb's shoulder, Natasha recognised the hulk, especially from his gait. 'Dodge?' His jackboots, black jeans and flannelette shirt, rolled up at the sleeves, made him look prone to violence. As his face set into a scowl, all doubt seemed removed. She'd heard his more colourful bikie acquaintances call him Brick.

'That you, Natasha?' He shielded his eyes from the bright shop lights to look closer.

'Yes, I was just about to call you.'

'Been a while, girl. Aren't you a sight for sore bloody eyes?' She slipped past Seb and gave the bear of a man a hug. When they broke apart, Dodge stepped towards Seb, who didn't take a step back but stood tall, glaring at Dodge. With both at their full height, they were eye to eye. Dodge was by far the broader, unquestionably a brick with eyes.

'Is this dickhead givin' you grief?'

'Oh God, no, Dodge.' She found herself stepping between Seb and Dodge. It was about now that Natasha was hoping that putting herself between Seb and her friends wouldn't become a habit. 'It's just a misunderstanding.'

Dodge nodded curtly. 'Good. If I remember right, you could handle yourself.' He gave her a broad, warm smile before his face dropped back to a scowl as he looked at Seb. The air boiled between the men. Now was not the time for pleasant introductions. Natasha didn't want either of them to get any closer. She steadied her breathing.

'Are you looking for Chevy?'

Dodge nodded. 'Yeah. He's such a worry.'

'He's here.' Natasha stepped aside.

Seeing where Chevy was cowering, Dodge's face brightened. 'Oh, thank Christ. I've been looking for him the last couple of days. Been pretty worried about him. He's such a problem child when he's off his meds.' Dodge pushed past Seb to help Chevy stand. 'Chev, it's Dodge, mate. You gonna come with me? Whattya think?'

Chevy eyed Dodge as he slowly stood, the fear in his eyes quietening. 'I know you. Yes, brother. I carried you when the jungle was on fire.'

'Yeah, we got out, mate. Thanks to you. It's all okay now. How 'bout I take you home?' Dodge supported Chevy as they stood together. 'The van's over there.' Dodge motioned with his head. 'I'm gonna take you to it, then you'll be safe, away from the fire. No worries. Okay?'

With childlike simplicity, Chevy said, 'Yes. But I need to thank that lady.' Chevy was built and looked like his brother, but his bulk hid a frightened boy. He didn't dare look at Seb as he stepped towards Natasha with unrecognising eyes. Natasha saw the battered man-child's true worth. 'Thank you.' He offered his dirty hand. 'You're the only one who was kind.' He suddenly beamed. 'Dodge, she touched my face.'

Natasha took his hand, understanding the gentle nature that existed within. 'Dodge will take good care of you.'

They walked past Seb. Dodge narrowed his gaze at Seb and rasped in a low, ominous tone, 'Don't you ever touch my brother or Natasha again. Hear me, Nancy-boy?'

Seb was quiet, staring sullenly at Dodge.

Natasha rushed her words, stepping between them again. 'Dodge, we're good.'

'As Natasha said, it was a misunderstanding.' Seb's jaw pulsed, grinding out his words. 'It. Won't. Happen. Again.'

'Good.' Turning to Natasha, Dodge squeezed her hand and winked. 'Don't be a stranger, girl. Come visit Sage, me and the big fella here sometime soon.'

Natasha smiled, nodding as she watched them walk off past the lump twins who were now standing closer. When she finally turned back to face Seb, he was glaring at her. She couldn't fully read the mixture of emotions. He looked more confused than angry. A strange attraction swept over her. Did she want to draw more anger out of him, or was it his passion to protect her that had her stepping towards him?

Seb was transfixed, wondering what heat it might elicit if he growled at her once more. He needed to find out. 'Let's go somewhere private to talk this out.' Steering well clear of junkies and any low-life was a non-negotiable for Sebastian. He needed to find out what her relationship with the biker was.

'Okay,' she said, still livid, yet still attracted.

'My place, we can get a taxi. I'd like to try and get past this.'

'Really?'

'I promise I'll be on my best behaviour. Let's talk about this in private, sort something out.'

'Yes, but stop with the bully-boy notions.' Natasha expected some other voices to chime in, but he had seemingly placated them by firing up her own voice. 'I'm my own woman. You. Don't. Own. Me.'

At hearing these words, he usually would have been done with someone. Instead, he was taking her to his home. A scorching fire as destructive as it was attractive raged in both as they walked in silence to the taxi rank.

Seb ushered her into the first cab. She was so in her head she missed the address he gave. Throughout the journey they were silent, brooding in the dark, preferring the company of their thoughts. Natasha couldn't believe he had reacted as he had. Then again, maybe it was true to type. The type Sage had mentioned – all brooding and dangerous. Confounding her principles regarding domineering men, she had agreed to give him the benefit of the doubt and talk it out.

The journey was short, her tone the same, but with an added dry edge. 'Naturally, you'd live at the Vergona Tower apartment complex.'

He rolled his eyes and escorted her across the foyer to the lift. She hesitated. Hadn't he heard anything? As she was about to turn and walk away, his gravelly voice stopped her. 'Natasha. Give us a chance.' A more potent force than her simmering anger took over, pulling her into the lift to be near him. He swiped a small fob over a sensor on the lift's control panel and stabbed the PH button.

'Of course it'd be the penthouse.'

He groaned. 'Yes, and the problem is?'

She mulled over what had happened as they ascended in suffocating silence, and her anger rose again. She couldn't control herself. 'Where do you get off at? Sure, you're rich, and your family own everything from here to kingdom come, but—'

'What? *You're* angry at *me*?'

'You're lucky Chevy or Dodge didn't bloody rip your head off. And to top it off, doing that after I'd told you I could look after myself. I don't need you or your misguided attempts to handle me. I'm not a victim.'

'Is that what you think? Did you hear anything I said? You're worth defending.'

'Did you hear anything I said? You don't need to defend me from any of them, especially Rick.'

He scowled at her. 'Look, screw Rick.'

'I already have,' she snarled back.

'That's not what I meant, and you know it. Fuck! What's going on with you? Why are you so mad at me?'

'Let's see. You've stopped me from giving my low-life, cheating ex what he deserved. You made me look weak and foolish. You've come on all chauvinistic and possessive when I was sidetracked from you for a moment to be with a friend. A *friend*, for Christ's sake. You don't own me, and Chevy needed help. I had this shit with my father and one other guy. Never again, understand?'

'I don't. Look, can't we ... why are you?' He made to step towards Natasha. 'I was defending you.' He glared. 'I don't like other men pawing at women. Is that so wrong—'

She put her hand up. Sebastian stopped as she continued her tirade. 'I don't care if you are a Mancini and can threaten people. You will not around me. It makes me feel awful. I didn't have the life you had with your perfect family and perfect dad. My father never gave me a break and he took my childhood away. He liked beating my mum and me to within an inch of our lives for sport. Excuse me if I refuse to have you treat me like anything other than your equal.' Natasha's hand rose to her mouth in a gasp. Suddenly she realised what she'd given away.

Seb glowered at her. 'Maybe before going off half-cocked, you should consider that you're not the only one who's had a shit life.'

They stared at each other, eyes blazing, blood pumping. But there was something else. Tension, more attractive than destructive, crackled around them. Neither understood what was happening or was prepared to give an inch. If anything, fighting drew them closer. *Oh God, this is tiring*, she thought. With any other person, each of them would have walked by now.

Nat and Seb seemed destined to be like two magnets with the same polarity facing each other. No matter how hard they tried to push towards one another, they just kept missing each other, sabotaged by a force stronger than their collective wills.

The lift reached the penthouse floor. The doors opened with a ping like the bell at the end of a round in a prize fight. They stepped out into their respective corners, escaping the oppressive atmosphere hanging in the lift. Standing in a huge alcove showcasing impressive highly lacquered black double doors, the pair settled.

'I guess after that outburst, coming in to sort this out over a quiet drink is unlikely?'

'You've got that right.'

'Should I order an Uber for you, or will you?'

Sullenly she said, 'I will.' Natasha was hurting. Her anger had finally left her, and now sadness filled the space. She liked being with him despite all of this. 'I'll wait for it in the foyer.'

Seb shook his head and turned away to the magnificent medieval castle-like black doors, fumbling with his keys as he opened the door.

# FIFTEEN

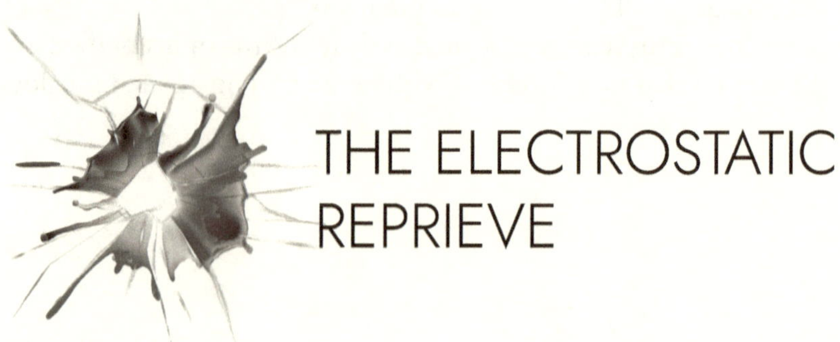

## THE ELECTROSTATIC REPRIEVE

'It's not how I wanted it to be.' His mutter was barely audible.

Natasha wasn't sure if she was meant to hear it or not. Turning to go, she brushed his lower arm and hand just as he pushed his keys back into his jacket pocket. It was a glancing touch, but there was a spark.

Easily attributed to science, Natasha thought, an electrostatic spark, dry weather, and synthetic carpet under her shoes. Yet this spark was more than just a scientific phenomenon. It spread through her as she noticed Seb jolt as well, giving Natasha the courage to look for a reprieve. Her voice filled with smoke.

'If it's not, then how did you want it to be?'

Seb felt the reprieve too. He swung around to take her hand, fixing her with heated eyes. Both acquiesced to the intense, primal attraction firing between them. His velvety voice murmured, 'Maybe this will answer your question.' Seb tugged her into him, wrapping his other arm around her shoulders, finding her lips. The force of his pull caused Natasha to fall into him. All the pent-up sexual tension between them went thermonuclear.

Natasha pushed him back through the door, their lips on each other hot and unrestrained. 'Yesss,' she whispered as they came up for air, and Seb back-heeled the door shut, swinging her further into the penthouse. Just like that, one of the magnets swung around. Finally, the purity of their attraction won out.

A tangle of bodies and yearning exploded. Lips lusted after each other's, teeth clashing, need and desire arcing like high-voltage electricity.

Seb was breathless. 'I want you. Now.'

'Please.' The sex-kitten Slut appeared even though Natasha wanted to do this for herself. Seb had released her, but this was different. Natasha was stronger and wouldn't acquiesce to The Slut. Nat wanted to hunt for ecstasy tonight, and with this man freeing her real self, she had the strength to push The Slut aside. There was no guilt, only a tiny piece of self-reproach, which The Slut clung to hungrily. She wouldn't easily give up such a thrill.

Seb's sensual ways and stormy brown eyes had unleashed Natasha's genuine deep sexual desires. When he rasped, 'Are you sure?' A heat filled her and fired The Slut.

The Slut chose Prince's 'Cream'. It pervaded Natasha's mind before she could choose a song, although she liked the choice. The Slut broke free and spoke. *Hell, yeah.* Nat yielded ever so slightly. Natasha's hands were The Slut's. They fisted his shirt, yanking it out of his trousers, finding their way to his chest. Finally, Nat had the chance, along with The Slut, to drag her nails through his chest hair. God, his pecs were glorious. He groaned against Nat's throat as she and The Slut rubbed their palms over his nipples, now tall and hardened. His hands were massaging Nat's butt, pulling her into him. She, with The Slut riding with her, could feel his erection at her hip. He felt sooo good, sooo big ... all so hard.

She peeled off his jacket as he growled, 'Upstairs. I want you there.' He bent down and lifted Nat, striding up the stairs that suddenly materialised. They burst through another door into a bedroom. Nat didn't really care where they were. All she and The Slut wanted to do was Seb.

'I want you,' she and The Slut whispered. They ripped his shirt open. Buttons flew everywhere as they stripped it back off his shoulders, pushing his arms behind him.

Seb's eyes were mesmerising pools of honest desire. 'Nat, I want you more than I've wanted anyone.'

Those eyes, those words, had Natasha believing. No other man had ever incited such feelings of power and confidence within her. She chained The Slut.

He spoke, 'You are stunning.' Trying to reach out, he chuckled, 'Natasha, wait.' Desire and humour danced across his face. 'My hands – they're caught in my cuffs. I can't touch you.' His shirt shackled his arms to his sides. 'I so want to touch you.'

'Oh baby, it's how I want you – for now, at least.' The smoky tone was pure Natasha – hers and only hers. It wasn't The Slut's. The Slut lingered, but it was Nat who pushed Seb, so he flopped back onto the bed. He laughed, and she, not The Slut, kept Prince playing.

Kicking off her stilettos, Nat straddled him. Her skirt scrunched up around her thighs. She gazed down at him. 'Trust me?'

His tongue ran slowly over his bottom lip. 'There's no place I'd rather be.'

With that, Natasha swooped down and gave his lips a swift kiss. Her blonde hair slowly swept over his bare chest, teasing him as it caressed his body. Nat felt a tremor run through him, giving her more confidence.

He moaned. 'I'm at your mercy.' God, he wanted this woman. The outside world, his family, it could all wait.

Shuffling back, Nat undid his belt, tossed it to one side and slid off him to unzip his fly. Lifting his hips, he allowed her to lower his trousers and boxers quickly, leaving them around his ankles. Seb was unable to move his limbs. His feet were bound by his trousers, his hands by his shirt, and heat darkened his eyes. His balls ached at seeing such an erotic creature hovering over him.

Marvelling at the glorious man submitting to being bound, she captured his long, full shaft in her talented fingers while moving to kiss him hard. More empowerment exploded within Natasha as she took control and released all her sexual desires with no guilt. This act was for Natasha, no alters.

Moving down his cut body, Nat swirled her tongue around the velvet tip of Seb's cock. He gasped and then released a groan through gritted teeth, writhing at Nat's touch and jerking his hips up. His manhood slid deeper into her mouth and she sucked harder. The erotic smooth tones and words of 'Cream' reigned supreme. The Slut was nowhere.

This time, Nat enjoyed the heat of the song and this, this right here – what she felt was all good. Natasha had mastery over her sexual acts for the first time since The Slut and Goldilocks had shared her mind. She wasn't going to settle and feel guilt.

Nat's mouth worked him, all the way down and up. It was hot, and Prince's voice was cool and sensual. Seb's eyes rolled up into his lust-heavy lids. Seeing the effect she was having on him turned Natasha on even more. Fuck, it was so good to be free, to revel in the sexual woman she'd hidden. All alters were left far, far behind.

Working him harder with her mouth, Nat was in charge as she took Seb again, deep and sensually, her sex creaming as she did. The real Natasha now stood alone. No Slut, no money, no filthy, dark rooms were needed, no disgusted guilt. Nat relaxed, taking him entirely.

As Seb hit the back of her throat, he groaned and found himself letting go. Wanting her to lead him to a place higher than he'd been for some time. He was losing his grip on suppressing his own dark predilections. Tonguing his silky, broad crown, Nat unsheathed her teeth, gently sucking and nibbling his shaft.

Seb huskily murmured, 'God, you're good.'

Prince's silky, suggestive lyrics and smooth orchestrations faded out, and only Natasha was left to drive Seb on. Buzzing, Nat found herself in control of her absolute sexual pleasure more than at any other time.

Seb was in a place he'd never been taken. The sensation of pure, unrivalled ecstasy had him cresting at the edge of frenzied climax.

'I'm going to come. I. Want to. Be in. You. Feel you, Naa ... tasha.' He moaned his words in time with Nat's movements of her mouth up and down his long, wide girth. She felt even more wanton working his cock with her tongue as she massaged his balls. Nat felt him ready to blow.

Pausing, she looked up and smiled. 'There's plenty of time for you to fuck me soundly, Dr Mancini, but for now ... my turn.' She took him again, and he groaned as searing pleasure had his body shudder. Nat twirled her tongue, pulling her teeth back so her lips were rigid around him. She sucked hard, luring him to an ecstasy where she knew he was only hers.

Her cheeks were sucked in, sealed tight around him. The pressure saw him start grinding in and out of her. Then, when he couldn't take the sensual overload any longer, he fired, releasing, again and again, calling out an erotic benediction to Natasha. She swallowed his thick, hot saltiness, delivering Seb total satisfaction.

Nat sat back on her heels, humming with sexual energy as she watched the show. Seb raised his nearly naked body up off the bed, rumbling his pleasure. 'Oh my God, Natasha,' he puffed, 'I haven't—'

'What?' With lustful eyes and a proud smile, she said, 'You haven't ever had a—'

'No, I mean yes. Never like … where did you learn to do that?'

Nat's voice was full of yearning, but a hint of The Slut returned in the reply. 'You don't want to know.'

Seb was overwhelmed, wanting more. 'You mightn't want me to own you, but right now, your mouth owns me.' After a beat, he took out his cufflinks and dropped them on the floor, pulling his shirt off. His perfectly formed washboard bunched as he reached forward to take his shoes, socks and trousers off. He stood magnificently naked before Nat.

A mist of sweat coated his skin, giving his beautiful form a glorious hue. Surprising her when he pulled her to him. Their foreheads touched as he slid his hands onto her hips with a deep, guttural, oh-so-salacious growl. 'I want you so badly.' Then his brow creased. 'But it's … I don't have a condom here. My wallet's downstairs in my jacket.'

Later, she'd think it was odd he didn't have any on hand in his bedroom. At the time, she dissolved as he kissed her, working his lips along her jaw. Nat couldn't contain her need. 'Dr Mancini, do you trust me?'

'Yes.'

'I'm a pharmacist. I know my pills. We're covered. I'm clean.'

'Me too.' Seb smiled at her hungrily. 'Smart, gorgeous and prepared.' Doubt swept his face. Should he allow himself to lead this beautiful creature down his tortuous path? Would he be able to control his family this time and most of all his own dark side? He had to ask, 'You sure?'

Nat wiped her fingers across her lips, removing the remnants of his arousal while the last trace of The Slut left her lips. 'Oh please, I've just rocked your world like never before. Don't talk. Throw me down and lay one on me.'

A roguish smile swept over Seb's lips, and Nat went from hot to steam. His eyes never left hers as he removed her scarf. 'My turn.' Those lips sipped at hers. Then he dispensed with her skirt, sliding Nat's knickers achingly slowly down her legs, trailing kisses up her thighs.

She almost collapsed as he brushed his thumb across her clit. He stood swiftly and slipped off her strappy blouse.

'No bra. Yesss.' Turning her around. 'I've wanted to get my hands on your body since I first saw you leaning on the bar at the Red Herring.' He stood behind Nat and wrapped his arms around her, pulling her against him. She felt his cock grow again as it bumped against her butt. Trailing kisses down Nat's spine, he dropped to his knees, kissing her tattoo and the arc of her butt cheeks. He turned her slowly to nuzzle her mound of curls. 'Mmm, you smell good. You're soaked.' He tantalised her further by brushing the pad of his thumb over her clit again before circling her folds. A throbbing wave pulsed through her when she saw sexy anger sweep his face. 'Why do you enjoy pushing me to the limit of self-control?'

'How do you know I'm doing that?'

'Because that's what I enjoy doing to you.'

Nat's heart lurched into a rapid-fire crescendo. The Slut didn't need to hold court as Nat did her own bidding. 'Ohhh, please push more.'

'Oh, baby, I'm gonna push a whole lot of different limits now.' Putting his hands on her shoulders, he toppled them onto his bed. Their bodies melded together perfectly as he ran feather-light fingers over her hypersensitised body.

With the promise of the exquisite act to come, Nat strained to contain the need sweeping her. Desperate for the ecstasy that had eluded her for so long, she couldn't hide the need in her voice. 'Please, Sebastian, I want you now.'

His fingers found her nipples while his lips smiled on her throat, his body hot against hers. No Slut required. Mercilessly, his fingers moved south and started massaging her sex. Seb wanted to explore her gorgeous body. It was going to take every fibre of his being to go slow. His lips and tongue took her left nipple. One finger circled the lips of her sex, possessively entering her.

As the need built, Nat craved him more than life itself. She ran her fingers through his hair.

The soft sounds she made, the way her body reacted, it was as if it was all new to her, making him want to give her more. He kissed down her body as electricity pulsed around them. He wanted to lure out their combined passion to have it blossom fully.

Nat couldn't help but groan and grind the apex of her thighs against his palm. The friction caused need to unfurl into an intense longing that rose from deep within her. She writhed and moaned, 'Oh yes, I want you.'

Removing his finger, he smiled before sliding his middle finger into his mouth. Their eyes locked as he removed his finger slowly. 'Yesss, you taste good.'

A shudder, but no voices. Nat smiled and licked her lips. Somehow Sebastian was a game-changer. Seb's touch had her giving herself unreservedly to him.

When he slid his finger into her waiting mouth, she fluttered her magic tongue around him before he withdrew it. Seb wondered, she had to have done this before, yet she yielded like she hadn't.

Nat saw the searing I'm-gonna- fuck-you-but-good look in his Old Gold chocolate eyes and welcomed it. Trailing kisses up her thigh again, finishing this time by nipping around her hipbone before he returned to worshipping her. Seb tongued her, pressing and circling her bud. She was ascending on a splendid journey to an erotic summit the likes of which she'd never experienced. He also had a magical tongue and mouth. She was delirious.

Seb raised his beautiful head, his ebony locks flopping over his hopelessly captivating eyes. He slid his body smoothly over her. It was like a dream, having a hot, hard lover hovering over her, wanting to share the journey with her.

Not being able to resist any longer, Seb sank slowly into her warmth. Nat gasped, and her core crushed him as he filled and stretched her to new limits. Before she could savour the feel of him, he withdrew. His absence left an impatient emptiness. He taunted her. Building the anticipation, toying with their discipline, stoking their erotic fires by stroking the crown of his cock agonisingly slowly at her entrance. Finally, he ground into her, deep. It was exquisite and tender. The silky end of his cock rocked into the most erogenous spot of her body as she sheathed him totally.

'God, you are so tight. Yesss. You never disappoint.' He started moving at a perfect rhythm that allowed Nat to savour him. Her core tightened further, fisting him.

Finally, his control acquiesced to their combined need, and Seb slammed into Natasha. She pistoned her hips up to meet his pace, losing herself in the glory of it. Their loving flowed, born from the beauty of the sensual dance they shared.

For Natasha, it was like her first time. Not the one she'd had, but the one every woman dreamed her first would be like. She was on her own this time, sharing the headiness with a worthy partner. She hoped that by not letting her alters take charge, there was no nightmarish Slut to cause the guilt of Goldilocks to rise. There was only Natasha, Seb and their pleasure.

He kept thrusting, his eyes lost in her saucers of blue. Holding his gaze, she was lost to the bliss, racing to the edge, thirsting for an exquisite release. Then it came in an erotic rush as she catapulted over the summit. Seb exploded, seeing colours more vivid than he'd ever known. He held on to Nat as their bodies and souls shared the deliciously long intimate detonation and aftershocks.

Every single carnal nerve Nat possessed fired, sending her flying beyond long forgotten limits. Time meant nothing, the power of the chemistry created when she held him in her was more incredible than seconds, minutes and hours. Eventually, he withdrew, and they lay on the bed facing each other.

On a half whisper, half giggle, she said, 'Oh. My. Fucking. God. Dr Mancini.'

Sebastian relished seeing her wicked smile. 'Pretty apt description. I didn't expect mind-blowing sex, given the ride in the lift.' Seb's voice became quiet and sincere. 'Honestly, I was only trying to defend you against Rick. And I thought you were being threatened by that guy, um, Chevy. I have a temper, and situations like that bring it on. I don't like to share.' Warily he offered, 'And after what we've just done, I never want to share you again.'

Natasha fired up. 'You haven't heard—'

'Okay, shh.' He glided his fingers over her sex-swollen lips. 'Look. I want to see you more. I shouldn't. Not with ...' Shaking his head, he managed, 'Forget that. I'll explain, later.' His brow furrowed as he looked around as if searching for something. Finally, he said, 'Be gentle with me here, but I need to know what I did to make you react the way you did. Most women are usually happy that a man comes to their rescue.'

His words doused her temper's heat.

Seb touched her cheek, not being able to resist the lovely glow their lovemaking brought to her skin. 'I was concerned, that's all.'

His disarming of her was complete. Natasha began to hope she could trust him with some of it. She opened the door a little.

'I had a rough family life. It's hard not to believe that you're anything but worthless and unlovable when your father is head of the kick-you-in-the-guts cheer squad. At times, my mum's caring voice was lost in the noise. I kept trying to prove my worth to him. Ultimately, I realised I never could, no matter what I did. He hurt me so often. I came to the conclusion that if I was going to make something of myself, I could only rely on myself ... fight my own battles. I will not be painted as a victim.'

She expected him to pull back. Instead, Seb reached for her, wrapping his warm body around her. Placing his forehead on hers, his eyes searched her soul. What he saw floored him. 'Natasha, never.'

For the first time with a man, Nat wanted to explain herself, give him something to stop the sadness that was spreading across his face to his eyes. 'Look, everyone has some sort of tragic tale. I decided not to ever let anyone treat me like they owned me. I've worked hard to become strong enough to stand up for myself. I don't need anyone.

'Today, when you went charging in to defend me, I know I should have been thinking it was great, but it just made me feel like a victim, and when you went off at Chevy, I felt like I was back with my father and another guy who bullied me – weak, unable to protect someone I cared about.'

Nat took his hands in hers, trying to make her point. 'Sebastian, I can fight my own battles. I'm not to be possessed by anyone but me. I'm free to talk to who I want, and nobody's going to tell me different. I don't care what your temper is like. Don't. Do. That. Again.' She found herself squeezing tightly and shaking his hands forcefully in time with her words. 'Oh, sorry.' She instantly let them go. 'And I am truly sorry for the crack about your family. I was hurt. My anger took over, too.'

'Don't worry, it's forgotten. But I will not forget your temper. It is certainly something to behold.'

'Excuse me. You were giving as good as you got, if I remember correctly. I do like the way you defuse an argument. The most agreeable way I've ever come across.' Nat grinned up at him.

With pride in his voice, he said, 'If I recall, we both found it a better way to come.'

'Cheesy, Dr Mancini, but point taken.'

They were both feeling sated and silly.

Seb ran his hand down her thigh. 'By the way, Rick's an absolute fuckwit. Your tatt's a turn-on.'

Nat instinctively grabbed at her lower back.

Seb's voice became husky. 'It's Celtic, isn't it?' His hand was soon on hers, and a tingle ran through her as his finger caressed her inked skin.

Nat was speechless, but her eyes spoke loudly.

Seb read what her radiant, blue eyes were saying. Round two, or was it three. He wasn't sure, and right now, as he found her nipple with his tongue on a journey south, he wasn't keeping score.

# SIXTEEN

## SOARING WITH A GOD, CRASHING AS A SINNER

'Pleease. No. Get off me.' It was useless. His sweaty bulk crushed Trixie. His erection ground against her thigh. His build wasn't the only thing that was thick and stumpy. One hand clamped Trixie's hands together, twisting them up in a precise move, anchoring them above her head. Nauseating, sticky beer breath flooded her face, staining Trixie's senses forever. The unknown shadow slammed the bottle down and snatched at her jaw with his other paw. He wouldn't be denied tonight.

Rough, greasy fingers deformed her cheeks. Grinding them painfully against her teeth, he snarled, 'Think you're too good for me. I told you I own you. You. Are. *Mine*. You can never leave.' The animal forced himself further.

*The Slut did this.* Goldilocks was unusually distraught as she directed her usual condemnation to Trixie the Slut and, therefore, Nat. *You sinned again, sewer rat – strayed. Now run, fight, run.*

*Screw yourself, Goldy,* The Slut screamed. *This is not my doing.* The Slut spoke to Nat. *I take your fear, your shame, take that burden from you. You survive because of me. Goldilocks only gives you guilt and punishment. But right now, you must fight, run, fight.*

Nat had deserted the scene and left it to Trixie to manage the shame, fear and pain. Only Trixie the Slut heard and understood what had to be done. She fought Goldilocks. This time The Slut momentarily won and decided they all would fight and then run.

Slipping his sweaty grip, Trixie freed an arm. Scratching out at the darkness, her fear consuming her, until scrambling fingers grasped an answer. Then Trixie felt pain as she rolled him. All she knew was to run – survive, find Natasha and a new life. Now she was falling, but the weight of her unknown attacker was gone. The terror remained.

Briefly touching reality, Natasha jolted up off the floor, shrouded in a thick, choking panic. She couldn't work out where the hell she was. All too soon, the smell of sticky, sex-soaked sheets, indomitable darkness and a deafening silence swamped her. Natasha was too far gone and sank back into the nightmare. Only Trixie the Slut and Goldilocks remained to rule.

Dirty, chubby fingers clawed at Trixie's face. Terrible dark images kept coming at her in a rush – the bars, the smell of stale beer, cigarette smoke and the strip club. The filthy rooms of the club and then the cold, eerie silence and blackness of one room. Terrible things happened there, when Trixie was locked in and they slipped the needle in. Her drug horror doubled. As helplessness consumed her, any power from free will and choice was yanked away from her.

Then there was blood, lots of it. No needle was stuck into Trixie this time, there was only blood. *What had happened? Was it from her cut hand?*

'No, no, no! Not this again.' Trixie never revealed her attacker's face to Natasha, even when Nat surfaced and Trixie dropped away. There was always just horrible pain and evil panic attacking Nat, which she always let Trixie handle. Tonight, Nat came back, it was a little different. Nat found herself wanting to break the surface of the tide of panic to understand if it was real or only her alter's trick.

Nat knew this nightmare and struggled to find a song to cling to and use to fight the terror of the panic attack. When fighting off a panic attack, some people tried to recite lists of things, like the title of every James Bond movie in chronological order. For Nat it was music. A haunting lament, 'Bring me to life', came weakly to her. She tried to cling to the melody, the fingering on her guitar, the timing wrapped around the lyrics. Could these things bring her to sanity this time?

From the chaotic noise thundering around Nat's mind, Amy Lee's evocative voice rang true like a beacon. The Evanescence singer's tone urged Nat to recite the lyrics to glue herself back together. She began stumbling over the words, attempting to stop shredding herself from the inside out.

Images were flickering fast and chaotic through her mind like a black-and-white silent movie; there was nothing she could recognise. The jaws of the panic came back to be baying at Nat's throat. She found the bedside light, fumbling it on. There was a large floor-to-ceiling shutter. No wonder it was so dark and quiet. Slender realisation pierced her mind. Seb's bed. She stilled her legs and arms, trying to settle the confusion, still bumbling through lyrics. She told herself to keep trying to remember, keep saying the lyrics, but she was losing, drowning in panic, leaving reality behind. Natasha couldn't grip onto the here and now. The sin of The Slut's deeds was too close, too strong.

Goldilocks was ready and waiting. *Pathetic women of your type can't fly with gods.*

Nat's heart and mind were still racing, she was panting, sweating. Seb's beautiful, loving acts blended with her murky, dirty past. Nat couldn't gain control by reciting lyrics or remembering how to play songs. She began to sink back into the panic.

Goldilocks morphed into her beast filled with revulsion, and its terror smothered Nat. Goldilocks crowed, *Just another jockey. You must pay the price for the sin you practice.* Nerves splintered, all fuelled by Goldilocks's pious taunts. *Filth. Stray, you pay. Trash.*

Nat had to leave to survive, so Trixie reappeared. Goldilocks was at her worst. Only terror and retribution existed.

Finding her clothes strewn across the room, Trixie tugged them on hurriedly. No shoes, no bag. Frantically, she searched the vast space in a state of robotic anxiety, feeling nothing but familiar, terrifying shame and guilt. She found her shoes. Suddenly it came to her in a nervous flurry. Her bag was downstairs.

Only the beast Goldilocks had become remained, biting and ripping at Trixie's sanity as she opened the bedroom door. There was no one in sight. She didn't care about her bag. Trixie had to go before she lost it entirely and endangered the lives of those around her.

She staggered towards the stairs. The waning moonlight streaming through a sizeable two-storey floor-to-ceiling window lit the room. It ran along the entire wall of the penthouse. A grandfather clock stood like a sentinel at the top of the stairs. The hands were at four-forty, causing the clockface to take on a look of disgust. The staircase and the room below warped and bent into her. Heart hammering, blood thundering, she took the stairs two at a time, looking to flee towards the door.

Sebastian appeared, standing in front of her. Trixie froze as they came face to face. The good thoughts he evoked briefly blunted Trixie's panic. His toned body was naked from the waist up. Pyjama bottoms hung divinely from his svelte hips. The moonlight made it look like he was chiselled from flawless grey-black marble.

'Natasha, what's wrong?' His handsome form was disturbed by the concern that marred his face. His voice stilled all elements of her body, soul and alter-filled mind. He grabbed her hand, spinning her around, away from her goal. She was now facing him, as he said, 'Natasha, please, what's wrong? Speak to me.'

'Sorry, got to go. Need to ...' Trixie couldn't let him see or bear witness to Nat's horror within. The panic monster was back, asserting its control, gnashing and tearing at her, driving more fear.

Trixie struggled against his grip. 'Please let me go.'

Seb's voice returned to her like a broken-up radio transmission, 'But why? Stay.'

'Please don't! Just let me go.'

'I'll drive you, or do you want me to call someone? Otherwise, how—'

'Let me go!' Shaking uncontrollably, her hands fisted. 'Please,' she stammered, nausea and mania rising as she threatened to come undone.

'Stop. I think you're having a panic attack.' Seb placed his hands on the rapidly rising and falling shoulders of the woman he knew as Natasha, but she wasn't seeing him. It was like she was someone else. Sliding his hands around her, he held her in his arms. Her eyes seemed unfocused but for the terror in them. It shattered him. There was too much pain for one so beautiful. He couldn't fathom what had caused this sudden change. It was like she'd awakened into some nightmare he couldn't see or share or help her escape.

Trixie was beyond the point of return. 'Oh, God, no. No!' She had to break free or she'd hurt him. 'Don't force me—'

He held her firmly to his chest. 'Breathe, Natasha, breathe. Take some slow, deep breaths. Go to a safe place. Think about a safe place.' Seb's words stilled her. 'Is there something you can take?'

No dice. The panic that caused Nat to disappear had overridden any chance of her returning. Trixie the Slut screamed, 'I have to go. Got to.' Trixie couldn't breathe. She didn't want Goldilocks's panicked beast to surface and hurt Nat and Seb in Goldy's fervour to punish the bad they'd shared.

He tightened his grip. 'I don't think you should—'

'Let. Me. Go!' Trixie shrieked and struggled against his arms, her dread mounting, eyes wild, not seeing. She squirmed and punched out violently. Natasha was in too deep, a red terror gripping her tighter than it had for ages, the savage monster feeding on her, so Trixie had to fight. Again, Trixie struck out madly, harder, trying to hurt, wanting to wound, needing to escape him.

'Your bag is near the door.' A blow to Seb's jaw saw him release her. 'I'll call an Uber.' He'd have to wake Paul. He could impersonate an Uber driver. Seb would make sure she'd be safe.

Trixie wasn't sure if she'd answered as she grabbed Nat's bag and headed out the door.

Seb was stricken. Every time they seemed to find common ground, it crumbled and she left. This time she was running away – in terror. He shouldn't care, especially if it was going to be this hard. But he did care – far more than he ever had before. Much more than he should, knowing his family's rules.

Finally, Trixie stumbled into her apartment. The Uber had arrived at Seb's almost instantly. The muscle-bound driver, dressed in black, looked like he'd just been woken up. It was early in the morning, after all. These thoughts didn't persist as she fought her panic. The streetlights and noise of early-morning Freo lessened the terror during the trip. She made sure of it by plugging in her earbuds to her phone and clinging to 'Bring me to life'. She shook uncontrollably, gasping for breath, her clothes drenched in sweat as she let the song numb her. Exhausted, a band of pain tightened around her head as she ran through her apartment, just making her bathroom in time to throw up.

Stripping off, Trixie collapsed into a cold shower, hugging her knees to her on the cold, hard tiles. A shaking ball of despair, sobs racked her body as the water washed away her tears. Eventually, the madness subsided, allowing Natasha to rise, brush her teeth, and rid herself of the stench. Staggering to bed, she rolled up around her iPad, searching for solace from the chilling dark of her mind.

Ultimately, escape from the suffocating smell, silence and darkness of her sin materialised. Nonetheless, Goldilocks's fierce demon of torture and trauma had subjugated Natasha once more. Scaring her with the one nightmare, or was it real memories of what had happened in that room? Why couldn't she remember why there was so much blood? Why wouldn't her alters let her see?

Not even Sage could help unlock the source of Nat's torment. Would she be free of her alters if she could unlock this unsolved puzzle from her forgotten past? Yet no matter how hard Natasha tried, she never had.

Not wanting to take an anti-anxiety pill and emotionally flatline, she decided to fight the panic and the shame and settle the attack herself. In her sanctuary, she could see the streetlights through the slender gap in her curtains. The light she needed. The smell of fresh air calmed her. Banishing the silence, she escaped into music's warm, protective cloak once more. She prayed and hoped it would be her narcotic, to be the potent cloak of oblivion she craved tonight.

Clutching her sin and her iPad, she scrolled through photos of the original Natasha. She drifted to a better time when she was happy to share a moment of peace with her younger brother and sister. Her mum was stronger then, and would take photos of them at these times, because they were at ease. Their dad wasn't around. They'd listen to their mum's old vinyls, sing and have fun. The slideshow began, which meant she wasn't alone anymore. Nat found the perfect song. She gripped herself tighter and plugged in her earbuds. This time Robbie Williams's eloquently penned 'Come undone' led her to safety, a theme for the damned and not quite beaten.

# SEVENTEEN

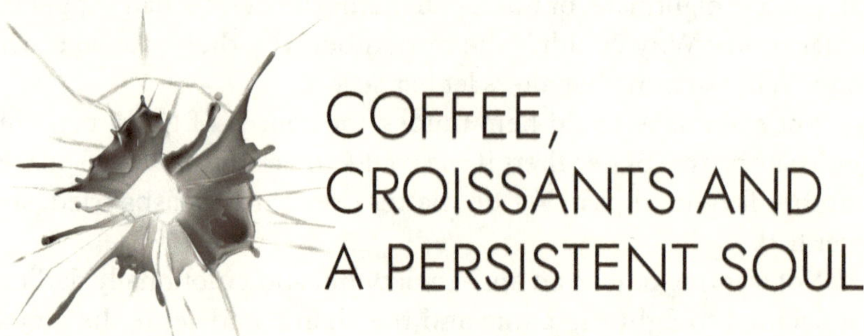

## COFFEE, CROISSANTS AND A PERSISTENT SOUL

There was a noise – an annoying ringing. It stopped, then started again, this time accompanied by loud knocking and then pounding. The shock jolted Natasha awake. The pain in her head yielded a little to the sounds of her apartment. Her doorbell rang repeatedly, and the knocking continued. She was naked and sprawled out on her bed. Her iPad was shut down beside her. One earbud was grimly trying to stay attached to her.

Natasha tried to reboot with movement, like her iPad. She struggled for a piece of reality, some reference point, but nothing surfaced. She grabbed her faux satin robe and moved stiffly through her apartment. The knocking continued. She froze.

Seb's voice, desperate and breathless, shouted, 'Natasha, are you there? Are you okay?'

The night's events collided with her like a bucket of iced water to the face.

'Please open the door. I need to make sure you're okay.'

Her immobilised body took many beats to jerk into action. She tightened her robe and opened the door. Sebastian's concerned face dropped a thousand floors. 'Jesus, what happened? Did I—?'

'You aren't responsible.' Her temper spiked. 'I hardly know you.' How dare he think he was the sum cause of her meltdown. She had no energy to sustain the anger. He stepped across her threshold, shutting the door. The smell of cologne and fresh coffee quietened her.

Seb set down two large takeaway cups of coffee and a paper bag. Before another word could be said, he checked her arms and torso, firing a barrage of medical diagnosis questions at her. She didn't answer, so Seb gently caressed her cheek. Only then did he find composure, the feel of her smooth golden skin under his fingertips.

His body was so close the fragrance of the man intoxicated her. His sky-blue button-down shirt clung to his muscular chest, accentuating its rise and fall. His grey trousers hugged him in a fashion that should've been illegal this time of the morning.

Stroking Natasha's hair back from her face, eyes glistening, his voice thickened, 'You didn't text. I called. And texted. And worried. I couldn't wait any longer. I had to see you.'

'Good God, Seb. I turned my phone off. I can handle things on my own. I don't need anyone's help.' She stepped away from him.

'Then tell me … what to do.' His voice was suddenly hoarse, filled with emotion. 'I'm going out of my mind here.' He stepped towards her. The space she'd just created evaporated. He took her in his arms, pressing her against his chest, where it was warm and safe. 'Natasha. Please put me out of my misery. What happened last night?' His chest expanded in a shudder.

'Look, let me handle this my way. I'm fine.'

'I can see you're not. Tell me. God, please, because I'd call getting through any time I spend with you that doesn't trigger an argument like World War Three, a success.' His voice was raw.

'I'm fine, really.' Without realising it, Natasha began rubbing her forehead against his chest. She couldn't do this, couldn't illuminate her dark, sin-filled past and entrust it and her heart to a man. He might rip away everything she'd fought to claw back. She wouldn't confide in him. She wouldn't make that mistake ever again, not like with Daddy dearest, not like with Archie.

Seb felt her pulling away from him again. He tried to thaw her, to bring her back to him. He rubbed her shoulders gently. 'Let me clean you up. Please. You look like you've been through hell.'

'Jeez, thanks.' Leaning back to glance across at the hallway mirror, she swallowed her pride. She was a badly drawn panda. Dropping her head she said, 'Seb, really, it's fine. Please don't fuss.' Her voice was full of despair. 'Please go.'

Standing close, he brushed his thumb across her lips, raising her chin. 'Hey, you look a little worse for wear, that's all.' Dropping his hand, he leaned in and kissed her lips. The solitary tender connection of only their lips caused the sweet release of forgiveness to flow. They both stilled, savouring the moment. 'Where's your bathroom?' he murmured against her lips.

Natasha took his hand and led him through her tiny apartment to the bathroom, where he lifted her up to sit on the vanity. With dabs from make-up remover wipes, he expertly cleaned the black smudges off her face, 'Ahh, there you are. That's the gorgeous, feisty Natasha I know.' He sighed before taking a deep breath. Her scent, even in her present state, was mesmerising. Blossoming jasmine caught in the rising sun filled his lungs.

Natasha brushed her teeth then rested her head tentatively on his shoulder. 'I'm so sorry it had to be this way. I can't let anyone see me when I get like that.'

The dark shadows under her eyes caused them to be filled with a deeper indigo this morning, like the blue in them held all her sadness and tears. They captivated him. Yet, as upset as she was, no tears fell. Maybe she was all cried out from the night before. He wrapped his arms around her.

She softened. 'I'm gutted you saw as much as you did.'

The tension left his body as he ran his fingers through her hair. 'Let's start with coffee and see where that leads.' Safe, strong arms lifted her like a small child and carried her to the lounge. Squeezing her, he placed another tender kiss on her lips, trying to overcome her desperation. He released her to the sofa, retrieving the coffee and the bag, which she discovered contained two fresh chocolate croissants.

'So what, um, set you off? Can you give me a hint?' He took a bite of his croissant, leaving a heavy silence to rest between them.

The warm cappuccino was hitting the spot, but not enough to loosen her lips. 'If I tell you, you'll hate me. I couldn't bear that.'

'Natasha, we all have a past. It's the future that counts.' He leaned across to meet her eyes, wanting to understand the fear she hid.

'I'm fucked up, okay. You saw that last night.'

'I want to know why it happened. How to help.'

'You can't,' she mumbled. 'Seb, please, not this morning. I'm wiped.'

'You can tell me now or tell me later.' Placing his coffee on a side table, he took her into his lap. Seb tried to reassure her. 'I want to see more of you. I'm not going anywhere.'

'You're like a dog with a bone. Some things are better if I keep them to myself. Anyway, I thought you said you wouldn't rush me.'

'That was before four-thirty this morning. Give me something. Enough to know I won't cause the hurt and fear I saw last night.'

Natasha saw genuine concern in his eyes. Something shifted within her. It made her want to believe she could trust him, to believe he wasn't a player, to believe he'd be the guy who'd stay. With a heavy sigh, she said, 'Look, the whole freaking-out-in-the-dark thing comes from way back.' She rolled her fingers over her face. 'I told you a bit last night. My father used to get blind rotten drunk and beat us, my mum and me. I'm the eldest. My brother and sister are younger, in that order. I tried to protect all of them from him. To punish me further, he used to lock me in our home's small cellar. It would terrify me to be locked up down there.'

Seb felt her shudder. 'It was so dark and too quiet. It smelt of him – stale beer and cigarettes. I would sit in the corner, clutching my knees, shaking. It was too low to stand up, and the floor was dirt. Things would crawl over me. I'd have to wait until he left or fell asleep. Then Mum would come and let me out. When Scott and Jess got older, we'd end up helping each other escape. Now remnants of that torture resurface.'

Seb's dark chocolate eyes widened, and he held her closer. 'Oh my God, how long?'

'How long would I be locked up, or for how long did it happen?' Her tongue rasped painfully over the words, like it had passed over splintered wood.

'Both, I guess.'

Resigned to reliving her dark past this sunny morning, she sighed. 'I remember the first time vividly. It was the first time I really put myself between him and Mum. I was nine. It was the last day of my childhood.' Her voice trailed off, and she coughed to move a lump in her dry throat. 'Times varied ... always felt longer. The longest was about six hours.

'As soon as I finished high school and said I wasn't going to be part of the family dry-cleaning business, he threw me out. He wasn't about to support a freeloader. I couldn't stay under the same roof as him anyway. The irony is, I did well at school. I was accepted to study medicine, but with no family support or money, that would only ever be a pipe dream.'

'So last night, what … what happened?' His heart was breaking.

'I've narrowed it down to some main triggers that need to occur together to set me off. If I'm alone in a very dark, silent room after a particularly harrowing emotional upheaval, like a fierce argument or guilty sex, I have what I can best describe as a violent panic attack. Last night ticked all the boxes. I sort of go into an emotional meltdown and relive dark traumas. I can hurt myself or others then.'

He rubbed his jaw, but soon forgot the ache, wanting to bring the light back to her eyes. 'I'm so sorry – about everything. After you had gone to sleep in my arms, I closed the shutter. I thought I was helping. You know, keeping the room dark and quiet. I left you because I was thinking about what was happening between us. I have some pretty confronting stuff to tell you too. Watching the ocean and the marina helps me think, so I went downstairs. I'm so sorry.'

'Seb, it's not your fault.' She didn't take in any of his words, only thinking that she wouldn't be painted as weak. 'I'm not your responsibility and I certainly don't want your pity.'

'It's not pity. I'm trying to understand.'

She pulled back, hardening her expression. 'I've fought my own battles all my life. Like I said last night, I'm not a victim.'

'I know.' His eyes were soft as he lovingly caressed her cheek. Now he understood why she didn't believe in herself and chose to hide. He twirled a strand of her hair around his finger before brushing it behind her ear. 'How have you grown into the strong, beautiful woman you are and not become bitter and twisted or just given in?'

'That's easy to answer. I couldn't give in. It was never an option. Dad would have won, and I was never going to give him that satisfaction. My father was my double-edged sword. My biggest curse, but at the same time, he was my biggest motivator. Without the one I may never have had the other.'

'There are easier ways.' Hesitantly, he said, 'Is that what kept you brave in the darkness?'

'That, and my guitar.'

'Your guitar?'

'My mum taught me to play. I used to memorise songs and their fingering, so when I had all those hours to myself in the silent darkness I could play. Retreating into music taught me that I could calm myself down and stop being so scared of the crawling dirt and the suffocating dark. I would play the notes on my air guitar, hear the music, and sing. I figured the cellar was soundproof. I couldn't hear anything from the outside world, so they wouldn't hear me. Strangely, the acoustics were fine. It kept me sane. Well, what that looks like for me.' Nervously turning away, she mumbled, 'There's nothing else.'

When he made to speak, she put her fingers to his lips. 'Shhh.'

Grasping her fingers, he said, 'I know there's more. I can see it in your eyes.' He opened her hand kissing her palm before holding it to his cheek, reassuring her.

It stilled and stirred her at the same time. 'Do you really want to know?'

'Yes, trust me to be here for you. I won't run if you don't.' He gave a sad smile, struck by her control, no tears. The only hint of vulnerability was her hoarse voice and a slight tremor. 'Don't hide from me.'

An unfamiliar emotion unfurled in her belly. 'The streets will do things to you. I grew up quickly.' She scrunched up her eyes and took a deep breath. Something made her want to believe that it'd be okay.

'I'd lived in Sydney all my life. After I'd been thrown out of home, all I had was a sack of clothes, some photos, my mother's guitar and not much money. I'm most ashamed of this time of my life. As soon as I saved enough money, I headed to Perth.'

'Why Perth?'

'Perth was the furthest city from Sydney. I figured it was the best place for me to start over.'

He gave a relieved, unconvincing smile. 'That doesn't sound too bad.'

Nat tried to swallow another hard lump burning her throat. She withdrew her hand and shuffled back, unable to endure his touch while she admitted how low she'd fallen. 'Before I came to Perth, I busked on the streets of Sydney. I couldn't live off what I made.' She wrapped her arms around herself, trying to withstand the embarrassment and failure that tormented her. 'There was no way my father would recommend me, even though I knew business and money. No one would take a chance on me. I was a troubled teen, fresh out of school, with no experience and no home.'

She took a breath. 'Look, maybe we should take a break.' A nervous hesitation grabbed her. 'Is that the time? I need to get ready for work.'

'Natasha, it's six-thirty. We've got hours.'

She couldn't even tenuously grasp what the attraction could be. Dr Mancini could have any woman.

He read her thoughts. 'You can't stop now. Don't let the car and the clothes fool you. We're not so different.' He leaned in and his lips touched hers, tender and soft. Seb lovingly caressed her cheek. 'Natasha, I'm on your side. You don't have to do this on your own anymore. Tell me.'

If it was one of his player lines, he was very smooth. No man had ever spoken those words to her. 'Oh, Seb, I don't know. I can't.'

He swung her around and lay her down on the couch, wedging his body beside hers, warm and safe. 'Please, Natasha. I can't tell you why, but I sense the woman here with me is far more than the circumstances of her past. That makes me want to find my way to the real you.' He wanted to unwrap her, peel off her mask and discover what it was about her that had him enchanted. He had her pinned down, literally and figuratively, 'There's no escape for either of us. I'm trying to recover from my past too.'

He was breaking her down. Given his family, Nat couldn't imagine anything in his past that could be as damaging as what she was about to set free. Her words came out in a rush, believing that if she said what had happened quickly, it would be less painful. Like removing a Band-Aid, she wanted to rip through her past and dispose of it quickly, limiting the pain.

'I couldn't find work. I was about to be kicked out of the grotty, run-down apartment I shared with a couple of equally desperate girls. A guy living in the apartment next door, Archie, was a bar manager and one time bouncer at a strip joint. He said he could get me work. He led me to believe it was as a barmaid. I was so stupid and naive. Apparently, I had a good body.' A pause shuddered through her. 'You can connect the dots.

'I became a redhead and danced under the name of Trixie. I got good tips. The pay wasn't too bad. And because of my father, I could handle myself. I was used to fighting off drunken men. I call the part of my personality that surfaced when Trixie was dancing The Slut. You met her last night for a little bit. I found I could only really turn on the sexuality while dancing if I wasn't, like ... me, Natasha. The Slut allowed me to work while the real me, Natasha, got out of her head and hid. I made better money with The Slut around. She'd help me disconnect from the guilt, allowed me to ignore the shame I felt when I saw the pleasure those horrible men were getting from ogling me.'

Nat gave a sad smile. 'Sage helped me recognise what was going on with my mind. She's been working with me to manage it. But there's one nightmare I haven't been able to unlock and understand. I had it again last night.' Any minute now, he'd want out and leave. No man wanted to hear that a woman he'd been with was a stripper, not to mention a crazy one.

'Natasha ... I'm so sor—'

'I know you're so, so sorry about my life, but you've got to go.' She'd make it easy.

# EIGHTEEN

## THE SHOWER-SHELF PRACTICALITY

She was shredding him. 'I … can't …' Half of him wanted to hold her and never let her go, to possess and protect her. The other half was sifting through which parts of her story his family would find the hardest to tolerate. He sure could pick them. Nonetheless, there was something about this woman. She was strong and had thrown off terrible circumstances to survive. His dad might admire that.

The reality was it could be a satisfying hook-up – great sex, better than he'd had in a while. He'd fulfil a need, kill some time. He'd let her down slow. He thought he had it sorted. Then she reached out. Her fingertips traced the line of his cheek and along his jaw to touch his lips, a feather-light touch. Her eyes were like mirrors. He saw himself – what he wanted and, more importantly, what he needed. It rocked him in ways he hadn't anticipated, like fresh rain reviving his barren heart.

Her voice was soft. 'It's okay. I understand, Seb. You don't owe me anything.' She straightened, defiant, trying to roll him away. 'Hey, let's leave it at sensational sex and move on.'

He fought to hold his ground. 'Nat, wait. I'm not leaving. Give me time to process this. Talk to me.'

She shook her head.

'Please, trust me. Help me understand.'

'Seb, face it. I'm not a woman you can get to know, not with your family's reputation.'

He kissed her, his tongue caressing hers, disarming her. 'How will you know unless you let me try to understand all of it.' Beautiful concern filled his eyes. 'Tell me.'

Nat weakened. 'Eventually, The Slut began appearing anytime I was experiencing any great sexual pleasure, even after I'd left the club.'

His eyebrows rose. 'Does that mean you can't … I mean, we shouldn't have …'

'I'm talking sheet-fisting, amazingly intense sex.'

'Okay?'

'Plain, mundane, domesticated sex is acceptable. It would seem I can't have wild, hot and untamed sex.'

'So last night was—'

'Yes.' Her insides clenched.

'Oh.' He gave a wry smile. Then sobered to say, 'So The Slut's bad?'

'It's not that simple. The Slut helped me survive. But I guess, yes, mostly, like an evil queen in a Brothers Grimm tale, she embodies all that's bad, but sinfully good too.'

Natasha seldom spoke about her alters. 'To keep The Slut and my sexual pleasure in check – for that matter, any real pleasure – my mind concocted Goldilocks. Somewhere in my fucked-up head, I took my feelings of guilt at dancing and my issues with my father and rolled them into one nasty package. I must keep The Slut on a tight leash because if she escapes, all hell breaks loose, and Goldilocks is upon me.

'Goldilocks isn't good to The Slut's evil, she's my puritanical punishment for The Slut's sin. I must abide by the Goldilocks Principle, a self-righteous, just-right path. Not too much and not too little of anything. Like nothing too hot or too cold, hence her name's Goldilocks. I've found I must repress wild sexual pleasure to stop The Slut from appearing. Otherwise, Goldilocks will surface and punish me. And it usually shreds me.'

Words tumbled out of her. 'The panic is overwhelming, like a horrific creature that smothers me – sucks the air out of my lungs in an all-consuming fear. It's like I can't have any pleasure without paying an awful price. Retribution for my past.' Another shudder racked her body.

'When I'm in the depths of a bad attack, I lash out. Sometimes I cause myself and others harm. At its worst, the panic and Goldilocks have dared me to take my own life.' She stopped, unable to delve any further.

'Natasha, I'm so sorry. I would never have thought. You seem so ... together.'

'I try.' Her voice was flat and bitter. 'After all, it's not like I'm going to go out into the world shouting, "I'm a nutter!" My mind is a very crowded place. Stay away.'

Ignoring her tone, he asked, 'Rick knows all about this too?'

She gave a frail smile. 'No. Rick never got me to any great sexual heights, and therefore no great guilt trips. It's just domesticated sex all the way with him. Being with him was even blander than bad vanilla sex. The Slut never had to come around. Goldilocks liked Rick. He was safe and ordinary.'

A fleeting look of pride rolled across Seb's face. 'So ... you mean ...' It was soon extinguished. 'Oh. Sorry.'

'Don't be. It was amazing sex.' She bit into her fleshy bottom lip. Her voice hushed. 'It was for me, at least.'

Seeing her bite down on her lip had him mesmerised. 'Natasha, believe me, it was amazing for me too.'

His heart ached as her eyes glistened and her face saddened. 'Last night, though it was beautiful, The Slut was there for a bit at the beginning, so my past overpowered the present, and somewhere inside my fucked-up psyche, it became guilty, dirty sex. I'm all mixed up, a hangover from my shameful past.'

'Another double-edged sword. Believe me, I know what that's like. My family isn't so easy either.' His voice was caring. He ran his nose along hers. 'But ...'

She let out a deflated sigh. 'But what?'

'Um, I wanted to. I mean, the vibe coming off you last night. God, I don't know how to say this.'

'Just say it. Get the bad stuff out in the open. You certainly can't stick around much longer. The least I can do is answer some of your questions before you go.'

'No,' he groaned. 'For you, let's stop with thinking I'm leaving, okay. I was going to say it felt like it was your first time. I mean ... wow!' Seb was regretting he'd started down this rabbit hole. Yet he couldn't stop. 'The way your body reacted to my touch. The wonder in your eyes.'

Her breath caught. She was taken back to the pleasure Seb had given her. Natasha, not The Slut. With a hoarse whisper, she softened. 'In one respect, and one respect only, it felt like the first time for me, that is, Natasha.' She thumped her hand to her chest. 'Yes, for the real Natasha, it was. It was new to feel like that with someone.'

He smiled sweetly. She was so complicated and yet so simply appealing.

He made her want to tell him more. 'I wanted to escape the club. I hadn't been there long when a new owner came. He was bad news and always carried a knife. If you disobeyed, he'd … well, let's just say he was a nasty piece of work who forced me to stay. Had his thug minders keep me in check, never let me out of their sight. I couldn't leave. He stole my money—'

'Couldn't you hide it somewhere?'

'Where? In my back pocket? I was stripping, remember. Not a lot of places to stash cash.'

'I see your sense of humour is returning.' He immediately regretted his words as a scared hurt rolled over her face.

'No, not humour.' She gathered herself. 'Not when I think about this guy. But yeah, I did manage to hide some money away. The ugly fucker said I was the jewel in his crown, his property, young and untainted. With me, he was going to make his club classier and make more money. He tried to own and control me.'

She grimaced. 'When this bastard took over, a lot of other shit went down. Drugs, BDSM and whoring. I tried to avoid most of it. He terrorised me, made my life hell.' Natasha felt herself shaking. 'People called him Wolf because of the large, black wolf tattoos he had all over his arms.' Just thinking about him caused a wave of nausea to pass over her.

Seb held her a little tighter, calming her with his warmth. 'Hey, I'm here for you. It's okay.'

Maybe he wasn't a player, she thought. It didn't matter. There was no way she could face telling him the rest, about the drugs. So she skipped over the worst chunk of her past. 'Eventually, I escaped and managed to get myself to Perth. That's when I met Sage. She took me under her wing. I worked at her clinic while she worked on me. Dodge got me some paying gigs and Sage encouraged me to enrol at uni, supporting me through Pharmacy, and here I am. She, Chevy and Dodge have been like a family to me. Other than Sage and Jo, you're the only one who knows.' But, unlike them, he didn't know the worst of it, and she couldn't trust him with it.

'Jesus, Natasha, I owe Sage.'

'No, Sebastian, not you. Me. I owe Sage.' Natasha raised her voice and slapped her hand onto his chest, trying to move him. 'You haven't earned the right to say anything like that or that I'm yours. Any of that shit you came out with last night.'

He stayed utterly still, absorbing her latest tirade, and shot back dryly, 'Really. You want to fight with me now about what *I* did last night.'

She tried to hide a wry grin. 'No, but you need to know. All right?'

'Okay, okay.' Seb sat up, raising his hands in surrender. He picked up the rest of his croissant. 'Do you want yours?' The atmosphere was now a little lighter, brighter even.

'No, you eat it. I'd better get going. I'll see you at work, yeah?'

'What, are you trying to toss me out again?' He started kissing her neck.

'Ahh, mmm ...'

She felt his smile against her cheek. 'If it's okay, I'd like to stay.'

'I need to shower. It could be a little while. I thought you'd want to go. Not be seen arriving with me.

'No, I want to stay. We can leave here together.'

Blinking she thought, *okay*, disbelief flooded her through her. *My God, he wants to stay.*

Natasha stepped into the warm, soothing water and felt the night's drama and dirt begin to wash away. She shampooed her hair into a rich lather. With her eyes closed, she raised her head to let the water flow over her. Her body began to uncoil as the warm lather slid luxuriously down her hair and back. Nat arched up, stretching out, enjoying the water's rejuvenating warmth. It was then she felt smooth hands on her waist. She jumped at his touch and her eyes shot open.

Pulling her gently back to his naked body, Seb wrapped his arms around her, murmuring at her ear, 'Shhh, you're safe with me. We'll take it slow. If they come, we'll stop.'

Nat rocked back into him as his loving words melted her heart.

'No sin, no Slut. No guilt, no Goldilocks,' Seb held her tight. 'Let me give you your pleasure back.'

Time was irrelevant. No more words were needed. Happiness, like the water, cascaded over them. A new feeling possessed her. Was this what safe and content felt like? She couldn't be sure, but it was beautiful.

He reached for the shower gel and poured it into his palm. With Nat's back pressed against his front, he worked the gel into a luxuriant lather over her breasts, hips and belly, cleansing, rinsing her body. His gentle, silken touch found her clit, sparking desire. He kissed her shoulder. She swept her hair back to allow him to trail more kisses along her exquisite shoulder and neck. Time stood still, only the water moved over them. She turned to face him. Their kiss had them forgetting the world.

Seb ran his hands up her sides tenderly until his fingers found her breasts, caressing her nipples. They peaked at his touch. She skated her hands around his body and up to his shoulder blades. Her breasts, full and heavy, brushed up against his chest. His hands massaged her butt cheeks. His desire, long and thick, fell against her belly.

Natasha's confidence in her enjoyment of their union was winning the battle. There was no music in her head and she didn't have to start any songs. His lovemaking was beautiful and elegant, making her feel wanton and sexy. The she-devils on her back were losing their grip.

Nat and Seb revelled in the skin-on-skin contact, kissing and savouring the desires rising within their bodies. Their tongues met with gentle licks as his middle finger stroked the tender folds of her sex before it slipped slowly into her. He withdrew, and her core ached with need and longing. His finger mimicked his tongue, slowly pushing deeper into her mouth as his finger delved deeper. As their hunger built, their kissing became more frantic. They became irresistible to each other. As he pulled his tongue back, she nipped the tip, which prompted him to growl before circling her clit with two fingers. He gently tugged the sensitive bud of nerves. The sensation was glorious, Nat's core pulsed, and he ever-so-slowly slipped two fingers into her, circling them deeper. He felt her tighten around them. Perfection.

Nat grabbed his hot, hard cock. She had an unashamed desire to work his magnificent shaft with her mouth, so she dropped to her knees. Seb's balls ached at the sight of her mouth sheathing his manhood. Flicking her tongue around the thick tip, licking and feeling his throbbing shaft with her lips, she massaged his cock with her hand as she tea-bagged his balls.

His breath caught before a primal utterance escaped his thrumming body. Nat pulled back to look up at him, this glorious man in her shower. Water cascaded down his toned torso while she revelled in the power of having him totally under her spell.

He swept her up, leaving her to wrap her legs around his lithe hips. Resting her on the narrow, tiled shower shelf opened her up to him. They both had needs and a desire to fulfil. Trust blossomed with unabashed pleasure. He was true to his word, taking his lead from Nat. She nodded, and he slowly slid into her hot velvet folds.

The second thrust slid deeper, driving her back against the tiles as the water crashed around his shoulders. They fused, and a charge swept over them, carrying the couple on a wave made of each other's pure pleasure. He worked his cock, grinding into Nat, finding her limits. Exquisitely chasing his need yet giving himself to her, they joined with such impact she had to rest her hands on his shoulders to hold on. Then she urged him on by dragging her nails down his back.

The beautifully sculptured muscles of his chest, arms and stomach bunched as he drove in and out of her. She found his darkening eyes, and they wordlessly begged each other for redemption as they scaled new heights. He made her feel so beautiful. He took her slow. He was tender, loving Nat so she could take the chance to enjoy unrestrained pleasure.

The slow, deliberate pace gave a raw honesty to their lovemaking. Seb rooted in her. His discipline was hanging by a thread as she drove him crazy. Her touch, her heat and her rippling around him brought him to the brink. He felt himself lengthen as he rooted in her, so deep, so tight.

Natasha tangled her fingers in his hair, pulling him to her. His pace quickened, chasing desire. Then she kissed him, before her lips nibbled down his throat. She felt his groan and her grip around him intensified. He couldn't hold the ride beyond the sun, she'd granted him any longer, finding release he poured himself into her, nipping her nipples as he did, sending her propelling towards the edge with him. There was just so much of him in and around her. She took all he could give her as she let herself go to fall into pure bliss. No voices, no sin, no guilt. They collapsed into each other, catching their breath. He pulled out and kissed her, forcing her back against the tiled wall. The water cleansed them both.

Time passed unnoticed until he reached over and turned the water off, helping Nat as she slid off the shelf and down his body. She murmured, 'You, you are amazing.'

'And you, Ms Perry, are indeed a rare breed.'

These were the first words they'd spoken since he said he wanted to give Natasha her pleasure back. His words called to her, resonating deep within.

Once they stepped out of the shower, she tried to dash out of the bathroom. Seb caught her by the arm, his face concerned and voice anxious. 'Hey, wait. Are they with you?'

'No, no.' Natasha stopped and hugged him in all his glorious nakedness. 'I was going to get another towel. You can use that one over there. It's fresh and clean.'

'Ah, of course. I can't read the signs yet.' He moved out of her arms but held her hands in one of his. He grabbed the towel from its rack and began drying her body. 'We can share. I need to spend more time with you to get to know the real you before you put your *all business* mask on.'

'Oh.' Nat was stunned that he got her.

'Oh, yes.' Seb wasn't letting her escape easily. His strokes of the towel were soft and tantalising as he dried her breasts and stomach. Not being able to resist losing himself in Nat's smiling blue eyes, he wrapped the towel around her hips, pulling her to his wet body.

'Seb, you're going to ruin all your good work.'

A wicked smile split his face. 'Do I look like I care?' He was growing again. His eyes darkened. 'I can't get enough of you.'

She took the towel from him and let it pool at their feet, leading him to her bed. This stunning man, who she'd bared some of her dark, dark soul to and he'd stayed.

# NINETEEN

## WHO CAN SEE WHAT'S HITTING THE FAN WHEN YOU'RE BLINDED BY DELIGHT?

Nat was now officially late for work, although she felt quite invigorated, which was rare after an attack. She hurriedly texted Jo.

> Sorry boss car trouble in by 9.

Seb and Nat drove to work separately. Arriving together in the same car would cause too many questions, akin to taking out a full-page ad in the local newspaper. She parked a couple of bays away before joining him to walk to the stairs together.

Alone in the stairwell, Seb pushed her back into the cinder-brick wall, madly kissing her. When he pulled away, she was breathless. He could only smile. 'Something to remember me by today.'

'Dr Mancini, my lips are not the only part of my body that will remember you splendidly today.'

They smiled at each like a pair of love-struck teenagers. It was soppy, but neither cared as they floated off to work.

Reaching the bottom stair, he opened the door for her. Husky lips at her ear, 'Natasha, I meant what I said. I *will* give you back your pleasure. All of it.' With that, he walked off, savouring the intense blue fire his words ignited in her eyes.

Nat leaned on the door, trying to regain her balance while her heart slammed against her chest. She wrestled with the possibilities. The wonderful possibility of having a man like Sebastian Mancini in her life. The lethal possibility of being betrayed by him. Natasha couldn't open her bruised and shattered heart to that again. Stalemate was where she settled as she hurried to work.

Walking along the glassed-in skybridge, she found herself face to face with a smiling Jo. 'I see your car troubles involved an Italian lube job.' She nodded her head in the direction Seb was walking.

Natasha instantly blushed, and Jo laughed. 'Confirmation. Okay, just don't go making a habit of it.' Jo was past Nat before she could say anything. 'I'll try and catch you for lunch to get the goss, but right now, I have a hospital management meeting. Must stay on the right side of the Cartwrights.'

Nat reached the oncology ward at around 9.15 am. Chelsea was on a day shift. 'Hey, what's cooking?'

'Not much.' Nat couldn't help smirking.

'Hang on. You look, ah, I can't quite put my finger on it. Like you've been cooking with some hot, hot stuff.' Chelsea Taylor no longer stood before Natasha. She had her Catherine Willows, forensic investigator, *CSI*-supremo babe on. 'Spill it. I want details.'

'Oh, please.'

'You seem a little too – satisfied – relaxed. Aha! It's Mr TDD.'

'Who? No.' A wicked smile spread unbidden across Nat's face. 'I can't stand around chatting. I'm late.'

Chelsea raised an eyebrow at Nat. 'Give it up, Perry. You're a lousy liar. You know I'll get it out of you a whole lot sooner than later.'

Nat gave her the abridged version. Lucky for Nat, the interrogation was short. Chelsea was distracted. She wasn't her usual full-on, effervescent self. 'Are you all right?'

'Don't try to deflect, Perry. I know there's more.'

'Look, I really am running late. Maybe at Friday lunch. Can you make it?'

Chelsea's face dropped. 'If I'm still working here.'

'Why, what's happened?'

Deep worry lines tracked across Chelsea's brow. It was a most un-Chelsea-like expression, her *CSI* investigator babe had evaporated. 'There's a problem with the morphine totals. We're missing ampoules. Quite a decent amount too.'

'What?'

'Late yesterday, we had a period when the DD keys couldn't be found, which meant we had patients in intense pain. We couldn't give them anything worthwhile. Averill went ballistic.'

'I imagine Sergeant-Major Avarice and Greed would've been on the warpath.' Nat's use of Head Nurse Averill Green's nickname didn't even crack a smile with the usually up-for-it Chelsea.

'Yeah. Avarice was right up there on her high horse. And as if that wasn't bad enough, when we did find the keys and start giving doses, it looked like there were a couple of mix-ups with some of the morphine given. We were all rushing around like crazy people.' Chelsea rubbed her brow. 'Dr Cartwright was up here checking her patients and right in the middle of it all, she demanded two new top-up doses be given. I thought Emma said she got Cartwright to witness her giving the doses, but there isn't any record. Of course, since we've discovered the totals don't match, Avarice and Greed has been on our backs all morning. Just when I thought I'd made headway with her.'

'What does Emma say?'

'Emma's not working today, so we can't check with her, and honestly, we were so busy, I don't know.'

She blew out a jittery, long breath. 'The only record is two signatures on the patient's chart, but I don't remember signing the chart. I believe someone forged my signature, and maybe Emma's, but there's nothing in the DD register. What a mess. Avarice is bound to ask you about it.'

'Is she talking to Cartwright as well?'

'Don't be stupid. You know doctors aren't ever questioned over things like this, especially one like Cartwright.' She caught herself and steadied. 'Sorry, Nat, I didn't mean to lump you with all my problems. I'll catch you later. And you *will* tell me *all* about Mr Tall, Dark and Delicious, but right now, I'd better get going. Lord B's ward round is starting soon.' She walked off, sending Natasha a troubled look.

Lord B was the classic ageing surgeon, a mix of fading brilliance and growing impatience mistaken for lost empathy. Natasha had seen it before. Guys like Byron Cartwright were desperately clinging to a time when they were the toast of the medical world, shiny and new. Gods of the scalpel. Now time was running short for them as retirement loomed. Their hands were as shaky as their failing knowledge. Natasha quickly checked the ward's drug trolley before going to the surgeon's round.

She hadn't gotten far when Head Nurse Averill Green stormed into the nurse's station. 'Ah, I thought you were here. Good.' She huffed her rotund frame about. 'I want you to look at something.'

Natasha felt like Avarice and Greed used her as a plaything, like a cat with a mouse before killing it. The nurses assured Natasha it was only because she was new to the ward. Averill headed to the ward's drug safe and the dangerous drug register. Nat felt something tear at her good mood. The drug procedures on the ward were as strict as those in the pharmacy. Lots of paperwork and careful record-keeping were required by law. All dangerous drugs had to be accounted for.

Averill opened the DD register and proceeded to lick her fingers, turning the pages with over-exaggerated flicks, a performance more suited to the importance of the director of nursing than a head nurse. With a huff, she said, 'Ah yes, here it is.' Averill opened the safe using the special DD key hanging from her neck on a red lanyard. Pulling out the morphine 100 mg/2 ml ampoules while a tetchy finger tapped at an entry in the register. 'There's a problem with these totals. As far as I can see, it came to light after two additional doses were ordered by Dr Cartwright. She was up here attending to her patients.' Full of condescension, she growled, 'I'd like answers.'

Natasha had a quick look. The tear in her good mood ripped fully apart. Sure enough, there'd been a mix-up somewhere. The totals were out. All dosage details should've been recorded in the dangerous drugs register, on the patient's chart, and signed off by two people. Glancing at the book, she saw no doses were recorded. However, the ward was down several ampoules.

Everyone was always more than thorough when handling DDs. Simple omissions did occur, but they were rare. Most times they happened when the ward was busy and many patients required pain relief simultaneously. That's when mistakes could happen with doses entered incorrectly. Four of the 100 mg morphine ampoules were missing, and there was the possibility of forged paperwork. Natasha prayed she could find answers and that they pointed to simple oversight; innocent human error.

If people figured out about Nat's past, she would be in the crosshairs of the investigation. Triggers would be squeezed, and being fired would be the least of Nat's problems.

Averill pounced on her concerned look. 'Ampoules unaccounted for, morphine usage not being recorded. It's just not good enough!'

'Yes, you're right.'

She hissed at Natasha. 'It looks like the morphine amount may have been incorrectly entered when you brought up the DDs from the pharmacy yesterday. I want it investigated. I don't think this is a nursing issue or a doctor's issue.' She sniffed, doubling her efforts to make Natasha aware of the importance of the situation. 'We wouldn't want you to have made a mistake so early into your time with us.' Averill started stacking the morphine back into the countertop safe before locking it. 'Must go. I have the chief surgeon waiting for me.' She spun on her fat heel and barrelled out.

Nat was just in time to take her place on Mr Byron Cartwright's ward round. She joined all his minions traipsing around after his coat-tails. Lord B always answered any question with a question. He liked putting people on the spot to prove his superiority. His passion for his craft was undeniable, but what made him hard to like was his treatment of the staff and his narcissistic air, which was as large and as distasteful as his extensively groomed, oily grey comb-over.

Lord Byron had started off his ward round by berating Chelsea. He believed his orders regarding the post-surgical pain management of a breast cancer patient had not been carried out. He was prattling on about the pain management findings discussed by an eminent visiting professor at a recent hospital lecture. No matter how often he dropped the name of the well-regarded professor, he had the gist of the lecture completely arse-about. That shaky ageing knowledge again. Everyone had been at the professor's lecture, but no one was brave enough to say anything as he continued to berate Chelsea. He was wound up.

Usually, the head nurse escaped his tirades, but he also started in on her. Now, even Head Nurse Green, who'd been hanging on his every word, pulled back. A steely concern transformed her face as he lectured her while diminishing Chelsea. 'Does this nurse know what she's doing? Is she even a nurse?'

Nat should have held her tongue. He was a Cartwright, after all. He could make sure Nat regretted saying anything. Nonetheless, she felt someone should defend Chelsea. If he insisted on his course of action, it would cause pain and unnecessary distress to the patient.

Carefully, she phased her words so she wouldn't embarrass Lord B, and let him believe he and he alone had thought of the right solution to the problem. 'Excuse me, sir, I couldn't hear you properly from the back here. I wanted to confirm that, like the nurses, you did agree with the professor's findings that a PCA, um, patient-controlled analgesia pump, should be tried first before any more invasive pain control?'

There was a disparaging twitch of his upper lip. 'And who might you be?'

'Natasha Perry, sir, clinical pharmacist for the ward.'

He cleared his throat. 'Perry, did you say?' He didn't want an answer. 'I'm glad to see that the pharmacists are up to date on the drug side of things. But do you know anything about complicated pain management like this?'

She held her nerve. 'Yes, sir.'

'I believe I'll be the judge of that. However, let me reiterate. Yes, of course, I was confirming that PCA should be tried first. Isn't that what I just said?'

Averill raised her eyebrows at Nat, giving a quick nod as a small, relieved smile settled across her lips. 'Yes, thank you for explaining that, Mr Cartwright. I will double-check that my nurses have followed the professor's instructions to the letter. The clarification is timely.'

Lord B puffed out his chest and turned to the rest of his minions. 'Can anyone tell me what the drug of choice and strength is for use here? Students only, please.'

With the DD issue playing on her mind, Nat decided she'd had her fill of pomp and stupidity today. She needed to find some traction on the DD issue.

Walking past the doctor's ward office, Nat saw that the overworked photocopier was free. Precisely what she needed. She walked briskly back to the nurse's station and grabbed the DD register. Nat slipped it into her file, along with the charts of the patients in question. She needed to keep close track of the records. Jo would need all this documentation, especially given what she'd said on Sunday night.

If they could reconcile the DD ward register with pharmacy records and the patients' charts, maybe they could show that neither Natasha, Chelsea nor any of the other nurses were at fault.

As the last page was copying, Holly came into the office with Mr Cartwright. She was all breathy and fawning over him, discussing a patient's progress. 'Oh, you're so right, Byron.' Holly's curves jiggled as a girly giggle rolled over her plump bosom, mesmerising the ageing surgeon. 'Do you think we could leave him on nourishing fluids a little longer?'

'Dear lady, what do you consider a little longer?'

Nat was thankful they were immersed in their conversation so she could gather her papers unnoticed and leave. The last thing she needed was another morning discussion with Mr Cartwright about patient pain control. Luckily, slutty Holly was like another redhead Natasha knew exceedingly well. They both had their uses for the powers of good and evil. While she was returning the DD register back to the nurses' station, Chelsea walked in.

'What are you doing with that?'

'Nothing that's not in my job description.' Natasha gave Chelsea a back-off stare. 'Leave it with me. I'm going to get to the bottom of it.'

'Hey, don't give me that look. I'm all for people getting to the bottom of things. Just don't put yourself in harm's way.' Chelsea glanced over her shoulder, motioning to the rest of the ward and muttering, 'Especially when no one else around here will stand up for us. It's not worth it.'

Giving Nat's hand a friendly squeeze, her eyes tearing up, Chelsea left. Nat busied herself with the ward's other drug trolley, feeling for the usually relaxed Chelsea. The DD issue and Cartwright's hissy fit had severely cut her.

# TWENTY

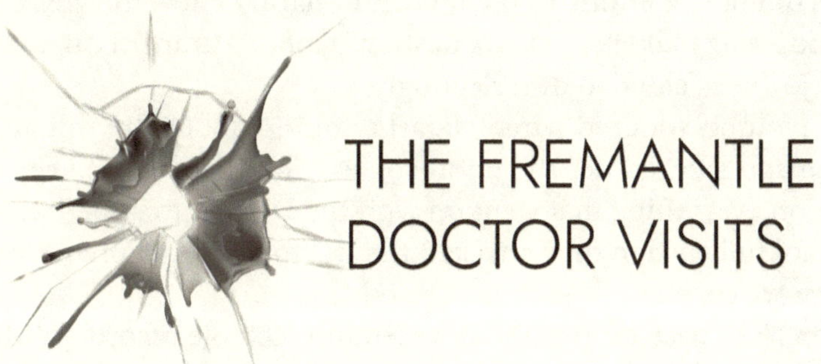

## THE FREMANTLE DOCTOR VISITS

Nat took a shortened lunch break, although she made time for Jo.

'You had an attack, and he came after you?'

'I know. Amazing, right?'

'You told him, *and* he stayed.'

'Yes. Blows me away.'

'How come you told him?'

'I'm not sure. He saw me at almost my worst and still came after me. For some reason, I wanted him to understand.'

Jo grabbed her hand. She wanted to believe too. 'It sounds great. But are you sure? You just met him.'

Natasha nodded. Her voice was small. 'I know. I only told him about the cellar and the stripping. Not the rest of it with the club owner and what he turned me into.'

Jo gave her a friendly nudge. 'Hey, it's a start. Oh my God, Nat. And he still said he didn't want you to fight it on your own? Wow—'

'And he wants to give me ... my pleasure back.'

'Nat, stop. You're making me go weak at the knees.'

'I know. I would never have imagined it in my wildest dreams.'

'And yours are scary wild. '

Nat nodded. 'Anyway, I never thought once I'd let some of my many cats out of the bag that a man would stay. He does something to me.'

'He's doing something to me too, and I hardly know the guy. Of course, the *taking your breath away* question is moot. Hmm ... I can only imagine.' Jo's eyes clouded over fleetingly.

Their mood sobered when Natasha told Jo about the missing morphine and showed her the photocopies. They decided to keep a close eye on everything that went on with the DDs on the onc/haem ward. Thankfully, when they checked the DD totals in the pharmacy safe they were correct.

Given Nat's past, even with her recent impeccable record, Jo still breathed a sigh of relief that everything added up from the pharmacy side of the transactions. Along with Rick's treachery, Nat going off the rails was the last thing Jo needed. 'Nat, report back to Averill that we will continue to monitor and investigate the situation.' Squeezing Nat's shoulder, 'You have done nothing wrong.'

'Thanks, Jo, that means a lot to me.'

Natasha finally made it home after being behind all day. She changed into her running gear, grabbed her water bottle and headed to the beach. The sea breeze was stiff as it whipped off the Indian Ocean. The fresh, salty ocean air revived Nat. The cooling breeze refreshed the coast and chased the day's heat away – it was why the locals called it the Fremantle Doctor. With its cool change, it relieved the day's woes, like that of a visiting doctor. Nat's run was going to be hard, heading into the Doctor, but she felt like she could do anything today. She was looking forward to it.

Half an hour later, she arrived back at her car, suitably exhausted but loving the satisfaction from the physical exertion. The wind cooled the perspiration on her skin, cleansing her of the last of the day's woes. When she was a teenager running was another release for her. It allowed her to escape her home life, freeing her mind.

She headed home to shower, not able to look at her shower shelf in the same mundane way she had twenty-four hours earlier. She'd always thought it was at an odd height. Maybe the interior designer wasn't so stupid after all. With Lady Gaga's 'Born this way' filling the apartment, she towel-dried her hair and threw on some shorts and a t-shirt, sans underwear. It was that type of afternoon. Soon she found herself dancing around her apartment with untamed joy to the anthem for individuality and self-empowerment. She walked into the kitchen shouting, 'Love needs faith'. It could be her new motto – *Mi amore vole fe yah.*

Thinking about dinner, she grabbed some ice cubes from the tray in her freezer and added them to a long glass of water. As she enjoyed her last mouthful, the doorbell rang. Assuming it was someone collecting for a charity, as she'd noticed they usually called at dusk, she grabbed her purse and headed to the door.

'Coming.' Fumbling with her purse, she opened the door.

'Hello, Natasha.'

There was no need to look up. A shiver of desire ran through Nat at hearing her name leave his lips.

Her power of speech almost disappeared. 'Hi, um, you.'

He hesitated. 'Were you expecting takeaway?' His focus drifted to her purse.

'No.' She couldn't believe how awkward she felt. There was a jitteriness between them. 'Thought ... um, charity.'

Seb took a deep breath. Telling her what he needed to would be harder than he had anticipated. He'd underestimated the impact of her large, soulful blue eyes. They made him feel like she could see all his weaknesses. By the same token, he'd seen a little of her soul. Maybe she was too brittle and fragile to have in his life. Yet staying away seemed far harsher. 'Um, I thought I'd come over to share a quiet night in. If it's okay with you, that is?'

'No ...'

His face dropped.

Her words rushed. 'I mean, yes. Please, come in.' Finally, Nat had managed to string more than two words together. He followed her into the lounge, where she began fumbling with her Bluetooth speaker and phone. When the music softened, she peeked up. A cheeky smile was spreading over his face. 'What?'

'It's good to be here again. I have fond memories from this morning. Although now it feels a bit more normal.'

The tension eased.

'If it's normal you want, I was just going to cook up some chorizo and mushroom pasta for dinner. Would you like some?'

'Sounds great, but only if I can help.'

'Sure.' She took his hand.

He wrapped her in his arms and kissed her soundly. 'Couldn't help myself. It means a lot to me to be able to do that.'

She steadied with a smile and led him into the kitchen. She was all hot again. 'I've just had a glass of ice water. Would you like one?'

'Great, thanks.'

Without taking too many steps she could reach efficiently around her small kitchen to place the ice cubes in a glass and fill it with water. Handing it to Seb, she said, 'Ah, um, my apartment is not as well-appointed or as big as yours.'

'Thanks.' Seb took a long sip. It gave him time to think. 'I'm sure it does everything you need it to do. Now, what can I do to help?'

Natasha was struggling to believe this Adonis was in her apartment again, and of all places, her kitchen. 'Um, alright. You can slice the mushrooms. I'll get the rest organised. Chopping board's there.'

She handed him a bag of mushrooms. He gave her a lost look. 'Knife?'

'Of course.' Nat rifled through a drawer to find him one of her sharper knives. She put a saucepan of water on to boil before retrieving the chorizo from the fridge. Her attention was drawn to how he was cutting the mushrooms. He was like a machine, a professional chef wielding the knife with precision. 'Oh, I see you can handle a knife like a pro.'

With a serious tone, he said, 'One of my lesser-known talents.' He looked down at the blade and thought she needed a better set of knives. A chef needed a good knife, like an artist needed a good brush. He forced a smile that grew to a megawatt Mancini when he saw the delight on her face at his talent.

Losing herself in Seb's handsome features and quick hands, she started slicing the chorizo. 'Ouch.' Her knife wasn't sharp, but she flinched, holding her finger up.

Seb dropped his knife and grabbed her hand. Then he did something that surprised them both. He drew her hand to him and soothed her finger with his mouth and tongue, gently sucking. Every part of her swooned sans guilt. Natasha couldn't believe how easily he was breaking her down.

The atmosphere sizzled. While his tongue was soothing her finger, it had the opposite effect on the two of them. He slowly slid her finger from his mouth. She tried to derail the runaway train that was her mind. 'Seb, I thought that was for snakebites.' Her voice betrayed her.

His voice betrayed him. 'Yes, but with you, I ...' Dark, smouldering eyes found heated blue. He was hypnotised by her. Stepping even closer, still holding her hand. 'I seem to lose—'

'Me too.' The kitchen scorched, but not from the weather or the boiling water. Nat wasn't experiencing any pain from her finger.

'Natasha, turn the stove off. I don't want to rush this.' She reluctantly broke free and turned the hotplate off. The heat subsided, while their need boiled over. It was the last time her feet touched the floor. Seb lifted her up, twirling her around as she wrapped her legs around his waist. Fingers twisting in his hair, she kissed him thoroughly, releasing boundless bliss.

Sweeping the books and magazines off her small kitchen table, Sebastian laid her down. With her knees bent and heels on the table edge, she was ready for him. He helped her pull her t-shirt off, hungrily looking down on her before his lips were everywhere. Nat lifted her hips as he slid her shorts off.

With a raised eyebrow, he almost hummed. 'As always you are full of surprises Ms Perry, commando. I like.'

She couldn't help a giggle. 'Dr Mancini, I didn't think I'd be receiving guests.'

He moved her knees apart with his body. She heard his zipper descending as his left hand dreamily worked its way down her body. His touch left goosebumps flowing in its wake. Seb arched back like a pulled bow.

She enjoyed the sight as he pulled his t-shirt over his head and tossed it away. All moving, muscular perfection, like a model in a designer underwear ad. Nat was distracted from her adolescent yearning as the afternoon sunlight caught his body. His olive skin stretched tautly over his muscular frame, all smooth and flawless, except for where his soft, curly black chest hair didn't quite cover a long scar that ran down the length of his sternum. Another scar of a comparable size rimmed his right hip.

Soon, Natasha was spread naked over her small table with Seb's heated body spread over her. There was no need for The Slut, nor music. Natasha wanted Seb for pure and honest reasons, not a transaction in sight.

The scent of jasmine and Nat filled Seb's lungs, driving him crazy. His lips found her breasts. He loved how they were so full and perfectly curved. The fingers of his right hand trailed down her body until they found the soft strip of sandy-coloured hair above her sex. His goal found, he rhythmically stroked her. As he brushed his thumb over her clit, it tantalised her, leading her arousal to awaken. Applying the right amount of pressure on one of the most sensitive parts of her body had Nat thirsting for the wonderous journey she knew he could gift her. Needing to intensify the friction of his touch, she writhed into his palm.

Seb wanted to tie her up, stop her squirming and control her, make her yield to him in every way. He couldn't, not yet, so he clung to the discipline he needed to hold his lust in check. If he truly lost his mind and revealed himself, he might lose her. Rolling her clit between his fingers, he held her a hair's breadth away from pain. Yet, she only felt exquisite pleasure. 'We're going to take this slow to savour it, no shame, only freedom.' His voice had her soak his fingers. 'What if I make you come this way.' In the throes of a searing lust, she just nodded.

In the past, if Nat was experiencing such sensuality, The Slut would have appeared many minutes ago. The veneration in his eyes was something new to her. Nat alone had control as pleasure usurped any thoughts of sin and persecution. Maybe this morning's sharing and Seb's decision to stay had banished her alters.

Moving his lips to her sex, his tongue rolled and licked its way around her erogenous bud. It was such an unbelievably carnal feeling. She writhed under his expert touch.

'Stay still, control it, before the feeling consumes you. Don't give in to them.' He growled between licks. Then he blew on her.

'Sooo good.' An intense yearning began to ripple through her body. Trying not to move, Nat's surrender to her desires showed in other ways. The little noises of pleasure, and the way a gorgeous pink blossomed over her skin as she started climbing. All of her reactions, were all making it difficult for him to maintain control.

He smiled. 'You like the cool change, huh?'

'Yesss. Mm-more, please.'

Thinking Seb would continue blowing, she waited for the expected thrill. Instead, he moved away. She was boiling water with its heat extinguished. Nat heard him in the kitchen. He returned, eyes on fire. Soon his mouth was on her, lips hot, consuming her. It was then she felt it, sharp and cold, like the edge of a blade at her breast.

# TWENTY-ONE

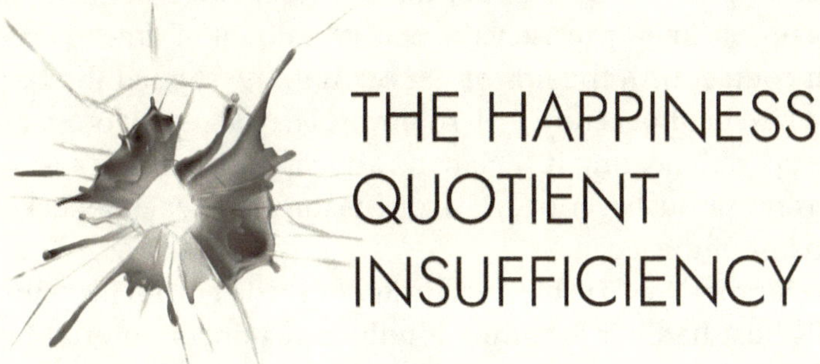

## THE HAPPINESS QUOTIENT INSUFFICIENCY

Nat's breath hitched as Seb expertly brushed an ice cube over her nipple in a perfectly timed, swift movement. 'Huhhh!' Her nipple hardened. A thrill of the most erogenous kind rolled through her, speaking directly to her sex, which fluttered in anticipation. Then his warm lips heated her nipple. The contrast sent more intense erotic shivers through her.

Not letting up, he repeated the breathtaking act on her other nipple, sucking and tugging gently. Wild desire drove through her core. He ran the ice cube over her torso, leaving a slow, meandering trail of cold over her hot skin. Skating the fast-melting cube around her belly button, Seb let it rest there as he attended to each of her nipples with his tongue once more. 'Hold still. Let's see if you have enough control over your body to keep the ice here.'

The melting ice at her navel did nothing to ease her cravings to have him fill her as exquisitely as he had that morning. 'Sebastian, please. I can't.'

'Shhh! You can, and you will. Natasha, if you control your desire, you will regain your pleasure. Don't come until I tell you to. Take charge of your mind, body and soul, then you'll take charge of your alters.'

While she stilled her body, her desires raged, barely contained and more concentrated than ever. It was agony and ecstasy all at once. Seb's direct tone had her holding her climb. All sensations were heightened while his tongue slowly found its warming way to her belly button. Delicately, he moved the melting ice cube further down her body with his skilled fingers, finding his ultimate goal.

Goosebumps cascaded over her torso as he blew on her clit. She moaned again. He knew precisely the perfect amount of time to leave the cold in contact with the lips of her sex until he slipped the fast-melting ice into her hot centre – all so slowly. His tongue followed the chilly, watery trail, heating it. The contrast gripping her body was a wickedly erotic, sensual overload. His tongue tortured her as he sucked on the remains of the ice.

'Come for me. Now.' He blew again and worked her with his skilful tongue. His heat had her groaning loudly as his finger entered her slowly and slid deep.

'Ohhh, Seb, this is …' She couldn't focus. Seb kept torturing her with his finger, driving her wild. She came, and he was there with his tongue and mouth working her, taking all she could give him.

She was shattered. 'Seb, that was …' Words failed her.

He didn't need words as his eyes spoke, wanting more. She had no use for sweet nothings either and when his lips captured hers, Nat's desires reignited from their erogenous ebb.

Seb pulled back and couldn't look away from the vision before him. She was radiant. Her tanned skin had an added soft glow. Her golden locks were fanned out around her like a halo. She rubbed one leg over the other, raising one knee up, covering the entrance to where he wanted to bury himself. Tease. He was at the limit of his control. 'God, you're … You don't realise how beautiful you are, do you?' he rasped.

'Sebastian, stop. Don't spoil it. You know my history.' Emotion filled her words. 'How can you say that?'

'Because it's true.' It had crossed his mind when she'd told him about the stripping that it might tarnish everything, that he'd see she was only putting on a show for him, all business as usual. Yet when Nat let her mask of control slip, it showed many things. The fear and pain were only part of it. When the real natural Natasha came forth, he caught a glimpse of her strong, sensual, untouched inner being. It devastated and inspired him all at the same time.

As he gazed down on her she sent him a sexy sweet smile. A searing charge drilled into his heart and ran down his spine to his balls. He was so hard, unable to resist any longer. He was lost to her – couldn't fight the need, didn't want to. Placing his hands on her thighs, he slid her down the table towards him. She wrapped her legs around his arms, allowing him to use them as levers. He bowed back again, this time arrowing into her.

Then, slowing, he exquisitely pulled out before plunging back into her. He repeated this cycle of rough pleasure, gradually getting faster and deeper with each thrust, divinely stretching and stroking the erogenous nerves, which had her core greedily grabbing him. His words, the syllables moved in time with his quickening rhythm. 'Nat ... Tasha. I. Can. Feel. Ev-er-y. In-chhh of you.'

Words she hadn't felt the need to honestly use, in a very long time jolted forth, 'Harder. You're sooo fucking big.' She was climbing to a new summit. He buried himself to the hilt of his long shaft, over and over, faster and faster. It was heavenly, the pleasurable pain flooding his senses, causing him to slam two final, fervent thrusts into her. Shouting something primal, Seb released again and again, his mind and soul blown away.

Natasha shattered and joined him, shrieking out her erotic high.

Bliss-filled heaviness caused Seb to collapse over her, sated, pressing her body flat along the table. After time had stood still, he planted a chaste kiss on her lips. 'God, you are so beautifully fuckable.' He raised himself up onto his hands, flexing his toned arms. 'Gorgeous perfection.'

'Sebastian, please, shh.' She lifted her hand to stroke his cheek. He laced his fingers around her hand and kissed her palm, holding it to his cheek. She sighed. 'Let's not get ahead of ourselves.'

They gazed at each other, caught in the moment, seeing deep into each other's souls. It was too honest. She broke his stare, trying to wriggle out from under him. Natasha was never going to give any man her trust and heart easily. She needed to slow this down.

Seb stepped back, offering his hand to her. 'How's the quiet night in?'

'Intense. But doctor, your house call involved helping me with dinner, which isn't finished yet. Back to work with you.'

Laughing, he said, 'Of course. What was I thinking?'

In no time, their pasta was plated up and ready to eat.

'Wow, this *is* good.'

'You sound surprised. Italians aren't the only ones that can do good pasta.' Her smile gave way to a soft chuckle.

He couldn't take his eyes off how her flushed cheeks made her eyes look bluer. How was it possible?

'If I sounded surprised, it's because I'm constantly surprised by your many talents.'

'Well then, thank you.'

At that moment, he weakened, hypnotised by her smiling eyes. He decided he needed to share some of his troubled past with her. Sebastian's demeanour sobered. 'I need to discuss something with you. Tell you some things about my li—'

Nat's phone rang. She automatically held up a finger, 'One minute.' Reaching down, she grabbed it from her bag near the table. 'Sorry, Seb, I've got to take this.' Before she could say anything, she heard panic.

'Nat, Sage needs you. Come quickly.' Dodge's voice was unusually rattled.

'What's wrong?'

'She's had some kind of fit and threw up.'

Happiness dissipated as she rasped, 'Oh God. Where are you?'

'We're at the clinic. I wouldn't normally ask, but you're the only one she'd let me call.' His voice hitched. 'She's groggy, not great. Can you come? '

Nat felt the joy within her wash away. 'I'll come right away.'

Seb had picked up on her concern. 'What's happened?'

'It's Sage. She's collapsed at the clinic. I need to go.'

'I'll take you. I can check her over.' Remembering Nat's I-do-things-on-my-own temper, he added, 'If that's okay with you?'

'Could you? It would mean a lot.'

Seb was already on the move, gathering up the plates. 'It's the least I can do.'

Natasha quickly went to her bedroom to dress – she needed underwear. She added a t-shirt, jean shorts and slip-on shoes and met Seb at the front door. He wrapped his arm around her shoulders, giving her a chaste kiss. 'You don't have to fight life on your own. Okay?'

She could only nod, her mind scrambling.

---

The powerful car glided through the traffic. 'What's the story with Dodge and Chevy?'

'They're good old country boys who grew up in the wheatbelt. Their real names are Charles and Donald Ford. They have a crazy love for cars and trucks, hence the nicknames Chevy and Dodge.'

Seb nodded. 'Yes, I see them much more as Chevy and Dodge.'

'Yep. They're *big units*, as Chevy would say. Both are motor mechanics. They can get anything working, from a washing machine to my Subaru Impreza.'

'Really, you let them loose on your car?'

'Yes, Seb. Dodge and Chevy have always serviced my car for a couple of home-cooked meals. They were the ones that found it for me. It needed a bit of work, so it was a reasonable price.'

'Don't you want a new car someday?'

'It's not a priority. I love cars, but I'm happy with the performance of the Impreza.' She smiled at him and used his words. 'It's got the grunt I need to eat more than enough road for me.'

He smiled. 'But wouldn't you like more money to do more, have more?'

'Not really. I don't want for anything. My needs are far more basic.'

'Like?'

'A job that makes enough money so I can live comfortably, and am reliant on no one but myself. One that allows me to go on the odd holiday.' She sighed and stared out at the traffic. 'I never want to fear where I'm working or living again. All I want is to feel safe in my own home with friends I can trust. Living a life where I'm in the light even if the sun isn't shining. Anything else is a bonus.'

'I understand. Really, I do.' Turning his head from the road, he pinned her with a soulful expression. The look in his eyes had her believe him.

He was floored by what she'd said. Had he finally met a woman who didn't care about his fortune? Holding her in his gaze for as long as he dared, he turned his attention back to the road.

'Have Dodge and Chevy been like your protectors?'

'Yes, the two of them and Sage have been my family. Sage is my rock.'

'What does Chevy suffer from?' *Keep her talking*, he thought. He'd seen how her face fell when Dodge called. Keep her mind from running wild with what was wrong with Sage.

'He has post-traumatic stress disorder, which wasn't diagnosed properly when he returned from the Vietnam War.' She found Seb's concern touching, given his reaction to Chevy the first time they met.

'On Monday night, he was ...?'

'Off his meds, yes. Now and then he goes off them, for one reason or another, and relives the war. He usually gets so scared he runs and hides. What makes it worse is he's very good at hiding. It takes a while, but eventually, he's found on the streets, disoriented and beaten.'

'Beaten by other homeless people?'

'No, beaten by life, and he's not homeless.'

Seb wisely changed the subject. 'What happened in Vietnam?'

'The details are sketchy, but Chevy and Dodge's platoon got caught up in a skirmish with the Viet Cong. Dodge was wounded, his right knee shattered by gunfire. It's why he walks with a limp. Anyway, in the middle of the fight, the platoon somehow got swamped by napalm fire. Dodge couldn't escape the flames. Chevy went back, picked him up and carried him out of the fire. After hiding for some time, they were rescued by an Australian helicopter crew.

'The experience of having to find and then carry his wounded brother out on his shoulders, coupled with the trauma of his face being burned before he found a way out, traumatised him. It's hard to know if he was already likely to be more prone to anxiety attacks before Vietnam. Certainly, once he returned, his experiences affected him severely.'

'Was he talking about the war on Monday night?'

'You mean his, *Chevy is the name of one who walked with his brother in the forest of fire* mantra. Yes. It's kind of hard to forget it when you first meet him and he's off his meds. Especially when he's saying it over and over.' She sighed.

'He's so big and looks hell dangerous. Truth be known, he wouldn't hurt a fly. Dodge tells me that many years ago, when he first brought Chevy to the clinic, he was rambling and unsettled, scaring the staff and patients. Sage, of course, walked straight up to him and started talking to him, calming Chevy. Both now work at the clinic as maintenance guys, and sometimes they double as security.'

'Impressive.'

'Hey, they're farm boys. They're always practical, handy guys.'

'How long have Sage and Dodge been together?'

'Not sure, about twenty years? They're an amazing couple, independent while being together. They both love Harley Davidsons, among other things. But boy, when they have a fight, even Chevy runs. They don't usually stay mad at each other long. Once in a while, they seem to need a big bang to clear the air. Then they move on, no recriminations or regrets.'

As they arrived at the clinic, she said, 'Park over there. See the Harley Softail? That's Sage's bike.'

A worried Dodge greeted them, eyeing Seb suspiciously.

'Dodge, this is Dr Sebastian Mancini. I've asked him to come to check Sage over.'

Dodge's face was still and sullen. 'Isn't he the guy from the other night?'

'Yes, and I apologise,' said Seb. 'I thought Chevy was going to hurt Natasha. I was just trying to make sure she was safe. It was my fault. But right now, I need to help Dr Thompson. Where is she?'

'Yeah, first things first. Sage's on the patients' bed in her office. I've been keeping her lying down. She knocked her head when she collapsed. She's still a little woozy.' Dodge shrugged his shoulders. 'But you know, it's hard to keep a good woman down.' He smiled, mystified. 'She wanted to get up to ride home. I persuaded her to wait until you got here, which was no mean feat. Nat, you were the only one she said she could stand, not even Dr Mike. I offered to call him back. He'd gone for the day, but she'd only let me call you.' Dodge paused, eyeing Seb. 'I don't know what she'll think of your Dr Mancini here.'

Natasha tried to sound calm. 'She'll see him. I'll make sure she does. Either way, it's no use standing out here. Let's go.'

Dodge steeled himself. 'Of course. It's just I've never seen her like this, so ... so ... defenceless. It's a shock, you know.'

It hadn't entered Nat's mind that someone as gruff and tough as Dodge would be this affected. She stopped and turned, giving him a quick hug. 'Come on, you big old softie. Seb will take good care of her.'

# TWENTY-TWO

## CHECKING OUT BUT NOT LEAVING

They entered the darkened room. Natasha had her heart in her mouth, as worries were swamping her. She held her dear friend's hand, speaking softly. 'Sage, it's Nat. I've got Dr Mancini with me.'

Sage tried to raise herself but flopped down. 'Argh, my head. I wish the room would stop spinning.'

'Hey, we're all very worried about you.'

'No need. It's … just. Need you … get me home. Sleep. Stop Dodge fussing. I'vvve jusss been very bussy … with … clllinic.' Sage paused, gathering herself. The slurring of her words rocked Nat's hopes, and alarm poked its ugly head into the mix of emotions.

Looking as if she was using every bit of energy she had, Sage spoke. 'No resss for wickedd.' Gathering herself she blurted out, 'It's not like my breast cancer's back.' She attempted to laugh, dearly wanting to put the people she loved at ease. She usually succeeded, but not today.

'Sage, please, I promise no fuss. I'm here, but I can't help you as much as Seb can. Please.'

'Natasha, I don't need—'

'Sage, don't argue. We don't have time.' Natasha pulled Seb over to Sage and took charge. 'We're doing this … now.'

'Only, agreed, to you, Nat. To get Dodge … off my back. Jeez.'

'Then let me help. I promise no drama, and it'll help stop Dodge and Nat worrying.' Seb knew how to reach her. Use the ones she loved to persuade her. 'It'll give you some breathing space. I think you know it makes sense.' Sage moved her hand away from her eyes and nodded slowly.

Seb conducted a series of neurological tests using some of Sage's medical equipment. A frown tarnished his face. 'Dr Thompson, one of your pupils is dilated. I'd like to call you an ambulance and get you to Aida immediately.'

'Don't fusss. Let me … sleep it off.'

'Dr Thompson, I must insist. I believe you know you need to be in a hospital environment for treatment. Let me help.' His eyes drilled into Natasha. 'While I phone for a bed, call an ambulance. You ride with Dr Thompson. I'll follow and bring Dodge.'

'I'll go call the ambulance.' Dodge hurried out.

Seb turned back to Sage. 'I'll admit you tonight to Aida, it'll be the easiest and quickest place I can get a bed for you. The sooner the better.'

Sage began to protest, then stiffened and dropped back onto the bed, shaking uncontrollably. Natasha held her as Sage leaned over the side of the bed.

'No, no, no.' It was hard to know if she was speaking to Sebastian and Natasha or trying to will herself not to shake. Sage held her head with both hands. 'Ahh, the pain. Quick, get me a bowl. I'm going to …'

Natasha held Sage as she used the basin. Hearing the commotion, Dodge was soon by her side.

Seb asked, 'Dodge, has Dr Thompson been tired, forgetful lately? Maybe a bit more irritable than usual, not herself?'

'Doc, what can I say? She's a woman.' He tried to sound in control. Although his real feelings overpowered his rough-diamond exterior and his voice wavered. 'I guess. Now I think about it, yes.' Natasha stepped back and let Dodge hold Sage. 'Come on, baby, it's okay. I'm here. Let's do what the doc says, hey?'

Within the hour, they were sitting in a hospital room on the eleventh floor of JCH at the Aida Foundation. Sage had been stabilised with anti-seizure medication and more medication to reduce intracranial pressure. Seb had organised for her to have an MRI of her head, which would help show anything sinister. Natasha was anxious, her foot tapping incessantly while Dodge paced. Seb came back into the room.

'Dr Thompson will be a while. Do you and Nat want to go and get a coffee? I can call you when Sage's back.'

Dodge gave him a stubborn look. 'You trying to get rid of us?'

'No, not at all. There isn't much to do here. I thought you might want a change of scenery.'

'I see that.' Dodge was, if nothing else, a practical guy.

'I don't want a coffee. I just want to stay.' Natasha's anxiety was consuming her. She had no tether to reality, making it easy for her to be engulfed by nerves and her alters.

*You need something way stronger than coffee. Take the edge off.* The Slut was at Nat's ear, trying to make her submit. *Let me take you there. Get your freak on. Forget your troubles.*

Dodge gave her a hug, bringing Natasha back. 'Yes, I see you want the doc all to yourself.' He winked at her. 'I'll make myself scarce. Coffee shop's on the ground floor?'

'Yes,' she mumbled.

As Dodge left, she grabbed Seb around his hips and turned him to her. 'Sebastian, how bad is it? She's had breast cancer. Granted, a while ago.' Nat sucked in a deep breath. Her head started to spin. 'Good God, it's returned. She's got some kind of tumour, hasn't she?'

He narrowed his eyes and his mouth formed a hard, downturned line. He didn't want to tell Natasha the truth. She didn't need to know just yet. He couldn't confirm what he thought the problem stemmed from, so he coated it in seven layers of sugar. 'I've seen her notes, and although she's had breast cancer, this doesn't have to be a tumour.'

He put his hands on hers. His touch quietened The Slut and her gnawing cravings. Even with Sage's illness hanging over them, the pull between them was irresistible.

'I'm not a doctor, but I know enough—'

'Let's not jump to conclusions. Wait until we get the MRI results back.' He wrapped his arms around her. His mouth remained in a firm, downturned line. To stop her lethal interrogation of his face, Seb rested his chin on her head.

Even with her capitulating neediness clawing at her, she'd seen it written on his face. Seb was being skinny with the truth. Desperate to stop her persuasions leaking out, she diverted her worries. 'Give me the truth, Sebastian. If you plan on telling Dodge and Chevy, I can at least be prepared and help you with them.'

He sensed the beginning of the same panic he'd witnessed a night ago. 'Shh, Natasha, you're safe with me.' Squeezing her gently, he kissed her, long and slow. 'So, truth?'

'Yes. I'm better with it than anything else. All my life, it's been the best—'

'She's seriously ill.' Seb mouthed, catching her close as she collapsed into him. 'Let's wait for the MRI. It's all the truth I know now.' He sat and pulled her onto his lap. Nat found herself curling around him. This was new, allowing a man to comfort her. Her emotions stilled as she laid her head on his shoulder. It wasn't that it felt right, but it did feel peaceful, and that was what she needed.

'Hush now,' he rocked as his warmth brought Nat back. Peace amid turmoil was new for him, too.

Dodge found the couple wrapped around each when he returned. His eyes widened. 'Natasha, Doc, has something happened?'

Nat had never heard Dodge's voice sound so stricken. Jumping up, she said, 'Oh hey, Dodge. Um … ah, it's fine, there's no change.'

'It's just. I thought because, um. I've never seen you, like, um, I mean … Nat with a bloke, um … ah. I'll just shut up, shall I?'

The awkwardness immediately subsided as Sage, looking groggy but comfortable, was wheeled back into the room.

'Hey, honey, how are you?' Dodge was by her side.

She smiled weakly, closing her eyes.

Seb spoke to the nurse and attendant who'd brought Sage back from her MRI. They nodded and left. Speaking to Dodge, he offered something so simple but so thoughtful. 'If you want to stay in this room tonight with Sage, I've organised a foldaway bed for you. PJs, whatever you need.'

Dodge stepped towards Seb, who stood to his full height. His eyes darted to Nat, a little wary as Dodge approached. She watched as Seb's somewhat worried expression turned to amazement as Dodge gave him a man-friendly bear hug, smacking him on the back. If Seb was looking to win the biker over, he'd succeeded and then some. Dodge sniffed as he pulled away. 'Don't worry. I wasn't going to hit ya. We seem to have gotten off to a rough start. I should've known Nat would only let a guy she liked and trusted look after Sage.' Just then, two attendants entered, bringing in a foldaway bed and sheets.

Natasha's cheeks ran hot. She had to stop appearing so wrapped up in Seb so that even a guy as hardened by life as Dodge noticed. At this moment, she felt she was beginning to crack. With her beloved friend being so broken and Dodge reading her like a book, Nat had to redouble her efforts to protect and hide the last soft, vulnerable pieces of her heart. If they were shattered she'd be lost. Before she gave away any more weaknesses, she needed to make an escape.

Too late. *Make it all go away the easy way.* The Slut seized her moment, returning stronger. Seb's peaceful vibes were out of her reach and it was easy to acquiesce to bubbling panic. It was a habit.

Seb spoke, 'We should go and let you two rest.'

*Just steal away downstairs. They've already had a mix-up. You know what to do. It would be easy. Go on. Do it. Make the pain go away. One little sting, a push, and we'll be flying.*

Seb's voice, first an echo and then a sharp statement of common sense, brought her back to the painful reality. 'There's nothing more that can be done now. Dr Thompson will be monitored all night. Dodge, I'll talk to you and her first thing in the morning as soon as I've reviewed the MRI results.'

Nat had to get away. The Slut gnawed at her. *I know your every move. We've been here before. I know you want it. It's the gift you need. Let it ride your veins tonight. Freedom.* The Slut had ascended. Goldilocks was silenced. Nat needed to get away and settle the racing dread.

'Listen, I need to freshen up. I'll meet you at the car, okay?'

'Sure.' He let her slip from his grasp. Nat took the stairs to onc/haem to give in and settle her needs.

---

Sometime later, Nat made it to the ground floor and hurriedly walked down the busy street leading away from ER. She desperately wanted to reach the carpark and Seb. A hospital orderly rushed past her. She was drawn to where he'd come from. Down a secluded alley off the busy street, a gaunt figure was arguing with a cap-wearing lump of a man dressed in black. The thug's broad shoulders bunched as he shook his fist. The woman stepped back into the shadows, remonstrating with him. The thug remained under the dull streetlight, pulling his cap lower and menacing the woman before shoving his hand in his pocket.

While the light from the street wasn't bright, it shone enough to glint off what he now held in his hand. He waved the blade around, threatening the stricken woman. With his free hand, he grabbed the poor woman's chin and cheeks. Nat took a step forward to run to help. Then a shard of unfathomable fear speared through her.

The Slut grunted. *Walk away. Not your fight.* The Slut had better judgement when it came to reading danger. Nat shuddered at the thug's threatening bulk. She couldn't hear what he was yelling. The traffic at either end of the alley was too noisy. The woman flapped her arms, the knife inches from her face. She quickly reached for something in her coat pocket. The sleazebag released her face and snatched at what she held. He stepped back. It looked like he had her purse and was relieving it of her money. He threw the distressed woman's purse back at her, picked up a dark bag, stuffed the cash and knife into it, and started to walk away.

Nat was glued to the spot as two hospital security guards ran past her into the alley. She noticed the threatening guy storming off through the congested traffic. Soon he was on the other side of the street, the river of cars flowing as the light turned green. His escape complete, he disappeared behind the hospital's multi-storey carpark. The heftier security officer started talking to the woman, drawing her out of the shadows. His size prevented Nat from seeing who the shaking woman was. It didn't matter. Fear sliced her. She forced herself to move, needing to find Seb and safety. She rushed to one of the carpark entrances.

As she neared the car, Seb was hunting through a black gym bag. When he sensed her close, he tossed the bag onto the back seat. Frustration tainted his words. 'You took your sweet time.' Realising his voice was harsh, he pulled back from the annoyance of his gym bag not containing what he'd wanted his bodyguard Paul to deliver to him. Taking a breath, he steadied. 'Are you all right?'

'No, not really.'

'You look strung out. Come here.' He wrapped her up in a warm hug, the act calming both unsettled lovers.

'Please take me home.'

He sensed she was struggling with more than her friend's demise. He kissed her forehead, not fully understanding but wishing he could. 'I'm here for you.'

'Thanks. Please, I just need to get home.'

After an agonisingly quiet ride where she was hurting and he felt useless, Seb decided there could only be one conclusion. 'I'll stay, shall I? So you won't be alone. I've got most of what I need to stay the night in my gym bag.'

'Not tonight, Sebastian. I know myself. My place is safe for me, even on my own. Thanks for all you've done today. The odds are that seeing Sage like that, I'll have a full-blown attack. I only want to have to worry about sorting me out, not dealing with the guilt and shame of having you see me fall apart – again.'

She couldn't tell him she was confident it would happen because The Slut had come to life tonight, at her tantalising best.

'Fine, suit yourself. I thought it'd be better if you weren't alone.' One thing he did know about was the darkness within and how easily it could swamp the person trying to keep it at bay. 'I understand more than you think.'

'Don't think you know me.' She needed solitude to deal with the path of synthetic temptation she'd been led down tonight.

'I only wanted to stay to make sure you'd be safe, that's all. Because ... because I care. I want to be a friend you trust.'

His use of her words and the care in his voice were a circuit breaker. She wilted. 'It means a lot, really. I've never had ... I've never had a guy say those words to me. There's too much for me to deal with right now. There's Sage, my new job, and now a DD thing at work.' She moved forward and cupped the side of his face. 'Let alone all these feelings you're stirring up in me.'

'Good feelings, I hope.'

'Yes.'

'In that case, I won't fight you. But if you need anything tonight, text or call, please.' Seb's voice thickened, 'Promise me?' He didn't think he could leave her, yet he had to respect her wishes if he had any hope of seeing her again.

She nodded. Sebastian reached across, finding her lips, and all too soon, everything heated and melted. Quickly, he found himself pushing her back into the passenger seat, and she was letting him. As passion rose, her angst dulled. He pulled back, his voice sexy, husky. 'You have no idea what you do to me, do you?'

A slow-motion, bewildered head shake followed. 'No, I can't understand why you're here at all. I'm such a mess.' She closed her eyes at her admission.

The air seemed to evaporate from his lungs. He wanted to stop her sadness. Holding her face, he kissed her chastely on each closed eyelid. 'Natasha, you must realise that everyone is a hot mess at some time in their life, even me. You're such a beautiful creature. Right now, it's taking every ounce of my control not to pull you out of this car and take you to your bed. But I will do as you've asked and go home and dream about you instead.'

Breathing hard, she spluttered, 'Seb ... I ...' She was spent and couldn't face any more of the emotions he was driving through her. She'd been running all her life, now would be no different.

Somehow, Sebastian knew. 'Please don't run from me.' Before she could open the car door to escape, he grabbed her shoulders. 'I get it – too much too soon.' He planted a soft kiss on her furrowed brow. 'Slow down, Mancini. Right?'

Her face lightened. 'Yes. Although, if you're going to dream about me, then know that I'll dream about you because you seem to chase away my demons.'

Seb took her hand, kissed the palm and placed it on his cheek. After her breathing steadied, he moved his lips to hers. Time froze, her world stilled, and his desires calmed.

Time returned on his whisper, 'Until tomorrow then.' She left the car, and with the roar of the Maserati's V8 they were anchored back into reality. Seb disappeared into the night and Natasha's darkness reappeared. Nat ran to the bathroom but this time she didn't throw up. He'd quietened her. Instead, she showered and fell into bed, exhausted. To stave off any visitors, she grabbed her phone and listened to a range of songs about redemption. She scrolled photos of Sage, Dodge, Chevy, Jo and Chelsea, her new family.

At about three in the morning, she had a fitful hour wrestling with Goldilocks. Haunted by chubby-fingered hands menacing her in an alley, grabbing at her, while shiny needles dug into her. *Run, whore, run! You listened to her, gave her oxygen, entertained the damned.*

Nat woke covered in sweat. She pushed Goldy aside before the panic took hold. Her haunting made no sense. The needles, yes, but she didn't recognise the surroundings in Goldilocks's apparition. It wasn't the usual dark, claustrophobic room of her typical nightmare. Maybe it stemmed from the torment she'd witnessed in the alley. Maybe Goldy was losing her grip on Nat's guilt.

Oddly, she hadn't punished Nat about Seb. Goldilocks also hadn't taunted Nat about the demise of Goldy's nemesis, Sage. As the choirmaster of the 'Stuff Goldilocks's chorus, Sage had been very much a conscientious objector to the not-too-hot, not-too-cold path. The more Nat went over the stunted attack, the more she relaxed. Maybe she was becoming more assertive. But was she? Nat had taken a step backwards the night before. She vowed it wouldn't happen again. She would stay strong for Sage and help her all she could.

The morning sunlight found Nat texting Seb, needing a hit. He was under her skin. Nat was beginning to like the fix he offered.

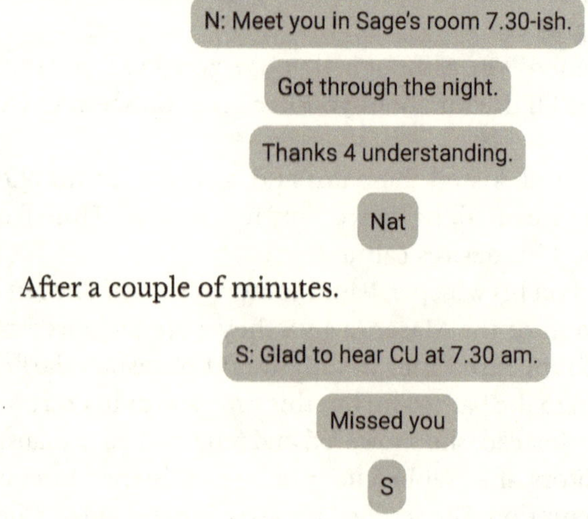


After a couple of minutes.

# TWENTY-THREE

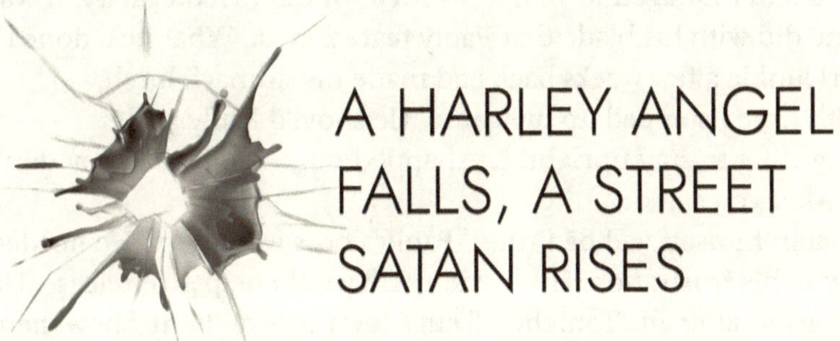

## A HARLEY ANGEL FALLS, A STREET SATAN RISES

*The Boss and Pauly: The day before.*

'Fuck, Pauly! If they want to party with primo product, these pieces of shit have to pay the going price.' The fibro wall cracked as his fist pounded on it. Proof of his power did nothing to quieten the rage-filled animal within. 'And this other little slut will pay the most. I've got her hooked good. Gave her some free stuff. Now she'll have to pay to get her rocks off. And pay she will. Family's got shitloads of cash. I'm back in town, and I'm taking it back. All of it.'

'She paid me some of it.' Pauly didn't mind beating up on the men who owed. He'd do almost anything his boss asked of him. Get him almost anything he wanted. But Pauly found it hard to hurt women. He was equipped with all bluster, but there was no bang. 'She said you'd get the rest soon, or she'd get some morpho for ya.' Pauly was sweating, his paunch and massive frame not dealing well with the hot spell. The heat from their cooking didn't help either. 'What else can I do?'

The Boss lunged, grabbing Pauly's throat, making his eyes bulge. 'Nothing, you dumb fucker. I'll do this one myself. It's time this little one-trick town woke up to my handiwork. It's been weeks since the first one – and not a mention. No respect. No fear.'

Pauly hated it when his cousin was in a temper. He couldn't do much about it, though. His cousin was more educated and a far nastier piece of work than Pauly. Pauly's cousin hadn't been back in town long, yet he'd still managed to inflict his form of depraved cruelty. It was what he did with his blade that Pauly feared most. What he'd done to the girl junkie a few weeks back had made his stomach lurch.

'It's time I stepped up my game.' He shoved Pauly aside.

Fighting to stay upright, he snapped out, 'Yes, Boss. They don't know what you can do.'

'Satan himself will be proud.' Pauly's boss was jittery. He needed to release his frustration. His hidden skill would help give release. He was an artist, after all. 'Tonight, I'll cut a few more of them. Show them all. *Don't mess with me.*' He was back, and he meant business. He'd kept himself out of the spotlight, but he could feel he was about to burst. His version of the Sicilian smile would permanently grace the faces of his clientele who didn't pay up. He would let everyone know, forever more, that these junkies couldn't be trusted.

'I'll see you later.'

'I'll come too, Boss.' Pauly hated the chemical smell of their cooking.

'No, stay here. Watch this latest batch don't burn. And *don't* call me the *Boss*. Use the one that's got the fuckers shaking.'

---

Natasha entered Sage's room to find Dodge having breakfast and Sage sitting up in bed, looking drawn and small but more reasonable – not so pained. Seb arrived, his professional poker face firmly in place. He looked tired, like he hadn't slept. He held Sage's patient notes and the telltale envelope with the results of her MRI scan.

To Nat's simultaneous embarrassment and pride, he slid his arm around her and gave her a quick peck on the cheek. 'Natasha.'

She just nodded, blinded by his light.

Dodge and Sage smiled at each other.

She was soft and warm, yet he saw increased steel about her this morning. Her perfume reminded Seb of the ecstasy they'd shared in her kitchen. He brought himself under control to attend to the business at hand. 'Dodge, Dr Thompson, good morning. How do you feel this morning, Dr Thompson?'

'I'd feel better if you called me Sage.'

'Only if you call me Seb.'

'Of course,' Sage smiled, but it was fleeting. An oppressive melancholy hung in the room.

Sebastian took a breath. The weight of the words he was about to deliver was heavier than usual. 'I have some preliminary results. Would you like me to discuss them now?'

'I'd like to know everything sooner rather than later. Don't sugar-coat it.' It was vintage Sage.

'Promise. No sugar-coating.'

'Doc, if you could keep it simple so I can understand, I'd appreciate it.' Dodge stood and held Sage's hand.

'Of course.'

Dodge nodded at Seb. Natasha, standing on the other side of the bed, rested her hand on Sage's shoulder.

'I believe you already have a fair idea of what's happening. You have a brain tumour.' They all gasped. Seb's gaze darted to Natasha, then back to Sage. 'It's most likely a result of your initial breast cancer metastasising, um, spreading to your brain and reappearing. I would like to do more tests to check if the cancer has spread anywhere else.' He flipped through Sage's patient notes and began a new page.

'What do you think, prognosis-wise?' Sage wanted to stare down her foe.

Seb explained, but the look on his face told Nat he was being light on the truth. With eyes narrowed and his mouth in a hard, downturned line, he said, 'I can't say with any great confidence – yet. I'd like to do more tests.' His sad, white-lie eyes flitted up to Sage's. 'Wait for the results of the blood samples and lumbar puncture from last night. I want to send you for a chest X-ray, an MRI of your back and hips. Then, I'll have a clearer view of what we're dealing with.' He dropped his voice and looked away from Sage to Natasha. 'I don't want to give you a number yet.'

'But it's not great.' Sage knew her body.

'Bloody hell.' Dodge's hard-knocks face seemed to crack.

Sage squeezed his hand.

The big guy's voice was barely a whisper. 'Babe, we'll fight it until we have nothing left, okay?'

Locking eyes, the couple nodded. The vow taken, they kissed.

Natasha found it hard to believe. Her indomitable friend and mentor was dying. The news immobilised her as sorrow swept through her.

Seb continued talking about the plan for Sage's treatment and management. After a little, he paused. They all took a deep breath. Sage spoke first. 'Sounds like a good plan, but I'll need someone to call the clinic and let them know. Especially Mike.'

The promise Natasha had made to herself the night before shot out, grabbing her attention like a red umbrella opening in a sea of black. It pierced the depressing fog that had enshrouded her. 'I'll do it. I'll call Dr Mike.'

'He'll know what to do.' Sage crumpled into her pillows.

'Is there anything else I can do, anything? What if I bring you some fruit or fresh nightgowns or something?' Nat tried to sound a little upbeat and carefree, but she sucked at it. Because while many women wore nightgowns, Sage would have only worn one when hell froze over, and Nat realised her mistake.

Sage understood Nat would be hanging on to normalcy by her fingertips. She needed her strong. 'Hey, you.' She tugged Nat's arm. 'Stop it. It's me here.'

Her tone hauled Natasha back from the edge. She stopped pretending to be some Florence Nightingale type. 'You stop it too. Because I'm not going to let you do this on your own. So get used to it.'

Sage smiled. 'Much better. Don't need you going soft on me. Got it?'

'Got it. What else do you need me to organise?'

'I'll let you know.'

'Ladies, we on the same page?' Dodge wryly smiled at Seb. 'Glad they got that sorted.'

Sage rallied. A little while later, Dodge and Natasha had their lists. Nat gave Sage a hug and took a step towards the door.

Amid ordering more tests, Seb looked up from his paperwork. 'Are you going?'

'Yes, I need to get to work and start busying myself with all these things on my list.' She gave Sage a wink.

Taking Nat by surprise, Seb leaned in and gave her a swift kiss on the lips.

'Oh.' Natasha was beyond embarrassed. She felt like he'd kissed her in front of her parents.

Sage and Dodge gave her knowing looks. They liked this one.

Natasha relaxed a smidgen and made a mental note. She needed to get used to Seb's tendency for public displays of affection. It was a significant change in her life. Glancing back at his cheeky grin, she knew the bastard fully understood what he'd done.

'Can I see you later, maybe tonight?'

'Um, I ... probably not.'

'Understood.'

She phoned Mike Hamilton. The jovial, middle-aged Englishman had taken to Australia like a fish to water, or a wannabe surfer to its fantastic beaches and waves. He was saddened, although he had suspected something was wrong with his colleague as her dynamism had waned. Natasha agreed to help at the clinic on weekends until they could find more staff to fill the void.

By the time she reached the onc/haem ward, Natasha was back on top of her work but not her emotions. She couldn't reconcile what was happening to Sage, and then there was her and Seb. She found Chelsea, and told her about Sage. Chelsea was shaken and saddened.

Head Nurse Avarice and Greed sought Natasha out. It seemed Nat wasn't alone in having a pain-in-the-arse, puritanical facet to her identity. Except Nat's was more treacherously unstable. However, Avarice was Averill today and much more receptive. 'Thanks for standing up for the nurses yesterday with Mr Cartwright.'

'Any time. I have some not-so-good news for the ward, though.'

'I think I can guess.' Averill braced herself.

'The pharmacy morphine totals match up, so the problem would appear to have occurred on this ward. We're going to keep investigating.'

With pursed lips, Averill spoke. 'I know I gave you a tough time yesterday.' Nat's stomach twisted as Averill continued. 'Now it's worse. We've got another dangerous drugs problem.'

Her admission shook Nat out of her funk. 'What now?'

'This time, it's me. I'm front and centre with Dr Cartwright – again.'

'Averill, I know you wouldn't. You're beyond reproach, surely.'

'I try to run a tight ship. I expect certain standards. Sometimes you rub powerful people up the wrong way when you ... well, let me just say, when you expose their weaknesses. Don't be so sure about me being untouchable. No one is, except maybe a Cartwright.'

'I'll keep that in mind. Tell me what happened.'

Averill started wagging her index finger at Natasha. 'Look. That doctor is alleging I witnessed her give a dose of morphine to one of the patients but—'

'Did you?'

Averill was walking the same worrisome DD tightrope Chelsea had traversed twenty-four hours earlier. 'Yes, I did for drawing it up, but no one witnessed her giving the dose to Ruby Brown. You know Ruby, feisty old girl. Room 17. Really with it.'

'Yes, I met her yesterday.'

'She's a favourite of ours, but last night we failed her.' Averill rested her hands on her hips in full defence mode, like a mother hen with its wings out, protecting her chicks. 'Late yesterday, we had several patients coming and going from surgery, new ones admitted very late, plus three patients were having complications.'

'You were flat out. How come you think Ruby didn't get her dose?'

'Ruby was having terrible, uncontrolled pain. She wasn't getting any relief from her PCA pump, even though she was pushing the pain-relief button to the max. The nurse looking after Ruby suggested Dr Cartwright order a top-up dose. I organised the drawing up of the dose with Dr Cartwright. I thought the dose was too much as well, but ... she's the doctor. She told me she'd get Ruby's nurse to witness her giving it because we were so busy. You know, to help out. I trusted her.'

'And Ruby kept having pain.'

'Severe pain. Ruby said that Dr Cartwright had not given her a top-up dose and that no one had been near her. Cartwright swore black and blue that Ruby was mistaken. It was bedlam. We knew if Ruby had been given the top-up dose, especially one that size, she wouldn't have been in such pain.'

'It's odd. Usually, patients notice a doctor giving them something.'

'I know, but I couldn't be sure. Dr Cartwright was very convincing. Saying Ruby was out of it with too much pain to know. She said she was suffering chemo brain, that she's old etc, etc, etc. For goodness sake, she's a doctor and a Cartwright. I trusted her. The one thing we were all sure about was that Ruby was still in a great deal of pain. It all just felt wrong. Something was off. You know how affected the ward is when a patient suffers, and we were still so busy. Ruby's sobbing put us all on edge.'

'A horrible night. Was there anything on the chart? There would have to be a signature along with Cartwright's, showing she had the dose checked. Whose was it?'

'Good question.'

'So?'

'That's just it. There was a signature on it, but at best, it was a signature that could've been any other nurse's. At worst, a poor attempt to forge mine. I didn't enter Ruby's room last night until she started sobbing with pain. I'd been admitting patients. Cartwright assured me she'd done things properly. I let go of my normal procedure of going with the drug all the way to the patient to make sure it's finished off properly.'

'Another mix-up between the nurses and a doctor,' Nat said.

'No! Another mix-up between different nurses and Dr Cartwright.'

'What do you think happened?'

'I believe Dr Cartwright thought she could just forge any old signature on the chart, and we'd fall for it. You know, not really check it because she's a Cartwright.'

'Not you, right?'

'Exactly. You have to get up pretty early in the morning to pull one over this old boiler.' Averill usually never gave much away from behind her mask of haughty bluster. Now cracks were showing as she worried over Cartwright sullying her reputation. She was concerned about what might happen to her, the nurses and the ward.

Natasha couldn't believe it could be this easy for someone to cause such confusion and get away with stealing a hit of morphine. 'Everyone is sure Cartwright didn't give the dose?'

'Yes.'

Nat knew that something strange had gone down, and Cartwright was in the middle of it. Frustratingly, it most likely wouldn't stick. After all, as Averill kept telling anyone who would listen, she was a Cartwright *and* a doctor. 'Has anyone told Dr Cartwright how important it is to follow the rules when it comes to the DDs?'

Averill huffed, turning up the corner of her top lip. 'Of course.'

'Sorry I had to ask. The chief pharmacist will ask me.'

'Oh, I understand. Tell your chief that Cartwright also seems to have this uncanny knack of wanting to give DDs on her own when we're swamped.'

'Really?'

'Yes. All the doses that have questions hanging over them have happened when we were busy, and lo and behold, Cartwright pops up.'

'But that doesn't link Cartwright to anything other than this ward, which is always busy with DDs. And you know as well as I do that mistakes happen when people are rushed, stressed and busy.' Natasha couldn't believe she was defending her. Maybe it was because she knew how horrible it was to be tarred with the brush about to tar Cartwright. However, if she was suspected, it would take the pressure off Nat.

'Is Ruby okay now?'

'Yes, although we had to settle her husband down too. He was distraught. He reckoned nothing like this had ever happened, and Ruby's been getting chemo for a while.'

'The whole thing's terrible.'

'Yes, and because of all the commotion, I must report this new missing dose to the director of nursing.'

'Naturally. And I'll have to collect and make copies of all the paperwork, med chart, DD register to give to the chief pharmacist.'

Natasha took a breath. She needed everything to slow down. 'Of course, you know we can't point the finger at anyone yet. We don't have enough. We need lots more evidence if we're going to accuse anyone of mishandling DDs, especially a doctor. And you can't alert Cartwright. Otherwise, she'll have us.' Nat began to think this would get much worse before it became better.

'Questions will be asked of all of us. It's good to know I have your support.' Averill patted Natasha's shoulder.

'Don't mention it.'

'I'll get that chart for you.' As she walked out, Nat saw Dr Cartwright materialise in the corridor just outside the door to the nurse's station. She gave Nat a death stare and followed Averill. It was odd for a doctor to be on the ward this early if she was on duty late the night before. Then, as a resident, she was probably on a long shift.

Averill dropped off Ruby's chart as Nat was photocopying the DD register. 'Thanks, I'll drop it back if you like? I need to start my ward round. I might as well start in Ruby's room.'

Averill gave a relieved look. 'Yes, thank you. I do have rather a lot to get on with. Already I can tell we're going to get along much better than the guy who was here before you.'

Natasha's pride was fleeting. It was swamped by how vulnerable this whole DD thing made her feel. At least now she had an answer to Averill's initial reticence. Rick had worked his magic yet again with the wily head nurse.

# TWENTY-FOUR

## THE FRIENDS AND FOES VORTEX

The previous night's unfortunate encounters could pose a problem, but Dr Rachel Cartwright had a plan. It wasn't anything she couldn't handle to her advantage. Fortunately for Rachel, and ominously for Freo, most of the talk around the hospital was focused on two knife-attack victims the ER had to deal with overnight. A bizarre assault had left the two victims horrifically maimed. Rachel breathed a sigh of relief. The fervour in the ER would smother any idle talk about her and onc/haem. She needed to shore up some minor annoyances before she felt comfortable. One was a visit to the head of hospital security. She was confident she could make him see things her way.

George was a respectful bear of a man. A powerfully built Māori, his arms were so muscular that just one was the size of Rachel's thigh. Beneath a gentle-giant outer skin, he had a rarely seen – or needed – threatening menace. Rachel followed George through the hospital's security nerve centre. She saw firsthand the extensive coverage the JCH surveillance cameras gave the security staff. 'Excuse me, George, is that how you knew something was happening in the alley last night, CCTV?' She pointed to the banks of monitors.

George ushered her into his small, windowless office. 'No, we don't have cameras in that alley. One of the hospital orderlies saw the start of your altercation and came running to get help for you.'

'I see. Good to know. Well, thank you.' She swallowed, and a weak smile threatened her lips. 'Please, thank him for me.'

The view and smell of low-paid human endeavour made Rachel thankful for her Cartwright name. She sat as George began. 'Can you tell me what happened last night?'

George was glad she'd come in so early. He thought she might make things difficult, having refused to be interviewed the night before. Fair enough, she did have patients to treat. Even so, George felt something about the whole situation and her reaction was off. He'd already been asked to supply some CCTV footage to the director of nursing. Some other shit had gone down on one of the cancer wards last night. 'I have to make a report, Dr Cartwright.'

Rachel deliberately painted a relaxed smile on her face and calmed her body. 'It was just a disgruntled patient's partner. He'd followed me out of the ER when I refused to give his wife stronger painkillers. Things got a little heated. I sent him on his way.'

'Really, because the orderly thought he saw the guy pull a knife on you and demand money.'

'No, nothing like that. Your orderly must've been mistaken. Just some heated words. If you had CCTV footage, you'd see that's all it was.' She met George's gaze confidently, adding, 'As you don't, I guess it's my word against the orderly's. And as I was actually there, I'm telling you that's all it was. I was fine. The guy moved off, especially when he heard your guys coming.'

'Are you sure?'

'I'm telling you, aren't I?'

George had a sinking feeling. The least he could do was cover security's arse. 'Would you like a formal report to go to the local police to continue the line of enquiry and maybe lay charges?'

'No, George, it's fine. Nothing to concern yourself with.'

'I see.' George was still wondering why she was attending to a patient in ER when she was working elsewhere in the hospital. 'Were you working in ER last night?'

'Just helped for a bit. They were busy. Then I made my way upstairs.'

He couldn't shake his uneasy feeling. 'Is that normal?'

Sitting up straighter to glare at him, she sniped, 'They. Were. Busy. I was helping out. Probably won't again, given all this grief.'

'Is there anything else you'd like to add?'

'No. George, you needn't worry. I'm not going to say your department was at fault or anything. Just because my name is Cartwright doesn't mean you're in trouble. It was a simple disagreement. End of story.'

His brow furrowed. 'All right then. I'll fill in a hospital incident form to that effect and get you to sign it. That will be that.'

She breathed a sigh of relief, 'Good. Thank you.' Now all she had to do was catch up with great-uncle Byron. Then all would be smooth sailing.

---

Natasha had only known Ruby Brown for a couple of days, but there was a certain fascination. She exuded a mischievous wisdom Nat didn't have, but would like to understand. Ruby and her husband, Jonathon, regularly flew to JCH from Karratha, a city in the north-west. They had no choice but to endure the travel. Ruby needed a complicated treatment regimen to keep her type of cancer at bay, which her local hospital couldn't provide. As Natasha placed the chart at Ruby's bedside, she sensed Seb's approach. A flutter of sensuality rushed through her. Ruby's medication chart fell to the floor. 'Ahh, Dr Mancini, I guess you'll need Mrs Brown's chart.'

'Yes, thank you, Ms Perry.'

She finally managed to pass it to him. His fingers lightly touched her hand, prompting another surge. Natasha desperately tried to control images in her mind of Seb, her kitchen table, and ice materialising on her breasts.

Seb was all business, seemingly unaffected. 'Ruby had a very rough night last night. Do you know anything about it?'

'A little. There was a mix-up with the timing of her top-up morphine dose.' Nat was trying to be diplomatic, with Ruby in earshot. Even though she knew Seb intimately, she wasn't sure how strongly he felt about the unwritten doctors' code of silence. 'The nurses couldn't get a clear directive about the dose. There was confusion over whether Ruby had already been given it or not.'

'I see. Yes, well, the resident doctor seems to have made a real hash of things. Can't understand what was so hard.'

*So that would be a no to upholding the doctors' code,* she thought.

'Yes, the nurses were very concerned. The dose may have gone missing. Nursing admin and pharmacy are investigating it.'

'Good.' Turning to Ruby, he ramped up his bedside manner. 'Mrs Brown, please accept my heartfelt apologies for the pain you had to endure last night.'

Ruby was all breathless, lost in the radiance of his charm. 'Thank you, Dr Mancini. I appreciate it.' She shot the young doctor a mischievous smile.

Natasha recognised the effect Seb had on Ruby because she suffered the same affliction, maybe more so. Not wanting to interrupt Ruby's moment, Nat stepped away quietly, moving to leave the room.

Mr TDD, in extreme professional mode, was having none of it. 'Ms Perry, just a minute. I need to talk to you about another patient.' Nat stopped and couldn't help but take advantage of the opportunity to legitimately watch and admire Seb as he finished up with Ruby and then glided towards Nat. They walked along the corridor in silence. Finally, he spoke. 'How are you holding up?'

'At the moment, I'm trying to keep busy, and there's this DD problem to investigate. If I don't think about Sage too much, I can function – just. Any more news?'

'Not any good news.' He took her by the elbow and gently steered her into the empty doctors' office. 'Are you sure you want to know now?'

'No, but if you don't tell me, it will only delay the inevitable and drive me even crazier.'

The knot in his heart wrenched tighter. 'The cancer has also spread to Sage's lungs.' It was the worst possible news. 'She's got months, given her age, how fit she is.' His words burned his throat. 'We'll try everything, chemotherapy and radiotherapy too.'

'Seb, nooo.' He caught her as she let herself fall into him, burying her head in his chest. 'What am I going to do?'

'I'm so sorry, Nat.' He nuzzled the top of her head.

'I can't. I don't know how ...'

'Hey, lean on me. Let me come to you tonight.'

'You mean another quiet night in like last night? I don't think my table could take it.' She smiled weakly, her heart crumbling.

His eyes were sad, his voice thick. 'As good as that was, I was thinking more along the lines of just keeping you company. Helping out.'

'Do we have to go through this again?' More forcefully, she said, 'I don't need you to babysit me. I can take care of myself.'

'I'm very aware of that. Let's just say I want to spend time with you.' He smiled softly, giving her a warm hug.

She pulled back, his warmth melting her resolve. 'Let me cook for you then. I owe you something, given all you've done for Sage.'

'You don't have to cook, or do anything for me. I'm just doing my job.'

'It'll keep me busy, keep my mind off things.'

His answer was to kiss her. She couldn't resist him.

After a beautiful moment together, she gently and reluctantly moved out of his warmth. Even though his embrace and kisses were tender and made her feel safe, her mind was in turmoil. Sage's situation had led to Nat's terrible addictive weakness bubbling to the surface. This vulnerability didn't align with the happy feelings she experienced around Seb. 'I'd like to visit Sage tonight and then cook for you. And it sounds like I need to cure you of your fixation.'

'Believe me, Ms Perry, I'm starting to think it's incurable. I crave you 24/7.'

Natasha found it hard to understand how he could know so soon. 'Dr Mancini, you need to seek a second opinion.' With a sad smile, she whispered. 'Don't you know any good doctors?'

'A second opinion? I'm sure you have one.'

Her face lightened. 'Yes, I do, and I prescribe four words to cure you.'

'And they are?'

'Too much, too soon.' Even though she tried to sound defiant, her tone was hollow, built on shaky, forlorn convictions.

'Alright then. I like your cooking. I'd like to sample some more of it, so I'll take you up on that offer.'

'7.30 pm, okay?'

He turned to walk out. 'More than okay.'

'Is there anything you don't like to eat?'

He turned back with a salacious smile. 'No. Nothing of yours that I've tasted so far.'

Nat's cheeks heated, and he was gone. Her pager beeped, reality barging back into her mind like Averill entering a room.

Jo had summoned Nat to her office asap. Nat left onc/haem armed with the photocopies and Averill's version of events. She found Jo sitting at her desk, and began recounting the events of the latest DD issue to her.

Jo gave a heavy, angry sigh. 'This is a right pig's ear, this whole scenario.'

She was more stricken than Natasha had expected. 'Yes, it's bad, but what aren't you telling me?'

Jo hesitated before gathering herself. A steely determination focused her eyes, and a hard edge sharpened her words. 'The director of nursing and Charles Cartwright have rung me about the two DD incidents. It seems pressure is being applied from above for this to be dealt with quickly. They want to send a message.'

'What does that mean?'

'I have to ask you some tough questions. As your boss, remember, not as your friend. Believe me, it's better coming from me than from the board or anyone else.'

'What's happened?'

Jo cleared her throat. 'Dr Cartwright has made a complaint to the hospital's head of surgery and board member, and by the way, her great-uncle Byron. She has alleged that the DD practices on the onc/haem ward are lax, and are threatening patient care. She apparently felt it needed to be brought to his attention immediately. He's taken it to Charles Cartwright because of the number of DDs that may have been misappropriated and likely poor patient care, especially pain control.'

'I see Cartwright nepotism is alive and kicking at JCH.'

'If you're hoping for a laugh, you're talking to the wrong hard-nosed bitch. I'm trying to make sure the truth is the winner here.' Jo's anger waned as she fixed Natasha with worried eyes.

It pained Natasha to hear Jo's tone and then see the disappointed look in her eyes. The hurt and shame Natasha felt, along with everything else she was dealing with, had caused her to slip into the mercy of her alters and now she had to deal with the consequences. 'Understood.'

'I know the last couple of weeks have been a roller-coaster for you. There's been the break-up with Rick, the new job, a new high-power relationship, panic attacks, and now Sage's tragic—'

'You can't seriously be going to ask me.'

'I am. And I must.' Jo growled. 'You know me, so stop thinking this is a witch-hunt. I must ask so I can wholeheartedly defend you should this get nastier and people, like the board, start asking tough questions.' Jo's shoulders rose on a deep breath. 'Is this you?'

Nat realised Jo was taking a whole lot of heat over her. They were both being pulled into a long, suffocating shadow of dangerous insinuations.

*Weak sewer rat. Not as smart as you think you are.* Goldy was in her element.

Nat shuddered and tried to push Goldilocks aside. 'But I'm the one who brought it to your attention. Way before Cartwright, did.'

'Let's look at the facts.' Jo deliberately moved some items around her desk, mustering her thoughts. Finally moving to her keyboard, she focused and began typing some notes. It wasn't personal, it was business, her business. Jo met Natasha's eyes. 'You still haven't answered my question. Over the last few days, have you been tempted to go back to old ways to solve new problems? I can understand if you have. We, I, can and will support you and get you help.'

'I haven't been on the ward when the DD problems occurred.'

'Ahh, you see, that's not quite right, is it?' Jo was saddened by Natasha's sidestep of the question. She was angry at herself for not seeing the signs – if they were there. It was rocking her faith in Natasha and in her own ability as a manager of people. 'All this only started *after* you started on the ward.'

'What are you suggesting?' While beating faster, Nat's heart sank, joining her pride and falling a thousand floors. 'Cartwright started at the same time.'

'Yes, but you see, the director of nursing has been in touch with hospital security to see if any CCTV vision could help get some answers. There's vision of you last night.' Jo had to pause, studying Natasha, searching for a flinch. The slightest sign of betrayal, a lie. The air stilled.

'I was up at the Foundation with Sage, my and your sick friend. She was being admitted. I was with Dodge and/or Seb all the time.'

'That's not quite true, is it?' Jo growled. 'You're not answering my questions.'

'Um, I was with them most of the time.'

'There's footage of you using the stairwell between Aida and onc/ haem just before onc/haem started having all their problems with the latest missing dose. You need to come clean.'

'It's not what you're thinking. Please believe me. If I'm evasive, it's because I didn't want to admit—'

'As I said, there's footage showing you, alone, in the stairwell entering onc/haem, and then leaving onc/haem, looking pale, sweaty and spacey.'

'Yes, I was badly shaken, that's true. As we were leaving, I was worried about an attack, since they've come easy lately. The toilets on Aida were occupied. I couldn't wait as my weaknesses were beginning to show. I went down to onc/haem ladies. I needed to try and pull myself together.'

'Why take the stairs?' Jo's eyes bit into Natasha's.

'Look, the lift was taking ages, and I was going to throw up – shaking uncontrollably. I didn't want to fall apart at work, in public, so I went down the stairs. Ask Seb. I met him in the car park. He'll tell you I was shaken and strung out.'

'From Sage, or something else?'

'Which do you think?'

'Answer me, for God's sake.'

'I just wanted to keep an attack private. I went to the onc/haem ladies. It was quiet there. I threw up, splashed some cold water over my face, rinsed my mouth, took more deep breaths and sucked a strong mint. I settled myself enough to stagger out to the carpark. Then Seb took me home. How dare you!'

'Stop it, Nat. Think. I'm trying to protect you here.'

'I haven't had any illicit drugs in my system for years.'

'No? I'm not talking about illicit drugs. I'm talking legal drugs acquired illegally.' Jo said.

'Why would I take such a risk?' Nat asked.

'If you were feeling so bad, so hurt, so defenceless?'

*Yes, sewer rat, explain. Sage can't save you now.* Goldilocks had come forth with the dig Nat had expected the night before.

'Is there footage of me entering the main part of the ward or near any part of the ward where I would have had access to the DDs?'

'No, that doesn't necessarily mean ... I need you to *answer* me.'

'I. Am. Clean. I didn't want it to come to this.' With a heavy sigh, Nat offered, 'I didn't want to admit to you that I'm still weak. I'm ashamed that I still have cravings like that. I fought them, and because I did, I had a small attack. Believe me, I would never betray your trust. Test my blood if you like.'

Jo had her answer and was relieved. 'You silly bird. Worrying about being seen as weak is the least of your problems. Given your past, if people suspect you of any of this, that will be the story. Not your brave fight against being tempted.' Jo squeezed her friend's hand.

Nat pulled away with a barb of anger and hurt at the unfairness jabbing at her. 'I haven't done anything bloody wrong. All I did last night was fight so fucking hard not to do what you're accusing me of!' She was speaking more to Goldilocks than Jo. Goldy fell silent.

Jo bowed her head, her voice smaller. 'I had to ask. You must see why.'

Natasha was back, slipping her mask, however brittle, back on, 'No. No, I don't. Not when that doctor is front and centre and dishing dirt on others. I thought you, of all people—'

'Natasha.' Jo reached for her friend's hand again. Her voice calm and authoritative but caring. 'Take a breath. I believe you, Natasha.'

Nat stilled. She swallowed a hard lump. Jo never used her full name unless she wanted Nat's total attention, like Natasha's mother used to.

Jo had been put in an unenviable position. It was all of Natasha's making. Jo had trusted Sage's judgement and given Natasha a chance when others wouldn't.

Nat realised she was venting to the wrong person. 'Jo, sorry. I may have recently thought about pushing something into my veins for release, but I fought it. And last night, I realised I didn't need to. I can get past the bad shit. Yes, I'm torn up about Sage, but I have great friends. I have a new belief in myself. I'm excited about the new job and the faith you have in me. And Seb. He's pretty helpful. I realised last night in the onc/haem toilet that I have too much to lose now, as shaky as that belief may be. I found my self-self-confidence. It got me through. That, and I thought I saw a drug deal going wrong in the alley near ER last night. It made me doubly sure I never wanted to go back to putting myself at risk like that ever again.'

Jo took a breath. 'Ah, the truth. I can see it in your eyes. As Chelsea says, you're a hopeless liar. I guess Mr TDD isn't such a bad accessory either.'

'Are all the nurses being asked questions? And what about Cartwright? She's in this up to her eyeballs.'

'Yes, the nurses are.' Jo threw her hands up, letting out a disgruntled groan. 'Byron Cartwright's actions have stopped any further questions being asked of his great-niece. It makes me so angry, their bloody doctor's code. It makes a mockery of everything. For all the procedures and careful recording of DDs, it seems they're important for everyone except this particular doctor.'

'Can anything be done about her? Are they asking her about her whereabouts last night?'

'No, not from what I've heard. Charles Cartwright isn't pleased with anybody right now, but it looks like if we can't get any satisfactory explanations, it will be brought to the attention of the full JCH board.' A cunning look spread across Jo's face. 'If that happens, I will recommend a hospital-wide DD audit. That'll allow management and the board to identify if any other wards have irregularities and if there are any common elements, personnel, or procedural deficiencies.' She paused and narrowed her eyes. 'Nat, would you say Dr Cartwright could be a user?'

'Maybe. Sometimes she's a bit spacey. She's thin and pasty pale, but let's face it, that describes most of the resident doctors. They're so overworked.' Shaking her head, she said, 'She's a Cartwright, isn't the world at her feet? Why would she need a hit to escape anything? It doesn't make sense.'

'People hide many things for many reasons, all behind masks of different shapes and sizes. Either way, I won't be able to do much about Cartwright unless she comes through the audit as a commonality. Then I might be able to turn up the heat. Cartwright has made this report, knowing her great-uncle would take it to the chairman of the board, probably to get ahead of anything that could damage her. You and Averill will be in the firing line because, in reporting problems to your superiors, you named Cartwright.'

'Shit. Does that mean I'm a problem for you?'

'I'm chief. I believe you. That's all that matters.' Jo's heart sank. 'You need to be very careful, though. If someone wants to make trouble for you and me, trying to link you more strongly with the missing DDs will do it. I'm not sure I'll be able to shield you. But I'll try with everything at my disposal.'

Even as Jo reassured Nat, a cold trepidation gnawed at her being. She was always skittish when her past looked like it would devour her present. Shit, if Cartwright was a user and found out about Natasha's past, the pharmacist would be the perfect patsy. Surely there was no way she'd find out? Sage or Jo wouldn't tell anyone, and Seb, well, he didn't know the drug part of it. She trusted him with the rest. Didn't she?

Nat was curious about making sense of what she'd seen. 'Is there any CCTV footage of the alley between ER and the carpark? Maybe a dealer could be identified, as well as a user.'

'No, there's not a camera there. From the management meeting the other day, I know the hospital is investing in more security cameras. George from security has assured the board it will all be covered in the coming months.' Jo tried to reassure herself. 'Ah, look, I had to ask.'

Nat was finding her new, confident feet. 'Yes. I guess I should have expected questions like that to be thrown my way sooner. As you said, better for you to ask them.'

'Good. Just be there for Sage. And any energy left over, focus it on that gorgeous doctor.' Jo's voice saddened. 'Actually, we'll all have to do what we can for Sage.'

'Yes,' Nat said softly.

'Do you think Sage will be up for a visit from all of us tomorrow?'

'That's an excellent idea. I'll check and let you know.'

'Good.' Jo sighed, rubbing her tired eyes.

# TWENTY-FIVE

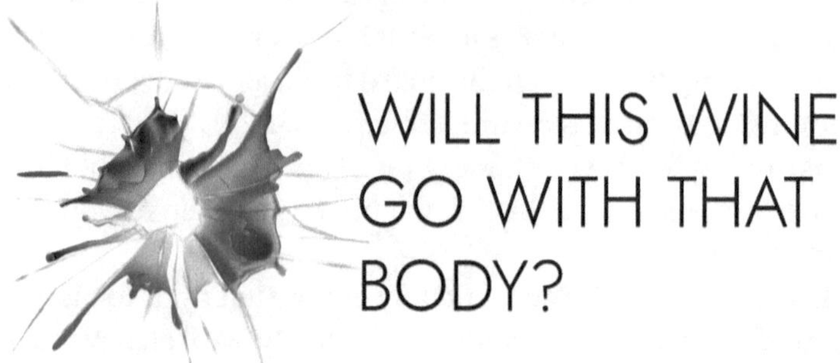

## WILL THIS WINE GO WITH THAT BODY?

The rest of the day passed uneventfully, but the damage had been done. Sage's demise was terrible enough, but now Natasha had a reminder of how wafer-thin the line she trod was. When she thought of the prospect of seeing Seb, having him again, her circumstances didn't seem so bad. Could it be this easy with him in her life?

Nat's mind was a pinball on the drive home from visiting Sage, ricocheting around a brain that felt like an old, over-used arcade machine, annoying sounds and all. She bounced between Sage, DDs and Seb – between pain, guilt and happiness.

Once she was home, Nat's thoughts and feelings churned inside her like the ingredients she stirred around the deep pan she slaved over. Deciding to lay low and trust Jo with the DD situation didn't help. Her emotions about Seb and Sage still yo-yo-ed incessantly. One minute she was happy beyond belief, and the next, saddened beyond disbelief. As she added the final touches to the paella, she still hadn't settled on any middle ground other than jittery, guilty confusion.

Her doorbell rang. Nat's heart missed a beat as she caught herself skipping towards the door. How old was she, five? She slowed to a walk and tried to appear nonchalant, opening the door with a smile.

'Hi.' Her breath hitched and any nonchalance dissipated. God, he was gorgeous. Nat lingered a little longer on his body as her eyes worked their way up to his face. He wore faded black-and-white DC shoes, tight blue jeans that left nothing to the imagination and a body-hugging white tee. To complete his runway-model appearance, his five o'clock shadow gave him a smouldering hot look. She could've jumped him there and then, but restrained herself. An image of a sick Sage extinguished her devious thoughts.

He was equally as beguiled, his chest swelling at the sight of her. Such a gorgeous body, and then there it was, her beautiful smile. He loved seeing the way it lit up her face when she saw him. Hopelessly captivated by her, Seb smiled back, holding up a chilled bottle of white wine. 'I hope this will go with dinner.'

Her thoughts purred. *Mmm, the whole package will.* But she managed to stick with the more controlled, 'I believe so.' Taking his hand, she led him into the lounge. As if to put up a flashing sign announcing her nervous disposition, she tripped over nothing except her own feet. 'Ooh, crap.' She stopped herself from face-planting on the carpet by grabbing a lounge chair and swearing under her breath.

Seb held his breath. He thought they were through all her nerves. Maybe this woman was too all over the shop. Then she stared up at him, and he became lost in her big, soulful eyes. All negatives were forgotten. 'You okay?'

'Yeah, just being a bit of a klutz.' She hoped some distance between herself and his deliciousness would help. 'I'll get some glasses for the wine.' Nat reached the kitchen and took a few deep breaths. Grabbing two glasses, she turned to find Seb right behind her. The glasses, jarring as they clashed in her hand, reflected her mood. 'Oh, you gave me a fright.'

'It smells delicious. What are we eating?' His voice was doing that treacle thing, again, where smooth, dark vibes drove to her core.

She tried to settle. 'Um, it's nothing much – just paella with prawns, chicken and chilli. I hope you don't mind. It's a little on the hot side.'

'I like the sound of that.' He moved even closer.

She tried to reel in her emotions with banality. 'Are you hungry?'

'Yes, for everything.' He wasn't helping Nat settle. Seb couldn't resist any longer, she was his weakness. He moved close so he could run his fingers down her cheek. Putting the bottle down on the kitchen counter, he held her face in both hands and kissed her, hypnotised by her scent and feel. Those full, velvety lips.

Nat shook her head and jerked away. Colliding with the kitchen counter, she made everything rattle.

'Hey, why so jumpy?' He reached for her again. He had to solve this. Resting his hands on her shoulders, he searched her eyes. 'What's going on?'

The timbre of his voice, thick with care, undid her. 'Um, I don't know.' His kind eyes had her babbling. 'One minute, I'm so happy I just want to jump your bones. The next, I'm so sad thinking about Sage, and then I'm overcome with guilt because the happiness you make me feel doesn't sit with the news about Sage.' She moved further out of his reach, robotically putting the glasses down. 'I don't know which end is up.'

'I'm a little scattered as well.' He moved close again, reaching out to reassure her. Her smooth skin warmed at his touch. It was perfect and protected such a beautiful, resilient soul. 'I want you all to myself, but I also know that it's a terrible thing that Sage is going through, and I see the pressure you're under. I don't want to cause you any more angst. So, Nat, I'll be guided by you. I understand.' He kissed her shoulder, moving to her throat, then the corner of her mouth. She sensed his smile. 'Relax. This is new for both of us. I'll ask things of you. You can ask things of me, but I will be totally guided by you and your decision on managing the too much and delaying the too soon.'

Surprised by the wave of relief that passed over her, Nat exhaled the breath she'd held. He'd said something that even Goldilocks might agree with. 'Yes. Wow! You get me.'

'Doesn't mean I'm not going to try to get you on your own as much as possible. Although I will be here, so you don't do this on your own.'

It's like he'd known her much longer than he had. 'Seb, you just keep surprising—'

His lips found hers and rendered her speechless. He pulled back. 'You don't need to say anything. I've had more experience balancing desperation and happiness than I care to tell.' Thinking about his past had Seb trying to hide the pained shadow that rolled across his face. His knuckles went white as they gripped the bottle. 'How about I open this and we settle down to what smells like another wonderful Ms Perry dinner?' She saw the pain. Recognising it, she briefly entertained the notion that maybe they weren't so different.

While the paella was hot, it wasn't until they finished eating that the sizzle came to the table. 'You're a good cook. You know that.'

'Thanks.'

'Are you doing anything tomorrow night?'

She dropped her eyes away from his heated gaze. 'Not after I visit Sage.'

'Will you let me treat you to a surprise?'

'Um, I'm not sure. What do you mean by a surprise?'

'You'll have to trust me. Hence the word, surprise.'

'Do I get any hints?'

'Before we get to that, would you also let me take you away for the weekend? Just you and me?' He had it planned. He needed her on her own, away from the city, to tell her about his past – all of it. 'We won't be far from Sage. You'll only miss seeing her on Saturday. As her doctor, I can honestly tell you she needs her rest. Missing one day so early in her treatment, will be okay. Plus, I asked her, and she also agreed you need a break.'

'Oh.' Her heart started drumming with a dominating beat.

'Natasha?'

'Um.'

'Your answer?'

She couldn't shake the crescendo of concern. 'What if I'm not here and something bad happens to Sage? What if I have an attack? What if I hurt you? What if you can't—'

'Forget about the what ifs and embrace the excitement of the why nots.'

'I'm not the kind of girl you do this with.' *Hell.* Should she dare tell him what was brewing at the hospital? 'I'm not the one you take on romantic weekends.'

'Yes, you are.'

'But you don't know.'

He fixed her with his bottomless brown eyes, 'I don't for certain, no. But I know I feel surer about you than I've felt about anyone, ever.'

His words dissolved her doubts. She decided to take a chance. 'You'll have to tell me something about it. Otherwise, how will I know what to pack?'

His glorious megawatt Mancini spread across his face and crinkled up his eyes. 'Let me give you some hints on what you won't be wearing.' He led Nat to her bedroom and had his wicked way with her. Although as she scratched her nails down his back, driving him to a new, higher place, he wasn't sure if he'd had his wicked way with her or she with him. Either way, when they shared being with each other, so close, so passionate, there wasn't any trouble in their worlds.

Natasha arrived at work on Friday morning feeling quietly excited about what the evening might hold. Of course, because she wanted the day to go quickly, it dragged until the four Amigos met in Sage's room. They were subdued by the cards that fate had dealt their dear friend. That was until Chelsea decided it was her lunchtime mission to lighten the mood by grilling Natasha about Seb. She wouldn't be deterred until Nat gave her the current status of their relationship.

'I have to ask, because if you were part of the twenty-first century, you'd be on Instagram or Facebook, and I could see what you're up to.'

'But this is sooo much more fun,' Jo interjected. She knew why Natasha was reticent to have any social-media accounts. Nat tried to satisfy Chelsea's curiosity by throwing her a few titbits, but nothing too concrete. She was finally placated when Nat told her about her upcoming mysterious weekend away.

'Oh, maybe I can find out a few things for you.'

'Chelsea, please. Don't go harassing poor, innocent doctors.'

'Don't worry, I won't embarrass you. I doubt Sebastian Mancini is innocent, and I know for certain he's not poor. I'd say he's fair game.'

Sage quietly smiled. 'From what I've seen, he can handle himself.'

'Yes, and then some,' Jo chuckled.

'I'm feeling distinctly outnumbered here. Why aren't we talking about how cosy Jo was with Charles Cartwright the other night?'

'Really? Where, when?' Chelsea pressed, 'Tell me. I need details!' Jo shot Nat daggers.

'At Nunzio's. The night we all went out to celebrate Rick's demise and my new job. Isn't that right, Joanna?' Nat moved closer, taking Sage's hand. 'I thought it was a coincidence that Jo just happened to book Nunzio's the same night the JCH board was there, but maybe it was all planned so she could hook up with Charles Cartwright, even if only for a little while.'

'CC and I are just good friends.'

Sage's interest, even in her dazed state, was peaked. 'CC, is it now?'

Chelsea giggled. 'Oooh! Now that sounds a little more than just board buddies.'

'Okay, okay. Nat has been very crafty in turning the spotlight on me. This is all I'll give up.' A hint of pride showed in Jo's voice. 'We've spent some time together, but our association is purely of a business nature. His wife passed away some two years ago now, and because we don't have partners, we often find ourselves together at JCH management functions.'

Chelsea quizzed mischievously, 'Well now, I don't know. It could be an innocent hook-up, although it depends on the nature of the business that comes up when you two are together. Is it purely professional, or are you colleagues with benefits?'

Nat enjoyed that finally someone else was being interrogated by the Amigos. Chelsea kept digging. The atmosphere in the room lifted. Soon they were all laughing and kissing a smiling Sage goodbye.

'Thanks, guys. I needed a boost. My mind is all mothballed up like it's been put in storage. I'll rest well now.' When Sage was alone, a soft tear rolled down her cheek.

# TWENTY-SIX

## WHO SAID ROMANCE WAS DEAD, BUT DOES KINKY COUNT?

He'd told Nat it was a surprise date. She realised that but … dress for the gym? What was that about?' What excited her was the need to pack a bag for a weekend at the beach. Of course, she'd invested heavily in a new G-string, athletic top and bum-hugging shorts, not to mention a new bikini. He was worth it. She hadn't worn anything remotely like it since her days at the strip joint. He'd made her feel more confident about showing off her body. Now, to see the appreciation in his eyes was a game-changer. It was real, not driven by money, and certainly not because he was a lecherous pervert.

All these heady thoughts faded as the butterflies in her stomach turned into bats. Seven o'clock eventually came around, the doorbell rang, and her anxieties intensified. She shakily opened the door but found Chelsea standing there.

Chelsea couldn't help but see Nat's disappointment. 'Nice to see you too,' she smiled.

Nat grumpily stood aside. 'Oh, just come in.'

Chelsea laughed as she walked past Nat. 'You should see your face. Am I that much of a disappointment?'

'With all due respect, yes. You know very well Sebastian's picking me up about now.' Then the bomb dropped. Chelsea was in her nurse's uniform. 'He's not coming, is he? He's come to his senses.'

'No, no, hold your horses.' Chelsea held up her hands, smirking. 'Stop, you're killing me. He's asked me to pick you up, but ...' she paused, playing with Nat's angst. With a flourish and a wicked grin, Chelsea then proceeded to pull a black cloth eye mask from her pocket. 'He wants you to wear this.'

'Just that?' A shot of hyper-nervousness ran through Natasha.

Chelsea was relishing her power and Nat's embarrassment. 'No, silly, but that would take things to a whole other level. No, no. Do you know what it is?'

'Yes. You ... and Seb want to blindfold me. You're kidding, right?'

'No, he was dead serious and said I had to get you to wear it. And tell you not to take it off or you'll spoil the surprise.' She lowered her voice. 'It's kind of kinky and really hot.'

'You don't know the half of it.' Nat tried to recover. 'I'll tell you some of the details you've been nagging me for if, and only if, you tell me where we're going.'

'You're going to wear it?'

'No, I didn't say that. I'll only wear it if you tell me where we're going.'

'Don't think you can negotiate your way out of this one, Perry. Come on. Do it. I haven't got time to argue with you.' Her voice was unashamedly salacious. 'You can spill the beans later, especially after this weekend. Then I'll want all the juicy details.' She winked mischievously. 'Come on, step outside your box.' Not bothering to suppress her mirth, she giggled. 'So he can get into it.'

'Oh, stop it. He's asked me to get dressed in gym clothes. I'm not sure what's going on.'

'Don't get all analytical about it. It's not a problem to solve. It's an opportunity.' Chelsea delivered the Wisdom of Chelsea, her very own life mantra that revolved around one thing and one thing only. 'Go eff your brains out with Mr TDD. In fact, it's the solution to all your problems. You finally get to have some fun and forget all the other crap. The DDs, Sage, Rick the Dick, Holly, or whoever else or whatever else Rick ... bonked.'

She may have had a one-track mind, but what she said resonated with Nat. 'Okay, I just have to know – do you think it's safe? Where we're going?'

'It's Seb. I trust him. You know I'd tell you if I didn't.' Chelsea lowered her voice. 'Hey, to do all this, he must be so into you. Don't spoil it.' She became scarily serious. 'You're going, *and* you'll leave this blindfold on.'

With Chelsea's last words playing a continuous loop in her head, all too soon Nat was blindfolded and speeding through the streets of Freo. After enduring about ten bruising minutes from being thrown from side to side, Natasha had had enough. 'Jeez, we're not in a race. Do you have to drive like this?'

Chelsea laughed. 'This is how I normally drive. Anyway, we're here.'

The car braked hard, followed by the ratcheting up of the handbrake. Chelsea opened the door for Nat and helped her out. Nat heard a strange man's voice.

'Are you Chelsea?'

'Yes. You're Paul?'

'I am indeed, and this must be Natasha. I'll take her from here. She's in good hands.'

'Great,' said Chelsea, holding Nat's hands so she couldn't take the blindfold off.

Nat was almost apoplectic. 'Hey. Don't you dare! All due respect to whoever you are, but ... Chelsea! You can't leave me with some complete random. Not like this. What do you think you're doing?'

'Making sure you have a good time.' Chelsea squeezed Natasha's hands, whispering in her ear. 'Trust me, trust him. I do. You'll be fine.' And she was gone.

Paul took Natasha's hands. 'Right, welcome. I'm taking you inside now. I've got your bag.' He gently moved her forward. By the noise, she could tell they were walking across bitumen. 'Three steps are coming up in front of you. I'll guide you. Step now.' Miscalculating the step, Nat fell into him, like falling into a brick wall. He was built for someone who had such a gentle touch.

She heard a door being pushed open and Paul guided her through it. Natasha was met with a familiar smell. She tried to place it. Then it hit her. It was the smell of physical activity and boxing gym leather, a scent she didn't fear, no bad memories. He wasn't joking about the gym. Nat wasn't sure whether she should be thankful or disappointed.

They walked further into the room. Paul grabbed her shoulders, and she jumped. 'What are you doing?'

'Take it easy. I'm just going to wrap velcro around your wrists.'

'No way.' She heard velcro ripping and tried to move away. He grabbed her hands in only one of his, which felt huge. Then he fixed the velcro in place.

'What the hell?' Silence greeted her. He gently pushed her back against a wall. 'This is ridiculous. What are you doing?' She tried to move away.

He grabbed her, holding her against the wall. 'Your bag is at your feet to your right. You're okay.'

'That's easy for you to say. You're not blindfolded.' She made to remove the covering, but he stopped her.

'I heard you'd be feisty. I'm going to leave you here. Just stand still. Someone will be with you very shortly. Don't move. Don't take the blindfold off. Otherwise, you'll spoil the surprise.'

Nat had had enough and tried to take the blindfold off again. Paul grabbed her hands and put them behind her back. She heard a click. Now she couldn't separate her hands. She was cuffed. 'What the fuck?' Her heart started pounding. 'Shit, shit. Is this for real?' She'd fallen for the oldest trick in the book – and done so willingly.

Paul said, 'I promise it's okay. Don't wander around. We don't want you hurting yourself.'

She heard him walk away. A door opened and shut, and then a lock was triggered. The sound echoed around Nat, warping like her nerves. She was thankful her back was to the wall. At least if anything was going to happen, it could only come at her from the front.

How fucking stupid was she? The Slut would be out dancing, and Goldilocks would have a field day stamping on Nat's grave. Was she still so stupidly naive? Dreading the worst, a shudder gripped her.

'Sebastian, please don't do this to me.' He wouldn't hurt her, would he? Shit. What did Sage say? Be careful, then something about him and his family. Sage had been too out of it lately to elaborate. Then she sensed someone was with her. She should run. Her breath quickened, becoming shallow and noisy until her panicky senses were overcome. His scent, that cologne, was both familiarly safe and exhilarating. Soft lips found hers. Surprised by his assault, Nat allowed his tongue easy access to her mouth. His tantalising licks mesmerised her. She found herself kissing him back. He moved to her neck, sucking and nipping. Why did she foolishly think she could withstand a frontal assault?

'Hello there.' There was no response. She started questioning herself as another frisson of alarm sliced through her. She hoped it was Seb. It certainly smelt, felt and tasted like him.

Madonna's dulcet tones began to surround them. Fortunately, the music was not in Nat's head. It was real, settling her into a seductive vibe. No Slut needed. The song was 'Secret', the first verse so perfect. Mmm! Madonna's sensual voice had affected her. Although wet with anticipation, she still needed confirmation from him – on everything. Then she'd feel safe.

She tried to push the body in front of her away. This action proved fruitless as it only served to help her seducer. His arm wrapped around her waist, pushing her hands away from her butt and pulling her to him.

'Is it you? Please, let me know. Sebastian, please?' Her voice was husky but concerned. A tender hand found the small of her back, slipping under her sports top where his index finger could slowly circle Natasha's tattoo.

Goosebumps travelled over her. What other male would know about her tatt? Some scumbags back in Sydney, and Rick, but there's no way they would be this thoughtful and gentle. Now she allowed herself to surrender to the feelings of pleasure unfurling in her body. His lips were on her neck again. His right hand travelled up her front, under her top, circling her left nipple, pulling it and rolling it to harden. She had never experienced anything like this. She was so hot, and he hadn't said a word.

Natasha didn't want to do anything but yield to his skilled touch. He lifted her top over her head, down her arms, and left it covering her hands. Now she couldn't see or use her hands or fingers. His seduction was overpowering. She was his willing captive.

His lips were on her nipples. His hands slipped under the waistband of her shorts, around to her butt cheeks, pushing her forward. She realised he was naked as his heavy arousal stood erect against her hip. He moved her hips into him. God, it was so provocative. This was pure seduction. His hands peeled her shorts and G-string down. She obliged by stepping out of them. He then removed her trainers and socks, spreading her legs.

She was now open and vulnerable to his every whim, and what a whim it was. Naked except for the cuffs and her top over her hands, she would normally have felt self-conscious and scared. Not with Seb. He pushed her back against the wall as his lips travelled down her torso. His tongue circled her belly button, and his hands and fingers massaged her thighs. Then he pushed her hips forward, allowing his lips and tongue to work her. His tongue encircled her clit and started an exquisite journey. Natasha was in ecstasy. She began to writhe against his mouth. His tongue penetrated her, and she ground against him and moaned loudly.

It only served to spur him on, and his middle finger took the place of his tongue, slowly entering her. Her legs were turning to jelly. Nat was climbing, building. He moved his finger in and out of her as he massaged her sex with his palm. All in time with the music, finger fucking her to perfection. She was so high and on the edge of an amazing climax until he removed his finger.

Nat thought she'd go crazy with need. 'Seb, please don't stop.'

His tongue returned, fluttering over her lips, his fingers to her other lips. Her lust reignited, and soon she couldn't take the ecstasy anymore. She finally shattered, falling through bliss. She was floating, her legs shaking. Natasha started to slide down the wall. He snaked his powerful arms around her to support her.

They took a few steps before Seb eased Nat onto his lap as they came to rest on a soft, matted floor. He still hadn't said a word. It was so hot.

She fell back from the stratosphere to George Michael serenading them. George's voice and the music were all sophisticated seduction. 'A moment with you' set the perfect tone for the unfolding erotic moment they were sharing. She would never have believed that the all-business, no-nonsense Dr Mancini was so into kink.

Right now, his kink was the least of her worries. She only wanted to share the erotic haven he'd created. He was teaching Natasha to control her guilty anxieties around sex while releasing her pleasure. Her alters were losing their grip.

A gentle hand lifted her chin, leading his lips to capture hers once more. The kiss deepened as his talented tongue played hers. The erotic keynote rocked her until he pulled back. She was left craving him in the darkness.

Her eyes may have been covered, but every other sense was hypersensitised. Seb's touch set fire to her skin. His hands skated over her body, leaving sparks of lust in their wake before they came to rest on her hips, urging Nat to lift. She instantly knew what he wanted to do. She rose onto her knees as he shuffled under her, between her thighs.

Then very slowly, he positioned her. As he motioned her down, she felt the head of his cock, notch at her entrance. It tantalised both as she slowly took all of him into her heat. His shaft was erect and unyielding. Not being able to resist, he drove upwards, filling her further.

She searched for some friction to move with him. It was difficult with her hands tied, 'I can't move for you..My hands like this make it difficult.'

Continuing to be her silent guide on this exquisite journey, he sat up to wrap his sculpted arms around her. She sensed his smile as his lips kissed her throat. He reached around to unclip her hands, taking them firmly in each of his and pulling them to the front. Holding his hands helped Nat balance, but his firm grip also made sure she had no chance of breaking free and removing her blindfold.

She didn't care. Nat needed him now, so she started to move, riding him. He thrust his hips up harder as they moved in perfect sync, faster and faster. George and Madonna were on a loop, and Nat was building again. Higher and higher, on a loop too, a harmonious, wonderous one. He became more and more urgent, and she rode him harder.

Seb was deep, the sensations she was riding into him off his scale. He pumped harder, faster, chasing his new ultimate end. For the first time since the seduction began, she heard him. Seb huskily shouted her name as he exploded. It was a sensual trigger, and she flew head-long into an eruption of desire.

Nat collapsed on his chest as they both steadied. George and Madonna had finished. A calming silence descended over them. She took off her blindfold and found herself blinking into his dark eyes.

'Hello,' he whispered.

She made out his smiling face in the muted light.

'You're so beautiful and brave.' He caressed her face. He was in awe. She'd taken this first mild kink in her stride. Could this woman take all of what he really was and return it with interest? Maybe history wouldn't repeat itself.

# TWENTY-SEVEN

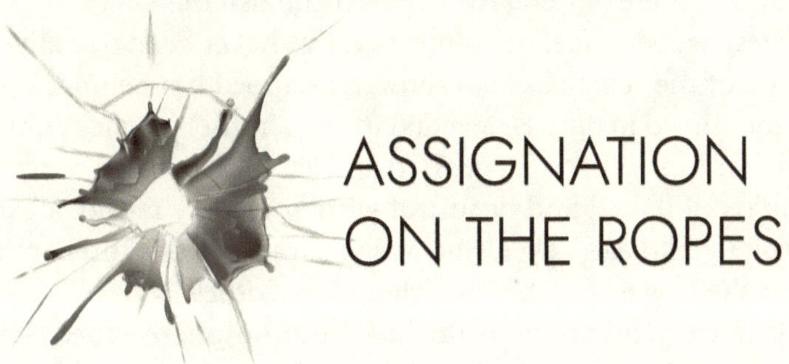

## ASSIGNATION ON THE ROPES

'What you do to me, Sebastian Mancini.' No other words could do justice to the emotions surging through her. Maybe actions would. Stretched out over him, skin to skin and still joined, Nat's eyes captured his. She threaded her fingers through his hair. Then slid her hands to hold his face before stealing his lips in an unhurried, tender explosion of adoration. As she drew back, she gently nibbled on his bottom lip, drawing it out between her teeth before releasing it.

When Natasha returned to the here and now, she realised they were definitely in a gym. It was dully lit by dozens of candles. There was a boxing ring with two chairs and a table with candles. She rolled off him and sat up, taking in the fairyland vision. 'Did you do all this?'

They stood, and with his chest against her back, he slipped his hands around her waist to nuzzle her ear. 'Yes, just for you.'

'Wow.' She couldn't believe it. It was magical, even for a gym. Odd setting that it was, she wasn't complaining.

'Are you hungry?'

'Yes.'

'Let's get dressed. The night and this weekend are just beginning.'

Before she could move, he hugged her almost too tight. His breath warmed her ear. 'I just can't keep my hands off you.' He caught her earlobe in his teeth and gently tugged. Natasha nearly collapsed as a charge buried itself deep within her core.

'Don't apologise. You make me feel ...' Nat sighed and struggled for the right words. 'You're helping me discover the real me.'

Seb's chest ached. 'I feel the same way. I've never been this alive.' Letting a little of the real Sebastian show, he slapped her behind. Yes, the desires she stirred in him. He needed to keep himself in check until he could tell her more. 'Let's get dressed and eat. Before I lose control because you're all naked and beautiful with your sexy tattoo, all so close. We won't get to eat – ever.' She wasn't sure if it was a threat or a challenge, so she moved quickly to pick up her clothes.

With distance between them, the intense atmosphere ebbed. Seb stooped to pick up his smartphone. With a swipe and a series of taps, Joan Armatrading's 'Love and affection' softly filled the room. The lyrics had always captivated Nat. More so now, with Seb's body flexing in the candlelight as he dressed.

Seb stepped onto the ring's side, grabbing the ropes. He offered Nat his hand. As he watched her walk towards him, long and toned, with skin aglow from fantastic sex. 'Please, Natasha, will you join me.' She moved to slip between the ropes he'd pulled open. He couldn't resist smacking her butt as she slid through, his control usurped by yearning.

Startling her, she jumped but smiled. 'You seem to like doing that.'

He rode his luck. 'You seem to like it as well.'

As he bent to slide through to her, she returned the favour, following the slap with a squeeze. 'Two can play that game, you know.'

'I know, it takes two to tango.' He smirked and thought maybe she was up for more of his type of kink.

'With you, always.'

At her words, his heart skidded. He quickly reviewed his words. No, he hadn't said out loud what he was thinking. Yet she seemed to confirm it with a dangerous smile. Seb shook his head, amused with her candour and his growing ... whatever this feeling was. He pulled back a chair. 'Please sit.'

As she made herself comfortable, he deposited a napkin on her lap and poured some Moët for them. Then he lifted the huge silver dome off the large platter gracing the centre of the table. 'Ta-dah!' He couldn't hide his pride. A sumptuous tapas tasting platter for two was revealed. There were prawns, stuffed squid, fried Italian sausage, roasted artichokes and aubergines, accompanied by various dips.

Seb was rewarded as Nat's glorious smile met her eyes. Her silken, beaming face was flawless, perfect for candlelight. They sat barefoot in their gym gear in the romantic sanctuary created by one for two.

The initial darkness and alarm gave way to a small, fleeting voice. *There's a catch. You don't deserve this.*

Grazing her cheek with the back of his fingers, Seb's warmth evaporated Goldy's negative presence. 'Hey, come back to me. Don't give in to her.'

And she was gone. Tonight, Goldilocks was no more than scattering vapours. Natasha sighed. 'How did you—?'

'Lucky guess. You seemed momentarily sidetracked. Your face dropped with worry.' When she looked away, he knew she didn't want to show her vulnerabilities. Something shifted within him. He reached out and gently tucked a stray strand of golden, sex-mushed hair behind her ear. 'It's okay. Let me see the real you. I like that Natasha, too.'

Her voice was small and breathy. 'Sebastian, I'm blown away by all of this. That you'd do this for someone like me.'

'Natasha.' He was dumbfounded she didn't understand. 'It's *because* you're the someone that you are.'

Before her feelings became too honest, she diverted the conversation. 'Why a gym?'

'I wanted to give you a night of pleasure that didn't set off any of your alter egos. I figured a gym was far removed from any place that could churn up bad memories for you. The only risk that worried me about the seduction was the silence and darkness. I hoped you'd be able to enjoy some real pleasure with the candles, the music, and if I made sure you were never alone.'

'Oh.' She was stunned at his thoughtfulness. 'You certainly know how to show a fucked-up girl a fucking good time.'

'I'm shocked, *shocked*, I say, at your trashy mouth. By the way, I prefer you just fucked. By me, and only me.'

'Off to a good start then, aren't you?'

'You seem to think you're not the kind of girl who could be swept off your feet, so I thought I'd take that as a romantic challenge. Have I succeeded?'

'Given I've never experienced anything like this before, I don't think I should be in any haste to comment. Ask me after we eat.' She brushed her fingers against his cheek. 'If we make it.'

It was his turn for his breath to hitch. Nat moved to take off the velcro cuffs. He growled, 'Leave them on.'

'But I don't want to get them dirty.'

'Oh, we'll get them dirty, but not how you think.' He rolled his tongue across his top lip, his mouth barely open.

Her mouth went dry.

'We really should get started on the food.' Seb shuffled his chair under the table, close enough for his knee to touch hers.

'What do you recommend?'

'I'd recommend the stuffed squid. I baked it myself.'

'Aha, you can cook. I suspected as much after seeing you handle that knife on the mushrooms the other night.'

He reached for her chin, gently tilting her head up to him. 'I have many talents I'd like to share with you.' He kissed her, long and easy this time.

'You're full of surprises. Who showed you?'

He couldn't suppress the pleasure in his voice as he thought about the power and control the blade gave him. 'My dad. To use a knife properly is a real skill.' His eyes sparkled. He was taken somewhere else for a second. 'To have a well-balanced blade in my hand and to control it so precisely is an art. At times, I find using them and the rhythm of sharpening them helps settle me.'

A little ashamed of his admission, he quickly returned to Nat. 'Learning the joys of cooking, that's all my mum's doing. She knew she was dying of cancer, so before she passed away, she taught me. Her way of making sure I could look after myself. As it turned out, she was right. I had a lot of growing up to do, and not just because she'd passed. The squid's Mum's recipe.' He smiled, but Nat could see the sadness in his eyes.

'Sebastian, I'm sorry. I didn't mean to—'

'No, no, it's okay, really.' He shook his head. 'I have good memories of her. Of course it's sad she's not here, but some of the best times we shared were in the kitchen, her teaching me to cook.' Natasha sensed that the sadness in his eyes was not all because of his mum. His heart carried an even more deep-seated sorrow.

In an instant, he cleared his mind of the forlorn thoughts that shouldn't be part of his memory of his mum. 'Try the squid. I wanted to share it with you. It's my speciality. I only cook it for very special occasions.' He offered her a piece on his fork. 'Try it.'

She took it in her mouth, and the flavours flooded her taste buds. She raised her glass. 'As ever, Dr Mancini, perfect.'

He smiled like a little boy who'd been let loose in a candy shop. 'Wait until you taste the Italian sausage. It's my dad's speciality. He makes it from scratch.' A proud smile graced his face. Seeing him fully relax delighted her.

Everything was so fresh and tasty. He was a good cook. They ate, chatted and laughed while beautiful music surrounded them in their very own boxing ring wonderland.

'Try the guacamole. I made it too.' He picked up a prawn, covering it in a large dollop, and then raised it to her mouth. She opened her mouth and closed her eyes. He proceeded to smear the guacamole along her cheek. She gasped, with her eyes shooting open.

'Where are my manners?' He smiled, sucked the dip from her cheek and continued kissing along her jaw until he reached the corner of her mouth. 'Mmm, that tasted almost as good as you did a little while ago.'

Her mouth dropped open. Taking advantage of her surprise, Seb placed the prawn on her tongue.

She bit it off at the tail and savoured it, once again captivated by his bottomless brown eyes. 'That does taste good.'

'Another?' he asked, smirking.

'No.' She grabbed his hand. 'If we're minding our manners.' Inspired by a confidence that had eluded her for a long time, Nat picked up a prawn and dipped it in guacamole.

With eyes hooded with lust, Seb opened his mouth and very deliberately ran his tongue across his lower lip.

She dabbed a blob of guacamole on each side of his lips. 'Not so fast, Mancini.' Her voice was laced with excitement. 'I have some tasting of my own to experience.' She licked up from his chin, his stubble tickling her until she reached the guacamole. She sucked it from the corner of his mouth. Reaching his lips, she allowed his tongue to tangle with hers before moving to address the spicy avocado still left on his face. Pulling away, she ran the prawn across his lips, where he caught it in his teeth and took it into his mouth.

After he devoured it, he placed his hand on the nape of her neck, bringing her lips to his, whispering, 'You. Are. Heaven.'

Amazed that his words could ignite such a sensual passion in her, her belief she could take chances with him and forget her alters grew.

Murmuring seductively, she placed her hand on his growing erection, 'Will you let me taste another very intimate speciality of yours?'

'Yesss. Just to be clear, never ask permission to taste it again.' His voice was low and full of longing.

Before he shuffled his chair out, she squeezed him gently, running her fingers along his shaft, feeling it harden through the material of his shorts. 'Please, can you take your shirt and these off?'

Dreamily, he took off his shirt and lifted his hips to take his shorts off. Nat dipped her finger, leaving a generous dollop of guacamole coating it. Dabbing it down his body, from between his pecs to his navel, Nat grabbed his hand, taking his index finger to dip it in the spicy avocado, bringing it to her lips. Her eyes met his sensual gaze, electricity crackling between them. She opened her mouth and sucked.

His eyes widened as he groaned when her tongue whirled around his finger. Seb's cock was becoming impossibly hard. Maybe he didn't need to be so gentle or controlled with this one. 'Ohhh, Nat.' He gasped as she withdrew his finger slowly from her mouth. He was filled with anticipation that her tongue would now work its magic on his thickening cock, which was about to burst with desire.

Dropping to her knees, she followed the trail of the dip up his body, licking and sucking her way to meet his lips once more.

The things he wanted to do to her. 'You are heaven and more.' His moan vibrated through her as she claimed his mouth again.

Moving to him, she sheathed her teeth, surrounded him with her mouth and sucked. Taking more of him in and then gently and slowly pulling her lips up him, she sucked tightly until she reached the velvet head of his long, magnificent cock.

Huskily he said, 'I love the way you let me fuck your mouth.' Sliding his hands into her hair, Seb gently guided her mouth over him again. It was so erotic for her to feel him reacting like this. With no guilt surfacing, she had absolute power.

Watching and feeling her take him all the way to his hilt had him lost to her. When he hit the back of her throat in a flurry of thrusts, she made him her slave. Seb wanted to serve and satisfy her every whim.

Losing some control, he pulled her up to stand with him. 'Will you let me try something with you ... with us?' His voice was heated velvet.

It made her want him more. 'Yes.'

'Follow me.' He led her to one of the corners of the ring.

Gently turning her around, he pushed her back against the corner padding, his body hard against her. He divested her of her shorts, then her sports top, expertly flicking the inbuilt bra up and over her breasts before throwing her clothes to where his had landed.

She couldn't help but notice his wild eyes. 'Stand up on the bottom ropes, a foot on each side of the corner post. Grip the padding between your butt and arms.'

Doing as she was told, Seb grabbed her arms, pulling them behind her and around the corner padding. His eyes were asking if she was sure. She nodded, and he felt the control of his kink side fracture.

He wanted to perform this act with her. She was bringing him out, as he hoped he was doing to her. Seb clipped the cuffs together behind her back. Her arms were over the top of all of the ring's four ropes but secured below the taught rope pulling back to the anchoring pole for the corner post.

'You're irresistible.' His voice was heavy with emotion. He kissed her belly button tenderly. His talented finger entered and slowly tantalised her, sending an erogenous wave through her.

The ropes began to rock in time to his ministrations. The sensation urged Nat to cream for him. Seb's touch and timing were exquisite. The familiar electric zing pulsed between them as his magic lips coaxed her nipples to harden. She was building. He slowly withdrew his finger, sparking an intense longing in her.

With her feet on the bottom ropes, they were eye to eye. The scent of sex, cologne and Seb was intoxicating, overwhelming any thoughts of guilty alters. Again, with heated velvet, he mouthed, 'Your body is glorious. My tongue wants to run wild over your skin, just to see it glow and shimmer.' He nipped, licked and sucked her breasts as her core seared.

Placing his feet on the bottom ropes on either side of hers, Seb pulled his body up. 'Take charge of your pleasure. The Slut and Goldilocks will stay away.' Wild with desire, he pushed up while leaning in, and he found his goal, spearing into her.

Seb thrust again, rebounding in and out of her. The elasticity of the ropes providing more force, more intensity and more pleasure than usual. She was immediately on a climb.

Seeing her skin bloom, Seb understood, she was one among no equals. Sharing this journey willingly with him, trusting him with her pleasure. It was exquisite. Keeping a slow rhythm, Seb rocked his hips up, in and back, making Nat want to call his name. Not because of some unspoken law of fucking. She wanted to because she was scaling new heights with this remarkable man. Seb kept thrusting, swaying and bouncing in ecstatic sync with her.

He let himself go, celebrating by driving into her deeper and deeper. She pulsed around him as he found intense release. She couldn't take any more. After kissing the stars, she came cascading down, over and over. They stayed like that, waiting for their emotions to ebb, enjoying the swaying afterglow.

Seb's feather-light lips on her shoulder brought her back. He hugged her once more before slowly pulling out and leaning over to unclip her. Blissfully spent, they sank to the floor to recover. When they finally resurfaced, the candles were burning low.

Natasha nuzzled his chest, not knowing but sensing he was unlocking a more intimate place in her soul while managing to warm her cold, shattered heart. She hoped he wouldn't break it further if the skinny trust beginning to grow within her was misplaced.

Seb whispered, 'Are you ready for another adventure?'

'I don't think I can move.' Nat blinked up at him.

He squeezed her tighter. 'Get dressed, grab your bag. I'll drive us to the *Brindisi*.'

Nat angled her head.

'She's my motor launch. We'll hang out on her for the rest of the weekend.' He was on the move, tidying up, blowing out candles and dressing, leaving them in the dull light of a distant fluoro.

She summoned the energy to dress, and once she'd found her bag, Seb set the alarm. Soon she was being whisked through the streets of Fremantle to begin another adventure with Dr Sebastian, tall, dark and delicious, Mancini, her very own Mr TDD. One thing was for certain: she was never going to be able to look at a boxing ring in quite the same way again.

# TWENTY-EIGHT

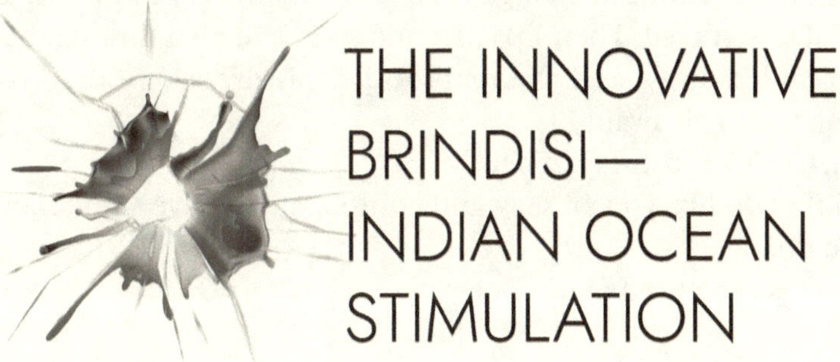

## THE INNOVATIVE BRINDISI—INDIAN OCEAN STIMULATION

The soft Sunday sunrise gently tugged at her eyelids, urging Nat to wake and believe she wasn't dreaming. They slumbered in the luxuriously appointed master cabin of the *Brindisi*. Nat had a naked Adonis wrapped around her in a bed bigger and softer than hers at home. The richly decorated master cabin was all cream and wood, with fine light blue and white Egyptian cotton bed linen. It belied the couple were on a boat.

She wasn't sure what to expect when Seb invited her for a weekend on his cruiser. Certainly nothing like this. The large ensuite made her feel like she was staying at a lavish hotel.

They'd spent a leisurely Saturday slowly cruising around Rottnest Island. The small, sandy islet eighteen kilometres off the coast was a beautiful getaway. It was every bit the fantastic weekend Seb had promised. He had navigated the fifty-foot white and navy-blue hulled Fairline Targa GT through rocky reefs and sandbars, mooring the boat whenever and wherever they liked. The hot afternoon sun found them swimming naked in the pristine waters off a desolate end of Porpoise Bay. The scenery, Seb's spontaneity and the scent of the fresh salty ocean air had Nat feeling free. She slid back into sleep.

Eventually, she was pulled from the depths of a sated slumber by the gentle tantalising brush of stubble on her skin as Seb trailed tender kisses along her spine.

'Good morning, Ms Perry.' His voice and lips caused a sensual shiver to flow through her.

While the atmosphere around the motor yacht was peaceful and calm, it was about to change on board. Nat turned to him as an emotional tide stirred. Their lips met and sparks tingled through her.

Seb pulled away, and she realised he was dressed. 'Come on, sleepyhead, brunch awaits.'

'Oh. Can't we just stay in bed?'

'While I do like you all sexy and compliant, we have some more sailing to do.'

'Don't get too used to it.'

'What?'

'Compliant.'

'Not going to happen. I like you feisty.'

'You sure you can handle that?'

'I don't know, but I'm going to love finding out.' He gave her a killer look that made her smile. Before she could give him a smart reply, he was gone, leaving her languidly spread across his bed.

When Nat met him up on deck, the Targa top of the *Brindisi* was open, the sun warming the deck. The salty ocean breeze caught her hair, gently rolling it off her face. Seb was naked from the waist up, all temptation and tone, while Nat wore a bikini under a long, flowing cotton beach shirt.

The galley on the boat was something to behold. He had prepared a beautiful spread of tropical fruit, yoghurt, croissants and fresh juice. As she moved past him to sit, he grabbed her by the hips, pulling her onto his lap. 'Tell me about your tattoo?'

Her bikini looked like it was painted onto her curvy, toned body. He glimpsed it through her translucent beach shirt. Clearly, the outfit had his approval.

'There's not much to tell.'

'How about you start with what it means?'

'It's a three-pointed Celtic knot interlocked with a heart. Depending on who you talk to, there are many meanings given to Celtic knots.'

'What's it mean to you?'

'It's not a traditional design, because of the heart. But I chose it to remind me that my spirit is eternal and love will constantly be interwoven with my life. I just have to find it through all the twists and turns.'

'Wow, really?' His eyebrows rose.

'Yes, with everything I've struggled through, I have to believe that if I keep persisting, good will come to me.'

Seb's fingers were on her tattoo, his voice husky. 'I get what you're saying.' He traced his index finger over the interlocking twists of ink, sending thrills radiating through her. He had to tell her. 'I have … you know, I should tell …'

She pinned him with her piercing blue eyes.

Seb baulked. He couldn't tell her his secrets. Not yet. She'd run. 'How about we finish eating, haul anchor, cruise around and see if we can find some dolphins.'

Nat's eyes narrowed. She knew he hadn't said what he'd been thinking, but she was in too good a mood to ask, so she said, 'Sounds perfect.'

After they cleared away their brunch Seb stepped away to the cockpit. The powerful hum of the *Brindisi's* engines signalled they were on their way again. The motor launch cut effortlessly through the waves, as she picked up speed, they enjoyed a rhythmic ride.

Seb called to Natasha, 'Come and steer her!'

Sitting between his legs on the cockpit chair, Nat took the wheel. Seb's chest was pressed against her back, his arms cocooned around her. He revelled in having her close. He loved the scent of her hair, the feel of her smooth, perfectly tanned skin and her taste. During the weekend, he'd discovered a greater depth of warmth, strength and humour in her. He was captivated, and then there was her as-ever witty and challenging mouth.

He instructed Nat on how to steer the *Brindisi*. As they reached open waters, he released the throttle a little more. It added intensity to the force of the boat hitting the waves. Soon Seb's fingers were in her hair, moving it from her shoulder. His keen lips were on her throat. With her hands gripping the wheel to stay on course, she was defenceless to his advances. Not that she wanted to stop him.

Seb pushed his hands up under her cotton shirt and, achingly slowly, pulled her bikini top ties undone. It fell away as his fingers found her breasts. She automatically sat up straighter, pushing her breasts into his warm hands. Skin to skin once more. His teeth nipped their way up to her earlobe, which he gently tugged. 'Has anyone ever told you that you're incredible?'

She shook her head, dropping it to look down. It was too much for her. Every muscle below her waist clenched as he worked her nipples.

'Seb, you're going to make me crash this boat if you keep—' Her words were trapped by sensation as his fingers skated down her body and slipped under her bikini to gently stroke her. She became hopelessly wet. He whispered breathlessly into her ear, 'Turn around and face me. You can still drive.'

'Drive what?'

'You'll see.' He smiled against her ear. He took the wheel as she slid off. He stood to shimmy out of his boardies, sat back down and steered the *Brindisi* out to deeper water. His darkening eyes flitted from the horizon to her and then lower to his stiffening cock.

She understood. 'Shall I climb on board, skipper?'

His carnal intent was reflected in her eyes. She took down her bikini bottom slowly and slunk out of her oversized shirt. As he watched her, his cock thickened. Now naked, she stepped up on the skipper's chair, straddling his legs. They faced each other as she slowly lowered herself over him. Nat's tenderness from their previous dalliances only made their union more intense. She took him slow – agonisingly slow, blissful inch by each slow, agonisingly blissful inch.

Seeing his cock disappear entirely into her while she gripped and pulsed around him had Seb craving she would never stop wanting him. He could be sure he'd never stop wanting her. When she rested her legs on his thighs, she understood what he had in mind.

As the *Brindisi* cut her way to the open sea, the rhythm of her crashing through the waves provided the perfect rhythm for their lovemaking. Nat was propelled up and down on Seb. Each time the *Brindisi* smashed into a wave, Seb rammed into her, exquisitely hitting her very end. His pounding into her was punishingly sensual, erotic poetry. Her tightness and depth had him climbing. She kissed him but was quickly bucked off his lips by the force of the leaping boat. Wrapping herself around him, resting her hands on his shoulder blades, she nuzzled into his neck, breathing in his heady scent.

He had his left hand on the wheel. His right arm snaked around and twisted a thick length of her hair around his hand, pulling Nat's head backwards and exposing her throat to his lips. It was just at the point of being painful, but strangely, it turned her on.

Seb fought to control the animal within. He tried taming it by sucking and kissing her throat and then along the sensitive line of her jaw, from her earlobe to her full, velvety lips.

He released her hair and opened the throttle up even more. His kink edged its way into his words. 'Let's explore undiscovered extremes and enjoy untapped pleasures together. No guilt, no sin. Keep them away.' Their ride became faster, and the impact even more fiercely erotic.

The ramming was causing their sexual pleasure to soar. Natasha was out of her mind with need. The fierceness of this brutal side of Seb had her grip him tighter, want him more, lose control like she'd never wanted to do before. 'What are you turning me on to?'

His thrusts became more fervent. He dipped his head, his right hand firmly pressing at her back to suck, taste and nip his way across her perfectly formed breasts. He wanted desperately to release his devious appetite, to bite and watch her skin bloom and blush. The pinpricks of red would brand her as his. He kept at her breasts as need and desire crashed over him. She moaned and pushed her breast to him to suckle on.

Seb lost himself in a rush to share the ecstasy with her. Later he'd feel guilty and ask her forgiveness. But for now, when they were like this, when brutal desire possessed them, and she seemed to like him possessing her, it was a need they could only quench with each other.

The sharp shards of pain drove her higher, adding to the sensuality of their union. It felt right. The spikey sensual pain broke her guilt trip. His eyes told her it wasn't violence for her submission. It wasn't what Wolf and her clients' eyes showed. With Seb, she saw uncontrolled adoration. A need only satisfied when they shared their dark inner tendencies and gave into the power that this new freedom released.

'Come with me now, Natasha.' The motor launch was still thrusting her up and down on his cock. He nipped her nipple, soothing the sensual sting with his tongue.

They let go of all the sexually intense pleasure they'd built. Sebastian shouted something unintelligible as he shuddered and came. Nat gripped him harder and hung on, before she screamed as her orgasm rumbled through her. 'Oh, fuck, Se ... bas ... tian.'

# TWENTY-NINE

## SEXTING THE NIGHT AWAY

Easing the throttle off in perfect sync with their ebbing passion, Seb eventually cut the engines. Other than the lapping of the waves on the hull, they were enshrouded in a silent afterglow of tangled, sated limbs. With her cheek resting against his soft chest hair, she could feel, as well as hear, his resonant voice. 'Ms Perry, that gives new meaning to, *come on my boat*. Fuck! That was so good.'

'Now who has a trashy mouth?'

'You're rubbing off on me.'

'How many other women have you lured onto your launch ... ooh!' She was pleasurably sore as she pulled off him, 'and made love to in such a torrid way? I thought men couldn't multitask?'

Seb saw through her. 'Are you jealous?' A slow, dreamy smile graced his face.

'I'm not sure what this is. Kind of ... maybe I am jealous—'

'Of nothing. Other than family, you're the only woman who's ever been on the *Brindisi* with me, and certainly you're the only woman to ever fuck my brains out on her.'

He reached for her. 'No need to be worried about any women I've been with. You're making me forget all but you. And you have no idea how good that is.'

'Good recovery.' Staying true to her MO, she couldn't take his words at face value. She overthought it. What had happened with a woman or women in his past? Why was he so keen to forget?

Her trepidation was brushed away as quickly as he brushed an errant strand of her unruly, just-fucked beach hair aside and said, 'Let's get tidied up. There's something we should talk about.'

Maybe he would tell her about what he was happy to forget.

As she stood before him, he was dismayed that he'd marked and bruised her breasts. A pang of regret lanced him. 'Natasha, I'm so sorry. I've hurt you. You're bruised. I can be, I mean, I … lose control, and with you, I'm in real danger.'

After a pause, he said, 'Is it okay, what we're doing?' He was hoarse. 'Sometimes I can't hold back with what I want to do with you. We've only scratched the surface of what I could do.' He needed to start the groundwork. 'I don't want to do something we can never come back from.' He didn't know how to deal with the emotions she stirred, but he knew he couldn't tell her all his secrets now.

'Stop, Seb.' Natasha was stunned. The atmosphere between them had become far too serious. She wouldn't hear any more. 'I'm fine.' Nat pointed at her breasts. 'Don't take on the guilt you think I have over these, please. I'm not doing anything I haven't wanted to do.'

Her eyes were almost as blue as the Indian Ocean surrounding the *Brindisi*. Nat skimmed her hands along either side of his jaw so he had to look at her, 'Compared to what I've been through, it's only ever beautiful with you. I don't feel cheap or dirty.' She put him out of his misery by giving him a long, languid kiss. 'You're teaching me to enjoy my pleasure for *me*, no sin, no guilt and no regrets, so there's no need for you to have any regrets either.'

His heart leapt while his eyes misted. 'Natasha—' Seb saw she didn't fully understand. She thought she was causing him pain. He was afraid it would be the other way around. If not now from his uncontrolled lust, it could very well be in the future when his family became part of their lives. Needing to stop the dark thoughts they were both having, he kissed them into oblivion.

The early afternoon sun found them relaxed on the *Brindisi's* sun lounge. The boat, gently bobbing to and fro on the water, wasn't the only thing becalmed. Seb sat with his head propped back on the luxurious lounge as Nat rested her head in his lap, her body stretched out along the lounge. His arms were spread along the top, soaking up the sun. That was until he started shuffling around behind her to grab his smartphone.

'Can I take a photo?'

'I guess so.' She sat up.

'I promise I'll send it to you.'

He gave her a swift kiss, pulling her to him, wrapping his arms around her to rest his chin on her left shoulder as he took a selfie. Seb looked at it and happily showed Nat the result. Feeling totally relaxed, Nat pulled back and laughed, her smile wide and carefree. He took another photo of only her.

Now was the time. As Seb returned his phone to his pocket, he murmured, 'I need to tell you—' His phone started ringing. Before looking at the screen, he said, 'I'll let this go to voicemail.' Then he glanced at the screen, and his face fell.

'Hi, Dad. Yes, I'm still out.'

Listening intently, Seb stood. His tone became serious. 'Certainly, as soon as I can.' He hung up and sighed. 'Sorry, I have to get to an emergency family business meeting. This afternoon is the only time we can all get together. Will it be okay if we go back a little earlier? Sorry.'

'We better get going then.'

Seb's heart swelled. A simple explanation was all she needed, he thought, uncomplicated, no argument. She was so different from the previous women in his life, especially one in particular. Then he wondered if his predilection in the bedroom had caused that mistake. Even with all her baggage, for him, Natasha Perry was ... amazing and brave. He whispered against her lips. 'You're becoming very special to me. You know that.'

Nat couldn't grasp why.

His lips claimed her mouth and had her toes curl. When he drew back, his eyes were filled with longing as he smiled down at her. 'Why don't you settle down on the lounge and enjoy the sun while I skipper us home.' He sauntered over to the cockpit chair, which now seemed very multifunctional indeed. He gunned the engines to speed off towards Freo.

Both had a feeling of impending loneliness as they walked hand in hand to his car. Nat sighed, not understanding how this could happen so quickly, while Seb yearned for more. He hugged her one last time, lingering, noting how perfectly they fitted together.

He was under her skin. Then she said, 'Dr Mancini, the answer to your question is ... yes.'

He slanted his head. 'Sorry, did I miss something?'

'It's the answer to the question you asked way back on Friday night.' She gave him a mischievous grin. 'The answer to sweeping me off my usually very unromantic feet.' She stretched up and kissed the corner of his mouth, hovering as his lips smiled under hers. 'Very much so.'

Seb relaxed, releasing the long breath that had caught in his throat. He swept her up and spun her around.

'Seb!' she squealed with delight as he set her down

He held her tight. 'Just the beginning, my lovely lady.'

The powerful growl of the Maserati accompanied their reverential silence as they drove off. He held her hand, wanting to have the feel of her with him for as long as possible. It was as if the wondrous world they had been sharing had imploded, crushed by the weight of their roles and responsibilities in the real world.

He parked the car outside her apartment. Before she could leave, he gave her a scorching, unchaste kiss. 'Can I drop by later?'

'I'd like that, but I'm going to visit Sage, so it might be best if you call first.'

'Until then.' Seb leaned over and gave her a chaste kiss. She wanted the other kind. Running her fingers through his hair, she pulled him to her, coercing and receiving a more sensual, sizzling kiss. 'Lord!' Seb broke away first to take a breath.

She winked at him, opening the car door. 'Just something to remember me by.' As her words settled, he grabbed her hand, running his thumb over her knuckles. 'I don't believe I'm in any danger of forgetting. There is one significant part of my body that will be remembering you intimately.'

She laughed. 'Mmm, haven't we been here before?'

He left her smiling and waving. He couldn't quite believe the emptiness filling him as the distance between them grew. For the first time in years, he wanted to blow off a business meeting.

Giving Sage the Little Golden Book version of her blossoming relationship, Natasha's joy was tempered by noticing Sage's telling complexion. The deathly white pallor of cancer was already taking hold. They talked, reminisced and laughed. As Nat was leaving, Sage squeezed her hand. 'Go have more of the fun you're having with Dr

Mancini.' Then she winked. 'And I don't mean the sanitised kind you've described to me.'

On arriving home, Nat was, as Chelsea would say, shag tired. She smiled to herself. It was so true. All the sun, sea and sex had clearly affected her. She settled down on her couch, which was suddenly not so uncomfortable. Hours later her phone rang, making her heart jump.

'Hey.' He sounded distant.

'Hey, Mancini. What's happening?'

With a sad sigh, he said. 'I'm not going to make it back to you tonight.'

'Is everything all right?'

'No, not really. It will take some time over the coming days to return things to where we need them to be to refinance this deal.'

'It's okay. It's not like you need to check in with me.' She was glad he had.

'But what about my incurable disease?'

'What disease is that?'

'My growing addiction to you.'

'Hasn't this weekend cured you?'

'No, if anything, it's made it worse. I need to find myself a good pharmacist to suggest something for it. Do you know any?' She heard his smile.

'Text me later when you're going to bed. No matter the time, I'll see if I can suggest something to give you relief.'

'Ah, Ms Perry, yet again, you keep me wanting more.'

Her voice softened. 'That's not so bad, I hope.'

His chest ached as his voice thickened. 'Never. I like it when you're bad with me.' Raised voices in the background had him hurry. 'I'm sorry, I have to go.' His voice became a whisper, 'Otherwise, there's no telling where this conversation could lead. And I'd have to play hooky.' He winced. Why was he acting like some awkward schoolboy? What was she doing to him? He was never frivolous, especially around Mancini Enterprises. The family business was sacrosanct. After what happened, what he'd done, the mistake he'd made, it had to be this way. No one would slip under his guard again. Not like Sofia.

Her breathy voice brought him back. 'I'm blowing you a kiss. Hope that holds you. No playing hooky. Until later, then?' She cringed, feeling embarrassed by her cheesiness.

'Justtt.'

She fell into bed with his voice still vibrating through her. It took her some time to settle down. Not because of her alters, but because her body was lusting in places the weekend had awakened. She eventually drifted off.

Around twelve-thirty, she was woken by the chime of her phone. A rush of excitement ran through her.

> S: Hi Honey, I'm home. I still have my symptoms ... bad

A sizzling night of sexting unfolded. They'd become so connected that with only sensual words, the memory and pretence of the other's touch, Nat climaxed, and Seb found an incredible release. Unbeknown to Nat, she gave him more than relief from his family's angst. She was softening his hard heart by beginning to claim it as hers.

The one thing Nat did know was that Seb was proving to be more than a game-changer. He was protecting her in a bubble of safety. Because bubbles were so delicate and easily burst, she left her curtains open the required sliver and had her phone ready. She drifted off listening to the Foo Fighters' 'Resolve', because that's what she hoped she was showing her alters.

# THIRTY

## SO CLOSE AND YET TOO FAR

By Wednesday, Natasha hadn't seen Seb since he'd left her outside her apartment on Sunday. Apart from their hot sexting on Sunday night, she'd only had a few apologising texts and one brief call. The family business issues were still proving to be time-consuming. Natasha tried not to be too hard on him. He also had to keep up with his work at the hospital and the foundation. The weekend's intimacy and excitement became a dim memory, easily smothered by Natasha's darkening thoughts.

The trust she'd granted him was trickling away with each hour, like water leaking through a crack in a drainpipe, faster and faster, more and more. All the while the weight of vulnerable feelings of worthlessness grew, faster and faster, more and more. On Tuesday night, Goldilocks had more than a little sanctimonious chuckle, then tore at her very being. Natasha tried to push back, but the pressure intensified within her. Trickle, trickle, ooze and surge. So much for thinking she was conquering her alters – and so much for his incurable disease.

By midday Wednesday there were no more emails or texts. Nat's new-found self-reliance was floundering. She started to drown in the growing flood of dangerous thoughts. Coward. He could have told her face to face if he wanted out, not ignored her. His ghosting of her did more than hurt, it devastated.

At lunch, The Slut gave up some unwanted wisdom. *If you had let me out to play and score, you would've had him more.*

Goldilocks chipped in with her own piqued rhyme. It was one of her solid gold hits. *Mirror, mirror, read the writing on the wall. He was the best chameleon of all. Too good to be true, too good for you.*

Natasha barrelled onto the onc/haem ward after lunch. The good news was she was angry, not cowering in a corner with her crowded mind. It may have been quiet on the ward, but Nat was in a mind-fuck tempest. Her irritation rose further when she couldn't find a couple of patients' med charts. The last place left for her to check was the doctor's office. She barged in, deep in her head-trip storm, only to find the source of all her angst. He hung up the phone as their eyes met.

Her heart spun. She wouldn't be distracted by any infatuation with Mr TDD's looks, not in this temper. She immediately turned and stormed out.

'Hey, Nat, come back.'

She heard footsteps behind her in the corridor. Then he was by her side, grabbing her arm. Nat shot him a glacial stare, a facade to stave off the intense attraction that took root and dared to thrive in his warmth. Wrenching her arm away, 'No, Dr Mancini. Just stop.' She hissed at him. 'Clearly, you've got all you need from me.'

'What the ...?' Even in her mood, she could hear the exasperation in his voice. She kept walking, steaming down the ward corridor. He grabbed Nat and shoved her through the ward's storeroom door, pushing her up against the door as it closed. His hands were on her arms, pushing them up over her head. He had her pinned against the back of the door. There was no escape, especially from his angry, heated eyes. They glowered at each other, chests heaving, each daring the other to bite so they could release some of the tension. 'Why would you say that?'

'How about not being able to keep your hands off me to just ...' She swallowed and rasped, 'Nothing, *zilch*, *niente*. What am I supposed to think?'

'That I've been swamped and completely honest with you.' He clenched his teeth. His jawline pulsed. 'I'm only seeing some of my patients for the first time today.'

'Sure.' She dared him. 'You had time to think about it and realised you'd taken everything you wanted from me.'

Seb's groan was laced with fiery attraction. 'Goddamn it, Natasha. Please don't do this.' He shook his head.

An odd thrill ran through her, a sad excitement at knowing she'd got a rise out of him. Was that all she wanted, his attention? Was she that needy? No, she'd just been let down too many times.

'Nat?' He jolted her back to reality. 'What are you thinking?'

'That you're through with fucking me.'

'What? No. Christ. I. Have. Been. Busy.' The angry sexual tension between them began to free itself from the restraints of rationality. Once more they pushed each other's dark and sensual boundaries.

'Get it over with then. Tell me.'

'Don't push me, Natasha—'

'Or what?'

'I won't be able to stop—'

'What?'

'Stop!' He took a rasping breath. His eyes were molten black. 'I won't be able to stop myself from showing you.' He moved in closer. 'I've been missing your ...' His lips met hers as their tongues tangled. His kisses burned and ignited her as they drove into her core.

'And I've been missing you here ...' He kissed her throat as her whole body sagged against him.

She began kissing him back, consuming his lips. Her blood was boiling with a fierce desire.

He pulled his mouth off her, running his fingers through her hair. 'I've been missing how you feel, your fine, smooth skin, the scent of your hair.' He was kissing her again. His hands were on her blouse, efficiently unbuttoning it and freeing her breasts from her bra. Her arms slid down. She dragged her fingers through his hair, tugging it by the roots and pulling his mouth to her naked breasts.

The sexy pain drove him to the boundaries of his control, the taste of her almost broke him, but once he saw the dull bruises of their erotic endeavours from the weekend, he lost control entirely. 'Understand. I. Want. Nahh. Need you.'

Seb wanted to freshly mark her. Nat would not only know that he wanted her. He'd make sure she felt him with every move she made. There would be no question, he could never be through with her. He sucked and nipped her breasts. She creamed as his nips marked her swollen breasts and hardening nipples.

'Sebastian, we're at work. We can't—'

Needy hands hitched up her skirt. 'I don't care. I want you now, here. You need to know how much. How much I'd risk ... for you.'

A spike of longing ran through her. She reached for his trousers, unzipping him, grabbing his heavy, throbbing cock through his boxers. 'Yesss.'

He smiled. 'I've missed your touch there more than you could know.'

Grabbing her left leg, he hitched it up over his hip. His hands were under her skirt now. She willingly obliged, opening herself to him. He deftly pulled her knickers aside while she guided his full cock towards her sex.

'God. I want to bury myself in you. But I don't want to hurt you.'

'Do it. I'm wet enough.'

He groaned as he swiftly moved their tangle of lusting bodies to the wall beside the door. Briefly, he let go of her leg to lock the door. Grabbing her again, he sunk deep into her, breaking through her taut folds. They moved together at a wild, intense pace. She nipped his bottom lip and dragged it back towards her. It drove him on as each thrust penetrated her more deeply than the last. He pushed her back hard against the wall. Each time he drove into her depths, desire ripped through Nat, and she fisted him.

'I was going to surprise you tonight.' He groaned through clenched teeth.

She rode him with her arms wrapped around his neck as a hoarse whisper escaped her. 'I need you too much. More than I should. It's too soon.' Her nipping his earlobe saw Seb almost shred her as he cannoned into her, trying to appease the intense passion flowing through him.

Hitching her leg up a little further, he ground deeper, exquisitely stretching the wonderful woman in his arms. She was balanced on the tip of her toes, the only part of her touching the earth. The rest of her was spiralling up towards the sun. His left hand had travelled to her right butt cheek, grabbing her hard, his fingers marking her as he increased the sexual force binding them.

His tongue flicked along the curve of her top lip in short strokes, the sensation sending her forth to touch heaven. They found release together. Wham-bam-thank-you-*very*-much-ma'am.

She stayed clenched around him for as long as she could, hanging on to the hedonistic feeling pulsing between them. He shuddered, enjoying the aftershocks as his vision returned to normal after blissing out.

'You. Are. Divine. How I've missed you.' Seb's husky veneration made her realise how foolish she'd been.

On one of the shelves was a box of tissues. Nat struggled to grab it. They cleaned up in silence while straightening their clothes and trying to achieve some semblance of professionalism.

As she started to button up her blouse, Seb rested his forehead against hers. 'I hope that allays any silly notions that I may have had my fill of you, Ms Perry.' Bringing himself back under control, he was in awe of her. She'd made him break every rule he'd imposed on his pleasure and his heart. Nat had her alter, Goldilocks. Yet he'd restricted himself all on his lonesome.

Seb was dumbfounded. He couldn't believe he'd not only lusted after her at work, but had been unable to resist fucking her. She was driving him crazy. Yet he had so much more life in his world because of her. It felt so right when it should have been feeling so wrong. Maybe in each other, salvation grew.

'I will see you tonight. Your place. You can be sure of that,' Seb murmured. 'Half seven.'

Nat could only dreamily nod as she tried to make her just-fucked hair look reasonably non-fucked and presentable. He gave her a tender kiss and unlocked the door to slip out. The ebbing of her thundering heart and churning emotions combined with the scent of wild sex were her companions as she tried to regain her balance.

A little later, she snuck out of the storeroom, hoping not to be seen. The door slammed loudly as it shut behind her. So much for a stealthy getaway. To make her jittery escape even more farcical, she heard a familiar voice behind her. 'Natasha Perry, my, my, what have you been up to in there?'

Bugger! It was Chelsea channelling Detective Catherine Willows, the *CSI*-babe herself. Nat turned. 'Umm, just looking for two patient's charts. Can't seem to find Mrs Mantle's and Mr Robinson's anywhere.' Natasha tried to keep a straight face, but she couldn't repress a grin.

Chelsea was in her element. 'Really? Is that the best you've got?'

Nat ignored her accusatory tone. 'I know it's a long shot, but I thought they might be in the storeroom.'

Not trying to hide her mirth, Chelsea gave a quiet chuckle. 'Oh, that's what they're calling it these days. Find the patient's chart in the doctor's trousers?' She walked past Nat, leaning in close, to whisper, 'My flustered friend, your buttons are all askew. I've just pointed out to Dr Mancini that he has a smudge of your lipstick on his collar.'

Nat hurriedly fixed her blouse, noting that the good doctor had cured her bad mood. His panacea, the scent of him and the feel of his merciless fucking, had soothed her bruised ego and needy nature.

Seb kept his word and dropped by that night, making time for her. He'd cooked his signature dish for Nat, so she cooked him hers. The cannelloni was her apology for having been so needy and angry. Notably, all signs of Goldilocks or The Slut had been dispatched to the darker recesses of her mind.

She was amazed at how natural it felt as the two cleaned up her kitchen after they'd finished eating. Happiness pervaded her apartment, culminating in carefree silliness as they had a tea-towel-snapping fight. Laughing, Seb tried to take a photo of Nat as she prepared to flick him with her tea towel.

'I'll need evidence that my attack on you was self-defence.' He laughed as his smartphone clicked. 'Not that I really need an excuse to restrain you.' His lascivious tone was easy to recognise. She pretended to fight him off, only to have him toss her over his shoulder on the way to her bed.

They always seemed to make time for great sex. As Nat fell asleep in Seb's arms, an unsettling ripple moved through her tranquil mind. Neither was prepared to face the nagging anxiousness that was building between the two of them – too much was left unsaid.

Late Thursday afternoon, that same nagging feeling had grown to a wave of disquiet that crashed over Nat. The JCH board announced several recommendations regarding the onc/haem's dangerous drug issues. Everyone had been dealt a crap hand except for Dr Cartwright. She sat pretty on top of her shiny white pedestal.

It wasn't unexpected, but all the 'little people' were hoping for was some semblance of equality. In their memo to the staff, the board, while not naming Cartwright in so many words, praised her diligence and integrity in bringing the slack DD handling practices on onc/haem to their attention.

Averill and Chelsea were on probation for six weeks, meaning if there were any more DD issues on the ward and either of them was remotely involved, they would be demoted or, worse, sacked.

Natasha joined them on three weeks' probation. Over these three weeks, Jo had to check all the DD orders Nat delivered to her wards, making sure what left the pharmacy with Nat was what reached the ward. If any DD problems occurred involving the pharmacist, she would be demoted or sacked. They'd all been tainted by the broad brush of suspicion at the board and Cartwright's instigation.

Averill was ropable, letting off steam by ranting at Chelsea and Natasha in the back room of the nurses' station. 'What's the use? I don't know why I bother trying to keep up the standards necessary to run a gold-standard ward when the whole ship is being sailed by a mob of monkeys.'

'And that ship's name's the *Titanic*. I can't afford to have this black mark against my name. Any opportunity for me to be promoted is gone.' Chelsea was frustrated and deeply disappointed. 'And I certainly can't afford to lose my job, especially over something where I did everything by the book. And that ... that effing doctor stuffed up and became a hero over it.'

'That bloody doctor.' Averill assumed her mother-hen pose. 'She hasn't got the smarts to know how to practice proper medicine, but she's certainly smart enough to know how to use the proper people to practice medicine at JCH.'

They both looked at Nat like she was about to come up with some pearl of wisdom.

Averill snapped, 'You're very quiet.'

Nat had nothing. A person in her position couldn't afford to make waves that could rock any boat, especially one sailed by monkeys. 'Look, let's just get through it. Jo says she will still try for board approval for a hospital-wide DD audit. Then we'll see if Cartwright has stuffed up anywhere else. We won't be the only ones feeling like we have an axe hanging over our careers.'

'Forget careers.' A nurse's call button lit up as it rang. Chelsea began to leave the room to attend to her patient. 'I feel like everyone is looking at me like I'm some kind of drug pusher.'

'Speaking of which. A word of warning.' Averill gave Nat a wary look. 'If the nurses' rumour mill has any truth to it, and it usually does, I hear that you're getting involved with Dr Mancini. Be careful there, him and that family of his—' A code blue alarm sounded from down the corridor. Averill's page started beeping incessantly.

Nat was stunned. 'What?'

As Averill turned to run in the direction of the alarm, she called, 'I'm not yelling it out. I'll tell you later.'

The ward surged into an organised swell of activity. Nat was left at the nurses' station with a very distinct sinking feeling. The boat she had been carefully trying not to rock seemed to have just been torpedoed.

# THIRTY-ONE

## SMALL WORDS, BIG ECHO

Averill's words were still echoing around her mind when Seb rang her doorbell. Immediately, it was weird between them. They couldn't seem to get comfortable. It had nothing to do with her lumpy couch.

Seb asked, 'What's up?'

'What do you mean?'

'Come on, you're all tense – wound up. Is it this DD probation thing?'

Her voice flattened, 'How much do you know about it?'

Cocking his head. 'All of it. Me, JCH board member – remember?'

Shit. Nat had forgotten all about Seb's other position at JCH. It had been lost in all their lust, his charm and her angst. 'You voted to do this. You were okay with giving Chelsea, Averill and me probation and letting Cartwright get off scot-free?'

'I wasn't happy about it at all. We only had Cartwright's report, even though Sharon Townsend spoke for the nurses and Jo spoke for you. Byron Cartwright used his influence with the rest of the JCH board to get it through. The Aida Foundation members were outvoted. It's like that saying, you know the one, um, *nothing appears as clear as blind faith*. That's what happened. They have absolute faith in the Cartwright name, a little less in the Mancini name.'

'Yes, why is that? Today Averill hinted that I should be careful getting involved with you and the Mancinis. Sage also mentioned I should be careful. Why?'

'How long has Averill been at JCH, you know, around Freo?'

'I'm not sure. Certainly longer than Jo, Chelsea and me. Probably even longer than Sage. What's that got to do with it?'

'Because the older staff, including Sage, may have lingering doubts about how we, the Mancinis, made our money. The younger staff will only see the respectable Mancinis, a family reputation my dad has worked hard to build.'

'What lingering doubts are they working with?'

He didn't skip a beat, although she sensed a lethal, icy change in his tone. 'It's a stereotype from the old days when any successful Italians were seen as being hooked up with organised crime, drugs, illegal gambling.' Tossing his head to one side, he quipped coldly, 'Like we're some old-fashioned Mafia family.'

'It seems stronger than a silly outdated stereotype. Averill's not an entirely unreasonable person. She wouldn't warn me if she weren't worried that there was something more to you, your family. And then there's Sage. Is your family mixed up with stuff like drugs?' This possibility scared her the most.

'You'll have to take my word for it. That's all there is to it.'

Nat threw up her hands. 'Come on. Surely you don't expect me to leave it at that?'

'You know as well as I do that Averill can be unreasonable at times. So if our family's word is good enough for the business community, it should be good enough for you.' His jawline started to pulse.

'Well, it's not.' Nat stood and moved away from his brooding frame.

His voice was Mancini menace with an edge of nasty condescension. It was the tone she hadn't liked when she'd heard it at The Norfolk bar on their first date. He used it then with Rick, and later when he was pissed at Chevy. This tone scared her more than his words.

'How dare you doubt what I tell you about my family?' He stood and stepped towards Nat, anger flowing through his body and arcing between them. While this anger had all the usual fiery sexual tension about it, it had an extra bite, an unadulterated, livid sharpness. It cut the air between them.

'Shit. You always think the worst of me,' Seb said.

'You and the rest of the world. Don't feel special. Just tell me the truth.'

'Look, if you're worried about being under suspicion at JCH with the DDs, don't be. We know how to handle stuff like that.'

'Tell me, if you aren't mixed up in anything dodgy, why would you know how to handle things like it?'

'You should shut your pretty little trap because it's stuff you don't understand. That is what it means to be part of a strong family that does everything for each other. No matter what.'

A surging crimson tide hit her. 'How dare you. Arrogant bastard. You think you know me. You don't know me at all.'

'And you don't know me.' His nasty tone prevailed.

She couldn't hold back the intensity of her rage at discovering this side of him. 'Get the fuck out. Right now. Before I kick you in your junk and roll you out of here.'

He clenched his jaw and steeled himself. Taking a deep breath, he calmed his voice, but the Mancini menace was not far below the surface. 'No. I'm not going anywhere, and you aren't going to do any such thing.'

'I will. You know I will. Or you could tell me what I need to know.'

His eyes darted around the room. He tried to rationalise his thoughts. A dark sorrow spread across his brow, but his voice seethed, 'Christ!' If he could only touch her, he'd be able to seduce her and then fuck them both into forgetfulness. 'Not now. I can't.'

'Why not? If you don't, it'll always stand between us.'

'I can't tell you until we both calm down.' His eyes never left her.

'Can't or won't.' Nat's eyes never left his.

'Both.'

'Both?'

Her defiance only fired his desire further. 'I won't tell you until we've had a chance to—'

'What?'

He leaned in close, she smelt so good. 'I can't tell you until we both calm down, and I know the best way to make that happen.' When they fucked, she forgot her questions, and he forgot his problems.

'Don't go there, not now.' She stepped back to lessen the hypnotic effect he was trying to wield over her.

'I won't tell you until we've got enough time and are in a quiet, neutral place. Then I'll explain it all. The Mancinis, how we work.'

'It's not like you haven't had the time or place before.'

'For fuck's sake, I've been trying to protect you.' He closed his eyes tight, wincing at what he'd let slip. 'It always comes down to this.'

She was about to ask what *kind of this* it was, but he cut her off.

'Natasha, my family is overwhelming.' He tossed his arms up in exasperation, flapping them around, finally slapping his thighs. 'They chew people up and spit them out, and that's just before breakfast. I want to prepare you for it.' He didn't have the energy now, and he needed to plan how, when and what he told her. He didn't want her alters appearing and ruining it for her – or him, for that matter.

'You don't need to prepare me for anything. I'll make it easy for you. Get the hell out before I scream so loud people will notice. Then you'll have to answer a whole lot of questions, whether you like it or not.'

He smirked. 'Come on. You don't want me to go. You need me to stay. So after we do what we do best, I'll be more in the mood to tell you about me.' The air instantly crackled as he turned up the magnetic tension to the max.

'Stop using sex to block any real conversation between us about you. It shows you only want me for one thing.'

He grabbed her by the shoulders. His voice was a husky growl. 'Look at me. Look at me, damn it. Does this look like the face of someone who only thinks that of you? Only wants you because you're a good fuck?' He took a breath, and then his voice was pure molasses. 'Might I add the best fuck I've ever had.'

She didn't dare look at him. He forced her to look into his darkening eyes, cupping her face with his palm, his manner desperate. 'Believe me, please. Saturday night. I'll tell you everything on Saturday night.' His dad was going to be the problem. 'I have family business to attend to tomorrow evening. They're coming to my place to put the final seal of approval on this South Freo deal, so I won't have time. But Saturday, I will. It'll be just you and me. We'll thrash it out. Trust me, at least until then. Give me that much. Please.' He tried to grab her butt cheeks to press her to him, his eyes smouldering.

She pulled away. Her crimson tide ebbed, yielding to the erotic wave that pulsed through her. Confusion scattered her thoughts. 'How can you be so fierce about something and then just brush it aside because your cock twitches?'

'Because it's what you do to me. I'm only a man, after all. That's why I need to have you in a neutral place to discuss this. That has to be Saturday night.'

'Okay,' she sighed, and stood down from their silly face-off. *Two can play this game*, she thought. Sebastian wasn't going to get what he wanted until Natasha did. 'Okay. Saturday night.'

'Really?' He relaxed slightly, hesitantly, wary of her sudden compliance. If he could only hold and kiss her. He wanted to bury himself in her and forget. All these questions were too much, too soon. 'You're okay to wait?' He reached for her, but Nat dodged out of his grasp.

'Yes, Sebastian, but you're not staying. I'm not feeding you, and we definitely aren't going to fuck. No matter how good it could have been.' She smirked inwardly. It was time to re-teach Dr Mancini a lesson. With no Rick to sabotage her plans, like at the Red Herring, Natasha was more than capable of being Sebastian's teacher tonight.

'You sure?' He was drawn to her defiance and strength, yet with a layer of vulnerability, all rolled up into one irresistible package. When they were this close and she was putting him in his place, he knew they were right for each other, although her being on probation wouldn't sit well with his family. He would work on them. Once they saw Natasha's inner and outer beauty and witnessed her strength and true nature, they'd be as hooked as he was.

'You know you're punishing yourself as much as me, right?' Seb asked.

'I'll live with that. Can you?' She left their hot and heated longing for each other hanging in the air and stormed off to her front door. 'Just go.'

He was in utter disbelief at her steel. He'd go, reluctantly, but wasn't looking forward to a cold shower extinguishing his desires rather than Nat's hot, supple body. There were other ways to release his frustrations. Maybe sharpening his knives and using them would alleviate the tension within him.

On Friday, the gossip about Averill, Chelsea and Natasha's probation was sunk. Overnight, ER had admitted two more knifing victims with the weird facial slashing. This news swamped the JCH rumour mill. Nat breathed a little easier. Maybe things wouldn't be so rough.

The story of the third and fourth victims in three weeks attracted everyone's attention, not least the local media. They'd christened the guy the Shoreside Slasher, aptly descriptive if a little graphic and morose. The news sites and the hospital were alight with the story. The furore and fear about the Shoreside Slasher made Nat rethink tossing Seb out the night before. Maybe it wasn't such a good idea.

A cold shudder shook her when, late Friday morning, it was reported that the Slasher was apparently only attacking junkies. Police thought it was over drug debts. None of the victims were speaking to them, so they were asking for the public's help.

This, on top of last night's unresolved fight with Seb, made Nat fear that history was repeating itself. The thug at the strip club liked using a blade. That was Sydney. She'd escaped. Now it was different. Her caring Mr TDD, while being able to handle a knife, also made love like a god. No, lightning didn't strike twice. Nonetheless, she felt terribly exposed, even if it was hard to know if the news sites were accurate.

Friday afternoon couldn't come quickly enough. Her last stop was Ruby's room. As usual, Jonathon, her husband, was by her side. He rose from his chair as Nat walked into the room. 'Hello, Natasha, good to see you, luv. Would you please excuse me? I should go buy some fresh flowers for my Ruby. These here are looking poorly.'

'Jonathan, don't make a fuss.' Ruby greeted Natasha with a bright smile.

'I won't be long.' He shuffled off.

Ruby shook her head, mouthing at Nat, 'Domestic deafness. Old coot.'

'How are you today?'

'Pain's been good. I'm more at ease.'

'I'm glad to hear that.'

'Yes, it's much better. Don't know what happened last time. I can tell you one thing, Dr Cartwright didn't give me my dose.'

'I'm so sorry you had to go through all that pain.'

Ruby clasped her frail hands together. 'When you're so distressed, you're desperate. You remember with a pain-driven clarity what is done to you and whether it makes the pain better or worse.' She shook her head. 'I know some people think I'm old and dithery, but I didn't get it wrong.'

'Ruby, we know you're very much with it. We all felt terrible about the pain you had to go through.'

'Natasha, could I ask a favour?'

'Sure.'

'Can you get me a bottle of sparkling water from the nurses, please? They keep some for me in their fridge. I like the fizz.'

'Are you sure? Fizz? Doesn't it upset your stomach even more after the chemo?'

Ruby's weary, pale green eyes creased at the edges from the wicked smile spreading across her face. 'Yes, fizz. Remember, I'm sleeping with a seventy-year-old man. I need all the fizz I can get.' Nat laughed. Ruby smiled. 'In all seriousness, I can't stand the taste of regular water now.'

'In that case, I'll get it straight away.'

On returning with the bottle of cool water, Natasha froze in the doorway. Ruby was smiling and batting her eyelids at Sebastian. He finished up and kindly squeezed her hand. 'Keep recovering this well and we'll see if we can't get you home tomorrow.' Natasha was sure she noticed a hint of pale pink spread over Ruby's alabaster cheeks. Ruby, who was more than pleased with Seb's attention, nodded and smiled coyly at him.

As he turned and saw Natasha, Seb's eyes narrowed. His face was stern. What was he going to do about her defiance? It spurred him on and made his devious mind want to push his and her limits further. They came together as they passed through the doorway.

'Ms Perry.' He ran two fingers along her forearm, up to her elbow. A zing ran through them both. Her breath caught. His chest tightened, prompting him to whisper, 'Remember. Saturday night. Your arse is all mine.'

Her insides quivered. Damn him. She wouldn't give in easily, particularly because Seb had so many questions to answer. That settled her.

# THIRTY-TWO

## TIME IS A VALUABLE CURRENCY

'Here's your bottle of fizzy water.'

Ruby smiled knowingly at Nat. 'Now there goes a whole lot of fizz in one very neat package, don't you think?' Ruby beamed at Natasha. 'Wouldn't you like to pop his cork?'

'Ruby!'

'That's the beauty of being old, my dear. Knowing that all too soon you have an appointment with your maker, you come to understand that time is a valuable currency not to be wasted on embarrassment, fear or regret.'

Her disarming stare and wise words caused Nat to loosen a little. 'I have got me some of his fizz.'

'I knew it. I've been watching the two of you over the last number of visits. Each time you seemed closer. A little smile here, a glancing touch, like just then. I'm so glad.' Ruby clapped her hands, bouncing up and down a little in bed.

'I see nothing escapes you. Be careful. I don't want to be responsible for any increase in your pain.'

'No, no. If anything, it's quite the reverse. I'm happy for you. You're much better off with Dr Mancini than with that drongo Rick.'

Natasha smiled to herself. Drongo was such a Ruby word. 'Hang on. How do you know about Rick and me?'

'Chelsea told me.'

Natasha had a slight chuckle. 'You shouldn't believe everything Chelsea says. But she's right about Rick.'

It was late when Nat walked to the car park. The sun was setting and the wind was cooling the day's warmth. Winter was on its way. Similarly, the warmth that had engulfed Nat since sharing with Ruby was cooled by the whole Mancini family secrecy thing. There were Sage and Averill's reservations, not to mention Seb's warning: 'Oh, but I've been about trying to protect you from my family.'

Natasha couldn't wait until Saturday night to find out. As the chill from the breeze ran through her, Ruby's words came to her. 'Time is a valuable currency.' Nat was emboldened by them.

She needed to pack up any thoughts of embarrassment and fear while shaking off Seb's misguided desire to protect her. She wanted answers, not just regrets. She needed the truth and to be in his safe arms tonight. The Slasher thing had her skittish. There was no way she would wait for Seb to orchestrate some alleged impartial environment. Neutral my arse, she thought.

She parked in the Vergona Tower visitors' car park and walked through the complex's foyer to buzz his video intercom.

'Hi, it's Natasha.'

'Natasha, oh, um.' Seb's voice crackled out through the speaker. 'Hello.' She heard the hesitation in it. Then again, they hadn't parted on the best of terms last night. Now she was surprising him – and his family.

'Hi, I thought I'd drop over, a spur-of-the-moment thing.' She could hear the growing trepidation in her voice. 'I wanted to talk about how we ended up last night.'

Yet, it was the trepidation in his voice that sank her spirits. 'No, umm, I guess, umm.' There was a long silence. 'Ah, yes, I suppose you could come up. I'll send the lift down.'

Her courage, born from Ruby's words, started to disappear as fast as the lift ascended to his penthouse. She knocked, using the large M-shaped brass knocker on one of the fortified black wooden entry doors. She was greeted with a puzzling sound of muffled voices and hurried activity beyond the doors. Eventually, Seb opened one door and slipped out through the narrowest of gaps, closing the door, determined not to let anything leave or enter his home.

He was genuinely surprised that she had the balls to turn up on his doorstep when he'd told her he would be with his family. Nevertheless, everything about her surprised and captivated him. He didn't want to put her through what he had planned for the next evening. But it couldn't be avoided. Without realising his face became sheepish, embarrassed even.

Not what Nat was aiming for at all. She was getting the same sinking feeling she had when she'd surprised Rick. Maybe he hadn't been getting on with paperwork with the family but getting on someone else. She should have learnt her lesson. Before Seb could say anything, the door swung wide open.

Standing before her were three dark-haired boys. The two smaller ones jumped up and down in front of Natasha, pushing each other while demonstrating various fighting poses. The third boy, the tallest, leaned on the door, sulkily folding his arms. She was speechless, if not a little relieved.

The tallest, she presumed the eldest, looked her up and down. The teenager was trying very hard for wannabe gangster nonchalance. 'Where's the pizza?' He pushed off the open doorframe, doubling his efforts at cool, adolescent detachment.

'Um, no, not delivering pizza. I'm, ahh ...' Words failed her.

'Boys, meet Ms Natasha Perry, a beautiful friend of mine.' Seb's charm bridged the awkward silence stretching out before them.

The smallest protested, stamping his feet, apparently not impressed at the sight of Natasha sans pizza. 'Aww, when's the pizza gonna be here? I'm starving.' The middle boy just appraised her silently, taking in everything. They all had dark brown eyes, like those that constantly trapped her.

'Do you still want to come in? You're more than welcome, but I suspect these guys are a bit of a shock.'

'Yes, they are.' She took a deep breath. A little bravery returned. 'If it's okay with the boys, I suppose I could stay a little while.'

'Alright, but as long as we get pizza soon,' declared the smallest.

She saw Seb's face relax, and he smiled, a gorgeously genuine, happy grin. They all peeled back from the doorway so she could enter the penthouse.

Her mind was falling over itself. Is this what Seb had to tell her? Are these his sons? Jeez, that'll do it for her. This was more family than she would have ever imagined. 'So, you guys are ...?'

Seb's eyes lingered on her a little longer, yet again surprised by her courage. She hadn't run. He decided to see how far he could push her. 'I'm glad you ask because I have three fine Mancini men here, who I have ... let me think ...' He drummed three fingers against his chin with a quizzical look on his face, then pronounced, 'Yes, I guess it's a pleasure to be babysitting them. Pia, her husband Tony and Dad have gone out to celebrate the closing of our real estate deal. They're having a break from this rabble.' Seb relaxed as he saw her face brighten. The boys quietened down as he spoke. 'Boys, introduce yourselves to our guest.'

The tallest grunted mulishly. 'Anthony Gallo.'

Seb deciphered his sulkiness. 'Young Tony, being a teenager, feels it's beneath him to be babysat by his uncle.'

Nat relaxed. Uncle, that's not so bad. 'I see. Pleased to meet you. I understand the eldest thing and always being saddled with what the younger ones are doing.' She smiled. The boy soon bowed his head, looking very self-conscious, both he and his uncle captivated by her smile.

The smallest boy piped up. 'Why are you here if you don't have pizza?' He was clearly intent on eating and was in no mood for chit-chat, especially with someone without pizza.

Seb chided him. 'And?'

'I'm Michael. I'm five. Do you work with Uncle Seb?'

Before she could answer, the middle boy interrupted, 'Don't be stupid, Mickey. It's too late for work.'

Seb interjected. 'And you are?'

The middle boy quietly answered. 'In case you were wondering, I'm Ren, short for Renzo. I'm named after my grandfather.' He looked shyly up at her from under his fringe.

'Pleased to meet you, boys.' She tried to sound calm. 'You're right, Ren. I'm not here for work. But I do work at the hospital with your—'

'Pizza!' The intercom had buzzed, making the boys yell. Nat was saved as the boys' focus turned to who was downstairs waiting to be buzzed up.

After they had feasted on pizza and garlic bread, the boys became restless. Seb organised for the youngest two to watch a movie. Anthony was in Seb's study on his PlayStation. While he was settling them, she cleared away the dishes and leftover pizza. Seb walked into the kitchen as she finished up. 'Would you like to finish the rest of your wine out on the balcony?'

'Sounds good. Only if you think the boys will be all right.'

He grinned, handing her a glass of red. 'They seem to be much easier to control when you're around. We can have some time to ourselves before I have to try and get them to go to bed.'

There was a cool, gentle onshore breeze. The moon was a large saucer of silver, bleeding shimmery platinum into the dark waves. They rhythmically crashed into the rock wall of the distant marina, throwing up a glinting froth. A shiver ran through Nat, causing her nipples to be on high beam through the thin blue silk of her blouse and bra.

Seb took one look at her in the moonlight, all curves and perfection, and he couldn't resist wrapping his arms around her. She jumped a little as he rested his chin on her shoulder. 'You look beautiful in the moonlight. Are you cold?'

'A little.'

'Let me warm you up.' He gently rubbed her shoulders, holding her close, her back to his front. 'You smell so good. I love having you so close.' He kissed the base of her throat, then the sensitive spot below her ear. Another shiver ran through her, but it had nothing to do with the chilly night air and everything to do with the hot man wrapped around her.

'Thank you, yet again.'

'What for?' She tilted her head to look over her shoulder. 'For not nagging you in front of your nephews? I didn't come over tonight just to get my rocks off. I came to get some answers. I couldn't wait. But they're a whole different family than I expected. Guess they put an end to anyone getting their rocks off here tonight.'

'I see.' He needed to slow her down. Kissing and grazing his teeth along her neck, he sensed her defiant stance starting to yield to his touch. 'I was thanking you for not avoiding me like the plague because you're angry about all the stuff I haven't told you.' He nipped her earlobe.

All the questions on the tip of her tongue the night before seemed unimportant.

He took her glass. 'Most of all, for not turning and running when you saw the troublesome threesome.' He set down her drink on a balcony table.

With his face turned away, she couldn't tell if he was joking or serious. Then his lips found hers. She swivelled around in his arms, deepening the kiss. What questions?

Once again, there was an intimate, unremitting connection buzzing between them. While claiming Nat's mouth, Seb pushed her back until she was pressed up against the balcony's glass balustrading. He let a groan escape his lips as he pulled back, gasping. He eyed her like he could devour her any second.

It loosened her lips. 'I want you more than I should. More than is wise.'

'Forget wise. Don't go home tonight.' His lips tickled her ear.

She pulled away, staring at him. 'Are you serious? Won't it be a bit awkward with your little guests?'

'Yes, I'm serious.' Desperate to stop her from getting into her head, he offered, 'I'll answer some of your questions if you stay.' He was so close that he ran his nose along hers.

'I have work tomorrow. I should go.' She wasn't going to make it easy. 'The boys have already answered some questions. And I guess I've been waiting this long, what's one more day. Tonight, you'll just use the boys as human shields anyway. Plus, they don't need to hear us argue.'

It was music to Seb's wary heart. If she just wanted information or to get at his money, like his father had suggested, she wasn't acting like it. He kissed her again.

She lost all ability to form words as his lips worked up her neck. Then his tongue began needily working over hers.

Nat fought back from the brink. 'No, Seb. Stop trying to derail my thoughts.'

'Again, with your all-so-hot defiance, not to mention your body is so bloody gorgeous in the moonlight. It's you who'll need the boys to shield you. And your oh-but-I've-got-work-in-the-morning bullshit won't save you either. Don't you start at nine on Saturdays?'

'I do, but ...' Her voice trailed off as she began succumbing to his lips working down her cheek and along her jaw, his hands stroking and enticing her.

'If you like, leave early in the morning,' he murmured before releasing her. 'Early enough to have plenty of time to get to work and not get caught by Pia when she picks up the boys.' He placed his hands on the top of the balustrading, caging her. She was trapped between his arms and his intense gaze.

Nat wanted to be wise, but she couldn't quell her desires. If she had to pick a song as a soundtrack to what was going through her mind, it'd have to be The Clash's 'Should I stay or should I go'. As flippant as it sounded, it helped distil her thoughts. She could lose herself with Seb or with Goldilocks. Either way, she'd be screwed, and she enjoyed his way a hell of a lot more than Goldy's. The breeze picked up, chilling her. It was like Ruby was talking to her. She decided to forget embarrassment, fear and regrets and not skimp on the happy.

'Sure. I'll stay.'

He took her head in his hands, pulling her lips to his, and then ran his hands down her body onto her butt cheeks. She willingly ground her hips against him. She felt him feeling her while she felt his growing erection strain against his jeans. The two of them forgot where they were and slipped away.

# THIRTY-THREE

## SLAP-HAPPY… WHO'D HAVE THOUGHT?

The sound of crying brought them back to earth. Seb moved away, hesitated, and then returned to kiss her deeply, leaving her grabbing the balustrading to stay upright. Ren came running into the large living area. Seb said softly, 'Hold that thought.' He slid the balcony door open.

*Which thought?* She gulped down the last of her wine and quickly followed. Seb was tentatively smoothing Ren's hair off his face to look at the young boy's forehead. As she came within earshot, she gathered, through the sobs, that there had been an altercation with a door and his older brother. As evidence of the collision, a reddish bump was growing on his forehead. While Seb was consoling Ren, Nat made her way into the kitchen. She dispensed some ice cubes from the fridge into a glass and grabbed some tissues on her way back to Seb and Ren.

Natasha had lots of experience in soothing domestic wounds. When she returned to the main living room, Seb was kneeling, hugging Ren as he sobbed on Seb's shoulder. Natasha wrapped an ice cube in a tissue. 'Hey, would you like me to put some ice on your bump?'

Ren nodded and sobbed once more as Seb released him. She knelt and gently placed the ice on the bump. He quietened down and his sobbing lessened. She sensed Seb's eyes on her. When she peeked up, he was giving her an intense stare, one she'd not seen before. She wasn't sure if it was for her or Ren. It was full of reverence and made her heart smile.

He sighed, 'I see you're in safe hands. I have a few things to organise upstairs while I get the other guys to bed.' Seb decided he'd test Natasha once more. 'Ren, when you're ready, can you show Natasha upstairs to your room. She can put you to bed. Brush your teeth, okay?'

In no time, Ren had settled, brushed teeth and all. He jumped into bed with a broad smile. 'Thanks.'

All she could do was smile back. Seb joined them, hugging Ren goodnight before closing the door. They were alone again.

'So much for thinking the boys would protect you.'

'Seb. Please. I should go. With the boys here, I'm not sure what you have in mind, but it probably doesn't involve answering any questions. To top that off, I don't think it's what we should really do with your nephews down the hall. You can tell me tomorrow night as planned, and then we can ... um, what will be, will be.'

Seb took her hand as they walked towards the top of the staircase. The grandfather clock chimed. Seb stopped. He was in his head. This woman didn't want him to give up his secrets for fear of upsetting the boys. He thought she'd have pushed him. She was motivated differently than other women he'd known. How could he be entertaining this?

Seb was fighting with himself. Descend to end the night or stay amongst the clouds and a shared carnal heaven? Nat could see he was torn, and wondered if he needed help from The Clash. He waited for the tenth chime, then turned and pulled her hands so his hips bumped hard against hers. His voice was as sexy as hell. 'Come to my bed with me.'

'Is that a question or an order, Dr Mancini?'

His eyes widened. 'What would you like it to be?'

'An order. I'm sick of questions. For now, that is.'

'Then that's what it is.' He guided her further along the hallway to his bedroom. A long, slow smile slid across his face. 'The walls are thick enough for what I have planned.'

His inner sanctum was gently lit by a bedside lamp. Locking the door behind them, he turned to say something, but Natasha couldn't wait. Her assault surprised him, allowing her to take his mouth. Silencing him, her tongue found his before sucking it into her mouth and nipping the tip gently as it slid out between her lips.

They wrapped themselves around each other. Seb needed control. Trapping her hands behind her back, his powerful biceps pressed on her shoulders, his eyes fierce and his voice hushed. 'Last time you were here, you bound me up in my clothes. It was beyond hot. Let me return the favour.'

'And I thought you were such a good boy, Mancini.' His words and the heat of his eyes sent a sensual rush through her. 'I think I can take you.' In fact, she was wildly turned on. Finally, she had the chance to do the bondage thing with someone she wanted. No ugly man-slob in sight. 'Haven't you already restrained me? The gym comes to mind.'

'Not in my bed, not how I want you tonight.'

Her sexual juices started churning. Seb moved away to a walk-in wardrobe. He reappeared holding her red silk scarf. 'I thought I should return this.' Wrapping the scarf around her hips, he pulled her to him, igniting an intense passion. Her body heated as she was overcome by the electrical charge between them.

Gazing down, he cocked his head to one side. 'You feel it too?'

'Yes, always when I'm with you, and only you.'

At hearing her words, he tilted his chin up to the ceiling and rolled his eyes upwards, breathing in as if his body was absorbing the divine energy sweeping over them. A low, guttural soliloquy escaped his lips. 'You are all mine. Slip off your heels. Just stand still for a moment, and that's an order. I'm going to do some things to you tonight that will test us both.' On hearing his words, another glorious sensual wave of arousal surged through her. 'You must promise to scream "stop" if you don't want to do what I ask.'

She sucked in a not-so-shocked breath. 'You mean a safe word, don't you?'

'That's for another time. Tonight, just use "stop". It should be enough.'

She could only nod as his feather-light kisses left a trail of erotic heat along her jaw and down her throat. He draped the scarf around his neck to let his fingers undo the buttons on her blouse. He slipped his hands up and under the silky material, gliding them over her shoulders so she could feel his warm palms on her skin. She loved the sensation of his smooth skin on hers.

He continued to slide her blouse down, leaving it to float to her feet. His darkening eyes darted to her bra. 'Wearing one tonight.' It didn't prove much of a problem as he soon relieved her of it and trailed more kisses down to her nipples. His balls fisted at the sight of the bruises he'd left days earlier. His brand of lovemaking. He sucked on her nipples until each tightened and rose. She nearly lost her balance as the sensation drove her arousal higher.

He scooped her up and laid her down on the bed. 'Give me your hands.' She obliged. He tied her hands, then threaded and tied off the other end of the red scarf through the metal strips on his bed's unique headboard. She was naked from the waist up and totally under his spell. With her hands tied and stretched out above her head, he stood and stripped in front of her – totally naked and very, very happy to see her.

'Now you've seen enough.' Seb's stare sizzled as he bent down to his jeans and pulled a black silk tie from the back pocket.

'So, Dr Mancini, do you think tying me up and blindfolding me will stop me from getting answers?' She was more used to the dominant role. Submissive men at the club never really got her going. Back then, she was paid to dominate. A means to an end, it allowed her to eat, to survive. Now it was very different. He had her heart racing with a yearning that awakened her soul. She played with him. 'What makes you think I like being tied up and dominated?'

As he heard her words, his face dropped, and he stopped. Shit! She was right. What was he thinking? Then she surprised him yet again.

'Don't stop.' Nat found she was surprisingly pleased to let him lead the way. It meant she didn't have to think about anything other than pleasure. 'Hey, I'm joking. I like it when you get hot and bossy. In the bedroom, at least.'

His smile returned. 'Then lie still and do as I say.' Seb wrapped the tie around her head and knotted it. Everything she felt and heard was amplified. The cooling material over her eyes only made her feel hotter.

To control her, to bewitch her body, captivate her mind and keep her alters away, Kylie Minogue's techno dance track 'Slow' began to echo around the room. The song was Kylie when she'd become an adult. Her seductive voice took Natasha higher. It may have been dark, but with Seb, Nat soared towards a light that chased away any demons.

His fingers lightly brushed between her breasts and agonisingly slowly down her body. He began to unzip her skirt as he followed Kylie's words exclusively. Kylie was directing them through an enchanting slow dance. Soon her skirt and knickers were gone. Only her stockings remained.

She was achingly ready for him. His tongue and lips were on her nipple. There was something in his mouth other than her nipple. It was slightly sticky. When he blew on her where his tongue had been, his breath created a totally erotic, supercooled sensation over her nipple. Now he started in on her other breast. It was beguiling and so arousing she could only moan as erotic sensations rolled over her.

Seb continued his captivating actions. Kylie's tantalising song took them deeper. Natasha couldn't writhe around. Tied tight, with this body pinning her, she had no choice but to absorb the magnificent rush gripping her senses.

'Control your need to feel guilt when you have pleasure. Enjoy the pleasure for what it is – an expression of what you like, what you want. Then when you come undone, it will be beyond what you've ever experienced.'

His hands were now on her thighs and his body was between her legs. His talented fingers slipped tenderly underneath the top of her left stocking before he slid the stocking down her leg and off, followed by his lips. The touch of his lips tantalised her skin as they travelled along and down her leg, Kylie's sultry voice setting his pace. Seb was in no hurry as he peeled her right stocking down and off.

She pulled against her restraints, the silk holding her hands and arms tight. Seb slowly palmed her sex and then circled his middle finger around her clit, signalling she was his. Her arousal soaked his fingers as his tongue moved south, kissing and blowing on her. Each breath left a super-cool trail once again. This was new. What was he using? He slid his middle finger into her, circling wider as he slipped in another.

'Nat, you are so wet and so fucking ready.'

'Don't talk. Just fuck me.' She was delirious from his slow, teasing touch. She arched her back, trying to contain the feelings throbbing through her.

'No, baby, not yet. You're gonna beg me even more.' He slowly withdrew his fingers, leaving her wanting and needing him. 'Remember, control your pleasure with me. It'll keep them away.' He grabbed her hips and flipped her over, slapping her butt cheeks – hard. Sending her into the grips of a new hot sexual arousal, he smacked her arse again.

The erotic sting drove her further along a path to ecstasy that made total sense. This was a way forward. It wasn't punishment. It was pushing her to her erotic best. In this moment, something snapped, releasing the real Natasha. It wasn't wrong – not with this man. Never. She wasn't being forced to do something against her will. And she wanted it. All he could give to her and all she could give to him. He was cleansing her of her thoughts of sin and guilt.

Grabbing her hips again, he brought her knees up, leaving her ass in the air, vulnerable and ripe for the taking. He slapped her butt twice. The sting was all erotic sensation, driving more pure pleasure into her. His erection rubbed against her clitoris, and she couldn't help but groan. He was seducing her slowly with his touch.

'Don't come yet. Control, Natasha, control. It'll drive us higher.' He nudged her knees apart. She was stretched out, leaning up on her forearms and knees. Ready for him to stretch and fill her. Nat waited for him to ram into her. Instead came his mouth. She felt his broad shoulders between her legs as his tongue went to work, licking and sucking on her. At this different vantage, she was so open to him that it drove her higher.

'Seb, this is ...' She'd never been eaten from this position before.

He blew on her sex. The super coolness that he had somehow triggered saw Natasha rippling with hyper-arousal.

She groaned out, 'Fuck! I can't. Please ...'

His tongue lapped, suckled and fluttered around her folds, finally penetrating her. His hands seized her butt cheeks, his grip commanding her to surrender her sex to his mouth.

His voice was a low, salacious growl. 'Come now. Give it to me.' The spiral of her climax was beyond amazing. It shattered through her. Nat's legs shook as sweet release claimed her, and she soaked him.

He moved around her. One strong arm snaked around her waist while the other gently soothed her butt, rubbing his palm over her. 'You're so brave. Stay with me, Nat. I want to give you more.'

'Yesss. Oh, please.' Now, all Nat heard was Isobel Campbell's breathy voice and Mark Lanegan's growls as they swept Seb and Nat up in 'Come on over (Turn me on)'.

Moving from gloriously massaging her breasts, Seb then took the head of his cock, and only the head. He pushed it slowly in and out, spreading the lips of the entrance to the most sensual part of her body. He coaxed her, and she began to climb again. He kept this torture up for a little longer. She started clenching around his broad crown. He slapped her twice more, before his hands gently slid over her skin soothing her butt cheeks. Beautiful agony and ecstasy flooded her.

Without warning, he slammed into her. 'Oh, fuck! Yes.' He slammed into her again, rough and hard, hitting her right there, all the right way there. 'You are sooo goood,' he growled. To keep the punishing rhythm going, he grabbed her hips, driving his fingers into her soft skin, feeling her toned muscles bunch as he hammered into her. He nailed her again and again, enjoying the red bloom of her skin under his hands. It was bliss as he rooted himself in her. His fingers tantalised her as they moved to strum her clit. She could just bear the overpowering feeling of eroticism he was creating.

Seb was so hard and big as he closed in on an unbelievable high. 'Give it to me, Nat. Give. It. To. Me. Let yourself go. Together. Fuck, *yeah!*'

The brutal purity of his loving was made sharper by being blinded to all but touch and its sensation. His ferocity for Nat allowed her to submit to her most natural yet most ruthless of cravings. She came, spiralling again and again around him. He poured himself into her with a flurry of thrusts and a throaty groan. He let the full weight of his hot body press down on her.

Collapsing onto his soft mattress, they continued to enjoy the heavenly contact of their sated bodies and the exquisite aftershocks. Sometime later, he pulled out of her and untied Nat's hands to lie beside her. She was breathless as he slid off her blindfold. She turned to face him, blinking. The bedside lamp was off because they were bathed in the pale moonlight streaming through the large floor-to-ceiling window.

They shared a tender, loving kiss. Nat broke away to catch her breath. When she peeked up at him, she saw the same intense, heart-wrenching look on his face as when she was soothing Ren's bump. This time it was even more powerful, his eyes glistening. Something passed behind them, an emotion she couldn't recognise.

Sebastian was overwhelmed. He'd let more of his kink out – and she'd taken it. He could only stare at the beautiful woman in his bed and pray he hadn't carried it too far. He'd let his proclivity bubble to the surface to redden and bruise her soft, sensual skin. Skin that was perfect except for the brutal marks left by his brand of sex. Now he had come down from the high they'd shared. It wasn't Nat that felt guilty, but Seb. He decided she had a right to know what path he could lead them down.

'Hey, are we okay?' she whispered breathlessly, seeing Sebastian's eyes clouding with apprehension.

He gently grasped her chin with his thumb and forefinger, the touch of her lips across the pad of his thumb, so full and sexy. He sought out her eyes so she couldn't escape him. 'The question is, are *you* okay?'

He brushed his other hand over the darkening bruises on her breasts, then splayed his hand over the marks on her hip. 'I shouldn't have … I'm sorry. I shouldn't have marked you.'

She surprised him, taking his hand from her hip, kissing his palm and raising it to her cheek. A reflection of what he had done to her to show he cared. She now returned the sentiments. 'You are … I don't know … wonderful doesn't seem to cover it. What you do, what we do. It frees me.' She continued to hold his hand in place along with his gaze. He was unbuckling the straitjacket of guilt that shackled her sexual freedom. In turn, she was liberating his kink, allowing him to finally truly enjoy what he was with someone who wanted to go there too. They were freeing each other.

He couldn't hide his amazement. 'I can't believe I found someone like you.' Seb's voice was hoarse with raw emotion. 'Natasha, I know we've only known each other a heartbeat, and there is so much I haven't said, but … I'm falling in love with you.'

It was a spectacular shock. 'Seb, you can't. There are so many things, questions, and reasons. I know what you want me to say, but I can't. You can't. I know people always say this, but … in my case, you know it's true. It's me. You can't.'

'Hey, I know it's too much, too soon, but I can't help myself.' He smiled. 'I don't need you to say anything. I thought I'd let you know. That's all. Maybe make some of your questions go away.'

'I'm a fucked-up piece of arse. Are you sure you know what you're saying?'

'Yes. And we do need to talk, so I can tell you all about me.'

Anticipating he'd reveal his secrets now, her heart stuttered while she let his hand slip from hers.

'But not tonight. It's late, you have work tomorrow. I keep my promises. Tomorrow night it is.' She frowned, and he smiled. 'You're going to have to try much harder to get rid of me. The stripping thing isn't going to do it either.'

'You're an idiot. You know that, don't you?' She brushed his fringe away from his eyes to stare at him with all the disdain she could muster.

He chuckled. 'Are you getting mad at me, defying me again? Because you know what that does to me.'

'Can you be serious about us for one minute?'

Sebastian could understand the fear in her eyes as they searched his. He decided to put Natasha out of her misery by soundly kissing her, taking her breath away, and yet again dissolving her questioning mind with his favourite tactic. Pulling back, he said, 'Your eyes are the bluest of blue when you think your past is going to affect us. You know that?'

'Don't be stupid. They're wishy-washy blue. If you want to see blue, you should see my mum's.'

'That's not so, and I don't only mean the colour, which is captivating, by the way. Sometimes there's such sadness that swims in them.'

'Seb ... I ... just let me get used to this ... you ... us. This is new to me.'

'Me too.' He exhaled, tucking a strand of her hair behind her ear as a dazzling smile creased his eyes. 'You're one in a million, and I'm not just talking about the fucking awesome sex.'

'Speaking of which, what did you use to make my nipples, and other parts of me, feel so super-cool and get me so hot?'

He reached for her as she rolled, pulling her back to his front and wrapping his arms around her. He nuzzled into her neck so she could feel his smiling lips. 'A strong mint. *Triple X,* baby! Now sleep, dear Natasha.' The distant sound of the waves rolling onto the beach and lapping at the marina wall was calming. She drifted to sleep as a warm, contented glow unfurled in her heart and soul.

# THIRTY-FOUR

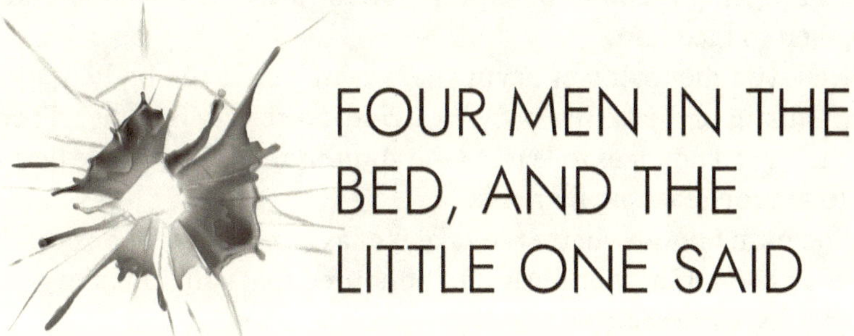

## FOUR MEN IN THE BED, AND THE LITTLE ONE SAID

The soft sound of Seb's breathing sent a thrill through Natasha as she dreamily woke. He was wrapped around her like a wisteria vine clinging to a tree. It was the first time she could have a proper look at his bedroom. It was very sophisticated and contemporary, like its owner. A low-backed white leather lounge snaked its way across the vast room with a curve that matched the curve of the floor-to-ceiling window. A lazy day of lounging on it would give front-row seats to the tranquil view up the coast to the marina, yachts casting blurred reflections on the calm water. Looking down the coastline, the viewer could be distracted by the golden sands and the glistening Southern Ocean.

The bed ran parallel to the rest of the window, allowing her to soak up the view while remaining where she was. The bed itself was a piece of modern art made of silver, aqua and white metal ribbons ornately fashioned to form a perfect, peaceful-looking wave frozen in a gentle rolling form.

On the far wall a magnificent painting of the *Brindisi* anchored in a quiet, aquamarine bay brought a tranquil atmosphere to the room. Underneath the image, stretching along the wall, was a bookcase overflowing with books. Her scarf lay discarded on the polished birchwood floor. The rest of their discarded clothes made a path leading to the bed, like breadcrumbs left by Hansel and Gretel.

She could picture the fun to be had in the room, especially on the rug that sprawled out in front of the fireplace. Her thoughts must have somehow delivered a message to Seb. He stirred and nuzzled her. A cascading, tingling wave of expectation unfurled through her body. She rolled to face him.

He loved the reality of having her warm, perfumed body nestled against him in his bed. 'Hey, baby, we made it through. Together. There are so many advantages to leaving the shutter open. One of the best is I get to see the real you, no mask.'

She didn't know whether to take that as a compliment or not.

'It's a good thing. Seriously, I'm honoured that you think I'm good enough to see the real you.'

Who spoke like this? No man she'd known. 'Seriously? What about your mask and secrets?' She found herself smiling at his handsome face.

'Seriously.' He smiled deliciously down at her. 'And I get to see your gorgeous body lying in my bed, your hair all mussed up from mind-blowing sex, in front of what is now the second-best view in my life.'

His words were so moving, and he looked so hot. Nat could just eat him up, so she started. The sprinkling of his soft chest hair tickled her lips as she trailed them down his chest. She felt the rough, hardened skin of the scar running down his sternum, continuing to trail kisses down his body until she reached her goal. Seb groaned as she gently caressed his growing manhood with her lips and tongue.

In one swift movement, his six-pack tensed and bunched. He grabbed her, hoisting her up to him while rolling over. Pinning Nat down, he started at her nipples, his tongue and teeth instruments of desire. 'I want to come in your tight cunt this morning.'

Before he could act on his words, there was a loud banging on the bedroom door. It made Nat jump.

'Shit! The boys, you distract me so much, I forgot.' He jumped off her. 'They get up so early. Stay there.' Like she had a choice, she thought.

She grabbed the sheet, pulling it up. Somewhere between a whisper and a shout, she called, 'Seb, I'm naked here.' She was suddenly in a state of extreme dread.

He ran to his walk-in wardrobe, grabbed a luxurious white Egyptian cotton robe and threw it to her. She pulled it over and around her. He was immobilised, too captivated by the sight of her pulling herself together as her fabulous breasts swung, full and aroused, monopolising his attention.

Another bang at the door jolted him into action. Natasha enjoyed the unfolding show. His superb abs rippled as he pulled on his boxer shorts, tucking his still somewhat aroused cock out of sight. It tented his boxers. He rolled his eyes at her as if it was entirely her fault. Grabbing his t-shirt from the floor, he pulled it on. Then trying to hide his excited manhood further, he pulled on his jeans. The show ended with Seb running a hand through his thick ebony hair as he walked towards the door shouting, 'Coming.'

Mmm, that's what Natasha wanted to do.

Seb opened the door. Not a good idea. The boys rushed in, pushing past him. Before either of the adults could say good morning, the kids jumped on the bed.

Nat tried to make sure she stayed covered as they bounced around her. She wasn't helped by Seb, who jumped on as well. Trying to regain her equilibrium, she said, 'Hi, boys, what time is it?' She tried to divert their gaze from her as she checked the clock on the mantelpiece.

Thankfully, it was only Seb's eyes that were lingering, travelling slowly up her body. Given his heated look, she frantically checked that her girls had not flown the coop. The last thing her nerves needed was an embarrassing Janet Jackson-type wardrobe malfunction in front of Seb's innocent nephews.

Anthony grumbled, 'Why aren't you up? It's seven. These two were up ages ago, annoying me. I'm starving.'

'I swear you guys have hollow legs,' Seb replied, looking so happy Nat's heart melted. For once he looked his age, every bit the young, cool, carefree uncle.

Mickey looked down at the floor and seemed stricken. Nat didn't think she could handle a five-year-old boy's curiosity about what they'd been up to in his uncle's bedroom. 'Uncle Seb, I'm glad my mum doesn't come in here. She'd get really mad. If I leave my clothes all over the floor, she yells at me, and my mess isn't this big.'

*Breathe, Natasha,* she told herself. There was relief on Seb's face.

'You're right, Mickey, and I'll pick them up as soon as I finish getting breakfast for you guys. Natasha needs to get to work, so let's get out of her way.'

Ren gazed calmly up at her, a question percolating. 'We don't usually see any guests sleep in here. You must be special or something.'

Seb jumped in to help. 'I guess Nat is all that and more, Ren.' And there it was again, that heartwarming, reverential look he had given her last night, just before he said he was falling in love with her. He turned to the boys. 'How about I get breakfast ready? Would you guys like French toast?'

Seb's suggestion was met with a resounding 'Yes!'

Thank goodness, saved by the promise of food, yet again. The boys jumped off the bed. Seb rounded them up and pushed them out the door. 'Go to the kitchen and get the bread and stuff out. I'll come and help you soon.'

She relaxed, swinging out of bed to cross the floor to Seb. 'That was close. I've never had four males share a bed with me.'

'Yes, you distract me from my duties, but I'm not complaining. I'd like to wake up next to you more often without the boys interrupting us.' His face was sincere and caring as he caressed her cheek with his knuckles, reaching for her chin, his lips softly meeting hers. She closed her eyes, wholly captured by him, sagging into him, holding his kiss.

'If we keep this up, I'll be late for work, and the boys will fade away.'

He pulled back. 'Yes.' He shook his head as if trying to clear a foggy thought. 'Yes, um, the shower is through there. You'll find fresh towels in the bathroom cupboard.' He leaned in and kissed her once more, lingering on her cheek. 'I love having you here. Is there a chance you can stay for breakfast?'

'Ah, no. I have to go home before work. I don't want to turn up in the same clothes as yesterday. That'd just be too much to explain. It'll have to be breakfast on the run. Sorry.' Reality suddenly hit her. Goldilocks and The Slut had been banished by a stronger Natasha, who'd emerged because of this beautiful man.

This realisation would have to wait. 'I promise I'll stay for breakfast some other time when I'm not so rushed.' She wanted him so badly, but she had to leave herself something to negotiate with to secure the answers she needed.

She brushed her teeth using his toothbrush. *What the hell,* she thought. They'd shared far more dangerous fluids than saliva. The shower was refreshing, her clothes not so much. She had to turn her knickers inside out just for the drive home. Better than going commando in front of the boys. She needed at least that part of her dignity intact as she left their uncle's, having spent a sin-filled but sensational night.

While she was in the shower, Seb had brought her bag up and left it on the bed for her. She retrieved a hairbrush and a hair tie. After brushing and fighting with her hair, she finally settled on a ponytail.

It gave off a neat vibe, not a fucked-soundly-all-night one. She added lipstick and decided she didn't look all that sinful.

In a moment of inspiration, she grabbed a pen and notebook from her bag. Writing a quick note, she kissed it, leaving an imprint of her lips, and placed it on Seb's pillow before leaving.

*You make me feel ... like never before. Give me time.*
*Yours, Nat. xxxx*

It was seven-thirty when Natasha reached the kitchen. To her horror, a woman she could only guess was Pia had joined Seb and the boys at the breakfast bar. Seb's jaw pulsed in anger. Even with his annoyance, Natasha appreciated his athletic form as he shoved back his chair and sulkily came to her. He was freshly showered, immaculate in blue running shorts and a white singlet. She figured he must have showered somewhere else in his vast penthouse.

Seb gave her a meek, almost embarrassed look. Her stomach did a jittery roll and fell. Who was he ashamed of? Pia? Or was he ashamed he'd been caught out with someone like Nat?

Shaky as she navigated the walk of shame in front of his sister, Nat managed a warm smile for Pia. She headed slowly towards the front doors, hoping for a quick hi and goodbye. Considering a quick escape as the best scenario, especially if he wanted to protect her from his family.

Despite his discomfort, Seb cautiously diverted Nat's path from the front door by taking her hand. He'd wanted to be in control of Natasha's first interaction with his family, and preferably not while she was leaving his house early in the morning. Now he had no choice but to introduce Nat to Pia, in under less than optimal circumstances. His sister could be an insufferable prude. Worst of all, he felt Nat slipping away from him, her mask of banality back in place. He knew Pia would try to pry it free. Nat lowered her eyes. He felt her reticence build as the distance between her and Pia closed. Seb and Natasha were both skittish. He thought, *How did this go south so quickly?*

Sebastian's words were firm when he spoke to his sister. 'Pia, this is Natasha Perry, the lady I've told you so much about.' Natasha's eyebrows shot up. She groaned inwardly, fearing Pia was bound to be disappointed. Natasha saw herself as a fucked-up pretender to a better life. Her troubled mind fixated momentarily on a positive – at least she was wearing knickers!

Pia stood and offered her hand. She was dressed in a tan panelled dress with a simple strand of pearls to add a sophisticated touch. She was a timeless Italian beauty. A young Sophia Loren came to mind. Only Pia's hair was darker as it flowed in waves over her shoulders. Her eyes were chocolate brown, like her brother's. She was so very elegant and adult everything Nat felt she wasn't.

'Pleased to meet you. It's nice to put a face to the name.' Pia's handshake was confident, as expected, but her caring eyes belied her firm, business-like grip. She seemed genuinely pleased to meet Natasha. 'I'm not sure what you've done to impress my little brother, but it must be remarkable. Every time I've been with him lately, he hasn't seemed to be able to stop talking about you.'

Pia was on a mission for the family. Not only interested in meeting Seb's mystery woman, but also extracting some face-to-face intel. He seemed madly smitten by this one. The first since ... the big mistake. This time Pia would be better at vetting any prospective partners.

Seb and Nat moved uneasily away from each other. Natasha twisted her fingers around her bag as Seb tried to hurry the chit-chat. 'Natasha can't stay. She has work.'

'Oh, where do you work?' Pia purred.

'I'm a clinical pharmacist on onc/haem at JCH and your foundation. But I suspect you knew that.'

'Yes, now that you mention it, I remember Seb telling me that.' Pia smiled sweetly. This one was sharp and strong-minded. 'You've certainly left a good impression on the foundation staff and my brother, but there's some trouble at onc/haem?'

'Not due to me. I've just been caught up in it as it involves drugs.'

Pia's eyes pinned Nat. 'Interesting that you mention it like that. But rest assured, I only deal with anything that affects the Aida foundation or Mancini Enterprises and of course my brother. Who seems taken with you.'

Nat nodded, a swirling dread now mixed with her jittery falling stomach. A classic, agonising silent awkwardness unfolded between the three adults, only to be interrupted by the sounds of the boys eating breakfast.

Pia broke the tension. 'I'm sorry. It's a Mancini trait. We tell it like it is. I didn't mean to embarrass either of you.'

This self-deprecating admission put Nat a little at ease. 'No, it's fine. I hadn't realised I'd made such an impression. I thought Seb kept coming around because I cook for him.'

Pia's eyes narrowed on Seb. 'Ah, I see. That makes sense.' Shrewdly, with a smirk on her lips, she interrogated further. 'But tell me, little brother, it must be more? It's not like you to have a sleepover – *here*.'

Natasha's mouth dropped. She was glad Pia was looking at Seb as her skittish ease dissipated.

Seb tried to laugh it off. 'And there you have it, Natasha, another example of the lack of a Mancini subtlety gene – or is it a total lack of any tact?' He tried to give Natasha a reassuring squeeze, but she moved further away from his touch. He was losing the battle with both women.

Pia wouldn't be derailed from her morning mission. 'Anything I should know?'

Natasha wasn't stupid. She knew what Pia was ultimately digging for and decided to forget subtly as well, 'You needn't worry, Pia. The only thing of Seb's I like spending is his time. You see, I like his smile, is all. *Not his money.*' The tension stirring within Nat now became a mix of boldness and insecurity.

'Oh.' Pia was momentarily knocked off her mission. 'I see. Well, aren't you a breath of fresh air.' This one was indeed astute and assertive.

Seb's voice growled, 'Sis, please leave it. There is so much I need to tell Natasha. I don't need you sticking your nose in.'

'If you've got a lot to tell her, why not ask Natasha to come to the family dinner tonight?' A mischievous smile settled across her face. 'That way, we can all help you tell her everything there is to know about you.' Pia was scheming.

Natasha didn't want Seb's sister to force him into something he didn't want to do. He had said he was taking her out, but hadn't mentioned it was a family thing. Jeez, what does one wear to a Mancini family do, especially if you're to be chewed up and spat out?

Crossing his arms, he snapped, 'Pia. Stop. You're certainly three for three. Firing on all tactless cylinders this morning, aren't we?' Seb groaned. He knew what Pia had planned on behalf of the family.

'Sorry! I'm just excited to meet your girlfriend, finally.' She folded her arms, staring him down. 'Natasha is someone who you should take to the family get-together, not the other pieces of media fluff you trot out to run decoy for you with the local women and the press. Stop hiding.' They stood glaring at each other.

Awkward and anxious were too pathetic to describe the atmosphere. Natasha took heart from hearing that Pia considered her his girlfriend, but it was time to breach the latest uncomfortable silence smothering them. Moving towards the door, she said, 'Really, I must go. I'm sure you understand I can't stay to chat. I love my job and can't be late. It's been nice meeting you, though.'

Pia ripped her eyes away from Seb. This one really did seem to be about work and not his money. Trying to reassure Nat so Pia would have another chance to interrogate her, she purred, 'Pleasure's all mine. Hopefully, I'll see you tonight.'

Before Nat could say anything, Seb was talking, flashing his sister a menacing stare. 'Nat, I'll walk you to your car. It's the least I can do after you've had to endure Pia so early in the morning.'

Nat resisted the urge to say yes, suitably chewed up and spat out, and all before breakfast. Instead, she managed, 'No, it's fine. I understand. A big sister must look out for her little brother.'

Pia flashed Nat her own megawatt Mancini. 'I like this one, Seb.'

Nat ensured her escape by calling, 'Bye, boys. It was lovely to meet you.'

They were still eating and could only wave and grunt. Yet, the usually quiet Ren gave her a big smile. 'Bye, Natasha. Thanks for helping me out last night.'

'Any time.' She returned his smile and turned towards the door.

Seb caught up with her, brusquely steering her out and to the lift. As they descended to the foyer, he was distant, frustration pulsing off him. Natasha was on edge from having met – or was it, having jousted with – Pia.

She was also unsettled by Pia's comments about the family dinner. Nat wanted him to ask her, but at the same time, she didn't want him to feel trapped into asking her because of Pia. The classic dating conundrum of wanting to appear above it all and not caring while deep-down caring and really wanting him to ask. Plus, there were the ghosts of Thursday night's conversation and questions about drugs that haunted her.

A shadow fell over her soul as her frail self-confidence and mind began unwinding in a familiar cycle of self-flagellation.

A distant, weak Goldilocks chipped in. *Come on. Stop dreaming. Sluts don't get taken to the ball by Prince Charming. They're kept in the dark. That's where your whoring belongs.*

The nagging doubt she had about Seb resurfaced. He was holding so much back, and so was she. How could they survive?

They'd been in a parallel universe over the last twelve hours. A place where they could have each other unashamedly, enjoying a tender, shared closeness. Now they were descending into reality. The stark differences between them must be heeded. Here, in this universe, their past lives washed away any future happy-ever-afters. The lift doors opened and they walked across the lavish foyer and out of the high-rise.

The heavy, muggy air, thick with stormy unease, reflected their mood. She reached into her bag and rooted around for her car keys. The tension between them stretched to a lethal breaking point, like one of her guitar strings stretched too tight. Natasha just wanted to make her escape.

Then it happened with a blinding flash and a deafening crash. The strain snapped with a flash, yielding to the stress atmospherically and gave release relationship-wise. A gum tree close by exploded into a twisted mass of burning, splintered wood and steam. She was knocked off her feet and into Seb's arms. He staggered a moment. Almost immediately, the bolt of lightning was accompanied by an ear-splitting, bone-rattling crack of rumbling thunder. Her head was spinning and her thoughts warped as adrenaline speared through her. Then rain, hard, full drops, showered down.

Seb yelled above the noise. 'Let's get to your car. It's closer.' She unlocked the doors as they ran towards it. They were both soaked when they dived in. Her ears were ringing, and her heart was pounding. A rush of excitement rather than any fear consumed her.

They were trapped in her car while nature's fury was unleashed around them. The rain was so heavy it was like a watery grey curtain had been drawn around the vehicle. Nothing could be seen for more than a few metres as the rain, thunder and lightning set in. Sitting in the driver's seat, her soaking wet silk blouse was clinging to her, her nipples on high beam again.

Seb couldn't resist her. Reaching across, he claimed her mouth. His fierce passion wedged Nat against the door. He was buzzing from the electric atmosphere and her absolute beauty.

She pushed him back. 'Sebastian, stop.'

He looked at her quizzically, panting, aroused and wanting more.

'Are we going to talk about what just happened? One minute you're all sulky, sullen and withdrawn, and now you're all hot, wet and horny.'

He grabbed her again, finding her lips. She was irresistible.

Shoving him, she growled. 'Stop. Give me some answers.'

'I said I wanted you this morning. What better time than now.'

Amid the storm – a perfect metaphor for their relationship – chaotic and uncontrollable, Nat tried to steady, moved aside, taking a deep breath. Her words came out in a quivering rush of raw emotion. 'Stop using sex to block talking about us. I've bared my soul to you, but you, you've refused to answer any of my questions. I'm not going to be some fluffy media fuck to throw people off the scent.'

'Natasha. That's not—' Another ear-splitting rumble rolled over the car.

By now, any positives had dissolved into her dark rage. 'What am I supposed to think? You've given me no answers. Every time I ask and we get close, we just fuck. And the way you acted just now. You got caught out by Pia, didn't you? Bad timing for me, but worse for you. You were embarrassed by me. Your silence in the lift and trying to jump my bones just now tell me you didn't want her to meet me. You only want me for one thing.'

'Nat, let me—'

'Sebastian. Don't do this.' She crumbled. 'Don't treat me like a whore. I can fight my past. I don't have the will or the desire to fight you for my future.' In his eyes she saw hesitation and dismay.

Seb quietened. 'You want the truth.'

'Yes. You know why.' The storm unleashed its wrath. She expected the same from Seb.

Instead, he cupped her face tenderly. His thumbs stroked each of her cheeks. He found tranquillity in all the turmoil raging in their minds and nature, settling her tormented soul. 'Don't shred yourself like this. Can't you see? I swear I'm falling in love with you. Believe in yourself. Me.'

He tried to find some common ground. 'When you said last night you couldn't say what I wanted to hear, I understood. You need time, and you certainly need time away from my family. They're something else altogether.' His words didn't dull her uneasiness and doubt. He continued, 'I wanted nothing more than to invite you tonight, but I didn't want you to feel like I was rushing or ambushing you. I was listening to you. "Not too much, not too soon, Mancini" – that's why I didn't ask you.'

She heard her warnings being turned on her. 'Oh.' He understood. 'So why so quiet on the way down here?'

'What can I say? I was overwhelmed. I want to answer all your questions about the Mancinis and me. I'd planned to do that tonight by missing the family thing to take you away. Then with Pia's outburst, which you handled amazingly, by the way. Anyway, I knew you'd think I hadn't invited you because I was embarrassed by you. And if I did after her outburst, then you'd believe it was because I was caught out by Pia, not because of my indecision. I'm so angry at her. She blindsided me and through me, you. I've been trying to weigh up being with you against subjecting you to my family and taking the chance they'll chase you away. And all this on top of all the things you need answers to. I didn't know what to do. That's all. It's the truth.'

Taking her hands in his, raising them to his lips, he kissed them tenderly. His eyes burned. 'Trust me, I do know what I want. It's you. It's simple, and for me, your past isn't a problem. But I don't want the Mancini family to be an issue in our future.'

She was struck by an unfamiliar emotion. *Our future* were words Rick had advocated and he'd cheapened them. But with Seb, the words were infused with such sincerity they soaked through to her heart.

He took her left hand in his, kissed the palm and held it to his cheek. 'I would be honoured if you would come with me tonight. If you think you can stand it.' His voice became sombre as he kept her hand in place. 'I haven't taken a woman who means anything to me to one of these things in over nine years, maybe never.' Seb released her hand and smirked. 'Fluffy or not.'

She let her hand fall.

'You must remember and believe the good stuff I tell you.' He couldn't help himself, chuckling. 'And I know I've definitely mentioned that you're anything but a fluffy fuck.' He kissed her lips softly. 'They will scrutinise you. It's a tough gig. My family are in your face. Pia was just warming up this morning.'

'If that's the real reason.'

'Yes, believe me, I'm asking more of you than you are of me.'

'Okay. I would love to go with you and take up the challenge. But if I do this for you, then you have to come clean about everything else. Deal?'

'Deal.' He ran his hand through her hair, gently pushing it from her face. 'Yes, dear Natasha, I will answer any questions that are left after my family has its way with you. We'll go where we can be alone, and I'll tell you everything.' He kissed the corner of her smile.

A shudder shook her, more to do with his lingering lips than the family thing. 'The things you do to me,' she whispered as his lips left hers. Relieved, deep blue eyes were lost in darkening Old Gold chocolate ones.

'Please don't ever think you are anything but light and love in my life.' His voice became laced with need. 'You're unbelievably irresistible and right now it's like my private wet t-shirt contest.'

'Dr Mancini, does your devious mind ever rest?'

'You make me forget everything but you and me. And right now, I'd like to finish what we started this morning.' He swayed back to look at her, this time asking permission.

'You had me at finish what we started this morning.'

When Nat next took a breath, they were on the back seat of her car. The storm was unleashing its fury. Seb had shed his clothes and shuffled forward, moving his hand up and down his cock with a searing look in his eyes, that mesmerized her.

Natasha was wet from more than the rain as she sat naked astride him. He trailed kisses down her chest. The storm, so primal and natural, broke around them. Thunder and lightning provided an unrestrained, natural backdrop to their own unrestrained, natural act. The most uninhibited, blissful tempest that two humans could share. The weather outside drove them harder.

With teeth clashing, and lips skating over hot skin, their dark needs complemented each other. For something so raw and animalistic, they knew they were also sharing something so pure and unique to them.

Natasha was delirious and drove for a higher climax by biting down on where the beautifully toned muscles of his shoulder met his neck. Her bite made him thrust faster and deeper. The last dwindling flash of lightning and boom of thunder saw Mother Nature's fury soothed. Sweet ecstasy was liberated within Natasha's WRX, relieving the once-intense atmosphere.

He huskily shouted something feral, and she screamed his name as her mind scattered. They came down gradually. The storm's fury matched their lovemaking as it also slowly abated.

Nat was totally beguiled. 'Seb, I know you say you're falling in love with me. It scares me because I'm not sure I'll ever be able to say those words to you. I don't know what love is.'

'Then let's learn together. Believe me, this is the first time I've ever experienced anything like this.'

'Are you sure? You've seen how needy I can be with my brittle self-esteem. You've seen it on show.'

'And I haven't seen anything I haven't liked.'

'Why me? You could have anyone.'

His astonishment was reflected in the lines creasing his beautiful face. 'I could ask you the same thing.'

She was baffled.

He sighed. 'How are you so patient with me? That's the question I want an answer to. You're intelligent and amazingly independent, and you do sexy so well. But most of all, you felt I was worth the risk to trust me with your past. I haven't given you anything, while you've given so much. You're willing to wait until I'm ready. That means so much.'

Natasha didn't know how to answer such a statement, especially being all post-climactic. Without realising it, she changed the subject, 'Shit! Look at the time. Your sister will think you got swept away in the storm.'

'I did,' he grinned.

She scrambled to pull herself back together. 'You're going to get me so fired, Mancini. Concentrating on work after this was going to be difficult.'

'Good, then I can keep you all to myself and enjoy you twenty-four seven.'

'Oh, you don't want to go there. Keeping me twenty-four seven isn't an option.'

He nipped her earlobe, sending pure ecstasy flowing through her. 'I like a challenge, and I wouldn't have it any other way.' Grabbing her hands, he stared her down. 'Now, about tonight, I'll pick you up from your place at six-thirty. Be ready only in your underwear with make-up on. I'll provide the rest. Your dress, shoes, everything else. Okay?'

'Don't be rid—'

He put his index finger on her lips. 'Now, before you protest, hear me out. Let me do this as a way of saying thank you for taking on my family. This way you won't have to worry about what you're going to wear. I'll pick out exactly what you need.'

'No, Seb, I don't need you to—'

'Please, I can afford this. Let me spoil you tonight. It might be the last chance I get. Once I've told you everything, it might cool your enthusiasm, so at least let this happen.'

His eyes implored her. She melted. 'Okay.' Although an underlying disquiet rumbled through her. 'I guess.'

'Excellent. And ... I have one other request.'

'Which is?'

'No matter what you think or hear, you'll give me time to explain, all the time I need. Give me a chance.'

'Um, all right.' A twinge of apprehension struck her like she'd signed a contract without reading the fine print.

# THIRTY-FIVE

## SOFT COCKS AND STIFF REWARDS

Natasha walked from the car park towards the skybridge just in time for work. The sun was heating the day. The smell of hot, steaming bitumen and evaporating rainwater greeted her. Her mind was drawn back to the morning's amazing car sex. Suddenly her arousal began feeding on the fragrance. As her belly and core rippled, Nat recognised the earthy aroma had become an aphrodisiac.

Her pleasurable thoughts were soon assaulted when punching in the door code to enter the pharmacy. A familiar, not-so-welcoming voice shattered her enjoyment.

'Are *you* working today?'

'No, I just come here for fun.' She opened the heavy door for them to enter. *Shit!* Rick must have decided to work a weekend shift for one of the other pharmacists.

It was early afternoon when Nat took a call from Chelsea. 'Hey, we're flat chat up here. Ruby's been prescribed a new drug. We need it right now. Can you deliver? Pleease. I wouldn't usually ask, but she hasn't improved. We need it to bump up her white cells. Otherwise, she won't be able to go home until much later, and you know how we like to move our immunocompromised patients out asap.'

Natasha stepped into the lift with the drug vials. Rick joined her. They hadn't been alone together since the break-up. When he finally did speak, it was to pick at Nat's scars.

'Since this dangerous-drugs fiasco, I thought I'd do a spot check to ensure other things weren't being missed on onc/haem. Let's say it's a surprise inspection. I haven't even told Jo. She supports you too much. If I were in charge, you would've been confined to the dispensary, not just on DD probation.'

She clenched her fists but remained silent. After all, she couldn't defend the probation by mentioning Cartwright's suspicious behaviour. She certainly couldn't mention his indiscretion regarding the pharmacy's security. She wouldn't let Jo down just to score some cheap points over Rick. He wasn't even worth cheap points.

Rick didn't have such lofty standards. 'Have you heard what Mancini's old dates call him?' Cheap points were his speciality.

'No, but I'm sure you'll enlighten me.'

'King Tut, like the Egyptian mummy, all golden and flawless on the outside. If you like that sort of thing. But I hear he's dead, dry and dusty on the inside. All very bound up in himself.'

'Oh, that's funny, ha ha, especially coming from you. Oh, wait. Haven't *you* heard?' Nat changed her mind and decided she could grab a few cheap points, especially at Rick's expense. She'd give him both barrels. Firing the first. 'You know what everybody calls your current fuck buddy?' With a deadpan face and voice to match, she said, 'Holly twenty-four seven'. Nat had sunk to his level, and she wasn't climbing back to nosebleed territory anytime soon. She cocked the second barrel. 'I hear she's open to anyone, anytime, to do anything.' As she'd fired the second barrel, the smug look on his face disappeared. Smiling sweetly, she exclaimed, 'It seems that while Holly twenty-four seven couldn't make it with King Tut, as you call him, I have had him many times – long, hard and very handsome, he goes forrr ... ever.'

Rick shifted uneasily and looked away from her. 'What would little frigid you know?'

'Enough to get a little ol' soft cock like you to come, and I mean *little*.' She was on a roll. 'Being with you was like the end of the Rolling Stones song, 'Start me up''.

Rick shook his head in disdain. 'Shut up!'

'No, not shut up, start me up, 'cos that's what I've been doing with you the last twelve months. You know, I was making a dead man c—'

'Shut the fuck up!'

'Now who's only speaking in clichés.' The lift chimed. Nat left him gaping as she stepped out into the fresh air of the onc/haem ward. She felt empowered. She'd never dared say anything so audacious to anyone at this job before, although she'd often thought it. However, she'd used similar smart-arse comments to ward off overly enamoured gropers at her previous vocation.

Nat found Chelsea.

'Hey, I see you rode up with Rick the Dick. Did you go all Kelly 'Since u been gone' Clarkson on his arse?'

'Yep. Very satisfying.'

Chelsea smiled. 'Speaking of satisfaction, you must visit Ruby – right now. Let me take those.' Chelsea grabbed the drug vials and shoved Nat off towards Ruby's room.

'Chelsea, what are you up to?'

Nat walked into the room, not really looking. 'Hi, guys, how are you?' She stopped dead in her tracks.

Standing at the end of Ruby's bed was Sebastian. Although she didn't look well, Ruby beamed at Nat.

'Oh ... my apologies for the interruption, Seb, um ... Dr Mancini.' Nat stuttered as her heart did a little twirl. When he was in his white med coat and all business-like, he was most definitely Mr Tall Dark and Delicious. Nat caught herself sighing as she remembered the sensual feel of his mouth on her while the lightning and thunder surrounded them. His lips on her lips – flash. His mouth on her throat – rumble – on her nipples – flash – and on her hip – rumble. *Oh, on my ... Oh* – flash.

'Hi, Natasha. Tash? Hello, earth to Tash.'

She was brought back to the here and now. 'Hi, Ruby. Sorry, just lost my train of thought for a bit.' She tore her eyes off Seb, who gave her a knowing smile.

'Yes, the view up here is beautifully distracting, isn't it?' Ruby smiled as she glanced from Nat to Seb and back again.

Smiling, Nat met Ruby's eyes conspiratorially before blushing. 'Yes.' She bowed her head.

Sitting next to Ruby, Jonathon surveyed the spectacular view from the window. The Indian Ocean glinted in the afternoon sun as it met the harbour city. 'Yes, it is a beautiful view up here. Fit for my angel.'

He'd missed the gist of the women's conversation, yet added a beautiful sentiment. 'Ruby's always been heavenly to me.'

Did real love between two people look like this, so palpable?

Nat couldn't help but glance across at Seb. His eyes fixed on hers, with his new intense, loved-up stare. She found herself smiling unashamedly at him. Before anyone in the room could do or say anything else, Rick barged in. Ruby's face dropped, as did everybody else's.

'Hello. Ruby, isn't it? How are you feeling today?'

'I'm okay.' A frosty change came over her.

'Remember me? I was the pharmacist up here. Rick. Remember?' She feigned bewilderment, and he patronised. 'I. Used to check. All your pills. And medicines. The things that make you better.'

Seb was appalled that Rick could be such a thoughtless idiot. Ruby was a wise woman who was ill. Neither deaf nor dumb.

They were all mute as Rick continued. 'I'm here to check on Natasha. See how she's going.'

'Natasha's doing fine.' Even though she was unwell, Ruby's spirit could not be denied. 'She's been like a breath of fresh air. Don't you think so, Dr Mancini?'

'Yes, most definitely.' Seb wasn't troubled by Ruby's cheeky question.

'Oh, er … good.' As always, Rick couldn't help himself. 'As her experience grows, she'll become more in tune with what the doctors and the ward need.'

Seb couldn't help himself either. 'I believe Natasha's experience and the doctors and the ward are doing just fine.' If this turned into a testosterone-driven arm wrestle, Seb would win easily.

Rick backed off. 'Okay, um, well, I'll keep moving and check the rest of the ward.' He made a quick exit.

Ruby breathed a sigh of relief. They all did. Nat had no idea what she had ever seen in him. She rationalised that now, having tasted Dom Pérignon, she could never go back to cheap, rough sparkling wine. The older couple were all smiles when Nat and Seb left them. They walked down the corridor towards the ward office.

'I didn't know you were working today.'

'I had a desperate call from Dr Cartwright. She wasn't well and asked if I could organise someone to take her shift. Pia had taken the boys, and I was shopping. It was a good chance to catch up with you. I decided to do it. Why should someone else have all the fun?'

'Oh, you know how to make a girl feel special.'

With a roguish grin, he grabbed Nat around the hips, steering her into the ward storeroom, where his lips passionately sought hers as her back hit the back of the door. She was precisely how Seb wanted her, sexily breathless. He mouthed hoarsely, 'I've got something for you.'

A pang of desire, reminiscent of the morning's, ran through her. Then thoughts of Rick being on the ward didn't only cool her desires, they iced them. 'Seb, we can't, not with him on the ward checking up on me.'

Shaking his head, his lips smiled on her brow. 'No, no. While I do find you irresistible, not now. I want you to wear this tonight.' He retrieved a small package wrapped in pink tissue paper from his med jacket pocket. He kissed her again as he left. Nat walked sheepishly out of the storeroom, relieved there was less staff around on the weekend. No one had witnessed their little tryst. In a daze, she put his present in her file and headed back to the pharmacy.

The weather had returned to being unsettled and rainy when she arrived home, forcing her to run from her car to her apartment. Being more excited than nervous, Nat changed from her typically late MO, and was ready early, dressed in the underwear and stockings he'd so keenly delivered. She'd tried to tone down her look to that of a family dinner, going for natural make-up. Her hair fell loosely around her shoulders in soft curled, golden waves.

The underwear didn't scream quiet family dinner. She suspected he had something else in mind after dinner. Seb's present was a red Yves Saint Laurent G-string with diamantes sewn into it. To complete the sexy look, he had included the matching red lace and diamante satin bra. She had never had such fabulous underwear, let alone a designer label. The satin was so cool on her nipples. It sent an erotic thrill through her when she put it on. Her mind drifted. She wondered if he was going to use ice on her tonight.

Given the underwear, she was more than a little troubled about the price to be paid by her for her outfit. Regardless of her background, she knew all too well that nothing in this world was ever free. Maybe the answers she wanted were too high a price to pay.

With her basement-bargain robe hugging her curves Nat grabbed her guitar and played to settle her excitement and nerves. A few verses of 'Permission to shine', the Aussie duo Bachelor Girl's inspirational ballad, seemed appropriate for the evening.

She kept strumming, no longer singing. Thoughts drifted around in her head. If his mask was the best of all, he could be playing the biggest con job ever on her. Yet it would be an exhilarating roller-coaster ride. If she decided to jump on board. As always, her playing soothed her.

Movement at the corner of her eye pulled her out of her musings. Seb was standing in her doorway holding two large bags, one in each hand, his black suit jacket folded over his right arm.

He looked divine. His wavy black fringe swept back off his face, slightly unkempt, yet hot. Natasha stopped playing to take note. Seb's stare was intense yet mystified. 'No, please, keep playing. It was beautiful. I hadn't realised how talented you are, well, musically anyway.' His eyes were filled with wonder but suddenly became hard. 'You shouldn't leave your door unlocked. You never know who might pass by and be lured to you by your beautiful playing.'

'Hello, Dr Mancini,' she smiled, glad he hadn't heard her sing. Yet happier she could enjoy the treat of watching his fantastic form stalk towards her, glorious in black dress trousers and a silvery-grey button-down shirt. She was somewhat defenceless against his powers, only in a robe, underwear and stockings. She knew he had planned this meticulously.

Seb crossed to her like a big cat hunting its prey, his predatory eyes locked on hers. 'I'm serious.' His voice was a little menacing. 'You should lock your door.' Seb's brow creased with concern, maybe frustration. 'You know there's this crazy out there slitting people's mouths wider across their cheeks, don't you?'

'How do you know the Slasher's cutting people's mouths, not just their faces? The reports said the police weren't releasing any specific details about the crimes, other than junkies were being attacked.'

'Must have heard it on the news on the way over. But you need to take care.' He shrugged her off.

She was moved that he was worried. 'Yes, you're right. I'll be more careful. Promise. If you must know, I was a little flustered when I got home from an eventful day at work.'

She stood and walked to him, putting her guitar down. Her robe slid open, showing him his purchases up close and personal. He wasn't the only one who could plan meticulously.

It worked. Seb moved closer to sweetly deliver an intimate kiss to the corner of her mouth, whispering, 'Oh, did something happen at work?' His face broke into a mischievous grin.

'Yes. I was felt up in the onc/haem storeroom by a hot doctor. My mind was a little scattered when I got home. Not to mention my growing concerns at meeting said hot doctor's family tonight.' She stretched up and kissed his lips.

Heat sparked between them. Bags and jacket slipped to hit the floor with a soft thud as Seb's hands slid through the front of her robe. She felt their warmth wrap around her hips, drawing her to him. His mouth moved along her jaw. He breathed against her ear in a deliciously seductive tone, 'You feel and smell sooo good. We really must get you dressed. Otherwise we'll have to ditch the family thing.'

'Let's do that.'

'Very tempting, but I promised you and Pia we'd go, and I don't break promises.'

Reluctantly she pulled away. Seb was right. They couldn't get lost in each other, otherwise she wouldn't find answers to any of her questions. He'd block her with sex again.

He stooped down to one of the bags and pulled out a raw silk Chanel dress. 'Voila!' He was so proud of himself.

A stab of anxiety pierced her. She didn't want to shatter the illusion, but she desperately hoped it wasn't too small.

The little black dress had a delicate pewter lace overlay, a level of classic sophistication like no dress she'd owned. It had a round neck, high at the front but dipping down at the back.

Seb's voice was husky, 'I'm told that as it's sleeveless, it will show off your gorgeous shoulders. Which are only one of the many things I'm growing to appreciate more and more about you every day.'

There was a silver chain waistband detail. This silver and diamond detail clasped in the front, drawing the eye and making the wearer's waist look tiny. A long, visible silver zip traced down the rest of the back of the dress. It was a practical, decorative detail in itself. It drew attention to the wearer's back, trapping the eye of the beholder on a journey downwards, accentuating a long and slender body that had an elegant conclusion at the derrière.

Seb slowly undid the zip, his eyes scorching her. She relished the appreciative look he gave her. 'Step into it,' he coaxed.

Slowly, she let her robe fall. It slid down her body to pool at her feet. Seb's eyes followed, drawn to her elegant lines. Standing in only her new underwear, she stepped into the dress. The silk lining was fresh and smooth against her skin. He gently slid the gown up and over her butt. Thankfully, it was a snug, elegant fit. She threaded her arms through the strappy sleeves. Seb sent thrills through her as his fingers brushed her spine, zipping her up.

'Stunning,' he whispered, moving her hair to kiss the back of her neck.

She turned to face him. 'I'm a little overwhelmed by your generosity. The only designer labels I've ever worn have been knock-offs.'

'Remember, you promised to accept whatever we did tonight, especially if you want answers. And you promised to hear me out and give me time to tell you all of it.' While he said these words, a flash of his don't-argue stare rolled across his face before his gaze melted and he kissed her cheek. She was speechless, and now more than a little stunned. He stepped back, seemingly enchanted by her.

It was uplifting knowing she was provoking such sensual need in him, which wasn't sullied by dirty money-changing hands. She had to believe these gifts were heartfelt and carefully chosen. A significant difference for her, and it felt so good. There was no reason to summon The Slut because Natasha was happy just being herself.

He bent down again and pulled a pair of gorgeous Christian Louboutin diamond and black leather stilettos out of the other bag. They matched the silver detail on the front of the dress. 'Sit.' Nat did as she was told, and like Prince Charming with Cinderella, he dropped to one knee and put the shoes on her feet.

Nat stood, somewhat stunned at how comfortable the shoes were given their ten-centimetre heels. 'How did you do all of this, sizes and everything?'

'Oh, I have my sources.' He rose, standing close to her. They were so enchanted by each other that they didn't even have to touch for the familiar sensual energy to pulse through them. He smiled dreamily. 'But let me say, Chelsea was very accommodating.'

'It all makes sense now, her desperate call for me to come to the ward.' She scoffed hoarsely. 'She knows my sizes and that I love heels. Today has been one surprise after another.'

'I'm not finished yet.' He reached into his jacket and pulled out a trademark Tiffany blue jewellery box. 'Remember, no arguments.' She was reeling, never having had such adoration heaped on her. She honestly didn't know how to handle it. Familiar with only one way, she tried not to let memories of that way taint the occasion. Maybe this wasn't so far from the business transactions she was used to?

*You're still whoring yourself. For you, silly skank, this is too elegant.*

Goldy was obliterated as he flipped up the lid of the box. Nat's gaze met a dazzling, finely crafted silver diamond necklace and matching diamond drop earrings. In a daze, drawn to its pure, elegant beauty, she moved her hand forward to touch it. And, in a *Pretty Woman* moment, Seb flipped the lid down on her fingers.

She squealed, 'I can't believe you did that!'

His eyes danced with laughter. 'I can't either, but seeing the look on your face made it hard not to. So worth it.'

His fingers skimmed her cheek as he moved her hair. The feel of them on her neck sent a further buzz through her. He clasped the necklace around her neck and gave her a swift kiss on her cheek. 'Here, you put the matching earrings on.'

Natasha walked to the hallway mirror with Seb following. She giggled, swaying a little more as a sexy, empowered feeling lifted her. Speaking over her shoulder, feeling his eyes firmly on her, she asked, 'Enjoying the view, Dr Mancini?'

'Yes, very much. Thank you, Ms Perry. You have a great arse and fabulous legs.'

Natasha didn't immediately recognise the woman staring back at her in the mirror. She was someone Natasha could only ever have hoped to aspire to be. Poised and elegant, she had self-driven belief and power. Nat would definitely give herself permission to shine tonight.

'You are truly a beautiful woman, Natasha. Don't let anyone ever make you think or feel otherwise.'

She dreamily nodded.

'Ready?'

She took a breath. 'Yes.' She noticed they were colour-coordinated. 'We're very dressed up. What kind of family event is this?'

'Oh, just the regular meeting of the family members and some employees ...' He paused, watching for her reaction.

Trying for calm, she quipped, 'So *not* just a small Mancini family thing then.'

'Ah, that would be right. Every once in a while, we have a dinner to honour some of our employees.'

'I was under the impression that when Pia said a family get-together, it would just be the family. How many is some?'

He stammered, 'Ah, just the family and about forty others.'

'What?' At least the family would be dispersed. 'I guess I can get lost in the crowd.'

He broke out a heated megawatt Mancini smile. 'Oh, I don't think a woman who looks as stunning as you do could get lost in any crowd, let alone this evening.' Her anxiety ebbed when he said, 'I'm looking forward to being by your side the whole time.'

While she didn't feel she could sing in front of Seb, Nat could be surer of his actions towards her in public than she ever felt about Rick. Then again, Rick never heard her sing either.

'I'll give you some background on the family and me in the car. I have to say I'm not sure how far I'll get.' He hesitated. 'Sometimes I find it too hard to—'

'Talk about it.' She reached across and kissed the corner of his mouth. 'Breathe, Sebastian. It's okay. I understand.'

He kissed her back, his lips soft before they formed a sad smile. 'That's why I keep coming back. You understand me.'

'And that's why I won't push you, but you need to tell me soon. Otherwise I'll make it up, and you know my mind. It always chooses the worst-case scenario.'

'Right, then. Well, we'd better get going.'

'And where exactly are we going?'

'The Duxton. Dinner is at a quarter to eight, but we're supposed to be there at half-past seven, so we better get a move on.'

Seb glided the Maserati through the traffic and finally broke his silence. 'Let me say this, I'm only involved in bits of the family business. I'm not involved in the importing, exporting and transport side. Dad and Dominic manage those aspects together, with Cole's help.'

'And the parts of Mancini Enterprises that interest you are?'

'We're all board members, but I only have interests in the construction, property and philanthropic areas of the company, like the foundation.'

Trying to sound on top of things, she murmured, 'It seems like a lot for Dominic and your dad to manage.'

'A little, but with Cole's help, it flows. They are smooth operators.'

'Cole, as in Cole Hexum?'

'Yes. He's the family's and the foundation's lawyer. He was Giuseppe's childhood friend, and he kind of became like the fifth Mancini child. Cole grew up with us. He and Giuseppe studied law and business together.'

'What does this have to do with your family's history?'

'When Dad first came out from Italy, he started the company with a friend. Then he met Mum and married her. As the company became more successful and complex, he realised that Mum was a real force, with a knack for business, and she should run it with him. Not the friend. Mum kept Dad on the straight and narrow. There was no place for his partner Carlo to fit.'

'What does that mean?'

He shook his head and snapped, 'I'm getting to that. Let's just say some of his business interests didn't fit with Mum and Dad's.'

Feeling his ire, Nat realised how much this would unsettle and cut him to the bone. That scared her.

'When Giuseppe and Dom were old enough, they began working in the business. Then, eight years ago, Seppe was killed in an odd accident at the Freo wharf. Mum died soon after. Dad wanted me to join him and Dom, but I couldn't.'

'Was it because you wanted to be a doctor?'

'No, I was already studying medicine, but at this time, there was a lot of family shit going on, mainly due to me. There was no problem with me being a doctor. Dad and Mum were happy for us kids to do whatever we wanted. They knew my heart was in medicine and the foundation side of the business with Mum and Pia, so Cole joined the company.'

'Was that a problem?'

'No, Cole's great.'

It was like pulling teeth with tweezers. 'The stuff surrounding you, has it got something to do with the rumours about your family being, well, I don't know – dangerous, trafficking drugs?' Bugger it. There, she said it. What would be, would be.

'Kind of, it surfaced that Dad's old business partner was mixed up in some bad stuff.' Seb couldn't stop the bitterness in his voice. 'It affected my ... my family.' A deep sorrow gripped him. No one outside the family knew about this part of his life. His father had forever hidden it.

He wanted to say more but didn't know how. 'My life was a mess. Then Mum was gone and ...' He was momentarily overwhelmed. 'I had a ... Nat, I can't. Not now, after. It's too much to go into. You'll only have more questions. Questions I don't have time to answer now. We're nearly there. I don't want to spoil this night for you.'

To see him hesitant and vulnerable had Natasha cautious and concerned. He was usually so well put together. She understood why he had baulked at telling her. Sharing the rest of his story was going to shake and drain him. Recognising this type of anguish and the energy required to confront it, she knew she could wait. Quietly, she tried to bring him back. 'Sorry, I didn't mean to upset you. Losing your Mum to cancer is as good a reason as any to need time to sort your life out. It's enough for now.'

He glanced across. 'Thank you, Natasha. I promise I'll tell you all about the rest of my baggage. You know enough to get you through tonight. I've organised the right time and place for me to tell you everything, but after this evening's dinner.'

Nat felt she needed to reassure him, as well as herself, so she leaned across. Resting her hand on his thigh, she kissed his cheek. 'Thank you for all the gifts you've showered on me. No matter what happens, I've never felt this special.'

He tenderly lifted her hand from his leg to his lips. He kissed the palm and held it to his cheek. 'The pleasure is all mine. You're very precious to me.'

'And you to me,' she whispered. She wasn't sure he'd heard.

Time, like Nat, held its breath until he said, 'You're my second chance.'

She was finding it hard to keep wading forward through all these half-insights and questions about his life. They were like waist-high mud, stopping her from moving with ease in his direction, and so murky she couldn't be sure of her footing if she chose a different path to the one Seb was leading her down. Everything that appeared so safe about him, the promise their future could hold, always seemed impossibly out of their reach. She felt she'd need a compass and shovel to dig her way out of this tonight.

Nat settled on humour. 'Dr Mancini, all I can say is thank God for double dates.'

'Yes, who knew I went with Ms Twenty-Four Seven and my heart left with Ms Smart, Caring and Sexy, the complete package.' He chuckled, treating her to his glorious megawatt Mancini. The atmosphere lifted as Seb was back. That was the Seb she believed in. So much for her mask. Seb had one equally as impenetrable.

# THIRTY-SIX

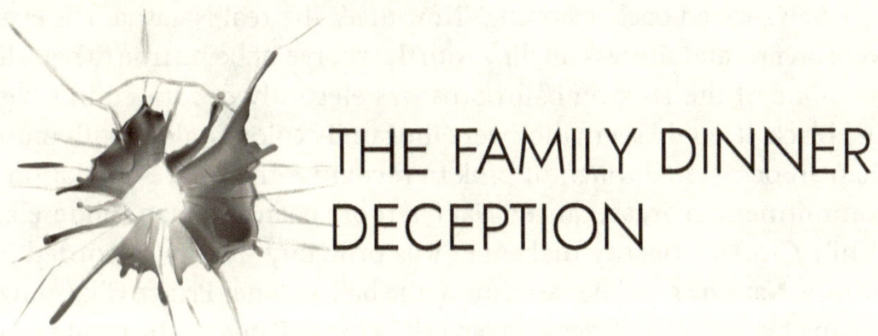

## THE FAMILY DINNER DECEPTION

They arrived at the Duxton at 7.25. By the time Seb gave the Maserati's key to the valet, they were right on time. He slipped his arm around her lissom waist, possessing her. Her stunning physical presence, the glide in her step, the scent of her perfume, the essence of her being, every inch of her had him feeling proud, powerful and at ease.

'You are so brave to take this on. If I don't say it later, thank you for letting me spoil you tonight.' His velvety words both levelled and inspired her, especially when he said, 'And, right now, I just want to be by the side of the most exquisite woman in the room.'

A thrill ran through Natasha. 'Oh. Thank you. Right back at you.'

Overwhelmed by her, Seb kissed her full on the mouth in the middle of the marble square of the very public Duxton foyer. He dipped her as his lips held hers. To his amazement, she didn't fight him. Her back formed a perfect arc in his hands, trusting him to hold her and not let her fall. They were underneath the grand chandelier, surrounded by the foyer's elegant columns. Well-dressed people bustled past them to begin their Saturday night.

Setting her back on her feet, he whispered over her lips. 'Where's the fearless lady I see first thing in the morning, the only woman, other than Pia, who dares to defy me?'

Seb's words were a shot of adrenaline. She straightened confidently and returned his kiss with interest, commanding his will, his attention and making his toes curl.

Seb swayed back, grinning. 'Now that's the real Natasha.' His eyes were on fire, and she was tingling with the charge of being true to herself.

One of the Duxton ballrooms was elegantly decorated in silver and black. It would seem they were the family colours, along with more than an occasional touch of pink to recognise the Aida Foundation's commitment to breast cancer. Nat felt more beautiful than Cinderella. While Cinders' beauty makeover was probably the first recorded in history, Natasha's had her arriving at the ball with her Prince Charming, leaving her rag-clad, fractured old self behind. Tonight, she would give herself permission to shine.

Pia came to greet them, all bubbly and smiles. She looked sophisticated and dignified in a vintage 1950s silver silk dress with small black polka dots. Her black hair was wrapped around her head in a classic updo. She was older than Natasha, but it was hard to tell how much. Her skin was flawless. 'Natasha, I'm so glad you're here. You look beautiful.'

'Thank you. As do you. Fabulous dress.'

She nodded and then, with a mischievous hum, said, 'Did you get to work on time? The weather was horrendous this morning. Seb came back all wet.'

Nat ignored her tone. 'Yes, I did, thanks. I apologise for the brief meet and greet, but I didn't want to be late.'

'Of course, I understand.' A playful look crossed Pia's face as she lowered her voice and came closer. 'I must confess, young Michael rang me early in the morning. He was very excited, telling me that his Uncle Seb had a sleepover all of his own. I had to come over to see. I couldn't resist the chance to meet you because Sebastian doesn't do sleepovers, not at the Tower anyway.'

Relief swept Nat like an incoming tide. Seb's silent frustration and brooding were because of Pia, not her.

'Hey, sis, you do know I'm here too, right?' Seb threw his sister a wry smile.

'Yes, but I see you all the time. Let me take your beautiful girlfriend around to meet everyone.'

'Pia, no.' Seb's voice was firm. 'I want to do that. After all, she's *my* girlfriend, not yours.'

'Of course. Forgive me.' She turned to Nat. 'It's just so good to see him with someone who makes him really smile.'

Nat sucked in a sharp breath. 'Oh … thanks, but I'm the lucky one.'

'Natasha, don't let Seb hear you say that too often. It'll go to his head.'

'Please, my friends, call me Tash.' Natasha liked that only Seb and her close friends called her Nat.

Pia was impressed, flashing a glorious smile. 'Of course, Tash. If Seb gets boring, come find me. We'll have some fun.' It was indeed a family trait. They all spoke so frankly.

A small crowd of people Natasha didn't recognise had gathered around. They soon moved aside for a handsome, fit-looking older gentleman with silver hair. He had a commanding, if slightly intimidating presence. The crowd parted as he walked towards them.

With a steely glare, his dark charcoal eyes fixed on Natasha and then Seb. 'Son.' His voice had a similar timbre to Sebastian's, although with a more resonant, staid tone. He smiled warmly as they shook hands. Nat was surprised at the formality between father and son. 'Are you going to introduce me to your best-kept but beautiful secret?'

Nat took his intimidating stare in her stride and extended her hand. 'Natasha Perry. It's a pleasure to meet you, Mr Mancini.' Who was she? A together Natasha, running on confidence, a little brave pretence and Seb's injection of faith and reverence.

'Natasha, my pleasure, but please, it's Renzo to you. Mr Mancini is my father.' His uncompromising charisma radiated power, trimmed with a formidable toughness. Seb was undoubtedly his flesh and blood. Then, chillingly, he added, 'You're the new clinical pharmacist on Aida. I've heard good things, and not only from Sebastian.'

Renzo looked at Seb. 'No need to ask how you are, son. I can see for myself. This new lady in your life must be rubbing off on you?'

Now, Nat understood who the Mancinis inherited their forthright manner from. The originator of the lack-of-subtly gene was Seb's dad.

Natasha blushed while Seb shifted a little from one foot to the other. 'You could say that, Dad.' His eyes darted to Nat, giving her the slightest hint of a cheeky grin. Silently they agreed. Yes, something like that.

'Natasha, sit by me at dinner and tell me all about yourself.'

Now, this was unexpected, but she didn't miss a beat. 'I'd be honoured.'

'Good. I still have a few people to catch up with before we take our seats. We will continue getting to know each other soon.' He walked off to greet a couple who had just arrived.

Seb was at her side with two glasses of bubbles. 'Would you like some Cartizze?'

Her head tilted a question on her lips. Seb elaborated, 'Cartizze Prosecco, one of the best Proseccos in the world, and we just so happen to import it. I think you'll like it. It's magnificent, like you.'

She took a glass, bumping into him playfully with her hip, relaxing after surviving her first encounter with the patriarch of this powerful family. 'Why, Dr Mancini, aren't you just the complete package – smart, caring and sexy.'

He winked, as a mischievous grin split his face. 'I couldn't have said it any better.'

Soon it was time for everyone to take their seats. Natasha was seated on Renzo's right, with Seb on her right. Dominic was on Renzo's left, and his wife, Elva, was beside him. Pia was next. She introduced her husband, Tony Gallo. Only one other non-family member sat at the table. Cole Hexum sat on Seb's right, completing the circle.

Seb introduced Cole. His shock of blond hair was perfectly sculpted, matching his tailored black suit, white shirt and silver tie. It completed a flawless, stylish look, but didn't camouflage an ominous, threatening power Nat sensed immediately when they shook hands.

His Scandinavian complexion was such a contrast to the Mediterranean Mancinis. As they shook hands, their eyes met. Natasha remembered him. It was his hooded, predator-like blue eyes. 'Mr Hexum, we've met briefly before, at Nunzio's. I believe you were finishing up a JCH board get-together.'

His eyebrows twitched ever so slightly but didn't give much else away. 'You have an excellent memory, Ms Perry. I remember you too. As I recall, Sebastian was quite generous that evening, buying some fine champagne for your table.'

She'd tried a little good humour with him, hoping to ease his aloofness. 'Yes, he did, and you, Mr Hexum, also have an excellent memory.'

In a very deliberate, if not intimidating, manner, he leaned in just a little closer and gave a curt nod. Hexum was a serious man, leaving Natasha in no doubt he'd be dynamite in a courtroom and an outstanding poker player.

Overall, the ambience in the room was relaxed and respectful. Natasha had never been part of such a gregarious family gathering. It struck her as unusual that a family could be so comfortable in each other's company. No longer on the outside looking in, she was part of the discussion, which at times was intense and raucous. It switched from business to family and back again.

They interrogated Natasha about what brought her to Fremantle. Not such a tricky question, as she had a stock-standard, sanitised answer. Then they moved on to her job, where Renzo and Pia became very interested. Because Seb had conducted the interviews, there was more than a little serious digging. Nat hoped she convinced them she'd been given the job on her own merits. It was all quite nerve-racking, however, when Pia quizzed Nat more deeply about her family, the scrutiny ramped up to another level. Seb stepped in, saving her from the awkwardness surrounding her dismal family life. He derailed Pia's interest in Nat by shifting it to business. It held Pia and she proceeded to give up some childhood stories about Seb.

Nat was touched that the whole room, led by the family, toasted the memories of Seb's late mother, Aida, and his brother, Giuseppe. Renzo's enduring love for his wife was unmistakable. His toast to her memory was warm and heartfelt. In contrast to his outwardly intimidating manner, he teared up when delivering the toast, as did the rest of the family. It was so moving, especially for someone learning about the love a family could share.

Dominic toasted Giuseppe's memory. There was another outpouring of warmth. Giuseppe lived for the business and never married, although he was quite the Romeo. His tragic wharf accident was still seen as a senseless loss.

With the family in full flight, Nat saw their all-consuming, uncompromising nature, where blood was undeniably thicker than water. She began to understand Sage and Averill's warnings. Being such a close family, there would be a price to be paid to hold their secrets. As she was on the threshold of discovering some of these, she wondered whether she could afford the cost – and if it was worth it.

Their sumptuous meal finished, they left their chairs and moved around the room, talking to various guests. Seb left Nat briefly to refill her glass of red, which she'd been drinking a little too easily. Like everything else, the wine was divine. While Seb was gone, Pia introduced Natasha to her personal assistant, Nina Panetta. Nat towered over her, especially in her skyscraper heels. She opened with a smile and the standard 'Pleased to meet you,' offering her hand.

It was met with a dismissive icy shake and nasal whine. 'Yes, I'm sure.' Right away, hostility was rolling off this diminutive but interesting-looking woman. Father Time had hit her hard with his ageing stick. She looked just a little too over-pampered and groomed. Too much Botox had been jabbed into her face, and an excess of dermal filler pumped into her lips. These gave her a very scary, plastic look. She had a skin-crawling dominatrix-Barbie-doll vibe, right down to the harlot-red fingernails and long, course black hair, straightened to within an inch of its life. It formed a curtain around a face heavy with make-up. Looking at her side-on presented the observer with an outline the shape of South America – full, rounded belly and big arse.

Their encounter consisted of small talk, stilted and grating. Nat was working hard to keep it pleasant. All she wanted to do was reach for that shovel to dig herself out of the plethora of awkward moments. When Pia moved away to talk to one of the waitstaff, Nina sighed, making no attempt to hide her boredom. She looked Natasha up and down with disdain.

Nat wondered what she'd ever done to Ms South American Barracuda.

The Barracuda spoke. 'How about we cut the crap? Who are you really? Are you anyone worthwhile, or just one of his many pieces of media fluff?' A twitch jagged across her upper lip. 'He brings them round now and then for a photo, then gives them the brush-off.'

'Pardon?'

'Oh, luvvvy, you are an innocent, aren't you? People don't usually have to ask me twice. They just know.' She stepped closer to Nat and folded her arms. It was an intimidating pose, territorial. Nat almost imagined Nina cocking her leg and spraying the spot with her scent.

The PA smirked. 'Let me educate you. I don't have the time or inclination to get to know you. Nor will Pia once he's done with you. If you're one of his media babes, don't call her office thinking I might be your friend, because I'm not. And I won't be getting you an interview with Pia or passing your CV on to anyone. I have no interest in helping you. Get it? Care factor nil.'

Nat did need that shovel. However, it would be better used to hit this woman about the head rather than any digging to get out of the uncomfortable situation. A slow, crawling vulnerability tried to claim

Nat. But tonight Natasha had a firmer grip on her worth. No one was going to put her down. Holding her head high, she said. 'Um, you're mistaken. I already have an excellent job. I don't need help from you or anyone, thanks.'

'Nina.' Pia had swung around. She growled while yanking Nina's elbow. 'You've misunderstood. Natasha is Sebastian's girlfriend. You don't need to be like this.' Pia looked sheepishly at Natasha. 'Sorry, Tash. Nina is sometimes too officious and protective.'

Nina seemed only a little contrite, bowing her head to Pia. She soon raised it to glare defiantly at Nat. As they eyed each other, Natasha noticed something odd about Nina's eyes. They were a deep brown, but not like Seb's or Pia's. They were fake, Nina wore brown-coloured contact lenses. Perhaps it was an attempt to make her eyes look closer to the telltale and unique Mancini dark chocolate brown. Nat wondered if this was an insight into Nina's personality. Was she that desperate to look like she belonged to this powerful family?

Either way, Nina was sly and cunning, a wolf wrapped up in the seeming respectability of a PA's clothing. Clearly, she wasn't about to let any blonde babe sweep in on her territory as she purred, 'You know, don't you, luvvvy, about his wife and his—'

'Nina! Play nice. Remember your confidentiality agreement. Maybe you should go home,' Pia growled. Sounding worried, she said to Nat, 'I apologise for my PA's rudeness.' Pia turned her back on Nina. 'Tash, there are a few other people you should meet.' Pia folded Nat's arm in hers as they walked away.

Nat was falling with no safety net. A wife. *What the hell?* Was this what he couldn't tell her?

'Sorry about Nina.' Pia picked up on Natasha's dismayed confusion and hurried her words. 'He hasn't told you. Well, that's for him to tell you about, not me. He will have his own good reasons.'

Natasha wasn't naive. She realised a guy as good-looking as Seb would've been involved with other women, even before mentioning his equally handsome bank balance. Why couldn't he tell her about a wife? Surely Seb wasn't still married? If he was, why was Pia, not to mention the rest of the family, so okay with Nat? This better not be some Jane Eyre scenario. This news would satisfy Averill and Sage's warnings. The question-filled mud Natasha had been wading through had risen towards her throat. No shovel or compass would help now. She glared at Pia in disbelief. 'What's going on?'

Pia cooed, beseeching her, 'Tash, I haven't seen him this happy in years. For that matter, ever. It can only be because of you. He was broken before.'

'Who was broken?' Seb was at last by her side.

Nat didn't know how much he'd heard. Seb handed Nat a full glass of red as Nina sidled up to him. She reached up to pull his arm down like a little kid would do to a parent. Out of reflex good manners, Seb turned to her and bent a little.

Stretching up on her tiptoes, Nina plastered a smoochy kiss over his lips. 'Hello, stranger.'

Nat took a large gulp of wine.

Seb stiffened and jerked back. 'Nina, uhhh.' His jaw set in a hard line as Mancini menace laced his words. 'I see you've met *my girlfriend, Natasha.*' He wiped his lips with the back of his hand, looking disgusted.

'Oh, you mean your latest piece of media fluff.' Nina chuckled, but there was no humour in her eyes. 'She won't be around long before you brush her aside.'

That was it. This shit-kicker had either had too much to drink or was just plain nasty. Nothing Natasha hadn't seen or handled before. She was sick of it all. Seb's secrecy, the unanswered family questions, and now this trumped-up tart of a secretary. If Nina wanted a pissing contest, she better have brought her A game.

It was Nat's turn to look Nina up and down with an unimpressed, condescending stare. She lowered her voice, the quiet ease of it more threatening than a shout. 'Oh honey, were you a bit of fluff cast aside? Having manners, I know now's not the time or place for that discussion. Don't get your knickers in a twist, though. You can fill me in later about how you didn't come up to scratch. Oh, but wait, that's right, *my* care factor's nil.'

Nina opened her mouth, but nothing came out. Natasha spun on one of her very impressive heels and walked towards the bar, leaving Seb, Pia and Nina in her wake. Nina was apoplectic.

Seb and Pia had a choice. The disagreeable, overly protective staffer or the new, indomitable girlfriend. Nat was angry, although she wasn't entirely sure about what or at whom.

Pia's voice sharpened, the familiar menacing Mancini tone slicing the air. 'I'd say you just got smacked down, something you deserved. Because you're drunk, you're in danger of breaching your CA. Go home *now.*'

As Nat approached the bar, she turned back to see Pia grab Seb. They both walked away from a glowering Nina towards Nat. She downed her glass, noting the score – Natasha one, Nina a big fat zero.

Pia whispered something in Seb's ear. His face fell as he broke away from Pia to be at Nat's side. 'You're full of surprises.'

Scowling, she growled, 'It would seem you are too.' She went to move away.

He grabbed her arm, turning her to him. 'Nat, in my defence, you know I was going to tell you all of it tonight.' A frustrated gruffness tainted his words, but he wouldn't let her out of his grip. The irresistible, fiery attraction surfaced between them. They stepped towards one another. This time Nat's temper subsided. After all, they couldn't have a sexually charged argument at family night. She realised she was more angry at Nina, not Seb, especially given what she hadn't told him.

'What can I do to make it up to you?' He leaned in, pressing his forehead against hers. Even in her super heels, he was taller.

She continued to ride her luck, whispering huskily, 'Kiss me.'

Relief flooded his face. 'With pleasure.' His words were the last sound she heard for a little while.

Pia brought them back, tapping their shoulders. 'You realise you're still in a public place, don't you, little brother?' She graced them with a relieved smile. 'And you, Tash, well, remind me never to get on your bad side. Way to put Nina back in her box.' She smirked at Seb. 'Little brother, you'll have to watch yourself. You have a true equal here.' Stepping between the two, Pia put one arm around each of their waists. 'Come on, let's have another drink with the family. The night's still young.'

'Yes, let's.' Seb said, smiling at Nat.

She needed to start drinking water. Otherwise this fantastic night and all the wine she'd consumed to keep her nervous hands busy would do her in, and she'd be at the mercy of her alters. Fortunately, her hands were the only part of Nat to give away any hint of nerves. It had been a near-faultless performance.

A crafty smile flashed across Pia's face. Instead of steering them to the family circle, she directed them towards the photographer who had been doing the rounds all evening. Pia took Seb and Nat's glasses. 'I'll get you a refill. You two should get your photo taken. Seb, it's time you let the world know about your gorgeous girlfriend.'

Nat cringed. She wasn't the type of girl the world should know about, media fluff or not.

Seb read her mind. 'It'll be okay. You know, it feels so right. Let's forget about everything else for now.'

Yeah. Of course, they could let the world know. The moment caught Nat, and she smiled warmly and confidently, sliding her arms around his waist, interlocking her fingers behind his back. He did the same to her. She was lost in his gorgeous eyes as their gazes locked. The air crackled, and their shared moment was captured by the snap and flash of the camera.

Natasha seemed to have passed some unknown test. A more natural conversation, with much less interrogation, flowed when they rejoined the family group. When Cole chatted with her, however, the awkwardness between them lingered. Then he stepped onto some common ground. 'I see you met Nina.' There was a hint of empathy in his voice.

'I apologise. I hope I didn't make a scene.'

'You didn't make a scene. It's my job to notice things, and I saw how well you subtly handled her. It was refreshing. Because, as you know, the Mancinis don't do subtle.'

'I seem to have done something to upset her.'

'It's not you.' There was no emotion on his face or in his words. Here was a man who only dealt with facts. 'She's like that with any woman who gets remotely close to Seb.'

Nat turned to face Seb. 'Oh, really.'

He held his hands up in a not-so-humorous protest. 'Come on, please. It's any Mancini man. She was the same with Giuseppe until he died. She didn't know I existed then. Luckily for Dom, he was already married.'

In what Nat suspected was a rare moment, Cole smiled, intimidation remaining in his eyes. 'You're certainly a good thing for this guy.' His general inscrutable demeanour made Nat realise he was a very polished attack dog.

Finally, Seb said, 'Right, family, I'd like my girlfriend back now. We've got to get going.'

Dominic remarked, 'So I've heard. I got a call to okay—'

'Shh. It's a surprise!' Seb cut in. Dominic smiled surreptitiously at Seb and then at Nat.

A chill ran down her back. What was it with this family and cutting people off mid-sentence when they were about to spill information Nat needed? All she could do was smile sweetly. She had absolutely no idea which questions to ask because she'd forgotten what answers she needed.

Before they left, it was like Nat was a very treasured pass-the-parcel. Each one of his family gave her a hug and a kiss. Pia couldn't help herself. 'I hope we'll see a lot more of you. Maybe Seb will let you out of his sight long enough for me to take you to lunch or a girls' night out.'

'I'd love that. But please, no PAs.'

'Yes, sorry about that.' They left each other giggling.

The last Mancini in line was Renzo. He gave her a kiss on each cheek. 'Thank you for coming tonight, Natasha.' In a deliberate tone, he said, 'I look forward to finding out more about you.' A chill gripped her.

Turning to Seb, Renzo's words gave a notion of caring, although they carried extra gravity. 'You have real potential here, Sebastian. Take care.'

Seb smiled politely with a solemn nod. They shook hands. 'All right, we have to get going.' Seb led her to the lift.

The doors closed and they were alone for the first time in three hours. He turned to her. 'Before tonight, I thought I wanted you in my life. But now I know I need you in my life.' Natasha had never heard words so tenderly delivered. 'Tonight made everything ...' he groaned breathlessly, with his lips on hers. 'Crystal clear.' His hands caressed her hips before pushing her into the corner of the lift. 'You make everything better.'

The desire they had for each other flared as they kissed. Nat yielded to an overriding need to be with him and the look of veneration in his eyes. The fire consumed any sparks of alter-anxiety due to her increasing inebriation. She reluctantly broke away from his lips to take a breath. 'I loved tonight. I don't think I've ever been so happy around a family.'

'I'm pleased, because tonight is only the beginning.'

They shared a kiss where desire wrapped around hope trapped in caution. Yet with Seb's lips so soft and reassuring, Nat once again lost her grip on any dark thoughts concerning Seb and his family. Being well on the way to the freeing wonders of tipsiness meant she was easy prey for his patented diversion tactic, but also for Goldilocks's freedom and she began to drift a little.

The lift doors opened.

# THIRTY-SEVEN

## WINDSCREEN WIPER PERSISTENCE

As the Maserati roared away from the Duxton, rain began to fall. Lightning cracked open the black of the night sky. Stormy weather continued to torment the city. Natasha hoped she wasn't riding into a Mancini storm.

With troubled eyes and a solemn voice, he said, 'To tell you the things I must tell you, I've made sure we won't be interrupted. I'm taking you away for the weekend and then some.' His eyes returned to the road.

'Jeez! Do you need that much time?'

'Hah. No,' he sniffed in light derision.

'Are we hanging around your place all weekend until we're sorted?'

'Something like that.' He then steered the Maserati onto the highway in the opposite direction to Fremantle.

'Where are we going?'

'It's a surprise.'

'You have to know this is driving me crazy.'

'Be patient. You'll have all the time you need to ask all your questions when we get to where we're going. I won't let you leave me.'

His unfortunate pause stirred the never-far slithering anxiety within her. He saw it coil around Natasha, so scrambled trying to stop it taking hold of her. 'That is, until you don't need to ask any more questions.' Seb turned the music up. The conversation was over.

Rihanna's 'Right now' filled the car, pulling Nat back to the high of the party. She let the music swaddle her in the joyful fearlessness of this right now, trying to trust him for a little bit longer.

She watched the windscreen wipers furiously working to clear the windshield, only to be thwarted and swamped by the persistence of the rain. Yet, they prevailed, faithfully protecting the couple with timely unobstructed glimpses of the safest way ahead. Nat tried to believe in the faith she had in Seb. It had shown her glimpses of a safe path forward. Yet, her trust in him was continually swamped by the persistence of his silence and the trepidation that rained down on her. She could only hope her faith, like the windscreen wipers, would endure until his silence, like the rain, stopped.

Finally, she had an inkling of their destination as they sped by a road sign pointing in the direction of the city's smaller airport. Nat's curiosity was so amped that any cat near her would've been on the last of its nine lives. Her angst eased a little as a black-and-silver plane came into view, lit up on the rain-soaked tarmac. They drove right up to it. Her eyes drifted over the sleek, wet fuselage. It wasn't a surprise to see the Mancini Enterprises family crest adorning the tail. Just how wealthy was his family?

A muscle-bound guy holding an umbrella waited for them, his bulk straining the seams of his black suit. No-nonsense, short-back-and-sides opened Nat's door. 'Hello, Ms Perry.' She found his voice familiar. 'Please step this way.'

Seb rounded the car. 'Paul, the bags in the boot need to be stowed on board and put the small grey satchel on the table in the main cabin. Thanks.'

'Yes, of course, Dr Mancini.' The guy smiled and handed Nat the umbrella. He set off towards the car's rear as suspicion sprouted wildly in Nat's tipsy mind. Her alcohol infused thoughts were fertile soil for doubts to easily grow.

The rain had eased to barely a touch upon her skin. 'Allow me.' Taking the umbrella, Seb nudged Natasha towards the stairs. Thunder rumbled in the dark sky and avgas filled the air.

'Hang on, wait. Paul?' She forced the guy to focus on her. 'Are you the Paul I kind of met at the gym the other week?'

'Yes, I am. Following Dr Mancini's orders, of course.'

'Of course. Well, that makes all the difference.' She rolled her eyes at Seb before returning to Paul, trying not to appear embarrassed. 'I'm pleased to meet you properly and finally put a face to the voice.'

'Nice to officially meet you too, Ms Perry.' He slammed the boot closed.

Seb glared at her. 'Now we have the niceties over with, Paul's got work to do.'

She couldn't help but notice he was a man mountain as he made his way up the plane's stairs. What the hell? She'd had this thought before – two guys in black suits. The men at The Norfolk and then at the Sail and Anchor. One of them could have been Paul. Had they been shadowing the couple? She'd seen him somewhere else but couldn't remember where. Was Paul Seb's bodyguard? Paul certainly seemed to be Seb's Man Friday. Why would he need bodyguards?

The scumbag owner of the strip club used to have thug minders, although he was a drug-dealing low-life. This realisation shone an intense spotlight on the suspicious anxiety growing in her darkening mind. She jumped a little too easily at the flash of lightning and crack of thunder overhead. The storm wasn't easing, nor was her brewing psychotic storm.

Paul disappeared into the plane as Nat narrowed her eyes at Seb.

'Don't make fierce eyes at me.' He kissed her soundly into wonderland, where thoughts of sinister persuasions disappeared. Then his Mancini megawatt appeared. 'I'm a lucky man to have you all to myself.'

And she was all gooey. Of course, Seb was a good guy. He'd said he was falling in love with her.

At the top of the plane's stairs, Seb shook hands with two guys. 'Good to see you, Garry, Carl. Thank you for flying us at this time of night. It's a terrible time to fly and a terrible night for flying. I really appreciate it.' He turned, 'Gentlemen, I'm pleased to introduce you to my girlfriend, Natasha Perry.' His smile was wide. 'Natasha, Captain Edwards and co-pilot Carl Johnston.'

They gave her a polite nod and shook her hand. Seb turned quickly and ushered Nat into the plane's main cabin, closing the door behind them. The click of the lock made her thoughts fall from the dreamy heavens to dark concern. How dare he corner her? This was the fine print she'd never sighted coming back to bite her. Seething, she hissed,

'I'm not flying anywhere until you tell me it all! I won't be trapped into staying with you against my will.'

'Exactly, that's what I have planned.'

There it was again, the arrogant tone she was rapidly beginning to dislike, along with his inconvenient pauses. She couldn't be sure which part of what she'd said Seb had agreed to – the first or the second.

She was about to ask when he said, 'Please, I'm doing this for your enjoyment. Relax.'

A cumbersome, strained atmosphere filled the cabin. Tipsy frustration bubbled to the surface. 'What the hell is this?'

He answered dryly. 'It's a plane. To be specific, our company jet.'

Natasha groaned and rolled her eyes, frustration only slightly quelled by the realisation that the mere-mortal males she'd known before wouldn't have been able to organise this type of surprise. Nonetheless, one suspicious thought persisted – neutral location, her arse!

There were forward and aft cabins adjoining the main one. Several elegant cream leather lounge chairs, a walnut table and a three-seat divan stretched before her. The sleek modern decor with walnut panelling and silver metal trimmings was a level of luxury Natasha wasn't used to, but Seb was the one acting like a fish out of water as he moved stiffly around the cabin.

She huffed, 'For God's sake, just tell me, Mancini.'

'I will. I will. Patience isn't your strong suit, is it?' Seb chuckled, 'First, let's change into something more comfortable. You'll find what you need in the aft cabin.'

'look, at this point I don't need romance, but I do need answers.'

He glared at her. 'We won't fly until there is nothing more to say, but there's no reason we can't enjoy this and be civilised about things. Meet you back here.' He exited through the door they'd entered.

Upon seeing the aft room, the lit match to her temper's fuse was snuffed out. Her emotions teetered between amazement and jarring concern as she walked into the small bedroom with its attached restroom and shower. The bathroom was fully equipped. He'd thought of everything, from high-end make-up, toiletries and clothes. Hanging near the vanity was a stylish satin slip with a matching robe and slippers, very 1950s screen-siren glamour.

She came to Natasha. On the rise, the room warped. *Satin to trap you. His spider, your fly. My beastly revenge, your fate. You're weak, and I can't wait.*

Goldilocks was talking in rhymes. With Natasha's inebriation and anxiety, Goldilocks had the keys to escaping Nat's control. The puritanical bitch's bad poetry made sense. Seb's mask might be the most deceitful of all. Natasha clasped her arms around her body. Breathe, she told herself.

Pushing Goldy aside, Nat gathered herself. Even if she stayed dressed in her pretty little party dress, would Seb let her go? Would she have to dodge Paul? She wasn't sure where he'd gone. He'd subdued her before on the good doctor's orders without questioning anything. No job seemed to be too unusual for Paul. His job description must make for interesting reading.

No, Seb was a good guy. Clinging to this thought, she decided to do as he asked and get comfortable. As she hung her dress in the slim wardrobe, her hand brushed against a gorgeous full-length pale blue overcoat. Nat's mind slowed to a canter. She'd wear the satin. He'd think she was staying and he'd relax, then maybe she would too. If she decided to leave, she'd make a more dignified escape by slipping the coat over her satin-clad body and go to the pilots. Surely, they'd have to let her leave if she asked. Then she'd run fast and far.

Shaking her head, Nat took stock of who she was with and where she was. She was being silly. Seb wasn't a monster, not like the strip club owner who'd abused her. No, he wasn't Wolf. Settling down, she hung the overcoat on a hook behind the door. Her breath stalled in her chest when she caught a glimpse of herself in the mirror. The look he'd created for Nat, while all seductive allure, had her at a disadvantage. She grabbed the overcoat.

The cabin was bathed in soft light and beautiful, albeit tormented music – the Pretenders' 'Hymn to her'. Seb was in the galley, dressed in black silk lounge pants and a matching long-sleeved shirt, unbuttoned to show his toned torso. Mr TDD was all draped in one attractive package of suave black. Maybe looks were deceiving. She hoped he was striving for lounge lover rather than lizard.

He gazed at her as she walked towards him, overcoat firmly in hand. Usually when he fixed her with such an appreciative, sensual look, she would revel in it. With so many unknowns circling the couple and her being well-oiled, Nat reverted to old guilty patterns and hesitated at his gaze. What did he want from her? When she was within touching distance, she expected him to reach out. Instead, his eyes returned to opening a bottle of Dom Pérignon.

'Classic, elegant satin suits you.' His eyes were captivated by her every hip sway and step. Seb's hands were uncharacteristically shaky as he struggled with the bottle. He wanted to reach inside her mind and bend it to his ways. He'd have to tread carefully, her mind being a minefield. Seb didn't want her to have an attack when hearing his truth. Resolute, he knew he would control whatever happened, the situation and her. He was sure he was prepared for whatever eventuated. Unbeknown to him, his words iced. 'Put down the overcoat.'

Nat froze as a harsher chill swept her. It wasn't from his tone but from seeing the small grey satchel sitting on a low table near the divan. Was it holding drugs? What type of drugs were in it? Then the coldness turned to lead in her gut as her eyes fell upon an ornate bottle filled with an alluring green liquid sitting beside the satchel.

He poured the champagne into two flutes and moved to the divan and topped both glasses up with the green liquid. When he poured more of the bottle's contents into her flute, alarm drove through her like a siren piercing Chrissy Hynde's beautiful lyrics floating around the cabin.

Then he offered her the champagne flute. 'Try this.'

# THIRTY-EIGHT

## OLD SINS AND PRESENT-DAY CRIMES

The green liquid floated momentarily on top of the champagne before mixing with the bubbles, leaving an eerie milkiness in its wake.

*He wants to fuck you up.* Goldy was back.

As was The Slut. *Hot damn, let me play!! YES.*

The weird colour descended to the bottom of the flute as a prickling sensation crept up Nat's spine. She snapped, 'What the hell is that?'

'Death in the Afternoon,' he pronounced, like he'd just poured her a glass of water. 'It's a cocktail made famous by Ernest Hemingway. It's also the title of one of his books about bullfighting, courage and fear. I've just finished reading it. I thought it had sentiments a bit like us—'

'Bullfighting?' Her eyebrow winged up. 'Really. Yeah, you've hit on something there. Are you talking about the manure you're spreading or is it just bull?'

'Ha, you're funny. The courage, the fear, it's us. Now you might want to bank some of that sarcasm for later and come and sit here. You'll be more comfortable.'

She tossed the overcoat over a lounge chair nearer to the front of the plane before moving to the divan. 'What's the green stuff?'

'Absinthe. The cocktail is sometimes also called Hemingway Champagne. It adds to the taste of the Dom.'

'Since Dom is so yesterday,' she whispered dryly.

'Exactly.' He chuckled with a short-lived smile. 'Trust me. The cocktail is something new and different to try. That's all.'

'My alters don't respond well to recreational drugs or too much alcohol. Nor. Do. I.'

'Settle down. I just want us both to be relaxed to tackle this.'

'Oh, for Christ's sake, cut the crap. You've had, or is it *have*, a wife?'

'You must understand I haven't told anyone outside the immediate family the full details about my past, about my wife. So, I'll most likely suck at it.' She gave him nothing in his attempt to ease the tension.

He felt like a noose was tightening around his neck. 'We've gone to great lengths to keep things hidden. This is why it's been so hard for me to tell you. Mancinis don't usually have to explain themselves.' He gritted his teeth. 'People like Nina think they know, but they don't. Cole and Dad worked very hard to protect the family's reputation from any fallout.'

'Am I fallout? That might be what you get if you try and keep me against my will. This isn't fair.'

'No!' he snapped. 'It's not. But I want every chance to convince you to stay, even if you don't like what you hear. I deserve that much, surely.' He glared at her. 'I've given you the benefit of the doubt. It's the least you can do for me.'

Silence screamed between them, and then she gave him a nod.

'Alright, here goes.' He took a gulp of his Hemingway Champagne.

Natasha followed his lead and took a long sip. An alcohol-driven wobble flowed through her mind as the glass slipped from her lips. Goldy was morphing into the beast, the alcohol helping her slip the chains of Nat's usually ironclad control. Both were almost free as The Slut begged, *Let me handle him. You know you want more of his hot, hot sin. I'll make his plane really fly.*

Goldilocks banished The Slut. *His plans are sick and twisted. Why drug what's already cheap and given? If we must fight and kill, we will. We've done it before.*

Nat had no way of grasping what Goldy meant, so she tried to concentrate on Seb.

His brow knitted. 'About ten years ago, when I was young and, as it turned out, stupid, I married a girl, Sofia. I met her when I was visiting my family's hometown in Italy, Brindisi.'

He kept the discussion on the straight and narrow, knowing it was best for 'all' of them. 'Sofia and her family were living in Brindisi, although she was the niece of a well-known Fremantle businessman, allegedly good Italian family stock. It seemed to be a good match all around.

'I thought I was in love. Dad wasn't convinced but let me lead my life. Mum told me she didn't believe Sofia loved me and that I was only in love with the idea of being married, not the lady. Thinking it was just the protestations of a typical over-protective Italian mother, I disregarded what Mum said. We had a small wedding in Brindisi. Only family. It was all her family could afford, and out of respect for her father, I didn't use my money for a bigger one. I didn't care, as long as I married her.

'Sadly, Mum's worries materialised when a few months later, Sofia and I were at each other's throats.' He blew out a defeated breath. 'There were many reasons. What incensed and hurt the most was Sofia admitting that she didn't truly love me. Her father had pushed her at me and into the marriage. His businesses were going broke. He thought my family connections and our money would solve it.' Seb's temper flared. 'It's always about the bloody money and the Mancini name. Always.'

'Sebastian?'

His name from her lips brought him back. 'By the time I found this out, Sofia was pregnant. We were still in Brindisi and decided to stay together, thinking the baby would help the failing marriage.' She held his gaze and didn't flinch. Grateful, Seb took her hand.

His touch slowed her panic, but not the fear. Nat grabbed her cocktail and downed a mouthful. She shouldn't drink any more, but The Slut was guiding her actions and Goldilocks was descending into Nat's hell. Seb finally sharing his soul may not be death in the afternoon, but Nat suspected it would lead to some tragic ending.

With alcohol warping her mind and her alters breaking free, she wasn't sure she was in any state to receive more news. Seb swivelled around to face her. His eyes held veneration amid a storm of pain. 'We stayed in Italy so Sofia would be close to her family until the baby was born and she got used to being a mother and me a father.'

It made sense. The telltale chocolate eyes, the subtle caring looks and the loving hugs. 'Ren, he's yours.'

'Yes.'

'But why is he with Pia?'

'I'm getting to that.'

Nat took another mouthful. All sensible thought was beginning to lose its grip on her mind. She was falling into the deep dark place where Trixie the Slut and Goldy ruled over her. Skittishly, Nat focused on Seb as the whispers of Goldy's building paranoia became louder.

'About six months after Ren was born, we all agreed, including Sofia, that her family, especially her older sister Gabriella, were causing trouble for the marriage. Then Mum was diagnosed. Dad had us return to Australia. We thought Sofia might do better with more opportunities to find her own way in Freo. I hoped the marriage might work with both of us more settled. It backfired. It turned out the only thing we were good at together was hurting each other.

'I was exhausted from studying medicine, spending time with Mum and looking after Ren. Then everything seemed to happen so quickly. Giuseppe and Mum passed away. I was in such a state over Mum, Seppe and, of course, Sofia. I could barely function and certainly couldn't help Dad with the family business. I was so angry about how my life was turning out. I blamed Sofia. Not Ren. He was the one piece of brightness in the dark.'

He all but snarled. 'Sofia chose drugs to escape. Seems she found more than enough to do in Freo to take her mind off any marriage troubles. It's not an excuse, but it explains my behaviour towards Chevy on our first date.'

'Oh ...'

'I have a deep contempt. No, actually, I *hate* junkies.'

Seb's anger and disgust over his wife's addiction gave fuel and voice to Goldilocks's dire warnings. *He hates junkies. No more pretending. This will have a nasty ending.*

Seb squeezed her hand as her eyes widened and lost focus.

He explained, 'Seeing you with Chevy,' he scrunched up his eyes, 'it brought me back to fighting with *her*. Trying to keep her away from dealers and junkies. I detested it all.' His eyes shot open, swimming with the deep anger they'd been hiding. 'It all came to a head one hot summer's night when I came home from work earlier than usual. I caught Sofia by surprise. She was in the driveway, about to leave our home. Ren was strapped into his baby seat in the back of her car. As she was reversing down the driveway she yelled that she was leaving to be with a real man. Her dealer.'

Seb's words cut him like razor blades. 'Worst of all, she screamed that she was taking Ren with her. If I wanted him, I had to pay and not bring the police into it. Before I could stop her she drove off, shouting that her dealer would call me to tell me how much money and where to drop it. Only then would I get Ren back.'

Now his voice was harsh and filled with loathing. 'Sofia didn't give a damn about the marriage, family, or our son. I couldn't let her take him. She was out of it. The meth, and God knows what else, had fried her brain. I called Cole.' Seb was trying to hold it together and judge what was happening in Natasha's head.

She was wide-eyed and breathing a little faster. He softened his tone. 'I was scared for Ren and so desperate to stop her. Cole already had a contingency plan in place. He had people watching her and urged me not to engage her further. He'd sort it. Ren would be safe.' Seb shuddered, still not convinced Cole had given him the best advice that afternoon.

Natasha's suspicions about Seb's family and Cole rose. Especially hearing that they had people watching Sofia and a plan for her already in place.

Goldilocks warned. *Don't be stupid all your life. They hated junkies, they hated her, and they had to get rid of her. Like he's going to do to you when he finds out your secret. You're a junkie too.*

Seb spoke coldly. 'I couldn't take the chance, so I followed. She barely stopped her car for the dealer to jump in. I didn't see his face. It all happened quickly, but he was a sleazy-looking, thickset bastard, wearing black clothes and gold chains.'

Nat was fighting for control as she seethed. 'What is it with dealers, the sleazebags? The guy at the club used to dress like that. Is there some kind of uniform shop they go to, like Sleazebags R Us?'

He cocked his head. 'Okay. But it doesn't take away from the fact that my son was still strapped into his baby seat in the car, Natasha.'

She checked her alcohol-infused comments. 'Sorry. I was just trying to empathise, obviously badly. I know what dealers are like. They are psychopathic, murderous bastards. Wolf used drugs and a knife to torment and control the women at the strip club. I know how you would've felt. You feel powerless.' She took another sip.

'Yes.' With a strained smile, he continued, 'I followed the two of them. I was out of my mind with worry for my son. As they travelled along the West Coast Highway, a truck-like SUV with a bull bar rammed into the driver's side of Sofia's car, T-boning it. I couldn't believe my eyes. The guys in the SUV got out and chased the dealer, who'd escaped

Sofia's car. It was a staged accident. They wanted the dealer, regardless of who died in the process.

'The dealer hailed down a car, hauling the good Samaritan out of it. He sped off, leaving Sofia and Ren. Fucking coward. The thugs got into another SUV that was following as support, and sped off after the dealer.'

Seb tugged on his untamed fringe, lost in the past. 'I parked my car and ran to Sofia. She was badly injured, bleeding and trapped in the front seat, wedged between the steering wheel and the twisted engine of the SUV, with electronics sparking around her. The sounds of screaming and the smell of petrol filled the air.' He shuddered, tormented by the memories.

'Ren was howling in the back seat. I managed to get him out and passed him to a woman who'd stopped to help.'

He was shrinking before her very eyes. Not the confident Dr Sebastian Mancini she knew. 'Was Ren hurt?'

'Minor cuts and bruises on his arms and legs. A large bump on his forehead. He was lucky, given all the flying glass and metal.'

A recent memory flicked through her fearful, red wine and absinthe-clouded mind. In the temporary quiet, she placed ice on the bump on Ren's head. No wonder it meant so much more to Seb than the simple gesture she had thought it was.

'Poor kid.' Her words wavered. 'You and Pia have done a fantastic job with him.'

He was too deep in the past to answer. 'I turned to run back to the tangled mess of cars for Sofia. She was screaming incoherently. That's what I remember the most – Ren's crying, Sofia's screaming, and I was so useless. Just pathetic. I couldn't do anything to stop any of it, the drugs or the accident.'

His voice broke. 'As I ran towards the wrecks, they exploded. I was blown off my feet and, from all reports, thrown back a fair way, my skull fractured as it crashed onto the bitumen. I was hit by shards of twisted metal blown out by the explosion. One lodged into my chest, another into the right side of my pelvis.'

'Your scars.' She ran her finger gently down the middle of his chest, tracing the rougher, tougher skin. They were the only two scars she could soothe with caresses to his skin.

Leaning into her touch brought him back to the now. 'I wasn't as close to the car as I could have been, but I was still in a coma for a few weeks. It was touch and go, and no one was sure I'd pull through. And, if

I did, what would be left of me. Ren was coming up to eight months old and very active. All the family, what was left of it, decided that the best place for Ren was in a stable home environment. Dad took over and—'

'Pia took him in.'

For the first time in a while, she tried to hold his gaze. 'Now I understand why you and Pia are so close. She's amazing.'

'Stop interrupting!'

Natasha pulled back. Goldy told her. *See, nasty, the real man comes through.*

'Sorry. That was uncalled for.' Seb winced. 'I just want to get this over and done with.'

'Sure, go on,' she whispered, trying not to have her sanity ripped away from her.

# THIRTY-NINE

## MORE THAN A NIGHTMARE ON A DARK AND STORMY NIGHT

'It's taken this long for Ren and me to get close. I was broken mentally and physically. It took me a while to get back on my feet and get my med degree. I spent some years overseas while Dad and Cole managed the gossip and fallout.'

'And Pia took over caring for Ren.' Nat shrugged her shoulders, 'Seb, this doesn't sound like something you should've worried about telling me, especially with my history. But how come people don't know about Sofia, or that Ren is yours?'

'Dad had the papers report I'd been injured trying to help at a bad road accident – nothing about it being my family, my whole life. Dad buried stuff to protect Ren, the family and me. Paid people to keep quiet, and he had them sign confidentiality agreements. Buried any story of Sofia's escapades.'

Her mind pounded as sanity started slipping from her grip. 'Paid people off, confidentiality agreements?'

'Not that many CAs. We were married overseas. Ren was born over there. Most people think he's Pia's adopted son. He kind of is. Sofia and I weren't much of a couple back here in Freo. She was only here a few months. It's long enough ago to be a hazy rumour and mainly people thought she was just another girlfriend. Social media wasn't a big thing. There's nothing much to find now. I only came back to work at the hospital about six months ago. I've kept a fairly low profile – until you.'

He met her eyes, hesitantly brushing a strand of hair off her cheek, his touch more desperate than intimate. 'I don't talk publicly about being a widower or a father. Dad and Cole saw to it that people don't know or don't ask.

'Ren knows I'm his father, that I was badly injured in the accident that took his mother, and we're working on the rest. When we work that out, he will come and live with me. Ever since the accident I've been living a safe life. Trying to be worthy enough to get Ren back and regain my family's trust. To achieve that, I decided not to allow my heart to be open to any hurt again.'

Teary, stormy brown eyes focused on Nat. 'You've made me break all my rules. I've never met anyone like you. A woman who doesn't care about the money.' He took a deep breath. 'Showed me you didn't want the prestige of the Mancini name. I was stunned you were more worried about your past being a problem for my family than what my family, the name, posed to your future.'

Goldy cackled, *If he finds out you're a junkie, he'll hate you, maybe kill you, like his wife.*

Natasha shuddered and her face paled. Seb reached for her, but she swayed out of his reach. He tried to reach her with words. 'I was amazed that in this age of instant gratification and status anxiety, I'd found a woman who confided in me that all she wanted from life was a home where she felt safe. That's what I want too, for Ren and me.'

Shaking his head, he sighed, 'So ... I let you into my life further than anyone since Sofia. You're the first woman I've let meet the boys.'

'Seb, surely ... with my history, you can't be serious. Letting me into your life is bad enough, but Ren's too? You don't know everything about my past.' Forget courage. She'd joined Hemingway in a drunken haze of regret. 'You can't have a broken person and nutter around.'

'You should be more worried about how my family will affect your life.'

She couldn't push her alters aside any longer.

*Now it's gonna get gooood. Can I play?* The Slut licked her lips.

Seb's voice was strained as he commanded her attention. 'Natasha, come back to me. Don't give in to them.'

'What?'

There was something in his voice. 'I want to explain the rest, so nothing is left between us. Not even the rumours about Dad and the family.'

'Oh, the rumours ...'

Seb squeezed her hands. She had to look at him. 'It sounds worse than it is.'

Dread took hold with a vicious bite. 'Why would you open with that. Nothing in the history of *it sounds worse than it is* has ever sounded better than it was!'

He rubbed his fingers across his furrowed brow. 'Point taken. Let me put it like this. Fremantle is a small place, you get noticed. People get jealous if you get ahead. You know, the whole tall poppy thing. Some small nasty people believed we made our money from drugs, but that was Dad's ex-partner, Carlo. Nothing to do with us. Those same small people call Dad the Boss and Cole the Vanilla Godfather and think we had Sofia and Carlo killed off to stop any public humiliation. It's stupid. There's nothing to it. Please believe me. Not Mancini Enterprises. Dad's not a drug dealer and certainly not a killer. Mum wouldn't have had anything to do with him if he was.'

Goldy drowned out Seb's careful words. *He's like Wolf. He'll fuck you up the same way to control you.*

'Shit! Your dad made money from selling drugs!' Fear needled up Nat's spine. There were too many things to dislike.

'No! I told you *no*. Stop, Nat.'

'But you do have a drug connection. And your dad made his early money from drugs.' Her altered state had no filter or resistance to panic. 'Holy fuck, you guys are the Mafia, all hitmen, thug minders. Hush, hush or else. Do you still do that?' The shriek echoed around the cold metal tube as the realisation hit. Paul was Nat's early-morning Uber driver. Jesus, of course, he was a drug dealer's minder. That's why Paul had no issue cuffing her at Seb's request.

Trixie came forward fully formed and purred as The Slut. *History repeats. He's tailor-made for me to treat.*

Goldilocks was in her element. *Is his thug bodyguard lurking? Will he restrain you tonight? So they can slip the needle in. That's what's in the satchel.*

Natasha had the pigeon pair, one on each shoulder. 'Is Paul going to cuff me tonight? Where is he?'

'No.' Seb's brow creased more deeply. 'He's waiting with the car in case you want to leave. Please don't.' He traced his fingers over her cheek, sweeping her lips with his. The pooling of an uncompromising emotion in her heart stalled her alters.

His care stopped Nat from retreating. For the first time, Natasha and The Slut were facing the growing overwhelming fear and danger surrounding Natasha, together. She was also fully aware that Goldilocks lurked with her beast. Nat had never had this kind of awareness so far into an attack. She was also aware of Seb's touch, and how at present it had momentarily stalled her alters' rise.

Seb was determined to reach her. 'Listen to me. We're not the Mafia. It's a stupid stereotype that ignorant, jealous people find easy to use against us. *Carlo* was the drug connection, *not us*.'

She cried, 'I don't understand. You're angry at Sofia and hate junkies. Yet your family's history is in dealing, which created the problem that ruined Sofia's life.'

'No, not me. On my son's life, on my mother's honour.'

'But what about your father?' Her mind was freefalling, remembering Averill and Sage's warnings. The panic Goldy brewed gripped Natasha like a long-lost friend.

*Ha-ha, history IS repeating,* Goldy crowed. *When will you listen? He's a dealer, like Wolf.*

Seb tried to wrench back control. 'Yes, but—'

'I won't go back.' Pushing him away, vibrating with fear. 'Not to drugs and a place where I'm locked in a forever-dark hole.' Her mind was circling the drain. 'I won't be forced into drug addiction again. Never, *no, never*.'

'What are you saying?' He was trying to understand her babble, 'Natasha?'

'I can't have that shit in my life. I vowed once clean, always clean.' Her eyes were wild as disgust clamped over her face like the armour of a hard-cold mask. 'Get away from me.'

'What the hell are you saying? Those people – junkies disgust me.' His voice filled with vitriol. 'They'd use no matter what.' Seb moved to her. 'Junkies rip families apart. Junkies need to be identified as users so good people can be warned and not hurt by them. I hate the idea of them for what she did to me and my family.'

Goldy screamed, *No. Not like Wolf, my God. He's the Shoreside Slasher!*

Nat was shaking. 'Like the Slasher. You think like him.'

'Natasha, you're not making sense. Carlo did all of this way before Sofia came on the scene; before I was even born.'

'I hear the loathing in your voice when you talk about junkies, about Sofia. We can't be together.' She was screaming now. 'Because I used to be one. I. Am. A recovering. Addict.' Her words rattled around the rapidly growing space between them.

The Slut yelled, *Why would you tell him that when he hates them!*

Natasha's paranoia grew as her alters fed her fear that she couldn't trust anything Seb said. Any rationality was lost. He wasn't who he said he was.

*Nooo. Not you too.* His body stiffened. There had to be more. Everything told him she wasn't like Sofia. He'd misheard. 'You were *what?*'

'I was a junkie. Wolf forced it on me. There, it's out. I'm never going back.' Fighting fearful thoughts of the Slasher, she yelled, 'I haven't used in way more than eight years.'

'I see.' He didn't fully.

'I can't have you around if you or your family—'

He grabbed her shoulders, commanding her to look at him. 'You can't leave. Not now, never.'

Seb's words were different, but not too different, bringing forth her unknown panic attack torturer. *You can't leave.* Goldy sent forth the words of Nat's nightmare. The darkness around her unknown attacker was lifting, but she still felt the crushing terror. The echo grew, and Natasha blinked, giving over to them. Goldy screeched, *That's right. You can't leave, never. Yes, your attacker said it.*

'I won't be imprisoned again.'

Seb couldn't stop terror seizing her. Anything he said only made her fear worse. He saw panic swamp her eyes, her body, her mind.

Goldy was finally in control. *Ha! You stupid bitch, he's not just Wolf in sheepish Seb's clothing. He's worse.*

*He's the Shoreside Slasher!* The Slut joined Goldilocks in screaming.

'Good God. You said it. You hate junkies. You can't possibly love me. Not if you're him!'

Her alters were mashing and mixing every fear and panic to devise the perfect formula for Natasha's demise. Holding hands with crazy, they were running around like the Mad Hatter, trampling any good Seb had said. Now he was in their sights.

Nat's paranoia over Seb was complete and unassailable. The Slut put it together. *He has those hell-fine knife skills. Now, he says he hates addicts and wants to mark them to warn people. How come he knew about the slashed mouths? He's never been with you when the attacks happened.*

Goldy taunted, *Ha, haa! He's on a crusade to avenge his life and take revenge on his addict wife, and now he has you to play with.*

Her alters had her believing his need for revenge surpassed everything, even his adoring words – or maybe because of them. They were just to lure her in.

*Finally, you've got it* her alters screamed.

She stood, grabbing the champagne flute, taking a step towards the overcoat and the forward door. Her mania took control. She couldn't see straight. Fears born from Wolf and the Slasher merged into one horrific scenario in Nat's mind. 'You want to control me, kill me if I won't stay.'

*He's like Wolf.* Her alters fanned the flames of her fear. *But he's really the Shoreside Slasher.*

Nat cried, 'If I stay, you want to make me a junkie again and mark me. Shit! Like the Slasher!' She backed up, trying to focus. 'Revenge for your wife. You're not pushing me back to drugs.'

'Natasha, stop. This is madness.' He could see and hear she'd slipped into that place where fear and panic ruled. The only story there was the one her alter egos spun. They were driving this lunacy.

Goldy twisted facts to suit her vitriol to control Natasha. *Like Sofia, they supplied her dealer. They want to do it to you.*

'I won't go back. I won't be Sofia.'

He had to haul her back, save her from herself. The danger needed to be nullified. He'd rid her of her demons. Together they'd reclaim what was theirs. The answer was in the grey satchel.

With regret crushing his heart, he grabbed what he needed. Seb turned and lunged at Nat. She jumped out of his reach.

There was something long and slender in his hand. It glinted in the muted shadowy light. A syringe and gleaming needle. Now she thought she had all the pieces of the Mancini jigsaw puzzle. They twisted together to form one overwhelming, horrific picture – not too dissimilar to her past. Now she had to fight for her present and her future, she would not be forced into using again.

*Fight him off. You don't know what we had to do to save you from Wolf.* Both alters screamed. *The things we covered up for you.*

'No, not this. Please, not again.' Her present began to schism away from her past. She wasn't in a dark room with her attacker. She was the screaming woman, the addict, dying in a car on a scorching summer afternoon. A well-executed hit. 'I've got to get out of here.'

'No, I won't let you leave me.' He growled.

His words fuelled her mania to a level of pure insanity. Reaching for her, Seb said, 'Over my dead body.'

Because this was the first time Nat was present and aware of it all, it forced her alters to yield the one last dark secret and Seb's 'over my dead body' freed it.

*Easily arranged. He's not your saviour, but your failure. Wolf used the same words. Tried to rape you in the dark. This one's the same. He wants to leave his mark on you. Wolf had a knife, drugs and rape. This one's the same. The Shoreside Slasher.* Goldilocks was in her element. *You owe us. We killed for you.*

Seb grabbed harder. 'Natasha, please come back to me. Don't let them win.' His arms were tight around her, stopping her. Squeezing the life out of her, a hand that belonged to a ghost gripped her cheeks.

'Let me go. Don't do this. No ... don't cut me.' She lashed out, trying to push out of his imprisoning hold. She was frantic, a writhing body of turmoil made all the worse by her fear of what he held in his other hand. *Holy fuck, he is the Slasher.* This was proof. Seb's mask *was* the most deceitful of all.

The Mancini menace was back. 'Don't fight me. You can't leave. Not like this.'

Wolf had said similar words, and what did she do? Natasha Perry had disappeared and let Trixie the Slut and Goldy handle Wolf. Natasha couldn't remember what had happened, but now she could.

Her alters were shining a light on her last, dark nightmare. The Slut and Goldilocks spoke together, hitting Natasha with the truth. *You killed Wolf. We made you kill, so you could escape. It allowed us to survive. That's why we'll always rule you. We feed on your hidden guilt. The man we've never let you see in your nightmares. The one hurting you is Wolf. And you killed him to be ours.*

The dark secret Natasha had blocked from the light until now consumed her. Her alters had repressed this murderous guilt so they could enslave Natasha. Wolf was the hidden horror in her panic attacks because she'd killed him. He'd finally been jolted into the light in her manic panic over Seb being the Slasher.

*Yes, kill again. Survive. It's what we ALL did last time,* The Slut screeched.

Her alters roared in unison. *You killed ... jagged glass bottle. You stabbed out, cut your hand.*

Nat was in a thermonuclear meltdown, yet everything was laid out before her with absolute clarity. All of the dark corners of her mind were lit by revisiting the terror of that night, because Sebastian Mancini was the Shoreside Slasher. History *was* repeating.

Any music or Seb's beautiful sentiments had been usurped by the horrific noises in Nat's head. She was in a full-blown psychotic mind fuck. She'd survived Wolf physically, but her mind hadn't slipped Wolf's bounds, and guilt had cemented its splintering.

The circle was complete. Seb was the same as Wolf and needed to be dealt the same death card. She lashed out with the champagne glass. Seb's grip faltered. She'd been here before. Her breathing became choppy and frantic as a cold sweat slicked over her hot face. The glass shattered.

Her alters yelled as one. *Kill him, stop the Slasher, his blade. Stop Wolf.*

The dull light and the blur of her panicked vision saw Nat stab out at the form in front of her, not really seeing. Her arm was knocked down, giving rise to a pain that ripped through her side, above her hip. Warm dampness coated her skin, and she smelt blood. The grip that was incarcerating Nat's body returned with more force. A radiating sting pierced her thigh. 'What the fuck?' she screamed. Nat struck out once more. Only then was she released. Finally, she'd done it.

*Run!* Get to the overcoat, the door, the pilots, get away from the Slasher. But she couldn't. Something was making her feel heavy.

Nat found herself drifting like absinthe in champagne. An ever-thickening, sinking cloudy shadow surrounded her. The sickening, all-consuming fog spread completely over Nat's mind and her body became too heavy. She had to escape the plane, get out and away. Her feet wouldn't move, she fell, and the carpet sped upwards to greet her. Nothing moved in the cabin as she slipped away.

At war with himself, Seb hoisted her lifeless body into his arms. He'd said they wouldn't fly until it was done, in his mind it was. He would possess her. As the dull screaming of the jet's engines filled the space between them he laid Natasha out on the plane's bed. They had a long way to travel on this dark and stormy night. As he staunched the blood flowing from her wound Hemmingway's words came to him.

*So far, about morals, I know only that what is moral is what you feel good after and what is immoral is what you feel bad after.*

*Ernest Hemingway*, Death in the Afternoon

**COMING SOON:**

Continue the *Too Much Romance* roller-coaster ride with Natasha and Sebastian.

**Deeply: Too Much Too Late.**

As Natasha Perry gets closer to the Mancini family, will her relationship with Dr Sebastian Mancini withstand the deadly plans of an unknown force hellbent on revenge? Will she be able to hold her own? Or will the vengeful past destroy them? Sometimes, no matter how hard you clean the slate, some sins stick forever.

# ACKNOWLEDGEMENTS

To the brilliant crew at Hembury Books, especially Jess, Grace, and Sinead, a big thank you for helping my words become published and seen. To my husband and our wily Westie, Jansz, thank you for the support, love, patience and when necessary, distractions to keep me sane.